Something wrapped itself around the tiller, nearly jerking the solid bar of wood out of his hands. Then the tiller jerked again, slamming hard against Torvik's chest. He heard ribs creaking, and was sure his spine had suffered grave hurt as his back crashed against the gunwale of the boat.

Then the boat tilted as one sucker-studded tentacle heaved the tiller completely out of its socket and brandished it in the air. A man rose to retrieve it. Another tried to pull him down. A third drew his sword.

Torvik shouted at all of them to get down, but it was too late. The boat had tilted beyond its balance point even before a second length of rank, sucker-studded flesh slapped over the gunwale with a hideous sound, like a man drowning in boiling glue.

Saga

From the Creators of the
DRAGONLANCE® Saga
WARRIORS

Knights of the Crown
Roland Green

Maquesta Kar-Thon
Tina Daniell

Knights of the Sword
Roland Green

Theros Ironfeld
Don Perrin

Knights of the Rose
Roland Green

Lord Soth
Edo van Belkom

The Wayward Knights
Roland Green

WARRIORS
Volume Seven

The Wayward Knights

Roland Green

DRAGONLANCE®
Warriors Series
Volume Seven

THE WAYWARD KNIGHTS
©1997 TSR, Inc.
All Rights Reserved.

Distributed to the book trade in the United States by Random House, Inc. and in Canada by Random House of Canada Ltd.

Distributed to the hobby, toy, and comic trade in the United States and Canada by regional distributors.

Distributed worldwide by Wizards of the Coast, Inc. and regional distributors.

Cover art by Todd Lockwood.

DRAGONLANCE and the TSR logo are registered trademarks owned by TSR, Inc.

All TSR characters, character names, and the distinctive likenesses thereof are trademarks owned by TSR, Inc.

TSR, Inc. is a subsidiary of Wizards of the Coast, Inc.

First Printing: September 1997
Printed in the United States of America.
Library of Congress Catalog Card Number: 96-60809

9 8 7 6 5 4 3 2 1

ISBN: 0-7869-0696-0

8383XXX1501

U.S., CANADA, ASIA,   EUROPEAN HEADQUARTERS
PACIFIC, & LATIN AMERICA   Wizards of the Coast, Belgium
Wizards of the Coast, Inc.   P.B. 34
P.O. Box 707   2300 Turnhout
Renton, WA 98057-0707   Belgium
+1-206-624-0933   +32-14-44-30-44
                Visit our website at http://www.tsrinc.com

So much history passed from human knowledge during the Cataclysm that we find it hard to realize just how much was lost. This is particularly true of the last few centuries before the dire event. Knowing what came to pass, we tend to ignore the whole era and fail to assemble even the few bits of knowledge we have into the best picture we can build.

A classic case: Sir Pirvan, called the Wayward, Knight of the Rose, and his associates, some of whom have come down only as names.

Various chroniclers have placed him at various times during the millennium before the Cataclysm. The best evidence, however, suggests that he was some thirty years old when he made his first appearance on the rolls of the Knights of Solamnia, in 181 PC. This would place his date of birth somewhere before 210 PC.

Such as Pirvan are undeservedly forgotten. When they were born, the kingpriests were not yet a menace. When they died, the kingpriests had become tyrants. During their lives, they carried the weight of the fight against that tyranny. They lost, but had they not fought at all, one wonders if the gods would have spared any part of their creation when their wrath descended upon Krynn.

> —From the Yellow Codex of
> Shtrenisalasandar Half-Elf,
> also known as the Palanthus Chronicler

Prologue

Torvik Jemarsson raised the dwarven-work telescope to his eye and peered northward, trying to pierce the haze. If they were not in sight of Suivinari Island—the Drowned Mountain, as some called it—then their navigation from Vuinlod had been fearfully inaccurate.

The young mate of the top would have wished for a spell in the telescope, to make it a mist- and fog-piercer. But it was only sound bronze and the best lens glass, worked with skills Torvik trusted, even though he had never met the dwarves who possessed them. Any dwarves who had won the confidence of both his father's old comrade, Sir Pirvan the Wayward, and his mother's present companion, Gildas Aurhinius, a retired Istaran general, had to be very singular dwarves indeed. Torvik would not have gone to sea in a vessel of dwarf making, for dwarves did not know the ways of water, but he would trust them for anything short of that.

He also did not wish for a wind to disperse the mist. This far north, it was summer or spring all the year round, with heat-spawned storms rising between one watch and the next, and reaching fearful intensity with hardly more warning. Torvik remembered an old desert barbarian saying:

"Be careful what you beg of the gods. They may send it."

So he would not risk the gods sending more wind than *Kingfisher's Claw* could endure. In these waters the reefs, the mists, and the minotaurs were enough danger.

"Ahoy, the foretop!" came the hail from the deck. "What do you make out?"

Being mate of the top, it had been only plain sense for Torvik to station himself atop the first of the ship's three masts. It had also put a safe distance between him and Yavanna, mate of the deck. She was half again his size and twice his age, and thought that his rank owed more to his lineage than to his skill. Most of the time she stayed within the bounds of manners, but sometimes she brooded until there was an edge in her voice, as there was now.

"Something too solid for a fogbank and too high for a reef," Torvik called down. "I will tell you more when there is more to see."

"How does it bear?"

"The highest mark is three points off the port bow," Torvik replied.

He could read Yavanna's unspoken thoughts after she growled acknowledgment. From that measurement, they might well be coming straight into the tangle of reefs off Suivinari's southeastern end.

If so, then straight on lay only destruction. Bearing farther to starboard put them on a long beat to windward before they reached the human beaches. Farther still to port, and they risked sailing blithely up to the part of the island that the minotaurs regarded as their territory—and defended with all the usual minotaur ferocity.

Yavanna must have already given orders, because as Torvik finished examining choices, he felt the ship heel as the helm went over. He had just decided to put the telescope away for a few moments when a rift appeared in the mist.

A cone of pale brown rock leaped skyward from the sea, as perfect as if it had been sculpted. Grayish smoke curled from the summit, and white steam from vents on the flanks.

"The Smoker, dead ahead!" Torvik shouted. His voice embarrassed him by nearly breaking.

The message still reached the deck. Yavanna called all hands on deck to prepare for landfall, and only then ordered the helm put over again. She knew her work; no need to weary the helmsmen or set the masts to swaying as if they were riding out a gale.

They had made a good landfall. Within hours—rather than days—*Kingfisher's Claw* would be anchored off a beach of white sand, with fruit-bearing bushes all around it, and a stream of the purest water known to sailors flowing within easy reach of watering parties.

She would also be days, rather than hours, from the minotaurs.

* * * * *

Kingfisher's Claw had only a short beat to the southeast before she was clear of the last reefs that trailed out to sea like the stinging tentacles of a jellyfish. She came about, and with a leadsman taking soundings, crept in toward Mikkledan's Cove.

The water was murkier than usual off Suivinari, and Torvik saw no dolphins, either dived or broaching. The other lookout saw the same, and did not care for it.

"They could have fled some rumblings of the Smoker," Torvik reminded the man. "Or they could all be Dargonesti who have changed back to their elven form and are somewhere off at a feast in the depths where we could never see them."

The man looked as if he craved further reassurance, but before Torvik could refuse it, the captain came on deck.

"Ahoy, the foretop!" the captain called. "See anything unusual?"

Torvik had studied the water until he had lost hope of finding anything there. Now he pulled out his telescope and studied the white sand. Parts of it seemed less white and far less smooth than usual, but that could be merely a recent ship with a lubberly crew. Mikkledan Cove had been known to host watering parties from three ships between one sunrise and the next.

Something long and dark lay at the water's edge, however. Long, dark, and with the sea washing over it so that Torvik could make out little. His curiosity began to itch. He licked his lips and called down: "Somebody abandoned a ship's boat on the beach. I can see that much."

A silence long enough to stretch men's nerves followed. Then Captain Sorraz shouted: "All hands prepare to take in sail and anchor. Landing party! I want volunteers, and every one of them armed!"

Torvik winced. The orders were what he would have given, but he would not have ordered the landing party armed where all could hear. Naturally superstitious sailors could easily become fearful of some unknown menace lurking in the cove.

* * * * *

The men scrambled out of the first boat to touch the beach almost before the boat had stopped. Torvik led. It seemed to him that they were less eager to be on dry land than they were to solve the mystery of the overturned boat.

It stayed overturned for some while after they reached it, for it was a massively-built craft, each plank as thick as a man's arm and each rib nearly as thick as a man's body. Only the youngest sailors failed to recognize minotaur work.

It did not ease anyone's mind to see that some of those thick planks and one of those stout ribs had been shattered like clay pots struck by a hammer. At last, enough men had mustered the nerve to find handholds, and at Torvik's signal they heaved the boat upright.

Those around the boat were not the only ones who gasped in horror. Yavanna's party guarding the way inland, and Sorraz's men resting on their oars just outside the surf line, also lost countenance at what the righting of the boat displayed.

It was a minotaur, well grown even for that massive

breed. He had plainly died fighting, with courage that would guard his honor, but had not saved his life. His foe had all but torn one arm out of its socket, crushed his chest, and bitten clear through one thigh and nearly through the waist. The minotaur's tough hide also bore gashes and round marks, a hand's breadth across. It was those round marks that finally loosened someone's tongue.

"I've seen those circles," he said. It was barely above a whisper.

"Louder," Torvik called. "What one knows about this, all must know. Would you steal a shipmate's knife? Leaving him ignorant is as bad."

The man swallowed. "I saw them on the hide of a whale," he said. "A whale one of my mates said had met a kraken."

That ill-omened name made everyone look toward the sea. Sorraz and Yavanna left their parties, hurrying to Torvik's side. Before looks toward the sea could turn into a rush toward the boats, Torvik whistled for everyone's attention.

"I've never heard of krakens in these waters," he said, "or this far inshore."

"Krakens go where they will," Sorraz the Harpooner muttered. The captain was a fine fighter and a better shark-chaser, but hardly a master morale-builder.

"So do we," Torvik snapped. "Or is *Kingfisher's Claw* a fat merchanter, thinking only of a safe profit, crewed by those who expect the sea to make itself safe for them?"

Those were much more florid words than his father would have thought wise for rallying frightened men, but at least they seemed to take men's thoughts off krakens.

"What I want to know is what is any triply-cursed bull-head doing on our beach?" someone asked.

"Could have been heading for the nearest land," Sorraz replied. "Habbakuk only knows I'd do the same with a kraken after me."

That seemed to ease the men, about minotaurs if not about krakens. Torvik was about to suggest that they draw the minotaur's body up above the high-tide mark, for an honorable burial, when one of Yavanna's men came running down from the tree line as if the flames of the Abyss were licking at his heels.

"There's another one up there!" he shouted. "Dead, and not a mark on him!"

"Another what?" Yavanna and Torvik snapped almost together. Torvik realized it was the first Yavanna had spoken.

"Another minotaur," the man said.

Both Torvik and Yavanna had the same idea at the same moment, and in the next, shouted the same name: "Beeyona!"

The ship's healer scrambled out of the boat and ran lightly across the sand to the mates.

"Your wish?" she asked.

Her manner was as gruff as one might expect from a woman of gray hair and large stature, instead of one short of thirty and barely able to look Torvik in the eye. But she had once studied to be a priest of Mishakal, and although she had taken no true vows, she still walked somewhat apart. All aboard *Kingfisher's Claw* agreed that her healing arts made it worth tolerating that minor vice.

Torvik wasted no more words than Beeyona.

"Learn how the minotaur died. The one inland," he added, as she turned toward the mangled corpse.

Beeyona had seldom enjoyed such a strong guard—or such a large audience—as the sailors who surrounded her all the way to the trees and afterward, when she knelt beside the dead minotaur. They did not much care to remain, for the trees might hide anything. The dead brown eyes of the minotaur stared blindly upward in a way that was the stuff of nightmares. Also, some of Beeyona's spells were rumored to be of her own devising, or even borrowed from non-humans—and there were folk aboard *Kingfisher's Claw* who did not much care for that last.

Whatever their origins, Beeyona's spells served as well as ever. When she rose from beside the minotaur, her face held what to Torvik seemed both dire knowledge and grim purpose.

"She died of fright," Beeyona said.

"She—?" Yavanna asked.

The healer pointed at the corpse and said, "She and her mate came ashore from a boat. She saw him taken by what pursued them, and saw him the way we saw. Her heart stopped."

"That's reading a good deal from a minotaur body, for human magic," someone said.

Before Torvik or Yavanna could identify the insubordinate sailor Beeyona shrugged and said, "Nor could I have done as much, had she been dead a few hours longer."

Torvik added what that implied—the killer from the sea could not be far away—to what he had already reasoned from the first minotaur not being devoured. The killer had not fed. The sun made the hot forest suddenly seem as cold as the face of a glacier, and nearly gave his legs the power to send him fleeing back to the boats.

Honor and good sense restored his wits to command of his body. "We have as much need of water as ever before," he said plainly. "I say let us fill our barrels and be off. I want an answer to this mystery as much as you do, but I doubt we'll find it on land."

"And if it comes back—?" the same voice that had questioned Beeyona's honor muttered.

"It is a thing of the sea," Yavanna said sharply. "On land we can choose where to fight, and none of us have weak hearts. If it comes by sea—well, *Kingfisher's Claw* is not a ship's boat, and our captain is not called the Harpooner without good reason. And that is the last word for laggards and cowards until we have watered. Any more backchat, and I won't be talking."

"Nor I," Torvik said. Several of the leaders among the sailors nodded assent, and Sorraz smiled enigmatically.

But even they kept looking from the forest to the sea and back again, as they rolled the empty barrels out of the boats and up the beach toward the spring.

* * * * *

The hours came and went, the pile of empty barrels shrank, and several boatloads of filled ones had already returned to the ship. The watering would have gone faster had the heat of the day not made the sailors as thirsty as if the springs ran ale instead of water, so that they drank nearly as much as they loaded.

Torvik took his turn at the hard labor, but both he and Yavanna spent more time watching the sentries, who in their turn were watching the tree line. Nothing had happened since they found the second dead minotaur, but Torvik knew that didn't preclude the possibility that something could happen and might mean the sentries were growing less alert.

Torvik was leaning against a tree when he felt a quivering—in the tree, not in the ground. He had just time for the thought that this was a most peculiar earthquake, when the sandy soil burst apart and a root as thick as his arm rose into the air, twisting and writhing like the tentacle of a kraken.

Torvik's sword rasped free. He had just time to take one slash before the free end of the root wrapped itself around his left leg. He slashed again, the root writhed more fiercely, and the tree shuddered again. Suddenly he was dangling upside down.

He slashed a third time, but only struck a glancing blow with the tip of his sword that barely chipped bark. Then the root was drawing back, still holding the young mate of the top, like a tossball player limbering up his arm for a throw—with Torvik as the ball.

Yavanna struck before the root could finish its work. Wielding a snatched-up axe in both hands she flung herself on the root. It jerked from one blow, spasmed from a second, tightened its grip on Torvik's leg so that he cried out after the third blow, and on the fourth blow fell severed into two pieces.

The portion still attached to the tree promptly vanished, like a sea snake diving into a burrow at the sight of a fisher hawk. Torvik thumped down on the sand hard enough to knock the breath out of himself, which was just as well, or he would have cried out again from the pain as Yavanna jerked the severed piece of root from around his leg.

"Don't touch it!" he finally managed to gasp.

"It's dead," Yavanna said.

"It shouldn't have been alive in the first place," Torvik said, and Yavanna had to nod.

"Far be it from me to expect gratitude for saving your life. . . ." she growled, turning away, axe still in hand. She looked at the trees as if daring one of them to so much as shake a leaf at her.

"I am grateful," Torvik said. "And don't you all stand around staring at me! Watch the trees or fill the barrels!" he shouted at a circle of wide-eyed sailors who had seemingly sprung from nowhere.

The sailors obeyed, and the withdrawal from the island was a retreat rather than a rout, in as much as they left no barrels or other gear ashore. No one turned his back on anything larger than a pebble or a strand of seaweed until they were all on the beach and ready to board the boats.

Nor did any of the watering party stop telling their shipmates about the magic loose on Suivinari Island, once they were aboard, until Sorraz gave the order to raise anchor and make sail.

* * * * *

At sunset, Torvik left the top to a lookout, because his bruised leg was more than a trifle painful and for another reason that he would barely admit to himself. The sooner the darkness swallowed Suivinari Island, the sooner he would feel safe from whatever lurked in the waters around it and the sand and rock inland.

He felt halfway between a coward and a fool for even thinking this, but he doubted that he was the only one aboard *Kingfisher's Claw* whose wits were a trifle blunter after today. It would be as well if they spoke to another ship soon, to carry the warning and perhaps learn if others had seen any strangeness in these waters. At the moment, most of the crew would willingly see even a minotaur ship lift above the horizon, rather than an empty sea.

The thought made Torvik lift his telescope, not that he expected to see anything that the lookout had not already spotted, but sometimes on a hazy night there was clear air on deck and fog around the tops, instead of the reverse.

Flickering, sinuous movement close to a barely-visible reef drew his attention. He swung the telescope to see why the porpoises were that close inshore, then saw that the sleek backs were too small to be porpoises. Seals or sea otters, most likely.

Then Torvik could have sworn he saw a faint ruddy glow in the water, where one of the seals had swum. The glow made a circle in the water, lasting only as long as a single deep breath—but out of it swam a human form. It reached the rocks with swift flashing strokes of long arms, then rose on long legs.

It was a woman, with hair the same color as the glow— a rich dark wine hue, and flowing all the way down to her knees, so that it alone cloaked her graceful form from Torvik's eyes.

Then she vanished so suddenly that Torvik suspected magic before he saw a rock pinnacle that effectively shielded anyone behind it from the ship. If there was anyone to shield. Torvik wrestled for a moment with the thought that he had in truth seen nothing. But if that were so, then his eyes and wits were both failing him. Better to accept that he had seen a seal—no, it would be a sea otter— change to a woman, and know that the Dimernesti also swam in these waters.

Which might mean they knew of the minotaur-killer? Yes, but it was far from certain that anything would come of that.

The Dimernesti were rarer by far in these waters than the Dargonesti. Few humans could find them, and the Dargonesti were not always willing to help. Even when found, the Dimernesti were slow to speak to humans, who had hunted seals and sea otters in a way that they had never hunted porpoises and dolphins.

Hidden by the darkness and his beard, Torvik's mouth twisted in a wry smile as a thought struck him. The captain would certainly know more of the Dimernesti than most, as he knew more than most of any creature that could fall to his harpoon. But in gaining that knowledge, Sorraz had most likely shed enough Dimernesti blood that the shallows-dwellers would see *Kingfisher's Claw* at the bottom of the sea before they gave anyone aboard her so much as a dead clam.

Chapter 1

About the same time as Torvik sighted Suivinari Island, the lord and lady of Tirabot Manor in the lands of mighty Istar received a guest.

Sir Niebar ducked his head gracefully to pass through the doorway into the narrow tower chamber where Sir Pirvan and the Lady Haimya waited. The two men, both Knights of the Rose, greeted each other formally, then embraced. Sir Niebar actually chuckled.

"It has reached my ears that your people are wagering on how soon and how often I will knock my head on your doorways," he said. Long before he wore any emblem of the Knights of Solamnia, he had been known as Niebar the Tall, and the years had left him much of that height.

Pirvan said nothing. He could tell that his chief and comrade had brought ill news and was trying to hide it behind lightness, as an army's scouts might hide behind the smoke of a grass fire. But Niebar had not succeeded Sir Marod of Ellersford at the head of the "secret work" of the Knights of Solamnia without the courage to tell plain truths sooner rather than later.

"If any contrive your downfall, we will punish them as they deserve," Pirvan's wife said, smiling.

"I am not so old that I have lost the power to judge the height of a door, or lost the suppleness to pass under it," Niebar said. He lowered himself onto one end of a bench that was, save for a chest and two fading, moth-riddled tapestries, the sole furniture of the chamber.

From the way Niebar moved, Pirvan judged that these words were something of whistling in the dark. Stiffness in the joints did not kill, the way congestions of blood in the brain did, but they could make a man miserable or even unfit for a knight's work.

When Sir Marod died three months ago, Sir Niebar had made no secret of preferring to let Pirvan step directly into command of the secret work. However, the Grand Master and the high knights disagreed; Pirvan rose one rung on the ladder rather than two.

"Would you care for refreshment?" Haimya asked.

Niebar shook his head. "The last stage of our journey was easy. Our stop for the night had ample water, kender left out fruit and bread, and word of our strength has reached all the bandits in this part of the country."

This was likely true. Niebar took even more seriously than most a knight's duty not to lie to another knight. Pirvan still thought that he heard more behind it.

So did Haimya. Her eyebrows twitched and one shoulder lifted slightly. She had a whole arsenal of these subtle gestures and movements, which Pirvan could read like a scroll after more than twenty years of being wed to her.

"The kingpriest is dead," Niebar said.

Pirvan made a gesture of aversion from the thieves' underground of Istar. Haimya made several of her own. Then she threw her husband a speaking look. Her right to be here did not carry the right to prod Niebar to greater eloquence. Prodding her husband was another matter.

"We heard not even the smallest rumor," Pirvan said. He frowned. "Was it sudden?"

"So sudden that tales of poison are already abroad in the streets of Istar," Niebar said.

Pirvan needed no further looks from Haimya to understand

where this was leading. He needed only to contemplate Niebar's too-carefully commanded face.

"Am I suspected?"

Niebar shook his head but simultaneously tugged at his beard. Pirvan knew a moment's wild temptation to tug at his own beard, then challenge Niebar to a beard-tugging contest that might go on until both were clean-chinned.

Instead, Pirvan shrugged. "What can I say, but this: I owe Sir Marod more than I owe any man, living or dead. Without him, I might at best be an aging thief in Istar. I would never have known Haimya, and the gods themselves could not reward the giver of such a gift."

Haimya actually blushed at those words, and squeezed her husband's hand.

"But I never suspected the kingpriest of involvement in Sir Marod's death," Pirvan continued. "Even had I done so, I would have thought of the honor of the knights, and my own. Also, I am no longer friends, as I once was, with the thieves of Istar. I have no one answering to me there who could poison the kingpriest, even if I were foolish enough to ask it. More likely they would buy the goodwill of the kingpriest by poisoning *me*, and taking my head to him in a sack of salt."

Niebar sighed, as if he had just laid down a burden. "I beg your pardon that I had to ask, but the orders came from the Grand Master," he said.

"Is he suspicious?" Haimya said. Had her voice been a sword, the Grand Master would have done well not to turn his back on her.

"No," Niebar said firmly. "But he needs to placate those who are, both in Istar and among the ranks of the knights themselves. I thank you for your frankness and even temper."

"Had anyone else come with such questions, they might not have met either," Pirvan said. "Now can we offer you that refreshment? We need to think what a new kingpriest may mean, which means more talking than I can any longer do dry-throated."

"By all means," Niebar said. "Or rather, by means of a

discreet servant. And—is this chamber warded?"

Pirvan pronounced four words, each rolling on through five or six syllables. He felt a prickling behind his ears and eyeballs as he pronounced the last word.

"Now it is," he said. "A gift from our old friends, Tarothin and Sirbones. They bound the room with the spell so that anyone at need could ward the room with those words I just uttered. They will come back next year to renew it. For now we are safe with what I have just done."

"I remember now, that you commanded a modest spell or two of your own," Niebar said. He sighed. "I would gladly command one myself, to bring down a pegasus to ride for the next few weeks. The death of the kingpriest will mean work for us all."

* * * * *

Even in the days when all of Istar's priests could meet in a single room there had commonly been one who was first among equals. His title varied. "Kingpriest" was only the most recent and still not accepted by all. It was also a recent development that this first-among-equals was considered a true office, to which a man was, for lack of a better term, elevated. Although in this case, "recent" was a relative term. Istar's priests had thought of themselves as a united body for several centuries.

The ways of becoming the leading priest in Istar had been many and various over the years. Once, it was said, a "principal priest" lived so long that by the time he died, so had all those who knew how to choose his successor, and the priests of Istar had no leader at all for nearly five years.

That would not be the case now, Pirvan knew. The dead kingpriest had reigned barely seven years, after being elected (it was said) through fear of a quarrel with the merchants over his predecessor's fondness for intrigues, assassinations, and general ruthlessness. If this kingpriest had not zealously sought to do good, he had at least cautiously sought to avoid evil. His death was hardly good news, still less so if it was by assassination.

"Of course," Niebar added, "we have only the priests' word that the death was sudden. It could well be that the man died of some common illness that he neglected until it was so far advanced that he needed a god, not a healer, to save him. He who sits on the kingpriest's seat must find room for more work in any given day than most princes."

"All of this is honorable to the kingpriest's memory," Haimya said. "But what it has to do with us, you have not made clear. Unless the succession to the high seat is likely to be bloody, or otherwise of concern to the knights?"

"Our best judgment is that it could be both," Niebar said. "The Servants of Silence were disbanded, true. Many then hired themselves out to priests with more ambition than scruples. Also, the street-corner howling that humans alone have true virtue in the sight of the gods is as loud as ever."

Haimya looked as if she wished to spit, but contented herself with suggesting that all such loud, wrong persons be drowned in hobgoblins' privies. Pirvan said nothing, but frowned. He kept that dour cast of countenance so long that Sir Niebar seemed on the verge of fidgeting when the other knight at last spoke.

"Have you come to urge us to abandon Tirabot Manor and flee into Solamnia?" Pirvan asked.

"I would not use the word 'flee,' myself," Sir Niebar said primly. "No one among the knights will doubt your courage in coming to Dargaard Keep, however, or some other place beyond the reach of the kingpriest and his minions."

"It is not certain that the next kingpriest will *have* minions," Pirvan said. "As for courage, I would doubt my own if I fled. So might those left behind."

"They are not of the knights," Sir Niebar said, then flushed as he realized how ill chosen his words might seem.

Haimya plucked his stammering attempts at an explanation out of the air, like a falcon swooping on a fat pigeon. "That does not mean they are nothing," she said. "I doubt you meant to say so. But too many among the knights these days seem to think only of what serves the Orders, forgetting all that the Oath and the Measure say about protecting those in need. Have you become one of those knights with short memories, Sir Niebar?"

"I have not," their visitor said. "Because I have not, I remember Sir Pirvan's rare value to the knights, and through them, to all under the knights' protection. Your duties to protect extend far beyond the border stones of Tirabot Manor, Sir Pirvan. Or has *your* memory begun to fail?"

"My memory is quite sound enough," Pirvan said sternly, "to tell me that Sir Marod forbade you to raise this matter with me, some while ago. He used rather strong words, or so I have heard."

Niebar's face showed the ghost of a smile. "From anyone else who used such language, I would have demanded satisfaction," he said. "Well, perhaps not from you or your lady. But Sir Marod—"

"If you say 'Sir Marod is dead' as an excuse for folly, I will carve out your tongue," Haimya interrupted in a tone that could have frozen a waterfall.

"I was about to say that Sir Marod was also concerned about your folk being used as hostages, to divert you from the concerns of the knights," Sir Niebar said, with the ghost of a smile. "Do you not have a duty to spare them that danger, if you can?"

"If I can, yes," Pirvan said. "Are you offering help to that end?"

"Were you really a thief, Pirvan?" Niebar laughed. "Or did you sell your father's candles and honey in the marketplace, always getting the best of the bargain?"

"Some call that thieving, too," Haimya said. "But I swear this much: I shall hold my tongue while Sir Niebar offers his aid."

"Then the gods are still among us, working miracles," Niebar said. "What next, a kender king—?" at which point Haimya drew her dagger (still sheathed) and mimed cutting the knight's throat.

Pirvan ordered more wine and a plate of dried gooseberry cakes, tested the warding of the chamber, and resolved to open his mind as wide as his ears, to Sir Niebar's offer.

He did not doubt that peril could come to the innocent from the ill will of the kingpriest. He merely doubted that he could do much against it by fleeing over the border into Solamnia like an escaping slave!

* * * * *

Night had come to Tirabot Manor, and with it sleep, to all except those whom nature made wakeful, or whose work kept them up nights. One of these was a shepherd, whose pipes floated on the breeze up from the pastures beyond the Silver Creek bridge.

Two others were those who listened to the piping, the lord and lady of Tirabot Manor. They sat side by side on a bench in a newly-carved window in their chamber, large enough to let in sun by day and fresh air by night. It was too high for rams or other siege engines to easily reach, and iron shutters lay ready to guard it against projectiles or intruders.

"Sir Niebar is not a fool," Haimya said at last.

"I did not say he was," Pirvan answered. "Did you hear me thinking it?"

"I heard you thinking that he was a poor guest for raising the matter again."

"I think less of that than of his not keeping his men-at-arms away from our table," Pirvan joked. "They ate as if they had starved for a week."

"Perhaps they had," the lady said, smiling. "Niebar is most likely here without a purse from the knights. We do not know how far his own silver runs."

"One more reason for not abandoning the manor. A landless knight is not the best fitted to pay for others' secrets out of his own purse."

"True," Haimya said. "But we need not abandon our people to spare ourselves abandoning the manor."

Pirvan looked at Haimya. He always took pleasure in that, even when as now she was swathed in a heavy woolen robe against the night's chill. Under that robe lay a woman whom he could hardly believe had been his wife and lover for more than twenty years, and mother of three children, two of them old enough to wed.

"I think what you have to say is too important to trickle out in riddles," he told her, "like a man disposing of a night's beer."

"How unfit for a lady's ears, such crudeness!" Haimya said, in tones of mock horror.

"Is the plain truth unfit for a gentleman's?" Pirvan riposted. It would be pleasant to set to one of their verbal duels, which at this hour seldom ended other than in bed. But they needed an answer for Sir Niebar before he departed at dawn.

"I was thinking of Vuinlod," Haimya said. "Any of our folk who could not live under the kingpriest could find homes there."

Pirvan understood. Under Lady Eskaia, the little port city in northern Solamnia had grown into a refuge for every sort and condition of folk who needed tolerant neighbors and few Istaran spies. Haimya's notion made sense, as Pirvan understood it, but it was not without flaws either.

"Aurhinius is no danger," Haimya said, as if she had read Pirvan's first objection on his face. "Eskaia has him eating out of her hand."

"A good way to find crumbs in the sheets of a morning, if I recall the days when we were young like that," Pirvan began. He broke off at a mock-slap from Haimya.

"Solamnia is still bound by the Swordsheath Scroll and the Great Meld with Istar," he went on. "What of them?"

"What of it?" she answered. "Have the kingpriests' notions of justice yet been enforced on Solamnic territory, even under the most zealous of the breed?"

"Not yet." He did not add that it would go hard with their people if this changed, because in such case it would go hard with everyone. There would be no safety for the just and honorable anywhere under the sun, or at least anywhere Istar's reach extended.

"I suppose we could pay Eskaia that visit she has been urging upon us these past two years," Pirvan said. "Take as our guards enough trustworthy folk so that they can bring back word of life in Vuinlod. Then those whom we urge to go will not be leaping into the unknown like apes from a vine."

Haimya patted his cheek, then drew him to her and kissed him. "That will answer Niebar well enough, I think. And now that we have done our duty . . ."

The kiss lengthened. Presently she led him to the bed and shrugged herself out of her robe. A warming pan in the bed had done its work, so that Pirvan was not cold even in the brief moment after he disrobed and before Haimya embraced him.

Chapter 2

The mounted company rode up to Vuinlod in a sullen twilight that made one suspect the end of day. The sun had not shown her face since before noon yesterday, and sometimes the clouds had shadowed the land more deeply than now. Altogether, it was a day to make even Solamnic Knights glad that their journey was near its end.

Three knights rode with the company, Sir Pirvan first among them. In the middle rode Sir Darin Waydolsson and his lady Rynthala. In the rear, the newly-sworn Knight of the Crown, Sir Hawkbrother Redthornsson rode with his betrothed, Young Eskaia. This young lady, eldest daughter of Pirvan and Haimya, was so called to distinguish her from the Lady Eskaia of Vuinlod, after whom she was named. Along with the three knights and their ladies rode a company of Tirabot Manor guards, chosen for their skill at arms, their sharp eyes, and their keen wits.

The task of spying out Vuinlod as a refuge for the Tirabot Manor folk would begin tonight.

Vuinlod lay hard on the Solamnic coast, rising from the shore of a sheltered bay up the sides of hills that formed a bowl around the bay. The landward slopes of the hills showed few signs that a town was nearby, being mostly terraced fields and orchards, with farmhouses and byres scattered about.

On either side of the road—well graveled, Pirvan noticed, and with drainage ditches to either side—stretches of forest lay scattered like swatches of cloth on the floor of a tailor's shop. They were mostly second growth, and to Pirvan's eye the trees seemed shrunken from the last time he had come this way.

Of course, that was some years past, and the mere need for firewood and building timber would take its toll of the woods. But it seemed to him that it was not always the trees best suited for hearth or home that had vanished. More than one strip of scrubby ogresnut wound its way most inconveniently across fields and along the banks of streams.

It was Sir Darin who gave voice to Pirvan's suspicions, when he and Hawkbrother rode up—as befitted junior knights—to confer with their chief.

"I think the Vuinlod folk have laid out defenses," Darin said, "to halt or at least delay any attack while they take to their ships."

"Who has so great a quarrel with them?" Hawkbrother asked.

Young Eskaia spoke before her father could. "The same folk who spoke against your becoming a knight," she said. "Or worse, if they are not bound by the Oath and the Measure, and have taken the kingpriest's silver."

Those words made the day seem gloomier still. The new kingpriest had the reputation of a fierce hater of all who lacked virtue, and might be one of those who thought only humans possessed it. Certainly he had publicly appointed several men whispered to have once been Servants of Silence; just as certainly, these dogs were not yet off their chain. Time was passing, and if enough passed, even kingpriests might gain wisdom.

At the moment, however, Pirvan unashamedly wished to gain no more than a roof over his head and something hot in his stomach. "Listen to your betrothed, Sir Hawkbrother," he said. "Now let us be on our way. And spread out a trifle farther. Trees can hide enemies as well as friends, and there has been ample time for word of our coming to reach the ears of both."

A mizzling rain blew in their faces as they urged their horses into motion once more.

* * * * *

Water dripped from Gildas Aurhinius's clothing as he climbed the stairs to Lady Eskaia's chambers. He left damp footprints on the polished wood. The lady met him at the door, holding out a heated, scented towel.

"Ahhh," he said. "You are my good spirit."

He must have read something in her face, because he stopped drying his hair in midstroke.

"Never be afraid to remember Jemar, no matter when or where," he said.

"I never have been," Eskaia said tartly, "and you can neither give nor withhold permission." Then she smiled and embraced him. "But I thank you for the kind words."

"You will be drenched, if you go on hugging me," Aurhinius said, with his mouth muffled in her hair. "It is the sort of day that cannot decide to be winter or spring. It ends by having the vices of both, and the virtues of neither."

"Then a soldier who does his duty out of doors on a day like this surely ought to have a warm woman embrace him when he comes inside," Eskaia said. She stood on tiptoe to kiss him, then led him inside to where a couch stood by a table holding a tray with hot spiced wine, strong tarberry tea, honey cakes, melon bread, and dried fruit.

"How fare our defenses?" Eskaia asked, when Aurhinius had drained two cups of tea and one of wine, and was halfway through a plate of cakes.

"All the necessary posts have sentries, and I would not ask anyone to face this weather otherwise. The tunnelers to the northwest are too busy bailing to dig. The rest are putting in extra props and moving stores and weapons to higher ground."

"No word of our friends?"

"None, but they are surely traveling more slowly than they intended. The roads are too thin for riding and too thick for rowing."

"As well," Eskaia said. She reached into her overgown and drew out an oiled leather packet. "We shall have more time to consider how to reply to this."

Aurhinius's eyebrows no longer rose when she handed him a letter concerning some matter of war or statecraft that she had already opened and read. He had accepted that Eskaia ruled in Vuinlod and he was her consort by courtesy; no less, but no more.

His eyes, however, seemed to move from her to the text of the letter and back. She realized then that his embrace had turned the thin silk of her overgown transparent. She wore an undertunic of heavier silk against the cold, held in place by a single thong around her neck.

At last Aurhinius placed the letter on the table. One of the cats crawled out from under the couch, perched on the letter, and started licking crumbs from the nearly-empty tray. Eskaia lifted the beast onto her lap and stroked it until it purred.

"This idea speaks well for whoever had it," Aurhinius said at last. "Have you any notion who that might be?"

"None," Eskaia said. "Except that it is someone who listens to the merchants of Istar. They would be the principal victims of Karthayan enmity, which would be certain if Istar sent a great fleet wandering about in northern waters."

"Whereas a call for volunteers for a voyage to Suivinari Island," Aurhinius finished, nodding, "could bring in Karthayans, rovers, even minotaurs. Can you ask among your father's friends, if they know more?"

"Most of them believe that they have long since paid all debts to one who has, after all, become a rival in her own right," Eskaia said. She did not keep a certain smugness out of her voice. Being a good steward of what Jemar left her had made her proud. Enlarging that fortune until she was called, only half in jest, "the Princess of Vuinlod" had made her prouder still.

It had not, however, made Gildas Aurhinius prince. His lack of envy of her wealth and power was another of his numerous virtues.

"More than an additional voyage each year or the price of tar could be at stake here," Aurhinius pointed out. "Can you ask, even if you expect no answer?"

"I—wait. I can ask Torvik and Chuina to ask their friends. Torvik will certainly get answers, now that he has been made captain."

Aurhinius stared. "You did not tell me that news," he said.

"It came only two days ago. He is leaving *Kingfisher's Claw*, to be captain over *Red Elf*. She is only a small ship, twenty crew at most, but she is his own, and at twenty-one—"

Aurhinius interrupted Eskaia by kissing her soundly on her lips, then her cheeks, then her forehead, while his arms went around her waist. The cat squalled a brief protest, then hastily took itself off.

Presently Eskaia realized that they were both on the couch, and she was nestled against his chest. It was a comfortable chest, rather like that of a large bear grown gentle with age, and warmed her almost as much as did her pride in her son.

"We shall need a banquet worthy of so much good news," Aurhinius said. "Your son a captain, our friends among us, and wisdom in Istar."

"I thought all wisdom had left Istar when you chose exile," Eskaia said.

"Oh, I am sure some remained who could find their shoes at dawn without help," Aurhinius said. His embrace tightened.

In time, Eskaia felt thick but still deft fingers undoing the thong around her neck.

* * * * *

At long bowshot from the foot of one of Vuinlod's shielding hills the road made a sharp bend. There, an escort met

Pirvan and his companions. They were three men and two women, mounted on shaggy, undersized horses, and had the air of being more at home on a deck than in a saddle. They took their positions like seasoned fighters, however, and the procession wound its way onward into the hills.

From here the hills were mostly bare. In spots, too bare to be natural, with hardly a brown and wizened weed rising higher than a man's calf. Pirvan mouthed "Fields of fire?" at Haimya, and she nodded.

"It seems they have cleared the ground to allow archers free play," Hawkbrother said. "If I were they, I would also have tunnels dug through the hills, so that my men could pass through and take in the rear anyone who thinks himself safe on the crest."

One of the escorts gave Hawkbrother a bloodthirsty look. Pirvan hoped it was over his chattering, not his being a "desert barbarian" wearing the marks of a Solamnic Knight.

Before Pirvan could inquire, Sir Darin fixed the new-fledged knight with a look only a trifle less hostile than the Vuinlodder's. "We know that you did well in the course on fortifications, at the Keep," Darin said. "We also know that by blood and training, your eyes are sharp. But you need prove neither of these, by blathering to all secrets that our hosts may wish to keep close."

Hawkbrother gave the wisest reply: silence. This left both his betrothed and her father without cause to speak.

Darin told the truth about Hawkbrother's study in fortifications, which to Pirvan was no small marvel. The Free Rider chief's son turned knight had been raised in a tent that could be struck in half an hour, and pitched two days later a hundred miles away. Pirvan had never known anyone with less experience of having a roof over his head, except for certain seafarers who never came ashore except to die.

But then he remembered the caves and tunnels within the sacred mountain of Hawkbrother's birth clan, the Gryphons. These showed magic or tools or both, so perhaps the ancestors of the Free Riders had not been strangers to permanent dwellings, and the memory ran deep without having died.

Meanwhile, the Vuinlodder who had glared at Hawk-brother was now trying to stifle laughter without falling off her horse. Pirvan labored as hard, stifling a sigh of relief. Knights of Solamnia, after all, did not admit to being so much as uneasy, let alone fearful.

The road now wound upward across slopes too steep for a more direct path, and straightened out only when it plunged into valleys between the hills. In one of these valleys, so steep-walled that it might have been gloom-shrouded even on a sunny day, a messenger from Lady Eskaia rode up to them.

The messenger was a kender, perched on a mule nearly the size of a horse, with elegant grooming that had suffered somewhat from the weather. So had the kender herself; her hair resembled a mop recently used to scrub the mule's stall and her clothes hung on her like wilted leaves.

"The Lady Eskaia bids you make haste," the kender said. "She bids you to a dinner, the knights and their ladies, and must know if you will come."

"Ask the road and the weather," Pirvan's chief guard said. Human stare and kender stare collided with an almost audible *clang*. Pirvan then saw the kender frown, and suspected she was waiting to see if the guards objected to being excluded from the feast or to receiving the news from a kender.

"Aye," the chief guard said. She was so short that some suspected her of dwarven blood, but no dwarf was ever that wiry or that fast on her feet. "We have duties to our knights."

"Duties?" the kender said, wiping hair and rain off her forehead and nearly poking herself in the eye with a thumb.

"Yes," the chief said. "Guarding our knights. As we swore to do. You've heard of oaths?"

"Oh, of course. Everybody takes some every week. But some of ours are not to harm guests. That's an oath even older than the Oath and the Measure of the knights. I can't imagine how anyone in Vuinlod would want to harm you.

"Or perhaps I could imagine it. But it would take a while. My imagination doesn't work well in bad weather, either. So would you like me to tell the story in a poem or a—?"

"What we would like you to do," Pirvan interrupted, "is tell Lady Eskaia that we accept her invitation as you have given it. We shall make all the haste we can. Meanwhile, we thank her."

"I go at once," the kender said, turning her mount. "My friends are laboring hard. They will be happy to know their work will not be wasted."

She dug in her heels, and had the mule up to a trot before she disappeared around the next bend.

" 'My friends?' " the chief guard said. "Are the kender preparing the feast?"

"They may try to, if we do not ride on fast enough to help Lady Eskaia stop them," Pirvan said. "Not that the kender would poison us, you understand. But I think we all want more of a meal than they are likely to have ready!"

* * * * *

Famine—or, at least, indigestion—was averted at the last minute. Kender are not the best folk on Krynn for keeping secrets, so Lady Eskaia's cook heard of what the kender planned before it was too late. A flying column of undercooks and scullions charged in one door of the kitchen as the kender fled with more haste than dignity out of the other.

The only irreparable damage turned out to be the biscuits, which Lady Eskaia suggested be sent to Torvik for ballast for his new ship. Surveying the rest of the scene, Gildas Aurhinius shook his head. "No one can say that kender are stupid," he said. "But they will try to be wise about six different things in the space of an hour. So nothing is done, or, even worse, much is begun but left unfinished."

The banquet ran heavily to fish, and Eskaia noted that this was not to the tastes of some of her guests. On the other hand, Sir Darin seemed to inhale broiled salmon and fried oysters, salted leefish and planked browser with spiced kelp sauce, as if he were having the last meal of this life.

"This is how we feasted at Waydol's stronghold," he explained. "Our feasts were few, but the sea served us most of them."

"You at least could not have been on short commons too often," Lady Eskaia said. She was applying herself to a bowl of pickled rockfish with a peppery turnip dressing. "Not and reach your present stature."

Darin flushed like a boy, which added still further to his notable good looks. He was far too young to stir her, even had they both been free, but he was a fine thing to see, like a blooded stallion or a vase of Ergothian alabaster.

"I have the parents I cannot remember to thank for that," he said. "That was a precious gift, too. Even from beyond the grave, Waydol was wise beyond the common run of men or minotaurs. He still might not have taken such care with me if I had been of more common human stature."

"And you are taking care that your line does not diminish, in any way," Aurhinius said, with that rumbling laugh Eskaia had grown to recognize as the sign to end his drinking for the night.

Eskaia called for spice water and turned the conversation to the affairs of Belkuthas. Darin and Rynthala had made it their seat, then left it under the care of the local dwarven thane when they came north.

"The dwarves said they could do more work on the defenses with us gone than they could with us in residence," Rynthala said. "What was it that they told you once, Darin?"

"They told me that they did not mind having humans loom over them like the cliffs of Bardrof, but when those humans knew not one stone from another, it was a trifle wearying," Darin answered. "Is there anywhere a man can expect courtesy from those who serve him?"

"Don't look for it at Tirabot Manor," Haimya said, and they all laughed. Indeed, there was a warmth in the air of the chamber that to Eskaia seemed to come from the presence of eight friends who were all more or less content with the courses their lives had steered. To be sure, Hawkbrother and Young Eskaia were young enough to be Gildas's grandchildren, and might never reach his years, but. . . .

Eskaia smiled, leaned far over, and planted a kiss on Gildas Aurhinius's cheek. Before he could move to return it, she turned to the assemblage and said, "I have news that deserves our attention. This letter—" she held up the report of the volunteer fleet's being raised "—and an announcement: Gildas Aurhinius has asked for my hand in marriage, and I have consented."

Then, as Aurhinius tried not to gape, she handed the letter to Pirvan.

It made the rounds of the six guests quickly enough. Eskaia was waiting for Pirvan to lead the replies long before Aurhinius had stopped murmuring what he was going to do to her for ambushing him as she had.

"Just be sure you keep those promises, and not only on the wedding night but afterward," she whispered back, then saw that Pirvan was ready to speak.

He spoke briefly, as usual, and wisely, as almost usual. "We cannot refuse this invitation," he said. "To do so, or to send only modest strength, would be to let the kingpriest's minions guide the fleet. We must do our best. Minotaurs dead on this island used so freely by both the Destined Race and our own people could lead us into a costly war. This is a matter of greater import than might be obvious at first from the situation at hand."

Darin nodded. "Indeed," he said. "Ah—I do not know much of magic, or those who work with it, but it seems to me that we now have a chance to send wizards and priests who are not in the kingpriest's pocket.

"If any such are needed at all," he added.

"Likely enough they will be," Haimya said. "I have heard from my kin in Karthay that two ships that intended to call at Suivinari are overdue. We still may not need magic-workers, but if we do not have them with us, we surely will."

"It could be minotaurs—" Aurhinius began, and was interrupted by Darin's clearing his throat. Rynthala put a hand on her husband's arm, and Haimya shook her head.

"That was thought, too, in Karthay, and asked of certain discreet minotaur captains," Darin said. "The minotaurs said that they too had ships missing or overdue in those waters."

"Minotaurs have been known to lie," Aurhinius said, and this time his look alone quelled any reply from Darin. "But not more than humans, and seldom in a matter of life or death at sea. They know that Zeboim has no friends among any land-dwelling race."

Eskaia nodded. "Then Gildas and I will see to it that Vuinlod does its share," she said. "With luck, we can put to sea with enough ships to hold our own soldiers, sailors, and magicworkers. We may even have room to carry the men whom the Knights of Solamnia will surely wish to send on such an important matter."

* * * * *

Pirvan stood in front of the silver mirror in its gilded wood frame and combed his beard. The mirror was one of many little luxuries in the chamber he and Haimya shared; small, but as snug as a ground squirrel's winter burrow.

Pirvan believed Lady Eskaia when she said that Jemar and she had made their fortune honestly. He was not so sure about her having done without help from her father's fellow merchant princes. It would be only wisdom for them to aid a sea rover and later his widow, so as to have their goodwill and some use of their ears and eyes.

The comb tugged at the knight's beard. For all the steel of Krynn, he could not have grown a proper knight's mustache. But his beard was more robust, gray as it was.

Pirvan finished combing and turned to the bed. It was of ebony inlaid with mother-of-pearl, with curtains of silk as fine as one of Haimya's summer robes. It was also so piled with quilts and coverlets that it was hard to tell which bulge was Haimya.

Pirvan walked to the bed and began prodding the bulges. At last he was rewarded by a murmured, "Ouch!"

"I thought you were asleep."

"Not quite." Haimya thrust an arm out and drew her husband onto the bed beside her. "Do you think Eskaia was jesting when she said she had accepted Aurhinius?" she asked.

Pirvan frowned. That was a question he had not expected, and for which he had no ready answer. "You were her attendant for two years," he said. "You ought to know her better than I."

"I attended her for two years when she was hardly older than our daughter is now, and greener than our Eskaia was at fourteen," Haimya explained. "And that was many years ago."

"You evade your duties well."

"When have I ever done that?" she asked. "Come here, and I will tend to them this very moment." Her grin and the tight grip on his arm showed what she meant by "duties."

Pirvan laughed. "If the question is serious—"

"To be sure," Haimya said.

"Then I would say that she does not jest. That she may speak of a previous proposal, but that she considers herself to have accepted it regardless. I think she would break Aurhinius's head if he refused now, as she would break his heart if she jested. Eskaia is not the sort to make such jests."

"I am of the same mind," she said. "As well, because with Eskaia and Aurhinius leading Vuinlod's volunteers, there will be space enough for the Knights of Solamnia."

"Why do you think any knights will come?" Pirvan asked. "Or that I will even ask for them?"

"Because I have heard you muttering to yourself, in a way you do only when you are composing a letter to Sir Niebar. If you did not intend to ask for knights, you would not be intending such a letter."

Pirvan felt that Haimya's logic leaped ahead at a pace that left him floundering far to the rear. He was, however, used to her mind working as the Free Riders raided: too fast for others to follow. She also made sense.

"If the knights sail to Suivinari in the ships of Vuinlod and its friends," Pirvan said, "then they will blazon their friendship with the town for all to see. For the town, and for all its folk, human and otherwise."

It occurred to Pirvan that the Grand Master might also listen to those who argued that the knights should declare no such friendship, lest Istar take it amiss. Pirvan hoped that no Grand Master could be such a lackwit as to confuse the kingpriest and his minions with Istar and all its folk, great or small, wise or foolish.

Hope was all that he could do, however. That, and not put his doubts into words. That would spoil the warm mood in the chamber tonight.

He realized just how warm it was, when Haimya gripped his arm again, and with her free hand tugged at his beard until he lowered his head to receive a kiss.

"I thought you were too weary," he said.

"Weary, but in need of soothing," she whispered. "I wonder how much of the light loving among the sellswords came from that need, after a battle or a hard march."

Pirvan let himself be drawn under the bedclothes. He wondered briefly if Haimya had a portion of the "light loving" herself when she was a sell-sword, then decided that it did not matter if other men had once held her.

For twenty years he and his lady had held each other, and held *to* each other. The gods might take away everything else they had given him, and he would still be richer than he had ever dreamed of being.

Chapter 3

Gerik of Tirabot halted his descent from the wall as a loose stair stone turned under his foot. He knelt to examine the stone more closely.

One more piece of work for the masons, he thought. A long list already, certain to become longer and costlier.

He wondered what it would cost to gird the manor house and outbuildings with a wall such as had once defended the old Tirabot Keep up the hill. Or one such as the dwarves were now finishing at the citadel of Belkuthas, far to the south. This would certainly be a sum far beyond his father's means, and likely to daunt even those Knights of Solamnia who supported the idea of a strong Tirabot.

Another reason for not submitting himself as a candidate for the knights, Gerik decided. If they did not think they owed his father protection, then certainly Pirvan of Tirabot did not owe them his only son.

He leaped down the last few steps, landing with flexed ankles and no unexpected pains. He was proud of being as fit and trained in arms as any knight—even Sir Niebar had called him so. Perhaps not having to spend so much time memorizing all the books that the Orders demanded helped, giving him more time for arms practice.

No, that was unjust to the Knights of Solamnia, and flattered himself. Gerik had not asked to join the knights because, as the son of Sir Pirvan, he was captain over the manor when his father was away. Even when Gerik traveled with his father, both Pirvan and his other companion treated him as a full-fledged warrior. To return to being treated as a child, as he would be during his training among the knights, was not something Gerik could face.

This was hardly a reason he could confess to his father. Pirvan had submitted to the training of the knights when he was rising thirty, a seasoned master thief of Istar and all but a married man as well. Pirvan would wonder (aloud) if Gerik thought the rule about learning to obey before you learned to command did not apply to him.

Footsteps behind made him turn. His sister Rubina was hurrying up to him, holding a pewter tray with a letter on it, the ink still drying.

"Brother, can you read this letter of mine to our parents before I seal it?" she asked. "I want to know if I have said everything as I ought to, and not written down any family secrets."

"I thought your tutor does that," Gerik said impatiently.

"He's asleep."

"Not drunk at this time of day, I hope."

"No," she said. "He complained of a headache, but I didn't smell wine on his breath."

"Good."

Chedishin (the short form of his name) was a half-elven retired man-at-arms, whom Pirvan kept on as a tutor for his children; one way of keeping him from starving. With no need to worry about food, Chedishin had for a while indulged himself in wine, until Pirvan frowned and threatened.

Gerik read the letter with great attention, not wishing to offend his younger sister. She wrote a very fair hand and seldom put a word wrong. It was almost as if the great learning of her namesake, a Black Robe wizard who had helped to win Waydol's War but had not survived it, had been passed on to the girl.

As for the rest, she promised to be sturdy rather than tall, and comely rather than beautiful, but Gerik was sure she would have as many suitors as a reasonable girl could wish. He hoped that his parents would live on for many years yet, so that all the work of telling the decent suitors from the others would not fall to him.

He finished the letter and handed it back to Rubina. She read doubt on his face. "Is it the part about how the walls are growing that you do not like?" she asked.

"Yes."

"I thought of that. But Father and Mother have been away long enough that matters have changed. Also, they talked much about strengthening this place, when they thought I could not hear. I know it is a worry to them."

"It is also knowledge our enemies might pay to have," Gerik told her.

"Yes, but if the king—"

"If 'our enemies . . .' " Gerik said, an edge in his voice.

Rubina shrugged, and said, "We know friends from ene-mies. Even I do. But I was going to say, if our *enemies* want to buy the knowledge, they can have it for pennies from any herdsman who has driven his cattle past our gate. They do not need to open our letters."

That was, unfortunately, true. Fortifying Tirabot Manor was not something that could be hidden—any more than could the fortifying of other farms, manors, and estates among their neighbors go unnoticed. A plague of building was abroad in the land, and Gerik thought that by the time it was done, the only folk left with any money would be the masons!

Rubina could send the letter, however. He was about to tell her so when a sentry hailed him from the roof of the manor. "Ho, Master Gerik!" the soldier called. "There's a woman coming out of the woods across the stream from the lower pasture. She looks a mite ragged and sick, and there's some children with her, too."

This was no surprise to Gerik. Tirabot Manor had a name for being hospitable to those driven off their land by local feud, natural disaster, or sheer ill luck. Four or five such parties knocked at the gate during the average month.

"Rubina," Gerik said, "go to the arms room and have the men there ready to ride. Then go to the stables and have my horse—"

Rubina looked rebellious, but before she could turn looks into words, the sentry called again. This time his voice shook with incredulity.

"By all the True Gods! That woman's got a band of *kender* with her!"

* * * * *

The shouts that sounded from behind the kender named Horimpsot Elderdrake grew louder. Either someone had seen him, thought they had seen him, or decided to shout just to encourage himself or his comrades.

The kender thought that the humans needed encouraging. Not so much that they caught him, of course, because if they did that they would surely kill him, and he did not want that to happen.

Not that he was really afraid of death. Kender do not fear death, in and of itself, so much as they hate the fact that death tends to keep them from finding out what happens next. Elderdrake had this curiosity as strongly as the next kender, and the next kender (and all other kender) were a race that seemed to have been created by the gods with an extra measure of curiosity.

However, he was afraid, though not exactly as a human would understand it, of failing his new comrades and their human friend. He had wandered onto the land of the Spillgather clan just after they had decided to befriend a young woman named Ellysta, who had offended the kingpriest, or a friend of the kingpriest, or someone who used the kingpriest's name a great deal.

The Spillgathers had not explained Ellysta's alleged offense in much detail. Elderdrake doubted that he would have understood it if they had. In spite of all the time he had spent traveling, he was still young, and not all of that time had been spent among humans. In fact, he made a serious effort to walk very wide of some kinds of humans.

Being properly brought up, Elderdrake had decided to help his hosts bring Ellysta to safety, which turned out to be Tirabot Manor. This seemed wise to Elderdrake, who knew a good deal about Sir Pirvan, Knight of the Rose and lord of Tirabot, and had learned still more from his own former traveling companion, Imsaffor Whistletrot.

All of which explained why Horimpsot Elderdrake was darting hither and thither in the forest. He was trying to keep the men who had come for Ellysta on his trail, and lead them away from the trail of the Spillgathers who were taking the woman to the manor. If he kept them chasing him long enough, they would never find Ellysta before she was inside the manor's walls and under the protection of its lord and lady.

More shouts echoed through the trees, now conveying more pain than enthusiasm. Stinging nettles grew freely in these woods, even if not so heavily during the late winter as at other times. It sounded as if someone had blundered into a patch of them, or maybe skewered himself on a comrade's weapon.

Elderdrake reached back to pat his hoopak. Even slung across his back, it was a trifle awkward in dense undergrowth, but he would no more abandon it than he would his pouches. It had been a gift from Imsaffor Whistletrot, when the older kender gave up traveling.

The underbrush gave way to a slope deep in dead leaves and the blackened remnants of last year's ferns. By crouching low, Elderdrake discovered that he could be almost completely invisible to anyone either upstream or downstream.

He had just made this discovery when men charged into the open from both directions. They seemed to have some idea of which way he was going, but not where he was. Elderdrake decided to use this fact.

He cupped his hands, pitched his voice to imitate a human's (as well as any kender could, and better than most), and shouted: "Down there! By the big redstripe!"

He had taken note that there were well-grown redstripe trees near both human parties. So naturally, both thought that the shouter was referring to the other redstripe. The range was long for spears, but easy shooting for both long-bows and crossbows.

So many arrows and bolts flew, besides the spears, that Elderdrake was amazed the humans did not wipe each other from the face of Krynn. However, few of the archers and none of the spearmen were true masters of their weapons. Only four men went down, and of these, two rose again. One of those who remained lying down howled and cursed like a man in rude health.

Elderdrake realized that he had not reduced the odds against him much. So he crawled down the slope until he had a clear jump to the other side of the ravine, gathered himself into a ball, and hurled himself across.

He landed sprawling and breathless, having made a very fair jump even for one of his nimble race. Shouts said that he was in plain sight of one human party, but only a few arrows flew his way and none struck close. Either the pursuers were short of arrows, or they were suddenly cautious about striking down comrades.

Two humans attempted to follow Elderdrake's leap. One of them made the jump and after much scrabbling and scrambling, managed to reach level ground. By then Elderdrake was again well hidden.

The other men failed the leap and plummeted into the ravine with crashing and screaming that suggested they would be pursuing no one for a while.

Elderdrake used the time it took the other humans to decide on evergreen whose needles would hide him, stout enough to support him at a great height, and close enough to other trees so that after dark he could leap into their branches and make his escape.

Of course, the humans might realize that his letting himself be treed was a ruse. But even if it only took them the rest of the morning to gain this insight, that would be enough for Ellysta and the Spillgathers. Meanwhile, Elderdrake intended to listen carefully to anything the humans said. The Spillgathers might think they knew everything necessary about their enemies, but Elderdrake's experience of war told him otherwise. Also, even if the Spillgathers knew much, *he* knew very little.

Picking a path through the underbrush, where a four-foot kender could slip along easily and a six-foot human would become hopelessly tangled, Horimpsot Elderdrake sought his tree.

* * * * *

The ship house smelled of fresh lumber, sawdust, paint, and sundry oils. Torvik stopped to watch two workers applying a foul-smelling concoction to the bottom of the ship propped up in the middle of the house, Gridjor Hem's *Flying Dart*. Hem himself was standing on deck amidships, and hailed Torvik when he saw the younger captain. Torvik sometimes wondered how much his acceptance owed to trust in his skill and how much to memory of his father—or even fear of his mother.

However, Hem seemed sincere in his affability and his fraternal embrace of Torvik, when he had scrambled down to the ship house floor. "Don't worry," he added. "We'll have *Dart* out of here within a day or two. Plenty of time for your little beauty."

Torvik knew undue optimism when he heard it, and besides, it was nearly the end of Brookgreen. Half the work on the ships gathering in Vuinlod was already being done outdoors.

"Don't cut yourself short for my sake," Torvik said, trying to sound wholly at ease. "A day or few more, and we'll be able to take her over to Hauldown Strand and do her bottom by careening.

"We might buy some of your bottom grease, though, if you've any left when *Dart* is done. It doesn't smell like you're using whale oil."

Sailors planning a long voyage in warm waters often smeared their ships' bottoms with poisonous grease, to discourage weeds, barnacles, and woodborers. The most common base for such grease was crudely-rendered whale oil, except in waters where the Dargonesti were known to roam.

The Dargonesti knew that humans hunted whales elsewhere, but in their home waters they regarded all the great sea mammals as under their protection. This had led to ugly, even bloody incidents more than a few times in the past, when the Dargonesti had been more numerous, better armed, and more widely scattered.

"I'm not," Hem said. "If there are Dargonesti around Suivinari they might help us, with knowledge if naught else. Small point to offending them. That's seal blubber that went into the oil. Takes more seals than it does whales, but we won't be in—eh, Torvik? You still listening?"

Torvik realized that his face must have shown more than it should have. "With all my ears," he lied.

"Didn't look like it. Your mind was—*ha!* Is it true what they say about Dimernesti around Suivinari?"

Torvik shrugged. "I only know what I think I saw," he said. "Everybody's used their own imagination on that, to spin tales. So what have you heard?"

Hem lowered his voice. "That a Dimernesti came aboard, in her woman shape, and—ah, what men and women do, she did with the men of *Kingfisher's Claw?*"

Torvik laughed. "Don't forget the other half of the story, the Dimernesti in man form who entertained all our women!"

Hem laughed in turn, longer than Torvik thought the joke deserved. When he'd caught his breath and wiped his eyes, the older captain shrugged. "I suppose the odd Dimernesti or two's nothing important," he said. "Not when Suivinari's grown magic that can kill minotaurs and make tree roots dangerous, and we've got to sail up there and put it down before the minotaurs blame us for it! But it's been so long since there've been any tales of the Dimernesti worth hearing that I'm curious.

"So you tell me what you remember, and I won't spread any more tales."

Torvik told of what he'd seen, and added, "We were so far off that I doubt the woman knew I was watching her, let alone whether I found her desirable. And I was so far off that I couldn't tell whether she had six toes on each

---

foot and a harelip!"

Torvik heard relief in Hem's voice, whether at the absence of Dimernesti or at Torvik's not having lain with one, the young captain could not tell. He hoped it was the first. Captains who believed the kingpriest's babble about "lesser breeds who stood beyond the law through their lack of virtue" would be a burden the fleet of Vuinlod did not need.

"So," Hem said. "Should I try tallow for *Dart*'s bottom? Stands to reason that the Dimernesti might feel kinship for seals, the way the Dargonesti do for whales."

"They might well, if there are enough of them to make a difference," Torvik said. "Remember, even if I saw the woman, she might be the only one of her kind in those waters."

"So she might," Hem said, plainly relieved. "I mean no offense to her folk, but if I have to scrape *Dart* clean and grease her again, I'll be another half-month before sailing.

"I've ordered some fish oil to add to our tallow," Torvik said. "It reeks so that only a god could smell anything else on a ship's planks. Let me give you some to mix with the seal oil, and what the Dimernesti don't know won't hurt you."

They shook on that, and Torvik left, much relieved. Hem was no hater of "lesser breeds," only a captain with much work to make his ship ready and little time to do it. There were many such about these days.

He himself had best learned to command his face better. Other captains, less friendly, might also read in it what he did not want known. Even captains spread tales, of his lack of self-command if nothing else.

Also, the Knights of Solamnia who would be sailing aboard Vuinlod's ships would be riding into town within days. And they worshiped self-command almost as a lesser god, and would expect much of it from the son of a man whose memory the knights mostly held in respect.

.* * * * *

Gerik had wanted to greet the woman—the lady, by courtesy—and her companions as befitted one who named himself Gerik of Tirabot.

He wished to ride up to her, dismount, bow, give his name, and ask hers as well as her reason for coming onto land given into his trust by Sir Pirvan of Tirabot, Knight of the Rose. Meanwhile, a mounted escort of men-at-arms would keep their distance, and hidden archers would keep an even greater distance—as well as keeping their arrows properly nocked and aimed.

Instead, everyone who could ride or run swarmed toward the gate, until the sergeants' rude language put a halt to the chaos. Even so, Gerik rode out with ten men instead of five, not all of them by any means fighters, and several other people rode or ran off toward the village.

Gerik only hoped that their riding or running would stop in the village, and that they were only going to bring the marvelous tale to friends and kin, not to those who would carry it to hostile ears. Gerik had no idea who this woman's friends or enemies might be, but he would prefer not to learn by having either of them sprout from the ground at his father's very gates!

It was a short journey to the woman, and the riders took most of it at a canter. As they reined in to a trot, Gerik saw that the kender numbered five, one of them a woman, and that all were armed: two hoopaks, two spears, and a crossbow.

They also took neither their hands from their weapons nor their eyes from the newcomers. Gerik had the sense of dealing with a trained war band, or at least with folk accustomed to working together—something not rare among kender, but seldom seen in daylight by humans.

He waved his men into a half-circle, facing the forest and well back from the woman. Then he himself dismounted and walked toward her, keeping his hands in plain sight, away from his steel. It did not take much learning to realize that the green grease on the head of the crossbow's bolt might be poison—or at least something brewed by a kender healer who intended it to be poisonous.

The kender archer would hardly need poison, however. Among the things forgotten in the rush out from the manor was Gerik's armoring himself. Besides a hastily girded-on belt with sword and dagger, he wore only a light helmet and his ordinary clothes.

"Greetings, mistress," he said, raising a hand palm outward. "And welcome to the lands of Tirabot Manor. I am Gerik, son of the lord Sir Pirvan, Knight of the Rose, and in his name and my own I bid you welcome."

The woman, who had been standing taut as a bowstring and with a hand inside her cloak, seemed to ease visibly. Her hand came into sight—empty—and the points of the kender weapons dropped by a whole handsbreadth.

"Greetings, Lord Gerik," the woman said. "My name is Ellysta. I claim your protection, in the name of justice and honor. I will explain why—" her breath caught and she pressed a hand to her side "—if you deem it necessary."

The woman spoke like one of birth and education, and her tattered, grass-stained gown and still worse-afflicted cloak were of good cloth. Her feet were not only bare but bloody, and plainly not commonly unshod.

A further look told Gerik that Ellysta was not much older than he, although at first glance this was not apparent. One had to look under dirt, cuts and bruises, a black eye, a split lip, and an air of fear, hunger, and weariness to see her youth.

"There will be a time and place for that, Lady Ellysta," Gerik said. "But not here and now. You seem in need of food at least, perhaps healing as well."

That meant a message to Serafina, wife of Grimsoar One-Eye, his father's old companion and formerly steward of the manor. Serafina was a singularly accomplished healer for one without magicworking arts. Indeed, she might already be on her way to the manor house, summoned by one of the riders to the village.

Gerik sighed. Serafina's coming meant having her husband hard on her heels, and Gerik would not thereafter be truly master in his own father's house until Grimsoar and Serafina returned to the village. That was one reason why he was glad his father had not asked Grimsoar to resume his office during Pirvan's absence; the old sailor and thief would have been as firmly in command as any sworn knight.

Before Gerik could choose a messenger, he heard a band of horsemen approaching at a canter. He turned to see his guards also hastily turning their mounts to stand between their chief and the newcomers. They did it with a precision and order that spoke well for their discipline, which had plainly returned now that the novelty of visiting kender had worn off.

The approaching riders also numbered five, all with breastplates, helmets, and swords. One carried what was either a lance or a banner, and all wore red and green armbands.

Those colors did nothing to ease Gerik's mind. They were the colors of House Dirivan, who held extensive lands in the area. They had also been well to the lead in fortifying their estates, and had been notoriously friendly to the king-priests for three generations.

Gerik was prepared to order the riders off his father's land on sight. He reined in his temper, however, so that he thought his first words came out with an air of reason about them. "Greetings, men of House Dirivan," Gerik said steadily. "What grave matter brings you here in such haste, on a day when a fair sky has not yet dried the roads?"

One of the men started to reply, but another made a chopping gesture that silenced him.

"We come for Ellysta," the second man said. "Hand her over, and there's no trouble for you, or for the kender."

Gerik thought the first might be the truth, but that the second reeked of lies. It was hard to tell what the kender thought, because they suddenly started scurrying around as if all of them had been taken with the purple itch, or a bad case of fleas.

Gerik saw neither plan nor purpose in their movements, until he suddenly realized that they were spreading out, so that they all had good shots but were a bad target themselves. Definitely these five were a trained war band, pretending to be the usual foolish, even witless kender that small minds expected. Proof of that: the five House Dirivan men were laughing aloud, one so hard that he could hardly stay in his saddle.

Gerik drew everyone's attention by drawing his dagger and rapping it against his sword scabbard. "Have you proof of your right to take Lady Ellysta?" he asked.

"We are House Dirivan, and one under our protection has been injured by her," the leader said.

"I should say that all the injuries were not on one side," Gerik replied. "Unless she was the one under your protection. If so, I think you need some help with the task."

Among the men passed looks that made Gerik raise his hand to keep his own men from drawing swords and nocking arrows. He decided to try one last time at settling the matter with words.

"If you have proof of that right," Gerik said, "I will not stand up for a criminal. My father holds land under the laws of Istar, and both as landholder and knight he obeys them. But if you lack—"

Five sets of spurs dug into five flanks. Then two kender began whirling their hoopaks, and five horses suddenly began dancing about at the weird howling from the kender instruments. Some of the Tirabot mounts also pecked and tossed their heads, but they had been trained to endure weirder sounds than hoopaks, at least with riders on their backs.

Meanwhile, the other three kender seemed to have vanished.

Before Gerik could wonder where they had gone, two of them reappeared, behind and in front of the leader's horse. The one behind prodded the horse in the haunches with his spear. The horse shrieked and reared. Its rider parted company with his mount and landed with a crash.

Before he could regain his wind or his feet, the other kender—the woman, Gerik saw—had the point of her spear at his throat. Her eyes were on the four House Dirivan men who were still mounted. Her voice would have made icicles drip from a knight's mustache. "Ellysta is in the hands of someone who promises justice," the kender woman said. "We know justice. He knows justice. You do not. Go away, now, or take this one with a hole in his throat when you go."

At a signal from Gerik, his own mounted men rode forward to disarm the House Dirivan riders. It was as well to do this before folly, pride, or mere disbelief that a human would fight for kender led them to try riding the kender down.

Swiftness prevented bloodshed; Gerik had often heard his father say this could happen, but it was the first time he had seen it happen by his own orders.

Once the men were disarmed and their leader remounted, Gerik faced them. "We do know justice here at Tirabot," he said, "and I will not stand in its path. You may know it too, but if so, then come with proof next time. Your deeds today have made me wonder.

"You will have your weapons back when you reach the borders of Tirabot land. As soon as I speak with Lady Ellysta, I shall write to your master, likewise to my father."

"That's right," gasped the leader. "Spread her lies across—"

He stopped, because the kender woman was looking at him again. She said something in her own speech, which made all the kender laugh—rather grimly, Gerik thought—then translated: "It seems you have so many holes in your head already that all the sense drained out, so I couldn't have hurt you by making one more. I'll remember that next time."

Gerik led the escort as far as the road. By the time he returned to Ellysta, she had fainted, but Serafina had arrived and she and the kender woman were busily applying salves and dressings.

"I don't suppose there's such a thing as a horse litter about," Serafina said. Her tone made it plain that it was too much to expect such a thing of mere men, and warriors at that.

"There is, and I will send for it," Gerik said.

"Good," Serafina said. "Oh, and for a few days at least, I

advise keeping men away from Ellysta. Those rogues—or some like them—gave her reason to fear men."

* * * * *

Horimpsot Elderdrake reached Tirabot Manor long after dark and completely covered with mud. He had fallen into a bog making his final escape from his pursuers, and had first thought to find a stream and wash. After all, Shumeen seemed to look on him with some favor that might turn into more. She would not be happy if he returned black as the dregs of tarberry tea.

Then he realized that he would be reaching the manor well after dark. The blacker he was, the harder he would be to see, even for alert sentries. The guards were keeping a close watch, but not close enough to spy out a kender clad in mud and dark clothing. As soon as he was safely within the guarded area, Elderdrake washed himself roughly at the handiest well. Now his earthy disguise would be more trouble than help, whereas if he appeared to be just another roughly-clad kender, the humans would take him for one of Ellysta's companions. Elderdrake had discovered that a good many humans could barely tell one kender from another.

Shumeen looked as happy to see him as he had hoped, but they had no time for words alone. Elderdrake was supplied with cold sausage and warmed-over soup, while the other kender took turns telling him of their day.

"So Gerik believes Ellysta?" he asked, finally.

Shumeen spread her hands and said, "He believes what Serafina tells him Ellysta said. He does not speak with her himself, because he and the other men are staying out of her chambers for a while.

"Why shouldn't they believe her, anyway?" Shumeen added. "It's true. It wouldn't seem true if you didn't know how strange humans are about possessions, but kender are born knowing that."

Elderdrake nodded. Ellysta's situation had come about because a widowed friend of hers had fallen afoul of friends of the kingpriest. The widow had been taken away, and her flocks were supposed to have gone to one of those friends of the kingpriest.

But Ellysta instead hid the sheep and goats, taking care of them herself even though her family had herders who could have done the work. She would not put them in danger, she said.

So danger came to her, and worse. She had looked half-dead when the kender found her, and it had taken days to nurse her back to enough health to walk as far as Tirabot Manor. Fortunately none of her enemies had actually come searching for her until she was actually on her way. Perhaps they had thought she was dead.

Apart from no kender having ever tolerated someone like the kingpriest, no kender had ever punished someone by saying that what had been theirs now belonged to someone else. In the course of a year, almost every sheep, goat, pot, pan, and kettle in a kender village made the rounds of every household. Sometimes they ended up where they had begun; other times they went with somebody who was marrying outside the village, or going traveling, or were stolen by gully dwarves.

This looked confused and complicated to humans, or so Elderdrake had heard. To him, it was the humans who had all the complicated laws, and all the worries about enforcing them, even when they wanted to be just, and all the opportunities for the unjust to make trouble. . . .

"We have one problem," Shumeen said. "Sir Pirvan is not at the manor. He was gone off again, on some quest, or matter of the knights, or spying on enemies, or whatever."

"Haimya too?"

"Haimya, and Young Eskaia, and more than half the fighters. Knights named Darin and Hawkbrother came, but went with Pirvan."

Elderdrake wanted to put his head in his hands, then realized that this would alarm his friends.

"Gerik is a seasoned warrior," Elderdrake said. "I have been on the same battlefield with him and seen as much. Also, House Dirivan will think twice before attacking the property of a Knight of Solamnia, even if the knight is not at home."

"If they can think at all," someone muttered.

Shumeen glared all around her, so that everyone except Elderdrake looked abashed. Then she smiled. "Now, tell us about your day in the woods," she said. She looked ready to hang on his every word, which she probably really wasn't, but Elderdrake was willing to be flattered. He was also willing to get his hands on another plate of sausage.

When somebody had handed him that plate, he stood up, waved a sausage for attention, and began: "Now, some humans are easier to fool than others, and these were the easy kind. But there were quite a lot of them, and I had to go on fooling them over and over again. If they started to learn from the time before and do better next time, I was going to be in a really bad situation. . . ."

Chapter 4

"Father, Mother, it is both our wishes." Young Eskaia said, hands on hips, daring her parents to contradict her.

Pirvan wondered where Hawkbrother might be. He did not question the courage of his son-in-law-to-be in light of the young warrior's absence from this confrontation. Rather, he thought it prudent, though he hoped it would leave no lingering resentment in Eskaia, to poison the marriage in later years.

"I believe that," Pirvan said. The alternative, calling both his daughter and her betrothed liars, was unthinkable. "I also ask you to believe that five days is rather an immodestly short time to make ready for your wedding," he added. "People will say that you are unmaidenly eager—"

"I am," Eskaia interrupted. "So is Hawkbrother. Ask Mother how she felt after your year of celibacy. Ask your memories how *you* felt, and remember that for my beloved it has been *two* years."

Pirvan flushed. This was partly from the memories, partly from hearing such matters from his daughter's lips, and partly because Haimya was desperately struggling not to giggle.

"I was thinking of more than modesty," he said, commanding his voice. "Believe me or not as you choose. I was thinking that five days is not much time to gather your wedding garb."

"Lady Eskaia has promised all the help in her power, including all the tailors and seamstresses either of us could wish. Her own preparations are long made, and Aurhinius has insisted on being wed in his best armor, much to her annoyance." The girl giggled. "Besides, you know full well how little garb a bride and groom need for their wedding."

Pirvan coughed. "I believe you are confusing the wedding with the wedding night. Not even the forest barbarians wed unclad, although on the islands north of Ansalon it might be warm enough to do so."

This time it was Young Eskaia's turn to flush. "I also remind you," he continued, "that if it takes place with Lady Eskaia's, only your kin will be present at the wedding. Would you rather not have your husband's kin standing beside him?"

"Sir Darin has already sworn to stand in place of Redthorn and Threehands for the giving of the necessary oaths," Eskaia said. "Both approved him at the time of our betrothal oaths. And you must remember that those oaths also give Hawkbrother and me the right to wed at any time and place we choose, according to the customs of my people. We need thereafter only reaffirm our wedding vows before witnesses of the Gryphons, at a time not later than the presenting of our first-born son to Hawkbrother's father or eldest surviving male kin."

It occurred to Pirvan, not for the first time, that the Free Riders were, in the matter of oaths, legalists who could contend with any Istaran law counselors or even one of the high knights. Moreover, wedding a Free Rider seemed to have corrupted the good sense and moderation of his daughter.

"Well, it seems we shall have to wait on Lady Eskaia to discuss this matter further," Pirvan said. "I would not wish to ask of her more than she is prepared to give, even out of old friendship."

"You will waste your breath and her time, Father," Young Eskaia said, but with a lilt in her voice that took the sting from her words. "However, it is not your wedding, so perhaps you will have idle moments."

She bowed so elaborately that it was almost a parody, the more so in that she was wearing tunic and trousers in the Free Rider style, but of silk and lace in the Istaran fashion. When she turned and strode out, the hard soles of her formal boots clicked on the stone floor.

Pirvan started to follow his daughter, but found that the floor had suddenly sprouted an obstacle. Namely, and to wit, his wife. She seemed suddenly as immovable as a granite block, and the idea of laying hands on her to move her out of his path was something else unthinkable.

"I think we had best let the young folk do as they wish, and as our old friend is prepared to let them do," Haimya said. "I do remember what it was like when you came out of your training." She hugged herself, and then, surprisingly, him.

"So, if we do not want them to take their betrothal rights before we sail," she continued, "for fear that their love will never be . . ."

"Consummated?" Pirvan put in, and was glad to see Haimya now blushing. She seemed a trifle more content with having a daughter old enough to think of wedding and bedding, but only a trifle.

"Yes," Haimya said, after a moment. "Also, consider that the wedding of Lady Eskaia and Gildas Aurhinius will be the talk of Ansalon for months to come. And they will say that Lady Eskaia allowed her namesake to stand up beside her and wed a desert barbarian, in the same chamber, on the same carpet, with the same blessings, while breathing the same perfumes . . ."

Pirvan held up both hands, to stop Haimya's torrent of persuasive words. "I begin to understand," he said. "Yes, it will do well to mark Hawkbrother's acceptance, and that can do him no harm among the knights.

"Nor can accepting him do the knights any harm," he added. "I will not mind hearing less often that

Hawkbrother's knighthood is a mere whim of Sir Pirvan the Wayward."

* * * * *

Sir Niebar stood in the middle of one wall of the chamber where the wedding—weddings, he corrected himself—would take place. Two knights stood on either side of him, and beside each pair of knights were two men-at-arms.

The nine men all wore their finest robes and most decorated (whether most useful or not) swords. The other six men-at-arms scattered about the chamber wore nothing to let anyone know that they served the Orders and Keeps. Their weapons were concealed, and their eyes continually roamed the room.

Niebar had come to Vuinlod with twenty knights and two hundred men-at-arms. When they heard of the change in the wedding plans, to the last man they begged the right to be guards on that day. Had he granted all those wishes, Sir Niebar knew, there would hardly have been room for the other wedding guests—although to be sure, they would have been very safe from hostile steel.

As it was, the fifteen were all who represented the knights. But they were not the only ones standing between the wedding party and any would-be assassins. Most of the men in the chamber wore steel, and not a few were of the host of Vuinlod that Gildas Aurhinius would be leading to Suivinari.

Even Gildas Aurhinius himself, although older and stouter than Niebar, moved like a man who would hardly be helpless in a fight. That hypothetical assassin would have a very short life, and probably not even the consolation of succeeding before that life ended.

But now the drums began muttering softly, the lyres and harps rippled like spring water, and the brides and grooms entered, each with his or her oath-witness. Torvik Jemarsson was standing up for his mother and Gildas Aurhinius, while Sir Darin loomed behind Hawkbrother and Young Eskaia. Lady Eskaia's youngest daughter followed, bearing both rings on a silver tray. Pirvan and Haimya, in the traditional array of the champions of the brides, brought up the rear.

As the wedding party stepped onto the square of carpet marked off by braided rushes and scented seaweed (all that the season allowed), a male singer in the gallery above began:

"Let there be man and maid, ho!"

A woman's voice replied:

"Let there be maid and man, ho!"

Niebar recognized the woman singing as Rynthala. Well, singing that well-wishing song was an honor, and Niebar had known women to assassinate at least one another's reputations over singing it at a friend's wedding.

How many times had he heard it, Niebar wondered. Twenty times at least, usually for knights, but never for him. Of course, if Gildas Aurhinius could wed at his age, there was hope for even the Niebar the Talls of the world.

But hope meant little without the time to seek a worthy bride—unless one sought you, as had been the case with Eskaia and Aurhinius. Niebar did not expect such luck for himself. The luck he hoped for now was that the Grand Master would allow this to be his last quest on the secret affairs of the knights. Then he could find his modest chamber in some keep, and leave the work in the hands of a man who would do it better than he ever had.

That man also probably did not much like the thought of the burden, of course. But if Pirvan the Wayward had not wanted the work, he should not have done it so well.

* * * * *

Nuitari and Solinari splashed light across the floor of the chamber. Faint phosphorescence from the sea added another tint to the light.

It was just enough for Hawkbrother to see his wife's hair spread out across the pillow. She had grown it for the wedding until she swore that it would be long enough to twine through his fingers, although she had not promised she would leave it that way. It would need to fit under a helmet before they had been wed a month, she said, and he feared she was right.

But tonight . . .

"Am I welcome in your bed, my wife?" Hawkbrother said. His throat felt full of hot gravel, so that he was sure the words came out a croak.

Eskaia seemed to understand even his croaking.

"You are welcome in my bed, my husband," she said.

He turned his back to remove his robe, but by the time he turned back, Eskaia had thrown aside the blankets—as she had already thrown aside her own robe.

"You are welcome everywhere you wish to go, in truth," she said, with what sounded suspiciously like laughter in her voice.

Hawkbrother stood and looked, and felt a gentle warmth flowing through him, unlike anything he had ever felt before. But then, he had never been wed before, so why should he not feel that he was entering a whole new world and time?

* * * * *

Gildas Aurhinius and Lady Eskaia swore that on their wedding night they would do what they had never done before.

Nor were they foresworn. Weary, filled with good food and better wine, and content with what they had done for themselves and for the younger couple, they fell chastely to sleep in each other's arms.

Torvik Jemarsson walked along the beach, listening to the thunder roll of the surf and watching the breakers fling rocks the size of his fist into the air like feathers. When one of them nearly parted his hair, he turned his course inland.

From the cliffs above the beach, he had a view well out

to sea. In the phosphorescence offshore, he thought he saw dark shapes rising and falling. They had to be whales, to be seen from this distance, and whales were kin to porpoises, and porpoises who spoke with the Dargonesti might carry messages to the Dimernesti. Were the whales here as scouts, to watch over the ships gathering in Vuinlod and bring word of when they sailed?

Torvik told himself that a long day and a surprisingly fine night for this time of year were filling him with fancies. He would go back to the town and find decent wine and perhaps a warm hearted woman.

* * * * *

Farther south, a messenger rode through the darkness. When he saw that he was approaching the hills around Vuinlod, he reined in, watered and wiped down his horse, and considered what to do next. The message he bore would reach Sir Pirvan if he simply rode into town and shouted it in the streets. So would it reach a howling mob of people, all eager to help or perhaps hinder him.

But how to go straight to Pirvan without anyone asking why he sought the knight? No one in Vuinlod knew him.

But Lady Eskaia was used to receiving messages, and would know where Pirvan was. She might even be able to summon Pirvan's men-at-arms, and once among those friends the messenger knew his secret would be safe.

* * * * *

Men had called him Wilthur the Brown because they could not come up with a better (or worse) name for a man who had worn the White, Red, and Black Robe, each at various times.

He had also commanded the magic of each, and forgotten none of it. What he had not commanded was himself, at least enough to avoid being corrupted by so much knowledge.

In the end he had fled beyond the knowledge of men,

and now called Suivinari Island his home.

From atop the dormant volcano men called the Smoker, he watched the world beyond through the most potent scrying glass ever made. He still had to use the eyes of his body, but that might be about to change, if the expedition coming to his island left enough bodies of other men behind.

He would say nothing and think only a little about that particular ambition, however. His robe now was Black, so the Dragon Queen should not (in theory) object to what he was doing. But a human mage who could transcend the limits of the body as far as Wilthur hoped to was no friend to anyone. Not even to gods. Gods whom he might soon be able to bring into or expel from the world at will. And of all gods, Takhisis was the least likely to endure such a challenge.

Meanwhile, dawn was breaking over Vuinlod. The scrying glass could not at such a distance show him single figures, but he could count the ships in the harbor.

Good. No more than the day before, although not all those who would be sailing against Suivinari would be coming to Vuinlod by ship. He considered taking a day or two to examine spells that might let him see farther into the town. Perhaps even, with luck, penetrate the walls of dwellings and stables, to count men and horses.

Yes. The close watch on Vuinlod could wait that long. Even longer, perhaps, for other towns and cities also demanded his attention, if he was to have some notion of what came against him.

Wilthur touched the scrying glass and it went dark. He breathed on a wad of cloth of gold hanging over the arm of his chair. It leaped into the air and set busily to polishing the glass, and afterward its wooden frame.

It sometimes amused Wilthur to think that the cloth now doing menial work held the spirit of a slain minotaur, who would have killed at once any human who asked his living self to labor so.

* * * * *

Pirvan and Haimya walked up into the hills above the town before they felt ready to talk of the night's news.

"Will our Eskaia know?" Haimya said. She pulled up a few withered brown grass stems and tried to braid them, but they were too brittle.

"Lady Eskaia wrote that the new couple were probably going to sleep late," Pirvan answered. "Even then, she promised not to tell them today."

Pirvan stood up. He had slept little and walked long and hard, but he was too restless to sit for long. Tirabot Manor in danger? His first thought had been that Sir Niebar would call him a fool, and while he was ashamed of the thought, it had not altogether gone away.

The older knight would not say, "I told you so," but everyone in the room would be able to hear his thoughts. Even now, Pirvan shaped the words slowly and reluctantly.

"The first person we ought to tell is Sir Niebar," he said. Haimya's reply was an eloquent look. Pirvan struggled on. "The men he has with him," he said, "knights and others alike, are his to send where he will. He can send—oh, two knights and ten men-at-arms—without weakening his strength for the voyage to Suivinari."

"That will put our son under the authority of a total stranger," Haimya said. "I thought we had decided his arguments against that had weight."

"They did," Pirvan said. "They do. But not leaving him with only the manor guards and staff to face a feud with a great house also has weight. More, to my mind."

"Private feuds are illegal," she said flatly.

"If that law still ran, why is everyone within a day's ride of Tirabot strengthening his defenses?"

"I was not putting more faith in the laws of Istar than they can bear, Pirvan. I was reminding you that we are also bound by the law not to fight House Dirivan over a small matter.

"But this may not be a small matter," she said. "It may not even be one in which the kingpriest is wrong. We do not know what the offense to the flock's owner was."

That sober reminder made Pirvan pause. It was difficult

to believe that no one ever suffered at the hands of the kingpriest, but fraud, theft, misappropriating funds, illegally pasturing cattle . . . one could not ask that enemies of the kingpriest go free over any of these. Not and observe the Oath and the Measure, as Pirvan was bound to do as a Knight of Solamnia. Or even listen to the voice of common sense, as he had tried to do even as a village boy some days' ride from Istar and a week from the nearest keep.

He sat down on the rock and put his head in his hands. The surest protection for Tirabot Manor and Gerik would be his own return. It would be a humiliation for his son, but a lesser one than ending up under the protection of total strangers, even if they were his father's comrades-in-arms.

It would also set chaos loose among the Vuinlod squadron of the expedition to Suivinari. Chaos there would weaken the ranks of the wise and honorable sailing to the island, and leave it under the command of those eager for reckonings with the "lesser breeds." A war with the minotaurs might be the least of the results of that.

No. He must go to Sir Niebar, swear that he will sail with the fleet, but ask that some form of protection be devised for Tirabot and its people.

Also he must pray that House Dirivan saw reason. They were as proud as the Silvanesti and as quick to take offense, but Pirvan himself had earned honors from those arrogant forest-dwellers. Perhaps House Dirivan could also be brought to see reason. Or at least not to see a cause for blood-feud in every petty slight.

"Well and good," Pirvan said, rising. "We go down and straight to Sir Niebar. Then, whatever his answer, we go to our Eskaia. She will not forgive our hiding the matter for long, and Hawkbrother hardly less. I do not want my next duel of honor to be with my new son-by-marriage!"

Chapter 5

When they were in residence, Pirvan and Haimya held formal manor councils once a month. Also once a month, they sat in some state to hear grievances and complaints from the manor's people. Istaran law, the oaths sworn when they took the manor, and common sense all demanded it.

Gerik was glad that his parents had held both councils for the month before departing for Vuinlod. With some luck, the manor's people would not feel the need for any more for a while. With even more luck, Gerik's parents would be home before the time appointed for the next council.

He knew that last hope asked a great deal of the weather, the Istarans, and the gods, to say nothing of the enemies he seemed to have made by taking in Ellysta. Everything would have to move like a well-ordered banquet for Gerik's parents to be back in less than two months.

In truth, he was of two minds about wanting them back. He had begun to realize that if he was not to enter the ranks of the Knights of Solamnia, he needed to find some other way to prove himself a worthy son of his father. His own honor demanded this, for all that his father had not demanded it, by so much as a single word or even a momentary look upon his weathered face.

Ordering the affairs of Tirabot Manor so that its quarrel with House Dirivan did not end in a bloody clash of arms would be proof of both courage and wisdom. These were two gifts that anyone would expect in the son of a Knight of the Rose.

However, if matters went so awry that House Dirivan continued to secretly wage private war against the manor, then Gerik badly wanted his parents back home and himself loyally obeying their orders. Attacking the son of a Knight of the Rose might seem to some folks unlike attacking the knight himself. By the time they learned the error of their ways, much harm might have been done.

So Gerik held council almost daily, with the chief of the masons, the steward, and the chief of the guards. Five days after he judged his message should have reached Vuinlod, he was seated in his chamber across a low table from Bertsa Wylum, commanding the guards. Her dark eyes flicked him like a riding whip as he poured more ale for both of them.

"You think I drink too much?" he asked, trying to keep challenge out of his voice.

"No," she said. "Just remember, though, that our enemies might try magic against our water. They did when your parents defended Belkuthas, and here we have no dwarves to save us."

"No, and the masons would not stay to work in the face of danger." He hesitated. "I would not ask them, either. They have families for whose sakes they must remain at peace with our enemies."

Wylum clapped Gerik on the shoulder so hard that he nearly choked on his ale. "Well said, and even more, well thought before you spoke," she said. "You needn't tell the masons that yet, of course."

Gerik didn't see where the "of course" came from, but Wylum was going on with the report he had interrupted by pouring the ale.

"No more 'ghost-riders,' by what my people say." Her tone made it plain that any of her people who saw riders with their faces painted grayish-white and did not report it would regret it, and possibly more.

"Somebody chased Pel Orvot's flock of geese all along the bank and killed a few," Wylum added. "But we don't know if that was enemies, common thieves, or children pranking."

Suddenly she was silent, listening, head cocked to one side. She mouthed "keep talking" at Gerik, then slipped off her boots. Three long-legged strides took her to the door. With one hand she jerked it open, with the other she jerked the listener outside into the chamber.

It was Gerik's sister Rubina.

She was well grown for a girl of not yet twelve, and would probably be taller than her sister Eskaia when she reached womanhood. Right now, however, she was as helpless as a kitten in Bertsa Wylum's grip. Wylum might be past forty, but she had come to the manor from a sergeancy under Floria Desbarres, and had fought in more campaigns than Gerik had years.

"How long were you listening?" Gerik asked his sister, to keep Wylum from erupting like a geyser.

"Awhile," Rubina said. She met her brother's eyes glower for glower. "I must have made a noise when I heard the part about the geese. It was other children, friends of Milnoran's. Pel Orvot caught him poaching on the fish pond and threw a stone at him. It hit and cut his forehead. Milnoran's, I mean."

"I doubt that Pel Orvot could throw a stone in a circle like the plains riders," Wylum said, obviously holding in laughter. "I also doubt that you should be spying on your brother's meetings with me."

"If he isn't bedding you, and you're just talking about war, why shouldn't I know?" Rubina said.

This time Gerik had the rare pleasure of actually seeing Bertsa Wylum lose her self-command. She laughed until she had to put her head in her hands to keep the tears from streaming down her cheeks.

By then, Rubina was addressing her brother. "I don't know about doing the spying myself, but I know about Pel Orvot's geese because I listen to the other children. They listen to their friends. Everything said to one child spreads all over the manor in a day or two."

Gerik frowned. "So you'd use your friends as spies without their knowing it?" he asked sternly.

"That's the best way. A spy who doesn't know that she's a spy can't tell anybody anything if she's caught."

"You know that could—you could lose friends, that way," Gerik said. Rubina was so longheaded in so many ways that it was sometimes hard to remember she was not yet a woman. All three children of Tirabot Manor had grown up with friends ranging from the swineherd's daughter to the steward's five nephews. Rubina was now offering to throw all this away.

"You are offering this, to help defend the manor?" Wylum said.

"Of course. I haven't quarreled with anybody. Yet," Rubina added. "It's never a really honorable thing to do. So I wouldn't do it unless it was going to be life or death for us. I thought you would know how matters stand, and what is honorable when they are at their worst." This last sentence took in both Gerik and the guard captain.

"May the gods spare us the need for you to sacrifice friendships on the altar of necessity," Wylum said. Gerik had been trying to put a similar thought into words, but realized that he had been hopelessly outmatched in eloquence. He merely nodded, then rose and gave Rubina a brotherly hug.

"Thank you for offering," he said. "Meanwhile, don't be listening at my door again. People might see you, then think you knew secrets. Our enemies would—"

"Try to carry me off and torture me for the secrets?" Rubina said. "If you gave me that dagger Mother won't let me have, I could be sure they wouldn't learn anything."

Gerik knew that Rubina was in dead earnest, and swore to strangle Bertsa Wylum if she so much as smiled. Instead the guard captain reached down into her boot and pulled out a dwarf-bladed dagger with leather bindings on the hilt that had a Kagonesti flavor.

"Try this one for its fit in your hand," she said, handing the dagger hilt-first to Rubina. "A friend of mine about your size left it to me, after she died."

"In battle?" Rubina asked.

"Yes. And if you're so curious about battles, I'll tell you a few tales. But only if you practice with this dagger for ten days. Your oath on it?"

Rubina swore by a number of gods, including some that Gerik did not approve of her knowing about. Then she departed, with more ceremony but no less speed than at her entrance.

"Warrior blood runs true," Wylum muttered. Gerik pretended not to have heard her.

"Is there anything else today, good sir?" the woman asked. It was a title that they had adopted for Gerik because she refused to use his given name and he refused to be called "lord."

"No." Gerik looked at the water clock in the corner of his chamber. That and the shadows on the floor told him twilight was near. "I am dining with Lady—with our guest Ellysta tonight, in her chamber," he said.

Something suspiciously like a cough escaped Wylum. "At her invitation?"

"At her invitation. Brought by Serafina and Shumeen," he added, remembering his father's words about being completely honest with his captains.

This time Wylum laughed. "Has Serafina ever—? No, I won't ask. You would be honor-bound not to tell."

If the question was what Gerik thought it was, the answer would have been "no." The wife of his father's old comrade was not yet thirty, and a very handsome woman. But she had never cast any encouraging looks his way and he would have been honor-bound not to even acknowledge them if she had, let alone talk about it afterward.

Besides, he was not such an innocent in the matter of women as Bertsa Wylum seemed to think. But if he tried to persuade her of that, they would be arguing over the ale until well past the time that Ellysta expected him in her chamber!

* * * * *

65

It had to be getting dark outside, Horimpsot Elderdrake thought. He'd been crouched here in the rafters by the chimney more than long enough for that.

Not long enough to hear what he wanted to hear, though.

None of these bumbling, drunken fools would say a word about being ghost-riders, or hiring them, or knowing who they were or who hired them! None of them!

Oh, they talked all around the ghost-riding, and one of them said something about children who could be frightened into telling tales by haunting their elders' farms. That made Elderdrake say things that would have singed the man's beard down to the jawbone if the kender had been a wizard. He tried to put the man's face firmly into his mind, but it kept getting confused with five or six other men with stubbly brown beards, red faces, and bald spots on their heads.

He'd begun to have the feeling that kender had as much trouble telling humans apart as humans did with kender.

He also began to feel a bit more warmth along his back and at the seat of his breeches than was comfortable. Warmth that hadn't been there just a little while back, and they hadn't built up the fire enough to make that much of a difference—

"Yeeoooohhhh!"

Elderdrake screeched in surprise and pain. Sparks flying through gaps in the ancient chimney had set fire to the thatch of the roof, the straw in the loft, and his own coat and breeches!

He swung on the rafters until he thumped back and his buttocks hit hard against the underside of the roof. That took care of the fire on Elderdrake's clothes.

It also served to spread it to dry, hitherto untouched thatch, and to draw the gaze of every man below who hadn't already looked up when the kender's screech tore at their ears.

Fortunately for both sides, no one had a bow within easy reach. Archery within the old farmhouse would probably have ended the life of both Elderdrake and several of the men. Everybody instead drew knives or scrambled for longer blades in scabbards hung comfortably well aside by men with serious drinking to do.

While the men were scrambling, Horimpsot Elderdrake was running.

He ran out the open door, turned hard to the left in case arrows, spears, or throwing knives were following him out the door, then remembered something he'd forgotten. To the left was a steep slope, dropping to the edge of the forest.

He tried to stay on his feet, but failed miserably. A smoking ball, he tumbled down the slope, bouncing off saplings and crashing through bushes in a way that would have broken the bones of almost any being save a kender or a dwarf. It was a good thing that he'd put out the fire on his clothes in the house, or he might have left a trail of burning sparks enough to start a fire even in the damp late-winter woods.

A squat, dark shape sprawled ahead: a stone hut that he remembered seeing on his way toward the house. Now he saw that it had a light roof of twigs and strips of canvas, and he was going to hit that roof.

He struck like a hailstone, crashing through the roof. Twigs and sod, strips of canvas and dead leaves rained down on him as if the whole forest had been upended, then flung down like a chamberpot from a high window.

Elderdrake rolled as he landed, which kept him from breaking any bones. He went on rolling, across patches of mud and through a puddle of rainwater, until he struck something hard, knocking all the breath out of himself.

What he'd struck was a small keg. It fell over and in its turn rolled, striking the wall hard enough to break open. Something grayish-white spattered everything inside the hut, including Elderdrake.

He lay still for a moment, knowing he ought to get up and run again, but also knowing that his legs wouldn't carry him more than a few steps unless he first won his breath back.

The pursuit Elderdrake had feared did not come. Probably the men were too busy keeping their house from burning down to worry about chasing kender. After a while, he was able to sit up.

As he did, he saw that the puddle had settled, until he could see a face in it. It took a moment before he could recognize it as his own face—the kender ears were the big clue—and then he wanted to shout all over again. This time it would have been a shout of joy.

His face was all patches and smears of the same revolting gray-white that the ghost-riders wore on their faces and hands. He looked as though some particularly gruesome fungus was eating away at his skin, and he smelled like a mixture of rancid weasel fat and aged pine tar.

He looked around for something in which to carry a sample of the ghost paint back to Tirabot Manor. After a moment, he decided to settle for what was on his skin—which was beginning to itch—and a barrel stave dripping with the muck. He couldn't even *think* of tasting it without his stomach twitching.

But if he could get a sample back to the manor, Serafina could study it. She was a better herbalist than most, which meant that she could learn what had gone into somebody else's medicine as well as making up her own. Although if she ever made up anything as foul as this, Elderdrake wasn't going to touch it, even if she said it was an elixir of immortality!

Shouts up the hill reminded Elderdrake that he had better be on his way, even if the forest was close. He scrambled up the wall, flung himself through the hole in the roof, and dropped to the ground.

"There he goes!" someone shrieked.

Several more someones had found bows. Elderdrake heard the twang of bowstrings and the whistle of arrows. Then he heard a series of blistering oaths, which stopped the archery as abruptly as if the archers had all been strangled with their own bowstrings.

Kender curiosity made Elderdrake halt and look back, not even waiting for a convenient tree. A small round figure sat on a small horse or perhaps a large pony. It held a staff out at arm's length, one end on the ground, the other sloping toward Elderdrake.

The kender ran. As fast as he ran, the fire bursting from the head of the staff would have overtaken him if it had been aimed properly. Instead, it seared through the base of a fir tree, second growth but stout and tall for all that. The tree wavered, swayed, then toppled.

It fell directly atop the hut. Whatever energies had gone into the spell, they multiplied the impact of the tree tenfold. The hut disintegrated. It also burst into flames.

No, it erupted into flames. The spell had multiplied tenfold the heat in the ghost paint and everything else in the hut. A fireball as tall as the tree had been sprouted where the hut had stood, like a hideous, eye-searing mushroom.

And the sound!

Once, on his first journey, Elderdrake had found himself hiding in a ceremonial drum during a particularly long ceremony. He did not care to remember the details even now, and had told them only to his old friend Imsaffor Whistletrot. But he had been deaf for a week after his hours in the drum.

This eruption of flame gave the loudest sound that he had heard since he was in that drum. It also sent out a wave of air like a charging herd of oxen, to fling him head over heels again. He landed rolling, but missed hitting any trees before a thornbush stopped him.

This time Horimpsot Elderdrake ignored the fact that he was breathless, that his clothes were in ruins, and that he had aches in his legs, his head, his stomach, and other places that respectable kender were delicate about mentioning. He lurched to his feet, put his left foot in front of his right root, and kept on doing this, faster and faster, until he was running.

Behind him he thought he heard a few faint shouts, or perhaps screams, over the crackle of the flames.

* * * * *

Gildas Aurhinius stood arm in arm with Lady Eskaia on the Drapers' Quay in Vuinlod. The sea breeze made the torches burning all along it flicker, but their yellowish light let even Aurhinius's dimming vision see clearly what lay before him.

The heavy trader *Long Sulla* was tied up at the quay, and from her upper deck a broad gangplank angled down. To either side of the gangplank, sailors were hoisting nets full of stores and ship's gear.

Four abreast, the foot soldiers of Vuinlod were marching aboard. Or at least they were moving in that direction; Aurhinius found it hard to describe their progress as a march. Even allowing for their being heavily laden, he thought they could have done a little more to keep in step, for the good reputation of their town if nothing else.

Those heavy loads, however, were good arms and sound armor, and he had seen that the Vuinlodders knew how to use them. Also, the fighting this campaign might see was not likely to require keeping fine formations or shifting from one to another at a run. It was most likely to be work aboard ship or from boats, and he trusted the Vuinlodders more in that kind of fighting than he would have trusted most of the Istarans he had led in his last campaign as a leader in the Mighty City's host.

"They may look like a mob, but I will be proud to lead them into battle," he said.

He felt his wife flinch. There, he thought. I did not have to think twice before calling her my wife. In a year or so, I will not think of her otherwise. Old dogs can learn new tricks, if they have a good teacher, and Eskaia is the best. Look at her children.

"I did not mean that I was going to put myself at their head every day or even in every fight," Aurhinius went on. "I am too old and fat to be a hero when one is not needed.

"Of course," he added, "being old and fat also means that I cannot run away. So I will have to bring up the rear in a desperate retreat, and let the younger men live to fight another day."

This time Eskaia did not flinch. She merely nodded. "Very well," she said. "But I will lead the younger men back to find your body when the battle is done."

Aurhinius did not quite sigh. His wife seemed determined to sail on this quest.

"I could hope you would not be anywhere near the battle-field," he said.

"I could hope that this matter was settled," she replied. "I must sail as far as Istar, at least."

"We are not going to Istar. Some who sail with us would not be safe that close to the city. Nor would the Istarans feel safe with some of us in their waters or even at their water-front."

"I meant," she said, "as close as the fleet goes to Istar, which is Karthay."

"I believe you when you say that your father and his successors have friends in Karthay, from whom we may learn much, but what if you cannot go ashore?" he asked.

"Then I will send—no, I will *ask*—Haimya. She has kin in Karthay, and no one will doubt that she goes ashore to visit them."

"No one except those who know she is the lady of Sir Pirvan, Knight of the Rose, and guardian of as many secrets of the Solamnic Orders as he is. Would she thank you for allowing her to go into danger for no purpose?"

"She would not thank either of us for even hinting that she has become a hearthwife." Eskaia's grip on his arm tightened; he heard steel in her voice.

A man could laugh, if the stakes in this gamble were not so high. "I believe that if the roads were not spring mud, you would long since have taken to your litter, bound for Istar," Aurhinius said.

He felt rather than saw Eskaia smile. "I would have ridden," she said.

"Of course. I forget. Litters are for ladies, which you are not."

"Have I not proved it often enough, by word and deed?"

"To be sure, and I look forward to more of both," he sighed. "But, beloved, consider that you are the shield of Vuinlod."

"The shield?"

"Yes," he said. "The town and the people who have

taken refuge here have more than enough enemies in the lands around them. As long as you are in Vuinlod, those who were your father's friends, and those who owe them friendship or money or favors—all of them will speak against moving on Vuinlod."

"It counts for something, I should think, that the town is across the border in Solamnia," Eskaia said.

"That border means nothing, if one cannot trust all the knights. You were not at Belkuthas, but you have heard of Sir Lewin. What if Sir Niebar is by chance leaving another such behind?"

"The folk I leave behind are alert."

"They will be more alert if you are watching them," he advised. "Also, only a fool will labor against Vuinlod under the eyes of its Princess.

"For now," he said, "I am the sword of Vuinlod, and we must allow other hands to touch or even wield that sword. You are the shield of the town. With the sword gone, you must remain fast to the other arm, to block blows until the sword returns."

"Gildas Aurhinius, you have turned poet," Eskaia said, so softly that her husband at first did not believe what he heard.

Then: "Very well. It shall be as you wish. I will remain here, and charge Haimya to visit Karthay in my name. Also, I will give you the names of certain friends in Karthay. If you have discreet persons whom you can send to these, you may learn more."

Aurhinius considered that if he had his old secretary Nemyotes, he could probably learn how many times Karthay's chief priest of Paladine visited the jakes each day! Nemyotes had not followed his commander to Vuinlod, however, but remained in Istar.

Well, that would have been another miracle, and Eskaia was miracle enough for one old warrior. That she would stay out of danger was almost another, so Aurhinius judged he should not really ask for more.

Chapter 6

Gerik wore his second-best tunic and hose and his best traveling cloak for his supper in Ellysta's chamber. Everything else fit for visiting ladies either direly needed a stiff brush and a hot iron, or else had been a winter home for the moths.

He doubted that Ellysta was expecting a fine Istaran gallant, in either manners or garb, but if she was, she would just have to be disappointed. There was too much work at Tirabot, and too few hands to do it, for him to devote much effort to his clothing. Indeed, he wondered what Ellysta might be expecting in matters besides clothing. She said she was a merchant's daughter, who had lived on in the country after both her betrothed and her mother died, for her father had wed again and Ellysta and her stepmother struck sparks whenever they met.

It was not an implausible story, but Gerik remembered how in old tales women who came out of nowhere with such stories so often turned out to be wizards, dragons, or even goddesses in disguise.

Gerik doubted that Ellysta was any such thing. He had heard enough about her experience to know that no one able to prevent it would have endured it. Therefore she was mortal, and likely to be offering friendship in return for his hospitality. From such an honorable beginning, they need not go any farther. But if they did, it seemed likely that they would be good company for each other.

At least that was what Gerik told himself, as he strode across the courtyard, conscious of eyes on him and even one or two grins hastily hidden as he passed by. He was also conscious that under his tunic was a chain of fine gold, with good-luck blessings put on it by both Tarothin and Sirbones.

He wondered if the Red Robe wizard and the priest of Mishakal were ever coming back to Tirabot, even for a friendly visit. Or perhaps, hearing of his parents' embarking for Suivinari, the two old magicworkers would find the strength to go along with them?

He would have to ask, in his next message to his parents, although it might not reach them before they sailed. Indeed, he had begun to wonder if they had received his first message. Certainly he had received no reply.

"Your pardon, good sir."

Bertsa Wylum stood before him. He halted.

"What news?" he asked.

"A hunter came in, with word of a great roaring sound over toward the Huichpa Forest."

"That's Dirivan land, isn't it?"

"Near enough," she said, nodding. "They try to keep anyone but their foresters from cutting timber in it at least."

Gerik mentally calculated distances. "If it was that great, shouldn't we have heard it here?" he asked.

"Sometimes sound travels in freakish ways, so that you can be standing right in the middle of the thunder and not hear it." She lowered her voice. "But a sentry said he saw a big cloud of smoke off that way, just before the light went."

Gerik looked up. The sky was not only dark but starless. The air held the smell of oncoming rain, and the wind was rising.

"Unless you hear more," he told her, "there's no need to send anyone out with a storm coming on."

"We can't send people into the Huichpa by day, I'm afraid."

"No, but there will be less wild nights. Besides, tonight all the Dirivan riders will be out and alert."

"They might also find us hard to see," she said, "in the storm."

"Or we might find it hard to see anything, including ambushes and even where the sound came from."

"There's sense in that," Wylum admitted, though she sounded as if there was not normally enough sense for her to follow Gerik's orders. If he had not been the son of her sworn chief and commander . . .

Gerik watched Wylum turn away, and wondered why he had so little fear of such women. Doubtless most of it had to be the influence of his mother, who never held back a word she thought needed saying. His father had played a part as well. He had never questioned Haimya's right to say those words, or failed to listen to them—even when he afterward told her they were nonsense.

* * * * *

Horimpsot Elderdrake had never been so battered and miserable in his life as on his journey back to Tirabot, and that was before it started to rain.

After it started to rain, he would have been the most miserable kender on Krynn, not to mention the most improperly clad (at least among those kender doing things that required clothing). Fortunately, he had a small turn of luck just before the skies opened.

The lights of a farm shone off to his left, and by those lights he saw a farm wife taking in laundry from a rope strung between two pear trees. Elderdrake quickly darted into the orchard, and came out at what he intended to be the end of the rope farthest from the woman.

Instead, he emerged from the trees practically under her feet. She screamed and threw up her hands. The laundry basket fell, and the laundry flew. The kender did not stop to sort for size or color. He merely snatched the first three pieces that came to hand and darted back into the darkness.

The woman's screams pursued him for some way, until the advancing thunder drowned them out. He hoped that the storm would discourage pursuit, until he was back at Tirabot and had explained everything to Lord Gerik, who should be able to explain them to the woman.

Elderdrake had the feeling that with the ghost paint all over him he had frightened the woman even more than he would have otherwise. Now, if he could just talk Shumeen into loaning him another Istaran tower's worth of copper pieces, he ought to be able to at least pay for the laundry.

Thunder tore at his battered ears. It would have torn more fiercely, if he had been able to hear it more clearly. Than a fat drop of rain struck his nose, and another trickled down one singed ear.

Elderdrake stopped to put on the stolen garments—or wrap them around him, at least, for he seemed to have stolen mostly the bed linens. He managed a semblance of garb by using his belt and the rags of his old clothes to tie the bedding on to himself.

Then he strode on, as the air turned to water and the ground to mud. He realized that he would reach Tirabot Manor as wet as if he had not stopped to clothe himself, and he might look just as ridiculous.

But if fear of looking ridiculous had ever stopped or even slowed a kender, the race would long since have died out.

* * * * *

The supper Ellysta had arranged was simple enough: stew, light cakes, and wine. But the stew and wine had traces of herbs Gerik had never encountered, and doubted were from the castle kitchen. The cakes were plainly not of the cook's baking, and Gerik swore that he would hire whoever had baked them to prepare his parents' home-coming banquet, even should they prove to be hobgoblins!

"They looted the cottage quite enough to please themselves," Ellysta said, in answer to his question about the herbs. "But they did not break all the pots and vials.

Shumeen snatched up a few before we left."

The old tales spoke of wine used as the base for magical potions to enslave men, but Gerik did not feel enslaved. He was not entirely sober, either, after the third cup of the herb-altered wine, but he was seeing the woman who was at the same time his guest and his host with clear eyes.

She had to be only a handful of years older than he, if that much. Even a few days free from want, war, and fear had taken the hunted animal look from her blue eyes and the gauntness from her face.

The visible wounds on her hands and face were healing under Serafina's deft touch and abundant potions; all the rest were hidden under one of Serafina's borrowed gowns. It was rather too large for Ellysta, and had not been designed to display the wearer's figure even when it fit.

Altogether, Gerik found himself enjoying Ellysta's company, with no sense of further obligation or fear of consequences. If this came from the wine, it was the most pleasant sensation he had won from the grape since he first tasted it as a boy.

He could spend half his evenings for a year like this, if they were all as agreeable.

Ellysta added details of her adventures, over the last of the wine in the jug. Some of Gerik's comfort departed, because he sensed she was holding things back. At last he held up a hand.

"Ellysta, you are telling me either too much or too little," he said. "Either too much for your peace mind, or too little for mine."

"I am not a spy for the kingpriest," she said, without indignation, real or forced. She might have been saying that the jug was empty.

"I was not even thinking that!" Gerik wondered how to put his next thought into words. "The—those who healed you—told me enough."

Ellysta closed her eyes. She also bit her lip. Before tears could trickle down her cheeks, she turned away.

Gerik wanted to brush a hand across her cheek or her hair. By Branchala, he wished he dared to take her in his arms and hold her while she wept, to tell her that with him she did not need to pretend to more courage than she had!

He reached for the napkin to shake the crumbs off it and hand it to her to wipe her eyes. She reached for it at the same moment. Their fingers brushed against one another. He felt her hand tremble, but she did not draw it back. After a moment, he decided to also leave his hand where it was.

They sat there for what seemed enough time for all three moons to go through their phases. In truth, it could not have been more than a few minutes, because a wine stain on the tablecloth was still damp when Ellysta moved her fingers on to Gerik's hand, then past his wrist and up his arm.

At the elbow, she stopped. She was trembling, her breath came short, and also Gerik's sleeves were tight above the elbow and loose below. That last brought a smile to both their faces, but Ellysta's faded at once.

Gerik was indeed no innocent in the matter of women, but was careful never to say so, knowing that few women liked to hear it. It often sounded more like boasting than a promise. Therefore, he knew something about when a garment becomes an obstacle. But now he found that he was far from experienced enough to know what he should do now, here, with Ellysta. He doubted that Paladine himself would know.

Gerik also resolved that although he was not a god, with eons before him, he would wait at least all through this night rather than give Ellysta a moment's unease. The honor of Tirabot Manor, and his own, demanded nothing else.

At last Ellysta reached out with her other hand, and moved it up Gerik's other arm. She tightened her grip, with a strength that surprised Gerik. A sudden picture in his mind made him laugh.

She almost glared.

"What's so funny?" she demanded.

"I remember a song, where the lady grips both the man's arms so that her friend can strike him down from behind."

"Not very honorable."

"No, but the man had treated the lady most shamefully."

"Then you have nothing to fear," Ellysta said. She pulled herself to her feet. Gerik thought she swayed for a moment, then she stepped around the table.

She did not sway as she stood there for another week's-long moment. Instead, she took three deep breaths. Then she stepped forward, into Gerik's arms.

"If I can be afraid of you, then I am too fear-ridden to go on living," she breathed. "Hold me."

Gerik began his embrace as gently as if he had been picking up a week-old chick. Ellysta quickly tightened hers. Indeed, she seemed almost angry until he replied with a firmer embrace of his own.

* * * * *

Elderdrake decided to make his way into the manor house through a window, rather than a door. Windows were less likely to be guarded by those who would ask questions or even halt him.

He wanted to tell Gerik and Shumeen at once about what he had seen and learned. But more than that, he first wanted to wash the grime off himself and put on at least one garment that didn't look like a stolen, sodden, filthy rag.

The luck that had walked with the kender so far tonight now deserted him. The only open window he could see happened to be Ellysta's. So he climbed to that.

Then his half-deafened ears did not let him hear the sounds from within the chamber, even when the thunder was not crashing and rolling. Finally, as he gathered himself for a leap into the chamber, a flash of lightning close by dazzled him. He did not see what the people within were about, and how little they would care to have visitors flying in through the window.

This time Elderdrake landed on his feet. It did not help much, because a scream battered one ear and a savage oath battered the other.

He found himself confronted by Gerik and Ellysta, both rather less clad than he himself. Each of them had snatched up a garment, although Elderdrake wanted to laugh when he saw that Gerik had snatched up Ellysta's shift and Ellysta held Gerik's shirt.

It did not make him want to laugh, however, to see the point of Gerik's sword a finger's length from his nose, and a dagger in Ellysta's free hand.

Then Gerik swore again, more softly. "By all the foul creatures of the Abyss, what are you doing here, friend?"

"Eh . . ." was the first thing Elderdrake said. He realized that that might not tell his hosts much, so he tried harder the next time.

It came out, "Ahhhh—" followed by "—choo!" as he sneezed violently.

Then he started coughing. Ellysta managed to pull Gerik's shirt over her head, ran to the kender, and knelt beside him.

"Mishakal be merciful!" she exclaimed. "He's burned, bruised, lame, and wearing what looks like someone's stolen bedclothes. Where have you been?"

Between coughs, Elderdrake tried to tell his story.

In the intervals between the thunder, however, he also heard shouts outside, and even worse, pounding feet on the stairs. When pounding fists on the door joined the pounding feet, Elderdrake wanted to sink into the floor. He started shaking, and found that he could not stop.

"Gerik," Ellysta said firmly. "Put some of our clothes beside the brazier. Don't set them on fire, just warm them up while I take our friend out of these rags.

"And call off those hounds of yours barking in the hall. They have no work here!"

Gerik laughed.

Ellysta stood up, and Elderdrake had a moment to appreciate the fine sight she made, with her hair spilling down her back and long legs thrust out of Gerik's shirt.

"Now what is funny?" Ellysta asked.

"The gods have put me in charge of commanding women, from the day of my birth," Gerik replied.

"You are going to regret that day, if your guards come charging in here like Solamnic heavy cavalry!" she threatened.

Gerik was still laughing as he moved to the door and shouted through it. "There is no cause for alarm. One of the kender was sick and lost his way. Send a messenger to Shumeen, and also to Lady Serafina."

Elderdrake heard mutterings outside the door. It sounded less like disobedience than who would have these unwelcome tasks. Shumeen was hard to find, like any good kender, and Serafina was not soft-spoken toward those who awoke her when her husband was visiting.

Finally the voices died away and departing footfalls replaced them. Elderdrake's one remaining dread was that Shumeen would come quickly and find him here, like this.

"Gerik, turn your back," Ellysta said. She went over to the brazier, picked an undershift and girdle from the pile there, and handed them to the kender.

"Put these on. They're warm, and they'll be a better fit than anything of Gerik's that I'm not wearing myself."

Then she turned her back, and Elderdrake endured another coughing fit.

* * * * *

Gerik feared that the kender would cough himself into exhaustion, but Elderdrake was made of tougher fiber than that. He managed to greet Shumeen in Ellysta's borrowed garments, rather than his bare and battered skin.

Shumeen did not help matters by laughing until Gerik was ready to shake her and Ellysta looked ready to help him. But she finally put an arm around Elderdrake's waist and led him off, murmuring things like "no more sense than a frying pan" and "soothing syrup" and "ask the cook for hot bricks."

When the kender were gone, Ellysta turned to Gerik. "We will be as chilled as he, if we stand about like this much longer."

Gerik nodded, groping for words. "If we wish—if we

don't wish to be cold—let me take the other clothes off the brazier—"

What he wanted to say was that if they were to go on, they could retire to her bed, and if they were not, he could retire to his.

Ellysta laughed. "I couldn't expect you to put on my shift the way I put on your shirt, of course. So perhaps we should exchange garments."

She drew his shirt off. Gerik swallowed, and dropped the shift.

"Beautiful," he whispered.

Ellysta flushed. "Even—the wounds?"

"Honorable wounds do not mar beauty." Gerik wished he could be sure that was original.

Then he knelt before Ellysta, and with great gentleness kissed each of the honorable wounds. She sighed. He stopped worrying about whether he was saying anything original. Shortly thereafter, neither of them were using words at all.

Ellysta did weep before they slept, but on Gerik's shoulder, with joy and hope. Then they fell asleep so deeply and so swiftly that they barely remembered to pile the bedclothes over themselves.

Chapter 7

To landward, Pirvan saw mostly the early-morning mist, hiding not only the hills beyond Karthay but the greater part of the city itself. Only the tallest towers and the topmasts of the greatest ships thrust dark above the pearly grayness of the mist.

To seaward all seemed brightness. A spring sun cast golden light that danced across the tops of the swells rolling in from the northwest. The swells hinted of storms farther off, but here they barely had the power to make *Wavebiter*'s deck sway under Pirvan's feet.

Indeed, it looked too peaceful a sea to bear the weight of a fleet sailing to war.

Pirvan forced his mind away from that thought, as he would have forced a stubborn horse away from a flooded ford in a river. Too many in the ships bound for Suivinari Island seemed persuaded that they were outward bound not to penetrate its mysteries but to fight any minotaurs there.

The knight did not know what the captains of the fleet might think on this matter. He was certain that if a fleet determined on fighting minotaurs met minotaurs whose honor would, as always, require them to fight back, much blood would be shed to little purpose.

It was a pity that Vuinlod's motley population did not include some minotaurs, but they had never been great ones for settling in human lands. Nor would free minotaurs have been welcome of late in those lands, and not only because they would have doubtless tried to liberate their enslaved comrades.

At least the fleet had Darin, raised by the minotaur Waydol and more capable of thinking like one than any human Pirvan had known. A pity that he was likely to find no counterpart among any minotaurs the fleet would encounter. Waydol might not have been unique in his notion that honor required one to learn as much as possible about one's foes before one drew a weapon, but his breed was certainly rare—and not only among minotaurs.

Pirvan thought of his son and home, now menaced by those who seemed unwilling or unable to learn. He hoped that Sir Niebar's knights and men-at-arms had a safe and swift journey to Tirabot, and that once there they discouraged House Dirivan and anyone else from folly.

Without foreswearing his part in this quest, however, Pirvan could do no more than hope that the loud beating of the drums of war would not drown out reason.

Someone was beating a ship's drum now, not far off. Pirvan heard a drum aboard *Wavebiter* reply, and looked over the railing.

Off to port, a high-prowed Karthayan boat was approaching under six oars, heading straight for *Wavebiter*. A man with a mate's formal sash sat in the stern sheets, with features betraying his sea barbarian ancestry, hung about with fine Karthayan weapons.

The boat pulled alongside; the rowers tossed oars. The mate leaped from the boat's gunwale to the ladder built into *Wavebiter*'s side and scrambled lithely to the deck. It was almost like watching the ghost of Jemar the Fair.

The mate's scramble was quick. For all her three masts *Wavebiter* was not high-built. She was of a new breed of ship, designed for sailing but with sweeps that could keep her off shoals in a calm, fit to carry loads that a galley could not with fewer hands than a galley needed, and at the same time shallower of draft than a deep-built merchanter.

Pirvan could see how such a ship might be useful, but also saw reason in the complaints of old sailors, that such a ship could be a villainously bad sea boat. No storms had blown to test *Wavebiter* in the voyage from Vuinlod, but Pirvan was aware that both he and Haimya had thoroughly lost their sea legs.

If a storm did blow, he feared that his lady would hardly be seen on deck. Even he might need luck to uphold the honor of the knights and keep down his own food.

But now the mate was striding aft, drawing his sword, and saluting Pirvan with the blade held against his lips. As was his own custom as well as that of the knights, he returned salute for salute.

"Sir Pirvan, Knight of the Rose," the mate said evenly, "you are bidden to accompany me in my boat, to the ship *Shield of Virtue*."

"Is this a council of war?" Pirvan replied. "If so, Sir Niebar is by law appointed to speak for the Knights of Solamnia."

The mate grinned—and Pirvan realized that the man could hardly be older than Gerik. Increased commerce by sea was doing more than creating new breeds of ship. It was making mates and even captains out of youths and maidens.

"A council," the mate said, "but those who invite you are not thinking of war."

"You make me curious. Have you names for them?"

"Do Tarothin Red Robe and Sirbones, priest of Mishakal, have a place in your memory?"

Pirvan's jaw dropped too far for a knight's dignity. He had heard in a letter from Tarothin that his old companion and his friend might be sailing with the fleet, but had thought this a pious hope. Neither was much in the grace of the kingpriest, and made no secret of it.

"An honored place," Pirvan answered finally. "But if they are asking for me, then Lady Haimya must be with me."

"Ah—I am in haste, with other duties—"

"She will not delay us. She will, however, push me over the side some dark night, or perhaps even some bright day, if I do not bring her to see our old friends."

* * * * *

Gerik lurched up from the depths of sleep like a drunkard climbing a hill. His first sensation was that he must have slept fearfully late for the day to be so bright. Then came a thought that perhaps they would have a fine day at Tirabot. Even this far south, spring did come in time, and with it such fine days.

At last came the knowledge that he was not alone in his bed, that the person beside him was a woman, and that she was holding him.

"Ellysta, I hope?" he whispered.

"You doubt it?" came her sleepy reply.

"I hope that any time I share a bed with a woman, I remember her name the next morning," Gerik added playfully. "To do otherwise is rude."

"I knew you were gentle of character as well as blood."

Gerik looked at the dust motes dancing in the sunlight. "Blood is what the council will have," he said. "Ours, if we are late for the meeting."

Too many thoughts of that meeting crashed in on his still half-mazed wits. He groaned.

"You look as if you would like to go back to sleep, meeting or not," Ellysta said.

Gerik sighed. "Perhaps I would. I was having a lovely dream. I was in a garden, and a woman and I were picking roses.

"I don't know if it was you," he added, and she stuck out her tongue at him. "She wore a veil and a long robe."

Ellysta sat up. Sunlight played across fair, freckled skin that had largely healed of its wounds and was hidden by neither veil nor gown. "Go on," she urged.

"We were picking roses, as I said. Then we found this purple one, as big as a cabbage. We wouldn't have dared pick it, but it floated off its stem all by itself. It floated up like a soap bubble, until it was between us, and its perfume—it drew us both toward it until our lips touched on opposite sides of the rose."

"And then?"

"I started waking up," Gerik said, climbing out of bed.

Ellysta propped herself up on the cushions, draping a blanket over her legs. "It's more than the meeting that troubles you, Gerik. Is it the message from your father?"

His suspicions that she was a spy for his enemies twitched briefly, but did not come back to life. "Yes," he answered.

"I do not ask more. If I did, and you answered because we were bedmates, others would be jealous."

Gerik grinned. "Bertsa Wylum, do you suppose?"

"Pah!" Ellysta said, miming spitting. "She is old enough to be your mother. No, I mean jealousy of what you tell me, not of what else we do."

Gerik realized that he had just been given an unsubtle piece of advice in a most subtle manner. Ellysta, he decided, could make her fortune going on embassies. She could probably persuade minotaurs that it was honorable to let someone else have what they wanted.

But he had now told her either too much or too little. "The message holds no bad news," he went on. "But it was—my father wrote it in a secret language, lawful only among the Knights of Solamnia. He also told me where to find the key that let me read the letter.

"I am the son of a knight, but not one myself. My father has—well, some would say that he has broken Oath and defied Measure."

Ellysta put her chin on her knees and wrapped her arms around her legs. This was her pose of meditation. It also dislodged the blanket, which made her a rather distracting sight for Gerik. He hoped she finished meditating soon.

"You are keeping a knight's holding, are you not? Or even the property of the Order of the Rose?" she asked suddenly.

"Some of both," Gerik said. "It would take too long to explain."

"I will listen some other time," she said, which was as close as Gerik could imagine to being an order without actually using words of command. "But the Oath and the Measure also allow you to act in your father's place in certain matters."

"Some, yes. Not all."

"Then by common law, responsibility implies authority and authority gives rights. Rights to know what is needed to carry out your tasks." ·

"And reading that letter was, therefore, one of my rights?"

Ellysta clapped her hands, then kissed him. Gerik stopped feeling like the pupil to her teacher and instead more like a man with a woman.

Ellysta's eyes widened, and she asked, "You have already read the letter, you say?"

"Yes."

"Good."

Then she kissed him in a way that made further talk both needless and impossible.

* * * * *

Tarothin and Sirbones were aboard *Shield of Virtue*, which was the largest ship Pirvan had ever seen. She loomed above the boat like a keep above a rider on a pony, and she seemed to have more people aboard her than Pirvan had hairs in his beard.

High-built from fore to aft, with a bowsprit as long as some seagoing ships and four masts, she clearly needed every bit of sail those masts could spread to move. Pirvan hoped her size gave her seaworthiness in proportion, or she would only be a way of taking more sailors to Zeboim's realm than any ship before her.

They met their friends in Tarothin's cabin, which was the only place aboard ship safe from eavesdroppers.

"Let us make haste," Tarothin began without preamble. "I have a warding spell on this cabin that not only shuts out ears and magic but hides its own existence. It only lasts about ten minutes at full strength, though, and renewing it would take an hour. I'm not as young as I was."

Tarothin had to be rising sixty, but looked far better than he had when he and Pirvan parted two years ago. Sirbones, on the other hand, looked neither better nor worse, neither more robust nor more frail. The priest, Pirvan decided, had doubtless looked middle-aged when he was an apprentice.

Pirvan spoke briefly of what had befallen him and Haimya during the last two years, of their reasons for sailing to Suivinari Island, and of the peril facing Gerik at Tirabot. He had no intention of spending more time than necessary in the cabin, spell or no spell. It had less than enough space and hardly more than enough air to keep four people comfortable.

Tarothin was reassuring. "It will be more than a while before the kingpriest sanctions private war," the mage said, "even for such as House Dirivan. New to his office, he cannot be sure that all who turn their household guards into private hosts and wall in their estates will be his friends.

"By the time he can tell whom to loose and whom to bind, you will be home and feasting by your own fire. And Grimsoar One-eye will stand strongly by your lad, if I remember rightly. A young wife will make an old man a lad again."

Sirbones looked eloquently at the cabin beams. "Doubtless you know better than I," he said.

Tarothin smiled, then continued with his old briskness: "I said we have little time, and here I am wasting it. The first and last message for you is that neither you nor Haimya nor Gildas Aurhinius should go aboard an Istaran ship, or ashore. Lady Eskaia might be safe aboard ship, but I would not wager for the shore."

"Eskaia remains behind in Vuinlod," Pirvan said. "She oversees the affairs of the town, and if need be its defense."

Everyone made gestures of aversion at the last words. Tarothin nodded. "A pity," he said. "We were hoping she would be here to bring her influence to bear on sending us aboard her son Torvik's *Red Elf*. It is hardly a secret that he is likely to be sailing in the vanguard of the fleet."

"Such a post of honor, for one not friendly to the king-priest?" Haimya asked. "How so?"

"The captains?" Pirvan asked, and wizard and priest nodded.

"They are all for virtue," Tarothin added, "but in unknown waters, prudence and experience are the virtues they prize most. Torvik has these, plus Jemar's blood. Perhaps you can speak in Eskaia's place, even if they do not listen as well to you as they would to her."

"As you wish," Pirvan said, as he and Haimya exchanged looks. Both plainly wished that their magicworking friends were not so intent on rushing into danger, and thought that it was as much curiosity as duty driving them. Just as plainly, they would be deaf to even old comrades' counsels of prudence.

"We will do what we can," Pirvan said. "And Gildas Aurhinius had Torvik's respect even before wedding his mother. Now he might even have the man's ear."

They went on deck after that, ducking under a netload of kegs thundering down the after hatch into some storeroom far below. Then Pirvan and Haimya strode to the railing and hailed the boat waiting a half-bowshot to leeward.

* * * * *

Unknown to Pirvan, his son was also enduring a meeting at Tirabot Manor with too many people in too little space. The warded tower chamber was cozy for three; it was definitely cramped for more than five. When there were seven and one of them was Grimsoar One-Eye, stout and sleek on his lady's cooking and potions, it grew positively stifling.

The weather did not help, for it had blown up a gale of wind, bringing rain that was rapidly turning to sleet. The temperature had dropped so fast that Gerik privately wondered if they faced weather magic or one of Chislev's bad moods interrupting the advance of spring. The closed shutter and door kept out chill drafts and spattering icy water, as well as every breath of fresh air.

"You ought to shrink down to normal size," Horimpsot Elderdrake told Grimsoar. "Then I might not have to worry about my ribs every time you took a deep breath."

Grimsoar snorted. "When I shrink down to common size, little one, it will be from decay after I die. Or from starvation after Serafina passes on. Starvation and grief," he added, squeezing her hand.

"We may none of us leave this chamber alive if we do not speak quickly and to the point," Gerik said. "Now, how do we stand if it comes to a fight?"

Bertsa Wylum shrugged. "No worse than yesterday," she said simply, "maybe better, but I don't know whose side time is on. We have forty men and women fit to fight, although we've weapons for more."

"Start training as many more as we can arm," Gerik said. "Take volunteers from the villages, as well."

"Some might be spies."

"They won't be inside the manor unless we stand a siege," Gerik said. "Riding the roads to halt bandits and chicken thieves taking advantage of troubled times will tell them none of our secrets. And make no mistake: our enemies will be counting on such penny-a-handful allies to wear us down."

Bertsa Wylum nodded. "There's sense in that."

"Forin?" Gerik said, looking at the steward.

"Forin" was short for an appallingly long name in the elven style, for all that the steward seemed to have more human than elven blood. But what a man chose to call himself was between him, his ancestors, and the gods.

"We do well enough, and would do better if we could hope this were settled before there's green forage around about," Forin said. "When they can feed their beasts, then they'll come. We're not worth spending stored fodder over, I wager."

Gerik hoped that was true. But it seemed unlikely that peace, if it came, would come so quickly. At least there was hope that the men Sir Niebar was sending would come before the campaigning season opened.

Gerik now read the letter from Pirvan. He did not mention

that it had been in one of the Solamnic's secret languages; what they did not know would not weaken their trust in him.

"Once the knights are here, I doubt we'll have much to fear. The weight of law, custom, tradition, and good sense are already on our side, simply because we hold a manor granted to a Knight of the Rose. With the weight of men actually sworn to the Orders on our walls, I think we are the masters.

"But they may take longer to come than our enemies take to gather. So Ellysta has suggested that we fight a war of laws and words, until we can take up the sword."

Forin's eyebrows rose. "How came she by this knowledge?" Gerik heard in the question the further query, "How came she to a place here, other than through sharing your bed?" But Forin grumbled much about women.

"My father was a law counselor, and my mother his clerk until they wed," Ellysta said. "I know the common law of Istar, and much merchant law."

Serafina nodded. "I begin to understand," she said. "Grimsoar knows more merchant law, and I know much of what governs the healers."

"I know the laws and customs governing sell-swords," Bertsa Wylum said. "And I know that if I say to Floria Desbarres that someone should be banned from her service, it carries weight."

"Good," Gerik said. "I think we can raise points of law in the path of any move against us, save by main force. It will be like digging ditches across roads an enemy may use to approach."

He looked at Ellysta and said, "Is there any chance of finding evidence that your friend was innocent of the accusation against her? If we do that, you become a valiant friend and a victim of injustice, and your questing here is no crime."

Ellysta shook her head. "That asks too much. Even if we could find it—"

"Does 'we' mean just humans, or are kender—?" Elderdrake began.

Shumeen elbowed him in the ribs, then put her hand back on his knee. The kender healer seemed to have laid claim to Elderdrake, rather as Ellysta had to Gerik. This did not keep her from backhanding him thrice a week or as more often as she thought his tongue wagged too freely.

"If you want to go spying again, once you heal, I doubt we could stop you," Gerik said. "But you could put all the kender hereabouts in danger, whether they are with us or not. Also, you would have to hold your tongue with those kender, and do you have that in you?"

"I can't not talk, but it isn't always important what I talk about. I mean, I can't be rude, but if I can be polite without telling them anything they shouldn't know . . ."

Shumeen looked ready to stamp on her friend's foot before he subsided. By then Gerik was satisfied that he could trust Elderdrake and the five fugitive Spillgather kender. He noted in his mind the need to keep watch on the rest of the clan, lest the fugitives' befriending Ellysta bring vengeance on their kin.

He would have a hard enough time defending Tirabot Manor. He would have little steel and less help from the law defending kender.

* * * * *

"So," Gildas Aurhinius said. "I am not safe aboard ships of the land I served in arms for nearly forty years. As a pension, it lacks justice."

"Who dispenses justice in Istar these days?" Haimya said. "Too many, I think, who would not know it if it came up and bit them in—" She made an explicit gesture.

"Too true," Aurhinius said. He looked out to sea. "Is Torvik himself vowed to lead the fleet to Suivinari?"

"I have not spoken with him," Pirvan said. "And rumor often lies. But it is what I would expect of him. As son to both Jemar and Eskaia, he has strong friends all through the fleet, as well as his own reputation."

Aurhinius nodded and added, half to himself, "And a mother whose heart would break if he falls leading the fleet."

"Her heart would break sooner if he held back from leading," Haimya said. Even Pirvan gave back a step at the edge in her voice. "Your head would break, too, if Eskaia thought you had aught to do with Torvik's holding back."

Pirvan remembered that Haimya had known Eskaia longer than any of them, from when both women were scarcely older than Eskaia's namesake was now. How much steel had always lain beneath that fair, even girlish outside, Haimya doubtless knew better than all of them.

"I will hold my peace," Aurhinius said, looking out to sea again.

Drowning out the rattle of blocks and oars, and the calls of the sailors, a long crescent of broad-winged birds soared overhead. The sunlight struck fire from their red wings, so that they held the eye until they were but distant specks on the horizon and their cries had faded to equally distant echoes.

"Red cranes," Aurhinius said. "Some fly north, out to sea, every spring about this time. Some say it is the females to nest on unknown islands far to the north, close to the minotaur lands. Others say it is only the old ones who fly north, to a clean death far out to sea. I like the second one better."

Pirvan stopped Haimya as she was about to reproach Aurhinius for ill-luck words or make a gesture of aversion, probably both. They were indeed old birds, some of them, but there were too many young ones making the flight to Suivinari for Aurhinius to have uttered a true prophecy.

Still, in his innermost heart and mind, Pirvan uttered a short prayer to Habbakuk, friend of those faring by sea, and Kiri-Jolith, friend of justice.

Chapter 8

Torvik looked aft from Red Elf's stern platform, wary of the swings and lunges of the tiller as the ship cut across the choppy sea under full sail. The fleet was steadily falling astern, with some of the smaller or more distant ships already hull down. He could still count seventy or more, from flyboats smaller than *Red Elf* and barely fit to be this far offshore, to *Shield of Virtue*, looming like a temple amid peasant huts.

Indeed, the fleet looked like a city afloat, and carried as many people, even if there were fewer women and hardly any children among them, and only the arts of war, seafaring, and magic represented. Torvik hoped that such strength would make even minotaurs think that prudence and honor together spoke in favor of peace.

Not that any number of human hopes ever moved a single minotaur, when he or she was determined on a fight. The best Torvik expected was that the strength of the human fleet would give the minotaurs pause, while they looked for weak spots at which to strike without sacrificing themselves to no purpose.

That might be enough, if a quick answer came to the mysteries of Suivinari Island. No sailor, human or minotaur, enjoyed dangerous mysteries that had already cost them a safe watering stop, and might spread farther out to sea. Even those sailors of either race who might in principal welcome war would in practice be content with being once again unable to sail safely near Suivinari.

The problem lay in the sailors not being altogether their own masters. War chiefs among the minotaurs and merchants and kingpriest's friends among the humans could both be ready to shed others' blood to pursue their own ends, which lay in the misty realms of racial honor and the pursuit of money and virtue.

Torvik wished he had been able to speak to his sister Chuina, serving as a corporal of archers aboard *Windmaster's Gift*. At her rank, folk doubtless talked more freely to her than they ever would to a captain. But the two ships had never been close enough for an easy visit, and letters or signals might be read or seen by unwelcome eyes.

Torvik looked forward. The waist of his ship was crowded with more than forty fighters sent aboard her from the rest of the fleet, and what planks the newcomers didn't cover, their baggage and weapons hid. He had asked that they all be fit to row as well as fight, because much of the advantage of a threefold increase in his fighting strength would be lost if the forty could not lend a hand at the oars. *Red Elf*'s own crew lacked the numbers to both fight and row, and facing minotaurs or unknown minotaur-slayers, she might have to do both at once.

That was as chance and the gods would have it, however. The fighters looked stouthearted and their arms were neither too shiny nor too rusty. As to their thoughts, Torvik would not have read those if he could have. He did hope that sharp ears among the loyal folk of *Red Elf* and prudence among the fighters would forestall any treachery.

He would gladly die fighting minotaurs or anyone else, as long as his short life would end with honor. He would shed neither his own blood nor his people's to provoke a war with the minotaurs from which others would reap the glory.

Beyond *Red Elf*'s raking prow, the peaks of Suivinari's mountains began to peer over the horizon.

* * * * *

Zeskuk's cabin was low for a minotaur's comfort, not surprising in a ship built for humans, however generously. It was likewise so dim that he needed a lamp lit even now, with full daylight on deck.

The whale oil in the glass globe of the lamp rippled as *Cleaver* rolled to the swell in the anchorage. Zeskuk scraped soot from the chimney with his dagger, and with his wrist wiped more from the inscription on the lamp's bronze base.

"To my brother Zeskuk. May his honor never be questioned."

The lamp was a gift from Zeskuk's eldest sibling, Yunigan, some twenty years ago, when the elder minotaur's honor was called into question. He had sailed out with two ships to silence the questions, and had done so, though at the price of his own life and one of his ships. The battle against the humans of *Golden Cup* and Jemar the Fair's squadron had, so the tales ran, been one for the praise songs. There had been honor enough for both sides before the battle was done and the last body cast into the sea.

Footsteps thumped on the deck outside and a heavy fist rattled the door on its hinges.

"Enter, Sister," Zeskuk called.

Fulvura strode in. She was tall for a woman, able to look her brother in the eye. She wore a kilt and tunic, a dagger on her belt, and a shatang slung across her back, as well as her usual sober look.

"The lookouts on the Green Mountain report the human fleet in sight. A scout is in advance, bound for the island," she said.

"Let him come."

"Even if he steers toward our anchorage?"

"Even so," Zeskuk said. "If the lookouts are alert, we will have ample warning. If they are not, I will have their heads."

"One of them is Thenvor's cousin. He might call challenge on you for his cousin's blood."

"Let him. I fear Thenvor somewhat less than I do the humans," he grumbled.

"What about dividing our ships," Fulvura offered, "sending half to the north of the island, to lurk inshore and thereby conceal our strength?"

Zeskuk considered his sister's suggestion. It smelled of prudence, even caution. Not something to let pass unnoticed in another minotaur—unless she was one's last sibling, most trusted adviser, and right more often than not.

"That hides," he said flatly. "It also divides, and in the face of what lurks below as well as in the faces of the humans."

"Who knows if what lurks below even has a face?" Fulvura replied. "The humans at least are known enemies. Hiding a portion of our strength works against them, unless they are uncommonly shrewd."

"They have been known to be so."

"Now who argues for marching with babe's steps?" Fulvura said, with a guffaw that made the lamp rattle on Zeskuk's table. "We are the Chosen Ones, the Destined Race. It was never written that any one of us could be sure of being alive to see our Day of Destiny. But I would be as glad as not to be alive on the day of victory, to hear the praise songs."

"Are you sure, Sister?" Zeskuk asked. "What if the praiser cannot sing?"

Fulvura had begun to glare before she understood the jest. Instead, she made the lamp flicker with her laughter.

* * * * *

Torvik had no orders about how to approach the island. This suggested either great trust in his knowledge of the waters, in spite of his youth, or a great reluctance on anyone's part to be responsible for his death through obeying their orders.

He would have liked to believe the first, and it might even be true for some. He suspected the second, but it might come as much from fear of the wrath of his mother, father-by-marriage, and friends among the Knights of Solamnia as from anything else.

Regardless, Torvik steered a course well to the east, to come upon the island as far from the common haunts of the minotaurs as possible. Whether this also took him far from the haunts of the minotaur-*slayers*, he did not know.

What he had seen and the tales he had heard all spoke of uncanny and deadly things haunting all shores of the island. So there might be a creature or creatures lairing in the reefs on every side of the island, like monstrous watchdogs set there by Zeboim or someone in her favor.

Or there might be only a single creature behind all the tales and the dead minotaurs, lairing where it could strike with equal speed in any direction. Torvik wondered at this. There were no tales of sea caves in the Green Mountain. Many were said to pierce the sides of the Smoker, but the heart of a volcano still seemed no place for even a creature created and guarded by magic.

Both mountains towered against the sunset before Torvik ordered *Red Elf*'s sails doused and all hands to the oars. Under those oars the ship glided swiftly across waters barely ruffled by the dying evening breeze, while the handful of crew not rowing kept watch and made ready to lower the anchor.

Torvik himself did a stint at the oars, to encourage the others. He came on deck afterward soaked with sweat, half-deafened by the clatter and squeal belowdecks, and ready to gulp in the sweet salt air of the evening as if it were the most delicate wine.

Now it was nearly dark, the wind altogether silent, and the only waves were those *Red Elf* made by her passage, rising white at her sharp prow and falling away into the purple twilight astern. Even on deck, the oars made such a din that Torvik was sure that only a minotaur too old and weak of hearing to be sailing in a warship could fail to hear them from the far end of the island.

Yet one sound did touch his ears, over the rowing, although so lightly that Torvik himself at first doubted what he heard. He also saw that no one else seemed to hear it, so he held his tongue.

Far off, from the direction of the island, he heard the yelping bark of sea otters.

* * * * *

The Dimernesti woman who named herself Mirraleen (when she did not wish to give her full name, not much shorter than a gnome's) was called the Red Walker by the true sea otters of her band. Walker for her shapechanging power, that let her take elven form and stride upright on the land, and Red for the color of her hair.

She did not know how she came by that auburn hair that flowed down to her knees when she let it fall free. There were many fewer of the Dimernesti, the shallows-dwellers, than there had been in the days when they and the Dargonesti ruled the seas of Krynn and even struck at the rule of the elves on land. Among those long gone were most of the Dimernesti elders who could have pondered or even explained why Mirraleen had auburn hair and a paler blue skin than all the others of her race whom she had ever met.

Not that these numbered more than ten, so they proved little. She sometimes wondered if that was all the Dimernesti now left alive, or at least all who still swam in the waters about northeastern Ansalon. Sometimes, she even feared that this was indeed the case, or the call for help she had sent out when she learned of the peril rising from Suivinari Island should have long since been answered.

It seemed too likely that the work here was in her hands alone, and that of any friends she could make. Nor did she have great hope of such friendships. The humans had slain so many shallows-dwellers in both elven and otter shape that it seemed likely they thought only with their harpoons and bows, where it concerned the Dimernesti.

But the barking she heard was a signal from her band of the approach of a lone ship. As she willed herself into sea otter form, she heard the watchers identify the ship, and then, much to her surprise, its captain.

They had recognized on deck the same young man who had been on the island less than half a year before. He had used wits rather than steel, and insofar as she could read his thoughts, they were bloodthirsty toward no one.

Mirraleen thrust her tail against the water and darted forward as if she were trying to reach the finest of oyster beds before her kin ate it bare. It might be foolish to trust any land-dweller, and it was certainly foolish to hope for more from him than learning of his fleet's purpose in these waters.

But even that would put the Dimernesti—would put Mirraleen, who here and now *was* the Dimernesti—well forward of where she had been.

She was listening now, for the sound of the ship's oars beating the water. Before long she heard it, even over the rushing water of her own swift passage. She rolled on her back to judge time by the moonlight on the surface, broached to judge the ship's course, and saw it proceeding as her friends had described.

Pursuing and meeting it might be easy. Meeting the captain alone would surely be otherwise, but far more important. Mirraleen eased her pace through the dark waters. She would need the strength to take her elven form and the breath to speak in it, when she met the captain.

* * * * *

The bow anchor line rasped through the blocks until the anchor splashed into the glassy waters of the bay. A second rasp and splash told Torvik that the stern anchor was also down.

Held at bow and stern, *Red Elf* heeled to the tide, for the moment the only movement in the water. It was a Solinari ebb, gentle enough that Torvik had no fear for the ship from it, or from the weather, unless the wind got up from the southeast in a way not common at this time of the year in these waters.

He told himself sharply that he was a boy whistling to

keep up his courage as he walked past the ruins of the ghoul-lord's castle. All the men aboard *Red Elf* together could probably not save her from what had slain the minotaurs.

The best he could contrive was to see that their deaths would not be in vain. The fleet was coming for knowledge. Very well, let him lead boats out to buy that knowledge—with blood if necessary.

Since even a son of Jemar the Fair and Eskaia of Encuintras could only be in one place at a time, he decided to begin scouting the bay with a single boat. Eight picked companions, all skilled as sailors as well as fighters, would surely discover what was there to be discovered. If they returned, splendid.

If they did not, *Red Elf* could still fight and sail.

Torvik thought of picking the boat's crew only from *Red Elf*. But that might sow distrust enough to make matters worse, and taking nearly half his people would leave the rest outnumbered four to one if treachery came to the minds of others.

So it was half folk of *Red Elf* and half the embarked fighters who grasped the oars of the ship's longboat when it finally splashed into the water. Torvik himself took the tiller, which was not so easy a task that he could be called slack, nor so demanding that he could not meanwhile keep a sharp lookout.

Now, if he only knew what—besides sea otters who might or might not be Dimernesti, and something that might have no shape ever seen by the eyes of gods or men—he was watching for!

*   *   *   *   *

Wilthur the Brown scried attentively. As his knowledge of the visitors grew, he regretted more and more that he had not given his Creation a shapechanger's power.

He had tried, but it had enough wits and will to call itself sacred to Zeboim, and threatened to invoke her aid if he changed its shape. Otherwise he would have gladly made it present itself as a band of sea otters, so that the Dimernesti among them would be speared as readily as their non-elven shapemates.

Wilthur could not be sure that his Creation was telling the truth, but he was always prudent in dealing with the evil sea goddess, daughter of the Dragon Queen herself. Zeboim would be a bad enemy for any mage whose use of all three colors made him an offense to gods of all three natures. She would be the worse, for his being on an island in the middle of her watery realm.

The scrying glance went blank for a moment, then a single colossal eye stared out of it, a green circle within a black circle, and around that a rim the color of old and ill-kept ivory.

"Seek the boat," Wilthur said, though not in words that it would have been lawful for any human to hear. "Seek the boat, and let it be as before. But wait until the shallows-dwellers are close enough to seem the cause of what befalls the boat."

The eye blinked. The intelligence of the eye's owner allowed it to be stubborn as well, and it insisted on understanding Wilthur's commands before deciding whether to obey them. By the time the eye closed in obedience, he wondered if the boat might have wandered beyond the range within which his Creation could sense and pursue it.

If he had to guide it by magic, anyone listening for his spells would hear far too clearly for his peace of mind.

* * * * *

Wilthur the Brown fretted to no purpose.

His Creation's senses were quite adequate to finding Torvik's boat, for all that it was moving along at a good pace, cutting across the tide rather than battling it head-on.

Torvik's first thought at the splash ahead was that they were approaching a reef.

So was his second thought, as a part of the darkness turned solid and jagged, like part of a reef thrust above the water. It was when the solid darkness moved, then opened to become a gigantic claw, that he realized they had found their quarry. Or, more likely, it had found them.

Something wrapped itself around the tiller, nearly jerking the solid bar of wood out of his hands. Then the tiller jerked again, slamming hard against Torvik's chest. He heard ribs creaking, and was sure his spine had suffered grave hurt as his back crashed against the gunwale of the boat.

Then the boat tilted, as one sucker-studded tentacle heaved the tiller completely out of its socket and brandished it in the air. A man rose to retrieve it. Another tried to pull him down. A third drew his sword.

Torvik shouted at all of them to get down, but it was too late. The boat had tilted beyond its balance point even before a second length of rank, sucker-studded flesh slapped over the gunwale with a hideous sound, like a man drowning in boiling glue.

It caught the man with the sword, who slashed at it. Purplish fluid oozed, the arm twitched but did not loosen its grip, and in the next moment the man was gone, over the side. He had time for one despairing shriek before he was pulled under.

Then the boat itself went over. Torvik had just decided to leap overboard and dive after the man, who could hardly save himself unaided, when he found himself in the water regardless. He was trying to count the heads bobbing in the water beside the boat's upturned bottom, when what might have been a band of iron gripped his left foot.

His father's sword was long and supple; it could thrust as well as slash. He thrust down, and the iron band's pressure eased.

Then a second took his other foot, and a third looped about his sword arm and squeezed. He had sworn many years ago to die rather than let the sword fall into an enemy's hands, but it fell out of his hand now because his fingers could no longer grip anything.

Fury and shame left no room for fear in Torvik Jemarsson, as the Creation's tentacles drew him under the water.

Chapter 9

Mirraleen had encountered Wilthur's Creation before, and so had the band with her. She had not seen it when it was killing, however, nor from so close.

The Red Walker knew that she must go even closer still, to try to snatch some of the human sailors from the claws, tentacles, and beak of the monster. She had not been able to do this for the minotaurs, or later with the folk of a human ship so small that she'd left no survivors. Those failures both shamed her, even considering how little she liked minotaurs. They were too quick with their harpoons, as much as the worst sort of human.

But failure tonight could do worse than shame her. If a single man survived from the boat and told of sea otters present when his mates died, surely someone would blame the otters. Then the sea otters of Suivinari would face a great hunt, which might destroy them, perhaps sweep up any shallows-dwellers who answered Mirraleen's summons, and surely distract human attention at the worst possible moment.

She did not know who would gain the most from the Istaran fleet sailing so far wide of its true course, Wilthur or the minotaurs. She hoped it would be the minotaurs, who had limits and knew it.

Wilthur was also bound by nature and the gods, but thought otherwise. Seeking to go beyond these boundaries, he could wreak far more havoc than a hundred shiploads of those who called themselves the Destined Race.

Mirraleen tossed her flippers, driving herself through the shallow water. After her the rest of the band splashed into the water. From offshore those already feeding at sea responded with the quick barks that meant they were coming in ready obedience. A moment later, Mirraleen knew that she was not as much in command of herself as she had thought.

She replied to the sea otters with the clicks and whistles her magic allowed her to use, the tongue of the dolphins. She had learned the language centuries ago, to deal with dolphins seeking to make a meal of a sea otter, as they sometimes did. It also had its uses in speaking to the rare Dargonesti sea-brother who had been in his dolphin shape so long that his spirit was more dolphin than elven, and his attention best gained with the dolphin tongue.

Mirraleen rose, inhaled the night air, and barked quick commands in the proper language for leading sea otters. Their replies gave reassurance. They would move against Wilthur's Creation from two directions, rescuing the humans first and fighting only if they must, to complete the rescue.

Mirraleen angled downward, into the deeper water beyond the reef. She went that deep only to feed or to avoid the Creation. Not only did it seldom pass beyond the reef, but its senses could not reach out past the reef to find those who swam in deep water.

The Red Walker had pondered more than a trifle on this mystery. Had she known more of magic, she might have set herself the task of solving it. But her powers did not allow her more than intelligent guesses. Also, she shared the temperament of those with whom she swam. Sea otters were shrewd and practical. They did not often allow themselves to be troubled by mysteries that did not directly threaten their survival.

A patch of warmer water ahead told Mirraleen that she was coming up on Fountain Grotto. A little farther on lay an underwater tunnel through the reef. Through it, she and her companions could return to the shallows, striking with next to no warning.

From mind to mind, Mirraleen sent her war cry. From mind to mind, it echoed back to her, as a hundred sleek forms surged through the dark water.

* * * * *

Torvik was an experienced sailor and a survivor of fights far more serious than tavern brawls. He was also the son of a father and mother who had not endured and prospered by losing their wits in the face of surprise.

After the first moment of rage and shame, his thoughts arrayed themselves for battle. He let himself be carried downward into the darkness without further struggles. His captor might eat only live prey, think him carrion, and release him.

Failing that, it might send some of its tentacles questing in search of further prey. Lightly held, he might break free. If he broke free while this deep, he might find himself underneath his attacker. There were few living things, whether creations of the True Gods or of twisted magic, whose bellies were not a vulnerable spot.

He had no sword (a loss that now only heated his rage), but he had two arms and two daggers. Anything that believed him helpless would regret that belief.

One tentacle loosened its grip and darted away, toward the surface as far as Torvik could judge. The other two still gripped him, however, and now he was deeper than he had reckoned on. He felt the pressure of water as well as the clutching tentacles.

How deep did this monster lair?

The pressure grew still further, and Torvik sensed invisible bands of something stronger than even magic-driven flesh tightening on his chest. He had breathed deeply before he went under and could hold his breath longer than most, but before long even his endurance would reach its end. Then so would his life, going out in a brief spate of silver bubbles that would never even reach the surface from this depth.

Something struck his leg. Then the tentacle holding his right arm jerked free. Able to use steel with both hands, Torvik wasted no time in drawing his handiest dagger. He thrust it hard into the tough flesh of the tentacle holding his left arm.

The second tentacle recoiled so violently that Torvik's deep-slashing dagger nearly went with it. As he clutched it, he felt the burning in his chest that meant the end of his breath. He had no time left to hunt his attacker or rescue any of his men. Not with his life measured by the remaining air in his lungs, which might not even be enough to take him to the surface.

This time it was more of a gentle bump than a hard blow. Torvik felt himself being lifted by two furry . . . somethings, one under each arm. A third, then a fourth, positioned itself between his legs, adding to the lift.

He was rising now, faster than he could have done by his unaided swimming. He was still holding the dagger, and his air-starved brain turned over wild thoughts of stabbing out at the beings lifting him.

Dolphins? Even wild dolphins with no elven selves or ties to the Dargonesti had been known to rescue swimmers in distress, or attack sharks and octopi. But dolphins had smooth, sleek hides. He had felt fur under his arms, and now felt it below as well.

Seals. No, sea otters.

It took all the wits he had left to make that distinction. It was beyond Torvik to carry his thoughts one last step farther, to realize how the sea otters must have come to his rescue, or to hope that the sleek swimmers would rescue his crew as well.

The bubbles of his last outward breath sparkled on the water. Before he could draw the inward breath that would have filled his lungs with water, his head broke the surface.

He did not know it. He did not feel the sea otters under

each arm or holding him up. Nor did he sense the one who swam up and took position under his chin, lifting his head out of the water.

His lungs drew in air, however, not water, with a noise like a sick whale. He would have heard similar noises from the water around him, had his senses been awake. Torvik heard none of the signs that others among the boat's crew yet lived. He also had no awareness of his swimming bearers guiding him away from the rest of his men, toward a beach at the end of a tiny, almost landlocked cove.

He was as one dead through the brief journey to the beach, dead to the pushing of whiskered muzzles and the heaving of agile flippers. He remained dead to the pricks and stabs of sharp rocks, and to the splashes as his rescuers slipped back into the water, their night's work only just begun.

He did not even sense a sea otter muzzle push above the water and suddenly change shape; nose, mouth, and eyes alike. Fur shrank away from the face, to instead flow from above as long auburn tresses.

But the owner of those tresses sensed that Torvik's life was safe, that he had passed from senselessness to sleep, and that she could now safely leave him. She left to the gods the question of her returning, although she knew what she wanted, in both heart and mind.

*　*　*　*　*

It had been arranged for small vessels with signal lamps to form a chain from within sight of *Red Elf* to the rest of the fleet. The disappearance of Torvik's boat was known aboard *Wavebiter* and the other principal ships of the fleet within an hour.

Gildas Aurhinius brought the news himself.

"This will kill my lady," the Istaran said, his first words after the bare facts that the lamps had already carried.

Haimya sat up in her bunk, snatching a sheet to cover herself. "You insult your wife and our old friend by those words," she said. "Take them back."

Pirvan looked from his wife to Aurhinius. Haimya seemed in deadly earnest, and Aurhinius more than a trifle taken aback by that earnestness.

"I know now why they call this the Bad News Watch," Pirvan said. "Even if the news is no worse than what comes in daylight, one has less strength to bear it."

Aurhinius sat down on Pirvan's sea chest and put his head in his hands. "I will beg my lady's pardon when I see her again," he said, "and I beg Lady Haimya's now. I—I have lost one who was no son by blood but might have been a son in spirit. How well would you have borne losing Sir Darin in the first year after he became a knight?"

Pirvan and Haimya exchanged glances. "Eskaia will hear nothing of your first words from me," she said, and her husband nodded. "As Pirvan said, bad news weighs heavier in the depths of the night."

Whether or not she had intended those words as a dismissal, Aurhinius took them as such. He bowed himself out, and Pirvan blew the lamp higher and took the Istaran's place on the chest. He did not, however, put his head in his hands.

"Are you thinking of Gerik?" Haimya asked.

"How not?" he answered. "We have it better than Eskaia. The land does not commonly swallow the dead of its wars, as the sea swallows those who do battle on the waves."

"That comes from *The Lay of Vinas Solamnus*," Haimya said. Her smile sagged at one corner of her mouth, but it was undeniably a smile. "You need more inspiration than such news, to be so eloquent at this hour of the night."

"Then inspire me."

"Perhaps I can."

She let the sheet fall. It pooled around her waist. Pirvan was admiring the play of the lamplight on his wife, when someone knocked.

The sheet rose to its former position. Pirvan opened the door on Aurhinius, who said, "More ill news. The minotaurs have sent a flyboat to our scouting line. They wish a parley. I agreed to be one of those going, suggested you, Haimya, Sirbones, and Darin for others, and wish your answer. Or rather, the council wishes your answer."

Pirvan wanted to suggest what the minotaurs could do with their parley and the council with its sudden need for delegates to it. However, that reply lacked a knight's dignity, if it was not actually unlawful.

Furthermore, minotaurs being the first to propose a parley was uncommon. It suggested shrewd leadership in their fleet, even if all their delegates intended to do was pound the table and bellow demands and threats.

Also, the human fleet's council was plainly not marching entirely to the beat of the kingpriest's drum, if they wanted any of the folk just named in their delegation. Surely there would be others, more in sympathy with the kingpriest—and still more if Pirvan and any of the others refused to go.

"I accept," Pirvan said, "likewise Haimya, subject to the approval of Sir Niebar. I must have that, by law. He should also be asked to join us, as commander over the embarked knights."

"Sir Niebar might command all the hosts of Ansalon, but he knows less of minotaurs than you do," Aurhinius said.

"I forged an alliance with one minotaur," Pirvan said. He knew he sounded tired and out of temper. He was. "One minotaur, moreover, very unlike most of his kind."

"That is still one more minotaur than most of us have dealt with," Aurhinius said. "But certainly I can ask Niebar."

"*Sir* Niebar," Pirvan said, but he was talking to a closed door, and Haimya had not only dropped the sheet again but climbed out of her bunk to embrace him. The embrace had just become mutual when knocking came again.

Pirvan opened the door just enough to see Aurhinius again.

"Yes?" He sounded as welcoming as a jailor hearing news of an uprising among his charges.

"Torvik's men are good, loyal stuff," Aurhinius said. "A new signal from *Red Elf:* she is staying to search the area, and has one survivor aboard already."

"As you said, good stuff," Pirvan said. "Or perhaps just with enough sense to tell ale from wine. I would not care to be known along the waterfronts of Ansalon as a man who abandoned the son of Jemar the Fair."

Pirvan took a firm grip on both the doorknob and his temper. "Now, my friend, a word of warning. The next person who knocks on this door before dawn, for anything short of the end of the world or the sinking of *Wavebiter*, will be bound, gagged, and hung up by his heels from the deck beams. Please send out the word.

"I can hardly be expected to bargain with minotaurs without sleep."

"Ah, but will you sleep more if not interrupted, or less?" Aurhinius said. With surprising speed for one of his age and bulk, he darted back before Pirvan could slam the door on his hand or thrust steel through the crack.

Haimya, meanwhile, fought so hard not to shriek with laughter that she finally had to lean on her husband to keep from falling.

"I—I suppose I said a word too many," Pirvan muttered into her hair.

"More than a few,"

Pirvan grinned and tightened his embrace. "Perhaps I lacked inspiration."

"Then pray let me provide it."

*   *   *   *   *

The first of Torvik's senses to awaken was his sense of smell. He smelled the scent of a tide-swept beach, overlain like silk by the perfume of tropical flowers, and also by overripe seaweed and other jetsam.

His ears came to reinforce his nose. Either he was on the beach of a landlocked harbor, or the sea was as calm as a pond. He barely heard the faintest gurgle and splash of water on the sand—fifty paces away, as far as he could judge.

He was not in the place where he had landed, he thought. He had a dim memory of gravel with as many teeth as a baby shark biting into his all-but-senseless body. Now he was on sand as fine as dust, with what felt like rushes in a bundle under his feet, to raise them above the level of his head.

Torvik was trying to pick out the scent of the rushes from the other scents on the breeze, when a new scent floated by. It had salt in it, and other smells of the sea, and also living flesh, sweet breath—he could almost say the smell of a woman.

Which was so unlikely here and now that Torvik decided to open his eyes, to see what was giving him the illusion of a woman's presence.

He opened his eyes, and found himself staring straight up into other eyes—two of them, vast and green, surmounted by thick eyebrows too brown to be called red and too red to be called brown. Above the eyes flowed hair the same color as the brows. Below was a face that lacked perfect beauty—the cheekbones were too high, the lips a trifle weathered, and the chin definitely sharp. The lips lacked nothing, however, including a gentle curve given them by a smile.

Torvik lay, wondering if he was the captive of an enchantress and if so, was this her real form? If the rest of her matched her face, his would be a joyous captivity.

He tried to move, to see the rest of his captor. His head moved, but his limbs refused to obey his brain.

"Lie still," the woman said. "You need to regain your strength. I will give you some water, if you can raise your head a little higher."

Her voice was low for a woman's, and although her Common was fluent, it held an accent he did not recognize. However, he had no trouble raising his head. At her command, he would have tried to dance on his hands.

He sipped fresh water, with a faint hint of herbs in it, which was all she allowed him to do. He would gladly have gulped the water down by the jugful, the more so when he felt strength creeping back into his limbs.

But that swiftly proved an illusion. He was glad enough to lie back down, head pillowed on the bundle of sweet-scented weed. It was only then that he noticed that the woman's skin held a faint but unmistakable tint of blue. It was a color he had previously seen only in the skins of the dying or the drowned, but this woman was plainly alive and in excellent health. She had strands of seaweed woven into that glorious auburn hair, rather like a high-ranking Istaran lady's hairnet.

His lips spoke without waiting for his mind to guide them. "My mother said that it is hard to wear blue and green at the same time," he said.

The woman smiled. "Your mother was wise. But I am also sure that she was human. What guides your folk does not always hold true for mine."

"Who are your folk?"

"We have been called the Dimernesti," she said, "the shallows-dwellers, and other names, some of them not friendly. The minotaur name for us means 'offal with flippers,' and that is not the worst."

"I suppose it would not be," he said. "The minotaurs are seldom polite, but still more seldom stupid." Minotaurs were the last folk he wanted to talk about now, but he did not wish to lie there with his mouth open like a dying fish.

Now his wits were beginning to move again, like the rowers of a galley falling into a faster stroke. "Was it you who saved me?" he asked.

"I did some work. My friends did more."

"Your friends? Other Dimernesti?"

She sighed, and for a moment he saw her looking far away toward something not in the world. He also saw crow's-feet at the corner of either eye. This sea-elf was no green girl—and at that last phrase, laughter nearly choked him.

The Dimernesti woman waited until Torvik got his breath back and sat up before going on. When he had, he missed her first few words. He realized for the first time that she was half a head taller than he, as splendidly formed as he had imagined, and quite unclad except for the net in her hair and a wide belt of fishskin from which hung several bottles and pouches.

"I am the only Dimernesti on this island," she told him. "But the sea otters and I are friends, and enemies to what

Wilthur the Brown has unleashed on these waters. We may not be Wilthur's only foes, but we are certainly the only friends to humans."

Torvik remembered the sea otters, who must have worked together as if trained to bear him to the surface and the life-giving air, "Did they—have you saved any others of my men?" he asked.

"All but three," she said. "We saw one hauled into a boat from your ship even before the Creation withdrew into its lair. Two were lost, one torn apart and the other drowned before we could carry him to the air. We have wrapped their bodies and will guide you and your men to them, if you wish it."

"I do." Torvik also wished to spend the rest of the day, and perhaps all night and the next day, simply staring at the Dimernesti woman, talking with her if she wished it but content to look if she wished silence. As for touching her—he did not think it prudent to even let that thought pass through his mind.

"Now, let me see how many of your host of questions I can answer," the woman said. "I am called Mirraleen among humans and elves, the Red Walker by the sea otters of Suivinari Island, and probably vile names by Wilthur . . ."

As she went on, Torvik wished he had listened more to his mother speaking of Wilthur the Brown, although she knew only what Sir Pirvan had written after the siege at Belkuthas. Still, he realized that he was learning much that neither Sir Pirvan nor anyone else had ever known, would give his eyeteeth to know, and would pry loose *his* teeth if he forgot.

When the image of Wilthur enslaving most living things on Suivinari and creating more to do his bidding was fixed in his mind, Torvik found himself growing curious. The question as it first took shape in his mind was doubtless rude; just as certainly he needed an answer.

"Your pardon, Mirraleen," he said. "But if you think that Zeboim herself does not favor Wilthur, how is it that you sea-elves have not long since cast down the mage? We shall do the work ourselves if needs be, but why is it yet undone?"

Mirraleen sighed. "Remember, the mage's work would also discommode Habbakuk, Zeboim's rival for domain in the sea. I doubt that she would openly attack one who is an enemy of her enemy.

"Besides, the Dimernesti, though not as much a legend among the sea-elves as we are among the dryfeet, have never been as numerous as the Dargonesti. On Ansalon, we lost more and more safe shores as the dryfoot folk grew in number. Some centuries ago, most of the Dimernesti swam north to shores even beyond the lands of the minotaur, and do well enough.

"I lost my family when I was young, and quarreled with those who reared me. So it was no great matter for me to swim south, find a home among the sea otters of this island, and watch dryfoot ships come and go."

"It sounds horribly lonely," Torvik said. "Like being a castaway."

"Ah, but I cast myself away—Torvik. Is that how you pronounce the name I heard your men calling you?"

"Yes."

"They called it in a way that shows they honor you, for all that they are of two—tribes—and you are young."

Torvik did not know whether to glow at the praise or flush at the frankness. Mirraleen smiled and laid a finger over his lips. "But hold your peace a little while longer," she said, "for I must finish my tale."

Mirraleen had not seen one of her own folk for more years than Torvik cared to think about, even though he knew that elves could live the best part of a thousand years. She did well enough, leading the sea otters of Suivinari, speaking to the rare Dargonesti sea-brother among the passing dolphins, healing sickness in others and in herself as needed, and altogether living the life of a contented hermit.

Then Wilthur the Brown took refuge on Suivinari Island, brought every living thing more than a few hundred paces from the water under his sway, and began creating monsters. The Creation that lurked in the shallows, with aspects of octopus, lobster, and poisonous reef cod, was only the latest. It would not be the last.

"We survive in the shoals because some power—call it Zeboim—will not let Wilthur intrude too far offshore. Had she done otherwise, I would be dead and my friends likewise, or even worse, slaves to Wilthur.

"Go back to your people," she finished, "and warn them not to simply debark and march inland. That is putting themselves into Wilthur's hands, and out of whatever protection the sea gods may offer."

"Such as it is," Torvik muttered. Among human sailors, Zeboim was the Great Turtle, mother of all that was evil about the sea, and protector of no one. Habbakuk was more friendly, but not always free to enter into human affairs.

Mirraleen stood up, and the sun on her made her so splendid that Torvik's arms and lips tingled with wanting her touch. If Mirraleen sensed any of this, she ignored it, only standing with her head cocked to one side as if listening.

"I hear a human boat approaching, Torvik. If you will hurry to the foot of the cliff to the left of the cove entrance, you will find ancient stairs there. Climb them, and wave to the boat," she said.

"Like *this*?" Torvik asked, looking down at the few tattered remnants of his clothes.

Mirraleen laughed, as sweet a sound as he had imagined it. "I have nothing you can borrow, I fear, and your own garb is at the bottom of the sea if not in the belly of Wilthur's pet."

She ran toward the water, more graceful than Torvik had believed any mortal creature could be. She sprang up atop a rock, then dived. In midair her arms became flippers, her legs a tail, and her body a sleek furry shape. A woman had leaped from the rock, but a sea otter entered the water.

Torvik wasted no more time. Even before Mirraleen vanished toward open water, he heard the horns and drums of the boat. He had best climb up to where he would be easily seen, as he had no way to make a fire, no mirror to flash signals, nor even a stitch of clothing to wave!

* * * * *

Mirraleen did not approach the boat closely until she was sure that it held humans, not minotaurs. The Destined Race might fling harpoons first and satisfy their curiosity, if any, afterward. Even after she saw humans, Mirraleen approached cautiously. She was alone, and while a dozen sea otters might raise no suspicions, after last night's events, a single one might still seem a portent, a sign, or something else to make tongues wag.

If there had been any way to help the humans overthrow Wilthur's enslavement of her island without revealing her own existence, Mirraleen would have chosen it. As it was, she would prefer to remain a secret until Torvik could tell his tale.

But at last it seemed likely that the boat would pass by, without seeing the small figure perched on the cliff or hearing his frantic halloos. Mirraleen swam up to the very prow of the boat, leaped half out of the water, barked three times, then dived back and away, in the direction she wanted to lead the boat.

At least last night's events had fixed every sailor's mind on the matter of sea otters. She heard shouts and urgent words from the boat.

"Hey! Sea otters!"

"Just one, though. Maybe it's lost."

"Maybe it's trying to help us!"

"Oh, you and your stories."

"No story. Remember what happened to Ligvur last night? When the boat went over, the otters came up under him and helped him to a rock. He'd have drowned otherwise."

"Yeah, and Jomo said he saw them going down and hitting that *thing* like sharks all over a dead whale. Wonder if somebody put them up to it?"

"Might have. Maybe not, though. Sea otters are pretty smart."

In her sea otter form, Mirraleen could not giggle. Underwater, she could not giggle even as an elf. She popped to the surface again, feeling safe and happy, and barked three times more.

It was while she was barking that she heard someone shout, "Hoy! Lookit up there! Somebody else from the boat. Get a rope so he can climb down."

Mirraleen thought kindly of the man who made that last suggestion. If Torvik had to retrace his steps inland, some of Wilthur's animal slaves might be across his path by now. Going down the cliff, facing the sea, he would likely be safe from everything except falling—and she trusted one of Torvik's years, strength, and experience to avoid that.

Her work with Torvik was done. Mirraleen dived deep and began swimming along the bottom. She might spend the rest of the day rallying her friends, counting their losses, and healing their hurts. It would be as well to find something to eat before she began.

Chapter 10

Nothing seemed to move in the world around Pirvan, save fumes trickling from the cone of the Smoker, well below the top. The knight half-hoped that the volcano would erupt in full fury, thereby settling the question of Suivinari's ownership in favor of the god Sargonnas, greatest master of destructive fire next to the Dark Queen herself, and one to whom humans, minotaurs, and any other seafaring race might cede the island with a clear conscience.

That the possession of the island by a god of evil might leave the mystery of what lurked in its waters unsolved was no matter. Sargonnas would allow nothing save of his own creation—and Zeboim seldom allowed any creation of fire to travel far through her domain.

Altogether, a battle of the gods over the corpse of the island seemed a fair way of saving humans and minotaurs the trouble of fighting their battle.

Pirvan shook himself, which made sweat drip faster down his neck and under his arms. It was hot enough for high summer in Tirabot, a damp heat that made one's clothes cling as if glued to the skin. He had endured such heat before, on his first quest with Haimya, but he had not enjoyed it then and enjoyed it still less twenty years later.

Not a breath of wind broke the stillness of air or water. Save for where the oars left their traces, the sea was as flat as a tavern floor and the color of moss-grown bread.

Pirvan looked toward the shade under the awning on the afterdeck and saw that it was as filled as ever, with folk who doubtless needed it more. The age of the four knights and Gildas Aurhinius ranged from barely twenty to more than sixty, but all were fitter than most of the Istarans. The minotaurs would surely refuse the parley if the humans gave them even the slightest excuse, such as one named delegate being unfit to speak.

It would be as well for everyone to reach Zeskuk's flagship fit to do serious work. It had certainly taken long enough to settle on who would represent the humans in the parley. The Istarans did not dispute sending all four knights and Gildas Aurhinius, but they insisted on sending an equal number from their ranks. Then everyone else who considered that he should be ranked equal with the knights, Istar, and Vuinlod clamored for representation.

If all claims had been honored, it might have been simpler to go to the minotaurs aboard *Shield of Virtue* herself. No smaller ship could have safely carried everyone.

After weary hours of debate consumed most of the night, they settled on four knights, four Istarans, two Karthayans, Gildas Aurhinius to represent Vuinlod, and Sirbones and the Istaran Black Robe Revella Laschaar representing the magicworkers. This already sizable delegation promptly grew by one, when word came at dawn that Torvik had been rescued and was returning to the fleet aboard *Red Elf*.

Not without protest, however.

"This gives Vuinlod an extra voice, in the mouth of a sea barbarian's heir who is not yet of lawful age," one Istaran all but gabbled.

Sir Darin looked for permission from the senior knights, saw it in their eyes, and brought one massive fist down on the table. Empty cups jumped, a half-empty jug upset itself into an Istaran lap, and the very deck planks seemed to groan under the impact.

"Torvik is captain of his own ship, by which he was declared of lawful age," Darin said. The senior Istaran, Andrys Puhrad, nodded. He was a merchant who had been a law-counselor in his youth and seemed the most level-headed from the city as well as the eldest.

Darin continued. "Also, he has priceless knowledge of conditions about Suivinari, and Zeskuk will know that he has such knowledge."

"All the more reason not to risk him," Sir Niebar said, which drew scandalized looks from the other knights.

"Your pardon, Sir Niebar, but that may not be the wisest reasoning," Darin replied. "Zeskuk may think that we do not wish an agreement, if we do not bring Torvik with his knowledge that may speed us along our course.

"Worse, he might think we hold back Torvik because we fear minotaur treachery. If he intends none, he will take it as an insult to his honor. He will have to, or some other minotaur will, and either challenge Zeskuk for leadership of the fleet or provoke us into a fight by some act of his own."

"Ugh," Sir Hawkbrother grunted. In spite of the reproving look he shot his son-by-marriage, Pirvan's unexpressed thoughts were much the same. So were most others', as far as he could judge from their faces. Fighting thirty shiploads (the best count so far) of minotaurs who thought their honor and that of the Destined Race had been impugned would have been an appalling thought in pleasant weather. In this heat it was enough to make a god cringe.

So Sirbones departed to see if Torvik was fit or could be made fit to join the delegation, and debate turned to picking a ship.

Some favored *Red Elf*, but she might be damaged, would be shorthanded, and was not yet up with the fleet. Others favored *Kingfisher's Claw*, but Sorraz the Harpooner was acknowledged even by his friends to be too hotheaded.

One ship after another was offered, usually by someone whose honor or fortune would be advanced by the choice—or at least by the payment for the ship, if she did not return. It was Pirvan who was finally able to at least begin closing the debate.

"We need something small enough to be no loss and large enough to hold all the delegates and their guards in some comfort, perhaps overnight," he said. "Above all, we need something too large to be sunk by accident. From what I know of minotaurs, their honor will forbid an open attack during a parley. But they will take it as a sign of their gods' favor if—oh, something heavy were to fall overboard and tear out the bottom of our craft during the parley."

"Will that not also tell them we do not trust them?" an Istaran queried.

"As with bringing Torvik, it will merely tell them we are not stupid," Darin said, uninvited. "Minotaurs despise dishonor. They despise stupidity almost as much."

To avoid even the appearance of stupidity, the delegation eventually sailed aboard a Harbor Watch galley from Karthay. Decked over for the voyage and towed most of the way, she was robustly built, light enough to be rowed easily without the rowers collapsing from the heat, and with room enough for everyone appointed to meet with the minotaurs.

"She even has room enough for Zeskuk and some of his companions to come aboard for the meeting," Darin pointed out. "I do not expect that he will do so, but we should ask."

"What about a meeting on land?" Andrys Puhrad said.

Gildas Aurhinius shook his head. "Each race has its own landing site," he said, "considered as much their property as the deck of a ship. The rest of the island—well, one reason we and the minotaurs are speaking to each other is that no one knows what is on the rest of the island."

From that painful fact there could be no appeal.

Nor could there be appeal from the old sailors' belief that it was bad luck to rename a ship. So when the luck of the draw fell on a ship named *Giggling Wench,* all efforts to dignify her with a new name (such as *Speaker for Knowledge*) fell on deaf ears.

So it was from the deck of *Giggling Wench* that Pirvan watched through sweat-blurred eyes Zeskuk's flagship rising higher and higher out of the torpid sea.

* * * * *

Zeskuk awaited the humans' envoys in the great cabin, rather than his own. It was the only space aboard *Cleaver* that in this heat would be endurable for both races for as long as the parley might last. Zeskuk knew that minotaurs smelled like a barnyard to humans; did any human know that to a minotaur a human smelled rather like diseased meat?

To be sure, there was no element of danger here lacking in his own quarters. The great cabin had three doors, and several ports whose shutters had been removed to allow what vagrant breezes might wander by to enter freely.

Zeskuk's cabin, on the other hand, had been rebuilt by *Cleaver*'s first minotaur captain to make it easy for him to hold against enemies. He had many, or at least enough that he was no longer among the living—but all the carpentry on his cabin had not saved him from a shatang in the back in a waterfront drink shop.

To Zeskuk's left stood his sister, Fulvura. To his right stood Juiksum, son of Thenvor. Loyal enough to his father that the loudmouthed Thenvor had agreed to let his son represent him, Juiksum was also ambitious enough that he would not go against Zeskuk merely for the pleasure of it. Not when Zeskuk's aid might speed his coming into his inheritance, or else give him wealth and power in his own right.

The humans entered, the knights armored and with their badges but not visibly armed, the others clad richly enough that their faces were already turning red in the heat. All except for the little man garbed as a priest of Mishakal, who looked as if he would have been equally at ease in the crater of the Smoker or in an ice cave beset by Thanoi. The black-robed wizard looked less comfortable, but held both herself and her staff as if they were weapons.

"I bid you welcome. I am Zeskuk, chief over this fleet, which has come by the emperor's command to Suivinari Island, to fight or make alliance with you as may seem best for unlocking the island's mystery."

The emperor had at least not withheld his consent to the voyage, or to others besides Zeskuk's personally sworn crews joining it. That should let Zeskuk's statement pass any truth-testing spell Sirbones or the wizard might have bound into their staves.

"My sister, Fulvura," the minotaur continued with formal gestures, "one of my honored warriors, Juiksum. What can be said for the fleet of the Destined Race here, we three can say."

Zeskuk thought that the humans were trying not to look impressed. His negotiating with so few minotaur witnesses implied great control over his fleet and great loyalty from those aboard it.

Zeskuk only hoped that what he implied did not run too far ahead of reality.

The humans introduced themselves. The names of the knights and the soldiers in merchant's garb were no surprise; the names of the others were of no interest. The only surprise was the wasted-looking young man (doubtless older than he looked) who named himself Torvik Jemarsson.

Curiosity as to his being the son of *the* Jemar would be ill-timed now, but the question needed an answer.

Fulvura for the minotaurs and one of the merchants for the humans in turn spoke of the reasons for their fleets' coming to Suivinari. As Zeskuk had suspected, both gave the same public reason—to end the mystery and menace now haunting an island useful to both—and both had other, hidden reasons.

The minotaurs had come to learn if there was any way they could ban the humans from the island. The lack of such a watering place would keep human ships farther from minotaur waters.

The humans, as far as Zeskuk could judge, had come for the same reason. If they could not claim Suivinari outright, they would be content with some other embarrassment or humiliation of the Destined Race.

It was Zeskuk's intent to see if the two fleets could be united behind their public purpose, with their private ones left aside until the first was achieved. By then the minotaurs should have learned the human fleet's weaknesses—

which might not be many, in a fleet of seventy ships carrying who knew how many fighters.

Still, one minotaur was fit to overcome at least four humans, if he knew where to strike at them. After some days of searching out the island's secrets together, the minotaurs should know some secrets of the humans'. Perhaps the humans might have learned some of the minotaurs', but Zeskuk trusted his people to keep their ears open and their mouths shut.

"I should add," Zeskuk continued, "that we know a trifle more than you of what is abroad on the island. We have watchers at a post on the Green Mountain. So we can see some of what moves on the island, and more of what moves on the sea around it."

He wondered if any human would be stung into saying something imprudent, by the implied accusation of treacherous scheming. None of them were, the warriors being too familiar with minotaur ways and the civilians being too ignorant to know an insult when they heard it.

This was not quite a surprise. The warriors, after all, had doubtless been taught by the gigantic Knight of Solamnia who had to be Sir Darin Waydolsson. By reputation, Sir Darin walked as much apart from humans as Waydol had from minotaurkind—but the humans had listened to him, and the minotaurs had not listened to Waydol.

What came as a surprise was young Torvik clearing his throat. "Pray tell how many fighters did you lose, posting watchers on the Green Mountain?" the young captain asked. "And how do you keep them supplied, with the island a weapon wielded against anyone traveling inland?"

"Yes," the wiry, graying knight who had to be Sir Pirvan the Wayward said. "Be warned, that if you do not tell us, we cannot help them. Not unless we read the messages they send by flag, or fire, or sun-mirror, and that would not be a course so honorable that we would choose it if we could do otherwise."

Juiksum snorted. Zeskuk was of the same mind. Sir Pirvan was flaunting his knowledge of how to threaten a minotaur without giving him cause to fight. Sir Darin, be it said to his honor, was giving his elder a slightly reproving look.

Torvik ignored both the knights and continued, "I am indeed the son of Jemar the Fair. If you know that, you should know the name of my mother."

"Lady Eskaia, of House Encuintras in Istar," Zeskuk said. He would not waste time by pretending ignorance.

"Indeed, although she is now wed to Gildas Aurhinius, who also stands here before you," Torvik replied, with a nod toward his mother's new husband.

Zeskuk inclined his head in the most minimal of gestures of honor. Then he inclined his head rather more, toward Torvik.

"Doubtless you wish to know how Jheegair and his son fare," he told the young man.

For the first time, Torvik looked bemused, but only for a moment. Zeskuk saw Darin struggle with the urge to kick the young man in the shins.

"Yes," Torvik said. "My mother dealt with them honorably. I do not remember her ever doing otherwise with anybody. Indeed, I have been curious to know if their lives were afterward filled with honor."

That was not a bad regaining of his feet after falling down; arena fighters had been cheered for less. Considering that Torvik had plainly not for many years thought of Jheegair, or the son of Jheegair whom his mother had saved from falling overboard from *Gold Cup*, it was a notable display of coolness and wits.

Jemar and Eskaia had between them bred a warrior to be reckoned with. Zeskuk would not delay in paying the first part of that reckoning, by answering Torvik's question truthfully.

"We lost four of the twelve warriors who set out for the mountain before they reached their post, although they tried to stay on bare ground. Another died of her wounds after reaching the mountain.

"They have water," the minotaur continued, "but scant food, save birds and their eggs. We are of divided minds about how best to assist them. Perhaps you have your own thoughts on the matter?"

This was addressed to Torvik, which was perhaps not altogether the wisest course of action. The oldest knight, second in height only to Sir Darin, looked sour, as did some of the merchants.

But Torvik was owed a debt of honor, for his mother as well as himself, and letting him speak first was the cheapest way to pay it. If he was as deep-skulled as he seemed, it might also yield results.

"I suggest that we send two, perhaps three columns inland," the minotaur said. "We find the safest path to the Green Mountain, and keep it open for your people there."

Zeskuk awarded Torvik additional honor for avoiding the insulting term "rescue."

"If we learn this cannot be done safely," Torvik went on, "we think of other stratagems. If the life of the island can be beaten down, then we should post watchers on the Smoker as well. With both mountains well guarded, the island should have fewer secrets, and less dangerous ones."

"Old wisdom often comes from young hearts," Zeskuk said, although he did not feel quite old enough himself to say that with a straight face. "I suggest that we discuss this proposal of Torvik's, and accept it or reject it. I offer you hospitality. Talking is dry work in any weather, more so in this, and I admit no weakness in saying as much."

Sir Darin actually smiled, and no one else seemed adverse to accepting the offer.

"I rejoice," Zeskuk said more formally. "If we agree, then after drinking, we can study ways to march inland without asking more of our warriors than honor allows. If we disagree, we will be refreshed and fitter to discover other courses."

It will also take all of the day and perhaps part of the night, was Zeskuk's unspoken thought to his companions. We are on our home deck, and it does not look to me as if the humans are united in their counsels, or had a good night's sleep.

*   *   *   *   *

The kender was running as fast as his short legs would carry him, but Gerik was still gaining rapidly on him. Gerik would have overtaken the fugitive long since, if he had dared to spur his mount past a trot. On this narrow, twisting path, anything more would risk the horse. Tree roots, rocks, soft ground, rabbit burrows—all lay in wait.

The kender turned and made an indescribable gesture at Gerik. The young warrior lowered the tip of his lance and dug in his spurs. The kender darted to one side. Gerik tried to follow him with the lance tip, and the steel rammed itself into a low-hanging branch so hard that the shock nearly unseated the rider.

Before he could recover fully, a noose dropped over his head and left arm, from higher up in the tree. His horse danced wildly, and suddenly Gerik was dangling in the air, as his horse bolted out from under him.

Before the noose could tighten dangerously, however, Gerik snatched a dagger free with his right hand. Two slashes, and noose and rope both parted. He landed spring-legged, without going down, and had his sword drawn the moment he had the use of both arms.

But the rope and noose were the last kender attack. By the time Gerik had retrieved lance and mount, nothing was left of the kender but shrill, mocking laughter and a few rude jests floating out of the trees. A snake would have found it hard to penetrate farther into the forest in pursuit of the little folk; this stretch had not been harvested or even much traveled for generations.

On horseback, all he could do was back his jittery mount until there was a widening of the path in which he could turn around. Then he trotted back to his comrades.

"Well done," Bertsa Wylum said. She wore light armor—a helmet and breastplate—and both her armor and her loose clothing showed a mixture of brown and green patches that made her hard to see from ten paces away.

"It would have been better if I hadn't skewered a tree, instead of that thieving kender." He recounted his adventures on the path.

"Better than I did the first time I practiced mounted

sword drill," the more experienced warrior said. "I clipped my horse's left ear clean off his head."

"Ouch!"

"The horse said something stronger, I recall. So did the riding master."

Gerik, Bertsa, and their five guards all turned their horses and rode at a walk down to the road. When the road had taken them far enough out of the forest that no unwanted ears could be hiding close by, they reined in.

"I hope I made it convincing," Gerik said. "My only fear is that I may have made it too much so. What if some of the Spillgather kin think I really do want a blood vengeance on friend Elderdrake? They will not be our friends if we are enemies to their guest."

Bertsa frowned. "Shumeen has done her best to make sure that the truth is spread far and wide. If you want to worry, rather worry about kender who are already friends to our enemies, and will bring word that the Spillgathers work for us."

Gerik grimaced. "Are any kender that foolish?" he asked.

"Your friends are never as good as you want them to be," Bertsa said.

"Does that mean that one's enemies are never as bad?" Gerik countered.

"It ought to. Sometimes it does. Whether it does here, we can only hope."

And pray, thought Gerik. He wished he knew more about whom to pray to, or that the local clerics could be trusted. Too many of them seemed to dance to the king-priest's tune—and was that a coincidence, so many of that breed tending shrines and groves around Tirabot Manor?

Somehow, Gerik doubted it.

But at least Horimpsot Elderdrake was well away, with every appearance of having turned against the folk of Tirabot, and could wait upon those priests with that known about him. Priestly indiscretion could be made to cut both ways.

* * * * *

"So it is agreed," Zeskuk said. "One column of minotaurs follows our original route to the watch post on the Green Mountain. A second column of humans blazes their own trail to the same destination, from their side of the island. When we have reached our comrades, we shall think about posting watchers on the Smoker, if the island has not resisted so much as to force us to some other course of action."

"It will take much resistance to turn either of us aside," the knight Sir Niebar said. "We did not sail all the way here to go home with the mystery unanswered and comrades unavenged. None of us."

"Also agreed," Zeskuk said. "Not that I ever expected there to be disagreement. We are all warriors with a knowledge of honor.

"But one matter remains. It is—"

"Shelter rights with each other's fleets if the weather gets up," a human merchant said. He was as fat and richly dressed, likewise as apparently unwarlike and landbound, as the rest, but something in his voice said "once a sailor" to Zeskuk.

The minotaur pitched his voice toward more respect than he would have commonly allowed to an interrupter and said, "I thought the law of the sea covered that. Or do some among you doubt this?"

If anyone did, he did not care to admit it—at least aloud, to Zeskuk, aboard his own ship. The minotaur sighed. "As well. At this time of year the weather off Suivinari is commonly fair for weeks on end. I hope we shall be done before the summer storms blow, but the magic at work here may have attracted the attention of the gods. . . ."

Zeskuk thought he saw Torvik's face twitch. Did the young captain know something he had not told the others? The minotaur studied the other humans, seeking for signs of knowledge withheld in a manner that must be denounced as treachery, lest his own fleet not follow him. Human faces were easier to read than those of minotaurs, from the thinner human skin and the more mobile human features.

No one seemed to be hiding anything, or to have noticed Torvik. Or if they were and they had, they would deny it. Calling one's about-to-be allies liars was the sort of mortal insult best saved until it could do useful work.

"The matter of which I spoke was that of observers with each column," Zeskuk continued. "Minotaurs with the humans, humans with the minotaurs."

Zeskuk hoped that no one would now breach the unspoken agreement to avoid using the word "hostage." The observers would be that in all but name, as well as what they were called. But both races had laws and customs that made it difficult to wittingly give hostages.

As she and her brother had agreed beforehand, Fulvura stepped forward.

"I am fittest among the fleet of the Destined Race to march with the humans," she said.

"Ah—if we get into a fight—" a merchant asked.

"If so, then I will be in the forefront, as I ought to be," Fulvura said. She put her hands on her hips, to let the humans see her full height and strength. Zeskuk thought that if they had seen his sister fully-armed as well, some of the merchants might have soiled themselves with terror.

"I stand forth, to march with the minotaurs," Sir Darin said. He stepped forward also, to within a forearm's length of Fulvura. He did not quite match her height, but he looked hardly less strong.

The speed of Sir Darin's action suggested prearrangement by the humans as well. That was as Zeskuk had expected. What he had not expected was Sir Darin, who would know far more about minotaurs than any other human and be likely to make "observer" really mean "lawful and honorable spy."

How to turn this danger aside?

"Sir Darin is not altogether equal to Fulvura, if one measures each by their rank among the fleets," Zeskuk said. "Will another of you with more rank step forward?"

Before any other human could have had a chance to volunteer, Sir Darin said, "I have a sworn and trusted comrade, veteran of battles beside me, who has spoken of our never being parted. Would that comrade's joining me make the human observers equal to those of the minotaurs?"

The way he pronounced "observers" darted close to the edge of scorn without flying into the forbidden territory of insult. Zeskuk looked at his companions. He was inclined to give Darin his wish, as long as neither minotaur nor human raised objections.

Both minotaurs nodded slightly. The humans were either nodding or unsure what to say. Zeskuk decided to take this for assent.

So did Darin. Captain Torvik left in haste, and Zeskuk called the servants in to bring more refreshments. Zeskuk would have no obligation to serve the humans dinner. He did not wish to have them aboard his ship that long, nor to burden his cooks with catering to human tastes, nor to serve them simple minotaur fare and watch them wrinkle their ridiculously sharp and small noses at it.

If Zeskuk wished to attack guests at his table, he would choose a more vital spot than their noses!

Knocking came. Fulvura opened the door to admit a tall human in blued mail, with plate covering the legs, arms, and head. Indeed, the helmet was so close-fitting that only the eyes were visible.

But Sir Darin undid the helmet fastenings with quick twists of his powerful fingers. The "comrade" combed long brown hair with her fingers, and grinned at Sir Darin as if they were alone, not only in the cabin but aboard the ship.

That smile told Zeskuk that he now faced Sir Darin's elven-blooded wife Rynthala. Her name was not unknown to Zeskuk, but he had never imagined that she would be so nearly of a height with her husband. He had encountered full-grown minotaurs of both sexes whom she could look in the eye.

Then he caught a glimpse of the humans. Plainly this was as much of a surprise to them as it was to him. To all, that is, except Captain Torvik. The others were straining, and in some cases exhausting, their self-command, not to gape and stare.

The minotaur chief decided to put his visitors out of their misery. "Sir Darin, Lady Rynthala," he said. "You are well suited for what you have come among us to do. I rejoice in your coming."

Another knocking heralded the scribes with the copies of the agreement, in both Common and minotaur. All that was needed was filling in the names of the observers and signing—Zeskuk and Juiksum for the minotaurs, Sir Niebar, Gildas Aurhinius, and two merchants for the humans.

It would not even be necessary, it seemed, to allow the observers time to pack their gear. Fulvura was already packed, and except for her weapons (two chests of them) always traveled light. As for Sir Darin and his lady, it seemed they had all they needed aboard the human vessel, carefully loaded by Rynthala in her guise of a "guardsman."

Zeskuk endeavored to end the meeting as quickly as possible without giving the appearance of dismissing the humans. The cabin was growing stifling, his stomach was rumbling for more than biscuits smeared with meat paste and ale from a barrel scarcely cooled under the keel, and the humans were looking very much as if they had things they wanted to say to one another without minotaurs present.

The minotaur chief did not dishonor himself or his guests. He waited until their ship had cast off before he put his head down on the cabin table and bellowed with laughter.

* * * * *

Sir Pirvan stood on the afterdeck of *Giggling Wench,* staring into the dusk as the minotaur fleet receded. The breeze was up, and the sails were full and drawing. The oarsmen were, for the most part, lounging on deck. The steersman was below and, Pirvan hoped, out of hearing.

Torvik hurried aft, as fast as he could without appearing undignified. Pirvan wanted to bark at him to hurry, but did not dare. He was angry enough that he had to look down at his feet to be sure his boots were not charring the deck planking.

"You wished to speak to me, Sir Pirvan," Torvik said. It was not a question. Indeed, the young captain sounded quite unrepentant.

Some of Pirvan's anger leeched away. Torvik sounded now remarkably like his father and mother, when they had chosen some course of action from which they would not turn aside, no matter what others thought or said. Blazing at Torvik would not only give mortal insult, but it would waste breath.

"Did you know that Sir Darin was bringing Rynthala, disguised, aboard the ship?" Pirvan asked.

"I suspected it," Torvik said. "But I could not be sure. Even had I been sure, would it not have been a matter to be judged among the knights? I could not withhold help to Sir Darin on such slight grounds. And are Solamnic Knights afraid of their wives?"

Pirvan nearly saw red for a moment, as cowardice could not be a jesting matter under the Oath and the Measure. Then he realized that the Oath and the Measure held no sway here.

"Yes," he said. "Or at least as much as any husband with wits in his head. You will discover that when you wed. I'm surprised that watching your mother has not already taught it to you."

Torvik grinned. "I will take your warning to heart," he said.

"Take another warning, too," Pirvan said, his smile fading. "Do not hold back knowledge we might need. I saw your face when Zeskuk spoke of the attention of the gods influencing the weather. I held my tongue, because your secrets may not be yours to reveal. But consider carefully the price others may pay if you are silent."

"I have," Torvik said. "It is true. I learned things during my escape from the sea creature that are others' secrets. But I am not bound by oath to keep them. Only by honor and good sense. I can tell you, and Gildas Aurhinius. I can and will tell anyone, if there is danger to the sea otters from my silence."

"You spoke freely enough about their driving off the monster, and your crew did the same," Pirvan suggested. "I think that most humans and even minotaurs would be fools to go flinging harpoons after hearing that."

"Both races have their share of fools," Torvik reminded the knight. "Gratitude might not be enough to spare the shallows-dwellers."

"The shallows-dwellers?" Pirvan said. "That, if I recall truly, is the old name for the Dimernesti."

"Yes."

Pirvan was tempted to ask for the rest here and now, but refrained. He suspected that he had already learned all he needed to know.

He also suspected that it was not only honor and good sense binding Torvik's tongue. The young captain's face reminded him of his own, when he had realized that he was falling in love with Haimya and she with him, while she was still bound to another.

Chapter 11

Sirbones stared at the clouds piling up on the northwestern horizon. Their tops were still foamy white, but lower they were shot with gray, and toward the bases some of them had turned black.

And was it just his imagination, or did he see flickers of lightning in the lower blackness? It would not be long before he could be sure, as the clouds seemed to have grown taller, closer, or both even in the little time since their appearance. Or was that, too, his imagination?

Sirbones turned to his companion, an Istaran priest of Majere, and said, "Has anyone tested those clouds to see if this is some magical storm conjured up to blow on us?"

The priest looked at Sirbones as he might have at a rip in a new robe. He was sweating, and his face was so round that Sirbones doubted that the other lived as simply as was expected of those who served Majere. "Why don't you do it yourself," the priest asked tersely, "if you've reason to fear?"

Sirbones smiled. "Mishakal seldom gives her servants serious weather magic, or even magic-detection spells," he said. "Healing demands too much strength. Majere allows one to cultivate the mind more widely, or so I have heard."

"Not widely enough to tell cloudbursts from chaos," the Istaran said. "At least not in this land. I've heard that it rains about every other day, except in the seasons when it rains every day. If you couldn't face that, why did you come?"

Clearly the Istaran had no fear that the god to whom he was sworn would condemn him for insulting another cleric. When younger, Sirbones might have envied the other how that freed his tongue. Age, however, had given discretion to Sirbones's tongue as well as aches to his bones. He smiled again and said, "Well, as long as the rain does not wash anyone away, it matters little whence it comes. I am too old to plunge into torrents and snatch people from their jaws."

The Istaran shrugged, uttered what was less than a word if more than a grunt, and walked away.

Left alone, Sirbones had a moment to look forward, at the slope up which the humans would soon be advancing. Fifty paces in front of him stood the vanguard, two bands of well-armed men.

The men on the left looked like a dozen brawlers abducted from the waterfront of Istar, but they had good swords and knives, sound helmets, and a double-bitted felling axe for every third man. Also, two of them had bows, and Sirbones doubted that he was the only man who wondered where they had come by those bows, if they knew how to use them, and where the arrows would go if they flew at all.

A dozen men and women from *Red Elf* held the post of honor on the right, as they well deserved to. Torvik himself led them. Sirbones would have been happier if Torvik himself had remained aboard ship. The young captain had not wholly recovered from his ordeal. But Torvik was adamant, resisting not only Sirbones's persuasion but Tarothin's blandishments and the next thing to a direct order from Sir Pirvan.

Oh, Sirbones thought. To be young enough to have that much strength to sacrifice in the name of honor! Two years' rest in his home temple had restored him as much as his years would allow. He feared that might not be enough to see him through to the end of this—battle? Quest? Expedition?

Before he could decide on a word, he noticed that a second, longer shadow had joined his. Then an unmistakable smell made his nostrils wrinkle of their own will.

"Can't stand the smell of honest work?" Fulvura said. She was doubtless trying to whisper, but a minotaur whispering could be heard in a blacksmith's forge chamber.

"Thinking of what we're about," Sirbones said politely.

"Finding out who wants both men and minotaurs dead," the minotaur said, not so quietly. She spoke Common well, although with a pronounced accent.

Heads turned in the vanguard. They, at a glare from Fulvura, turned back to look ahead to where the ground began to rise and tangles of brush, vines, and scrubby trees covered more of it. Even without magic, Sirbones suspected they would lose people to the serpents that brush undoubtedly hid.

"Then I'd best be well up toward the front," Sirbones said.

"I'll guard your back, if I may," Fulvura said. Sirbones looked at her, decided that the offer was serious, and knew that it could not be refused.

"I'm grateful," Sirbones said. "But don't turn your back on those Istaran bravos."

Fulvura snorted. She sounded remarkably like a bull about to charge.

"They had better watch theirs," she said, loudly enough for Sirbones to see Istarans flinch. He looked at her weaponry and decided that she could well be right.

She carried a bundle of three shatangs (minotaur throwing spears) across her back, and a double-edged battle-axe in her right hand. On a metal-studded leather belt she wore several katars (minotaur daggers), with blades of varying length and elaborately decorated hilts. She also wore spiked metal wrist guards on both arms, and a tunic of sharkskin sewn with steel disks. Sirbones suspected that the tunic alone weighed more than he did.

Altogether, he would wager that the humans would be glad Fulvura was with them, and their enemies would regret it. Any humans attempting treachery against the minotaurs would also regret it, if they lived long enough.

* * * * *

Drums rolled—at first only a few, then a dozen, then too many to count. A trumpet blared, but the bellowing of two hundred minotaurs drowned it out almost at once.

The ground seemed to shake as the minotaurs surged forward, toward the foot of the trail to the Green Mountain. The sun sparked fire from the weapons all of them carried, from the helmets a few of them wore, and from the great banners clustered at the head of the column.

Sir Darin Waydolsson hoped that the standard-bearers would not be so zealous in competing for the lead that they fell to fighting among themselves. This was not a contest in the arena; today no minotaur should make himself enemy to any other. He also knew that to ask this of minotaurs, one needed to be a god, not a mere Knight of Solamnia.

The standard-bearers did not come to blows. Axes and clabbards, the saw-edged minotaur broadswords, had widened the path enough to let the whole band of them strike the slope at once. There they halted, while warriors flowed forward to either side of them to take the lead.

More axes and clabbards danced in the warriors' hands, and at least one tessto. The great spiked club with a thong at its hilt was the one minotaur weapon even Darin had not been strong enough to learn well, and it seemed in any case more suitable for the arena than for the battlefield. But again, only gods could safely give a minotaur unasked-for advice about fighting.

Darin felt his wife slip her arm through his and rise on tiptoe to whisper in his ear: "The minotaurs seem a mob rather than a war band. Is this their way?"

Darin nodded. "They train mostly to fight in the arena," he told her, "where even melees take place on level ground, or ships' decks. Also, a minotaur is not at ease submitting to discipline in ways that give another authority over him.

"Much as I honor Waydol's memory, I always thought that was as important as any other reason he had for fleeing south. But do not judge too soon, or by the minotaurs you may have seen as slaves in Istar. The minotaurs do not call themselves the 'Destined Race' or the 'Chosen Ones' for their prowess at berry picking or lute playing!"

Rynthala's grip tightened almost painfully, and Darin remembered that she had never been to the Mighty City in her life, nor seen much of its settled lands except Tirabot Manor. Minotaur slaves were rare in Solamnia, and Sir Pirvan would no more have kept one than he would have made a human sacrifice of his wife or daughter.

"You can see Istar for yourself when this is done," he said. "I have some honor time coming to me."

"If we can trust the Istarans to be good hosts," Rynthala murmured. "But we go together there, too. Guard each other's backs again."

Darin smiled. "It was not always at your back where you wished me close," he said. Then he looked at the sky. Half of it had now vanished behind the oncoming clouds. He had not voyaged far enough to see such a warm-seas storm for himself, but Waydol had memorably described them.

The question tonight might not be guarding one another's backs from minotaurs while they slept. The problem might well be sleeping at all.

The clouds had begun to blow wind on the marching column. Darin and Rynthala had nearly closed with the vanguard when the first attack came. The humans were close enough to see the minotaur with the tessto whirl it, and see something fly into the air, caught in the hilt loop.

It was a snake, easily twice as long as a man. Darin had just time to see that before lightning flashed from the clouds above. The bolt split into a dozen spears of raw yellow fire, and half of them lashed the ground. Sand turned suddenly red hot and flew in all directions; minotaurs bellowed as pain seared even their tough hides.

Most of the other bolts seemed to strike where Darin could not see the results. All except one.

That one took the flying snake in midair. The blaze of fire briefly dazzled the knight. When he could see again, he saw fifty, a hundred, perhaps more snakes flying through the air where there had been only one.

They were not as large as the first snake. They didn't need to be. What they lacked in size, they made up for in viciousness. Also, in the length of the fangs that flashed in the sudden twilight as they opened their mouths to bite.

Darin felt something slap his shoulder, then a *whick* of disturbed air as steel flashed within a hairsbreadth of his neck. He turned to see Rynthala, face the color of a snow-field, stamping on the two writhing halves of the snake she'd slashed off his shoulder.

Before it could bite? He felt his neck and looked at his upper arm. Rynthala interrupted him. "It didn't bite you," she said. "Let's go help our friends."

Darin wanted to laugh at his wife pulling him out of a battle-daze. But she was right. Minotaurs had thick hides and thicker clothing, but that did not mean they had no vulnerable spots for a snake to thrust its fangs.

He drew his sword and prayed to Kiri-Jolith that the island's wizard had not used this same trick on the human column on the other side of the island.

* * * * *

One arm of the storm had advanced faster than the others, bringing rain down on the human column by the time the magical attack began.

The snakes here wriggled out from under bushes rather than sailed through the air. The shadows, particularly under the trees, made it hard to see the dark-scaled crea-tures, as long as a man's arm, attacking in a frenzy.

The humans fought back in an equal frenzy, but they had thinner skins than minotaurs, and not everyone wore boots or heavy clothing. Fangs sank deep and human fighters screamed and clawed at flesh turning purple-black or red-orange around the twin fang marks.

Some people slipped on the wet ground and fell in the

path of the snakes, to be bitten on the face. They did not scream as long as the others, but nobody could look at what had been their faces after they stopped moving.

Pirvan was fighting in as close to full armor as he ever had. Past fifty, he was still faster than most warriors, and preferred to rely on that speed. He wore boiled-leather breeches and a boiled-leather tunic almost as rigid as steel, but a good deal lighter and nearly as proof against fangs and thorns. What else he might have to face, he would worry about when it came at him.

He also wore a leather helmet that protected most of his head and face but let him see to either side. That kind of vision had been life or death to a thief in the streets of Istar. It was the same to a Knight of Solamnia in a battle against who knew what sort of evil on a strange island in the hot northern seas.

His hands held a shield, with the edge sharpened for striking, and a short, heavy-bladed sword. He had been offered an axe but knew he could use any sort of sword better. He had never been muscular enough to wield armor-chopping weapons anyway.

A man ahead clutched at a bush that Pirvan half-expected to attack him with writhing, thorn-studded branches. The man fell into the bush and managed to entangle himself as thoroughly as any foe could have wished. A snake lurking under the bush attacked. It struck first at the man's booted foot, then at his leg, loosely garbed in sailor's trousers. The fangs missed flesh both times.

Foiled in its early attacks, the snake started crawling up a branch. Pirvan saw that the man might not untangle himself from the bush before the snake reached striking distance.

"Don't move!" Pirvan shouted. The man struggled more frantically. Branches waved. The snake fell off, nearly at Pirvan's feet. He stamped down, and felt the spine snap.

Good. The snakes might have magically-enhanced poison, but they were still of the same flesh and blood as nature had made them. Pirvan leaped back, dragging the man with him. The man howled as broken branches ripped his skin.

He stopped howling when he saw the writhing snake. Instead he drew his own curved sword and slashed down. The snake stopped writhing as its head flew from its body.

"Thanks, Sir Pirvan," the man said. He rushed on ahead, vanishing in the murk before Pirvan could reply.

Scorpions followed the snakes, but the rain seemed to slow them until they were almost easy prey. A few men were stung, however, by scorpions perched on branches at face level. They did not die—the scorpions being less poisonous than the snakes—but only wished they could die. Some of them begged for friends to kill them, and one or two found friends who were willing.

But even Istaran healers were equal to the scorpion stings—when they came up and started to work. Pirvan wondered if they would refuse to heal "sea barbarians," Vuinlodders, or others without virtue. He thought the best cure for that reluctance would be a foot or two of steel fed to enough Istarans to improve the manners of the rest.

But that would take the approval of Sir Niebar and Gildas Aurhinius, at least, not to mention his own conscience. The two senior leaders were well back in the column by now, as speed came to mean survival and youth, in most cases, meant speed.

Pirvan decided to catch up with the vanguard before his seniors caught up with him. He really wasn't supposed to be that far forward, but in for a piglet, in for the sow.

He took two steps, and a branch above dumped a bird's nest onto his face. He wiped dead leaves and bird dung out of his eyes with the back of his hand, then held his face up to let the rain wash it clean.

A hand clutched his arm.

"Where do you think you're going without me?" Haimya said.

"Forward."

"To the lead?"

"I'm not going back to Eskaia and tell her that I didn't try to be at her son's side," Pirvan said.

"Then I have an older right to go up there than you do." Pirvan spat his mouth free of foulness and grinned. "I don't think we have time to argue," he said, looking at her. Wrinkles and crow's-feet, gray hair and thickening waiste vanished in the rain, and he saw again the battle maiden, Haimya.

"Pity you don't have a shield," he said. "We've never gone into battle with shields locked."

Haimya kissed him. "It's not as useful a way of fighting as you think, against most opponents," she said. "Now let's waste no more time arguing."

They did not lock shields, but they took their first few uphill steps hand in hand.

* * * * *

Sirbones was using only his staff for healing those stung by the scorpions. He had enough different potions to fill several cups, as well as many pouches of herbs. He did not want to expose any of these to the wind and the rain for anyone not already sliding into the Abyss.

The staff did not completely heal the scorpion-stung; they walked haltingly and with pain written large on their faces. But they could walk, away from the battle if they had the sense the gods gave lice, and back to more potent healing.

If the Istaran healers honored their vows to those not of Istar. Sirbones had heard too many tales of the kingpriest demanding that healers and others violate their vows, to have full trust in those who lived where the kingpriest held sway. He also had too much work at hand keeping his own vows to spend much time worrying about those who would break theirs. Indeed, Sirbones had so much work that he did not see the new attack before he had become its first victim.

Twenty paces ahead of the vanguard, consisting of two of Torvik's fighters and an Istaran, all apparently at peace with one another as they fought the common enemy, a stout tree branch bowed upward. It went on bowing upward until it snapped, to dangle by strips of bark and a few fibers of wood that seemed to glow in the storm-murk.

Then the lower portion of the branch, closest to the trunk, reared back. It hurled the broken portion forward like a plains rider's throwing spear. In midair, the broken portion spun end over end, until the jagged end was fore-most.

It was this jagged end that drove spearlike into Sir-bones's chest. It struck with enough force to knock him off his feet, but as it had pierced his heart as well as driving shattered ribs into his lungs, he felt no pain from the fall.

Indeed, he had only time to feel surprised, before he lost the power to feel at all.

* * * * *

Fulvura was not quite up with the vanguard of the human column. She did not entirely trust her back to this many humans in a battle so confused, deadly, and dark. It would be far too easy for someone to slip close in the rain, the wind, and the rest of the battle-din, and hamstring or even kill her.

She wished to avoid this, although not out of fear, being of a line that had never flinched from battle, raid, or arena, and produced at least one emperor they were willing to ac-knowledge. She was instead loyal to her brother's plans, which hung on some measure of peace with the humans, at least until they could all quit Suivinari Island with their work done.

Those plans would go sadly awry if Zeskuk had to avenge her death or wounding. Of course, he would also be without her help if she were killed or wounded in an or-dinary battle, or merely fell overboard and drowned. But he would have no blood-duty of vengeance.

It was as Fulvura considered these matters that Sirbones died. Indeed, his body landed almost at her feet. Two long writhing tree roots snaked across the rich soil, gouging the leaf mold, reaching for the human healer's body and for the living man he had been trying to heal.

Fulvura stepped over Sirbones's body and chopped down with her battle-axe. The wounded man screamed, convinced that the axe blow was for him. He was still screaming when the descending blade hacked through the first root.

The minotaur jerked the man to his feet with her left hand and sent him stumbling toward the rear. Then she stamped hard on the other root, as it groped for either Sirbones or his staff. She could not be sure which was its intended prey.

The root stung her exposed foot, as if its sap were an acid. She smelled even in the storm the reek of scorching hoof. She was bending over to snatch Sirbones clear of immediate danger when the root brushed against the dead healer's staff.

There were legends of how the priests of Mishakal bound into their healing staves secret spells that kept anyone else from using their magic. Whether the legend was true, or whether the collision of healing magic and killing magic was simply too violent for matter to endure, Fulvura had the sense of standing on the lip of an erupting geyser.

Wood of every kind and in every form from whole trees down to splinters, mixed with sand, mud, hot water, steam, dead creatures and bits of creatures that the minotaur neither could nor wished to name—a mighty column of all these and more towered an arm's length from her. It soared into the treetops, then started to collapse.

Before a ship-long and minotaur-thick tree trunk fell where she had been standing, Fulvura had leaped backward, with agility more like a leopard's than a minotaur's. She had Sirbones's body firmly clutched under one arm and the battle-axe was still in the other.

"Hope I won't have to do that again, to prove anything to anybody," she muttered. She did not dare look about her for humans who might relieve her of her burden, but she hoped they would not be long in coming.

She would not leave the healer's body prey to twisted magic, but this was no battle for even a minotaur to fight burdened and one-handed!

* * * * *

Pirvan saw Zeskuk's sister standing with Sirbones's body under one arm about the same time as he noticed three other things.

One was Hawkbrother and Young Eskaia hurrying to catch up with him and Haimya.

The second thing was a quivering in the ground, not far from Fulvura.

The third was a misshapen form crashing through the undergrowth, ready to burst out of the trees. What it had been before magic transformed it, Pirvan did not know. He was only sure that it was no friend to anyone in the column.

Lightning flared again. This time it flung no snakes or anything else. It nearly dazzled Pirvan, but the remnants of his vision let him tell what was coming at him.

Once it had been a wild boar, or at least a wild pig. Now its snout was a razor-sharp spur of bone, its tusks were barbed, its teeth were pointed like a shark's, and its hooves left red smoke curling up where they touched. Pirvan rather hoped that its hide had not been turned to armor as well.

" 'Ware!" he shouted. Fulvura turned, and so did Hawkbrother, who had a throwing spear in one hand, which gave him the readiest weapon. The spear flew. It struck the once-boar in the left eye and stuck in the socket. The boar outbellowed a minotaur and charged the nearest enemy, who happened to be Fulvura.

The quivering ground flew apart in a shower of dirt and things too long dead to be looked at, let alone smelled, without revulsion. Fulvura reeled backward, nearly losing her balance. The monster boar turned aside and caught sight of Pirvan.

As the glaring yellow eye steadied on him, Pirvan wondered if Wilthur the Brown's magical creations were falling afoul of one another. This would not save him from the boar without some further exertion on his part, however, so he leaped, slashed, fell, rolled, and sprang to his feet again in a single flow of movement, knowing as he did that he had been as fast as he had ever been. He had also hamstrung the boar, but it seemed to be quite as fit to charge on three legs as it had been on four. Pirvan, on the other hand, doubted that he could death-dance with the boar for as much as another minute.

He did not have to. Before Fulvura could fall, Eskaia and her mother caught the minotaur and steadied her. She rumbled something that did not seem to convey gratitude, but then being rude to lesser races was sometimes a point of honor with minotaurs.

Meanwhile, Fulvura flung the axe down, all but threw Sirbones's body at Hawkbrother, unslung the shatangs from her back, and snapped the finger-thick leather thongs binding them as if they were pack thread. Then she put one shatang between the boar's ribs. As it staggered around to face her, she put the second into its throat. It fell too quickly to need the third.

Fulvura and Pirvan met, facing each other over the boar's body. They fell somewhere between shaking hands and glaring at each other, until at last Fulvura jerked her head. Pirvan saw, and wondered how he had escaped noticing it before, that one of her horns was painted in spirals of red and gold, and the other in purple and green.

"Well struck," she said, looking back at the trio grouped around Sirbones's body. "Stop gaping and either get out of the fight or find someone else to oil and wrap him. I'm done with scavenging this thrice-cursed battlefield!"

Then she stared, as if she could not understand why Pirvan was shaking with laughter, and many more than three humans were shouting her name as if it were a war cry.

* * * * *

Tarothin wished he could shout louder than the storm and the battle together. Then this Istaran witling might listen to him!

Instead he turned away, to nearly run into a medium-sized, sharp-faced woman wearing a robe that sun and salt air had faded from black to a dubious gray. The Red Robe almost made a gesture of aversion. Revella Laschaar, the oldest and most powerful Black Robe woman with the fleet, had come to the battlefield.

Karthayan by birth, she now lived in Istar. It was said that she was much in favor with kingpriests over the past twenty years, and Tarothin suspected this was true. She would never have risen so high otherwise.

"Tarothin, friend of the wayward and the unvirtuous!" she called.

"I do not answer to those titles, O servant of Nuitari," he said.

"So be it," Revella replied. "Waste my time, waste your time, waste the lives of those who need our help."

Tarothin bit down on another sharp reply, so hard he thought for a moment he had broken a tooth. Well, there was Sirbones to put it right if so. Meanwhile, no one ignored Revella Laschaar without paying a price.

"Reverend Lady Revella," he hissed, "do you wish to speak, or may I?"

"Answer a question first, then I will listen."

"I will tell all that I know."

"All?" The Black Robe laughed, throwing her head back so far that Tarothin half hoped something would fall into her mouth and choke her. Then she pierced him with an arrow-swift glance.

"We have no time for that much," she continued. "Only tell me this: When you and Rubina fell out with one another—was that feigned or real?"

Tarothin groped for his scattered wits, trying to throw them back across the years to the Black Robe who had been his lover during Waydol's War. As he groped, he looked more closely at Lady Revella. It seemed now that something about her features echoed Rubina's, or perhaps the other way around. Almost certainly a blood tie, somewhere.

But that was a mystery whose answer could wait. An answer to Lady Revella could not.

"It was all an act," Tarothin said. "Well, perhaps not wholly on her part. She did take another lover, until we met again. After that . . ."

Briefly, Tarothin was glad that it was raining. Otherwise someone might have noticed that his eyes were wet.

"Ha!" Revella spat. "That is the answer I hoped for. Now I can help you."

"Help?"

"You haven't changed your mind about needing some magic worked for more than healing, have you? And stop gaping as if you didn't have a mind to change!" The lady's tongue certainly lived down to rumor.

"We certainly need all the help against Wilthur we can find," he said. "What is your price?"

"Already paid. You made Rubina happy. Darin trusted her. Pirvan honored her with his youngest daughter's name. Gildas Aurhinius would have saved her. Your stand at Belkuthas avenged her."

Tarothin's memories had now caught up with the Black Robe's babble. It had been the unlamented Captain Zephros who killed Rubina at the end of Waydol's War, and met his own end in the siege of Belkuthas.

"She wished us no ill, and helped us when she could. More than we would have asked," Tarothin said. "Why should we not honor her?"

"Too many people these days give reasons or excuses why not!" Revella snapped. Then, without waiting for permission as wizardly custom required, she touched her staff to Tarothin's.

He neither sprouted wings, fell senseless, nor began to speak in the tongues of the gods. But Rubina's old spell for linking his magic to another's thundered back into his mind, like rampaging minotaurs. He pressed hands to his ears, in a futile effort to fight a noise that was trapped within his skull.

"Hold Rubina's spell, and let me give you one of mine, that we can cast linked," Revella said. "Well, what are you waiting for? Is your brain so soft Rubina's masterpiece has sunk out through the bottom of it?"

Tarothin shook his head and was surprised when it did not fall off his shoulders. "No," he said. "But—I won't ask why you do this. I will ask that if we are not enough by ourselves, will the rest of Istar's magicworkers follow you?"

"They had cursed well better," Revella snapped. "O have a good explanation. Now, put your staff across min just there . . ."

* * * * *

Sir Darin was not the first to notice the break in th storm. The minotaurs had thrown out scouts to the flank as well as to the front, and in between hacking at mad dened vegetation and poisoned monstrosities of animals they felt the wind and rain ease.

Then they saw breaks in the clouds, and began bellow ing the news, loudly enough to be heard over the last of th storm and the battle. They had to outbellow the battle fo quite a while.

Darin had never fought side by side with Rynthala i such a deadly fight. He found that it was a curiously inti mate experience, in which he could feel as close to her a when they were wrapped in each other's arms.

It did not, fortunately, affect the iron detachment Waydo had taught him to bring to war, and which helped mak him almost as formidable as a minotaur. Minotaurs migh be stronger, but they fought, too often, in hot fury.

It was in that hot fury that the minotaur column se about clearing a path to their comrades high on the moun tain. Some minotaurs fell, past healing; others fell and wer carried to momentary safety. The enemy's magical cre ations gave way before trampling hooves and flying stee Darin even saw minotaurs using their horns, to hook ani mated branches away from comrades, or gore sorcerou beasts trying to leap down from above.

Darin and Rynthala had armor, while the minotaur often relied on their tough hides, so the humans kept we to the forefront. It was just behind the head of the column indeed, that they saw an obscenity with wings and teet swooping down on a minotaur.

Rynthala had long since shot off all her arrows, retrieve

none, and found no far-striking weapon lying on the battle-field. Minotaurs, of course, were not much for archery, except sometimes at sea—which Darin thought just as well. He did not want to think of the power of an arrow shot from a bow that a minotaur could honorably wield; it would go through plate as if it were cheese.

But a shatang lay near, the head bent but otherwise service-able. Darin snatched up the fallen weapon, hefted it to judge its balance, then threw it.

The bent head sent the shatang a trifle awry and the winged creature had time to claw at the minotaur's eyes before the shatang transfixed one wing. Darin ran in and chopped off the other wing with his sword, then jerked the shatang loose and pinned the creature to the ground with it.

Meanwhile, Rynthala was trying to wrap an herb-steeped dressing around the minotaur's bleeding, blinded eyes. It was her last one, but Darin judged the risk was fair. The battle must be close to a lull, if not an end, regardless of who would claim victory.

The herbs were supposed to bring calm, ease pain, and stop bleeding. It was a formula handed down from Ryn-thala's parents, and Darin had seen it save lives before.

It nearly cost him his.

It had not occurred to him that the winged creature might have a mate or at least a companion. He only thought of that in the moment after claws ripped at his ex-posed cheek and hand, leaving both feeling as if they had been branded and set aflame.

Rynthala cut the creature out of the air with her sword a moment later. It screamed in dying, and Darin wished the scream would go on long enough so that he himself could cry out without being heard. Instead, he bit his lip until blood came, then tried to force out sensible words that would keep Rynthala from lamenting her ill-timed gen-erosity.

"As long as it's not—poison—" he said, feeling as he spoke a chill that gave the lie to his words.

"It is," a voice rumbled behind him, in the minotaur

tongue. Darin wanted to turn, but knew he would faint if he tried, so only stood, swaying gently, until the speaker came around to his front.

The minotaur wore sandals, an apron with many pockets, and a sleeveless vest hung with pouches. In his prime, he must have matched Waydol's height, but now that his muzzle was gray and his russet hide speckled with white, Darin could almost meet his eye.

One eye only—the healer wore a patch over the other, taken by some injury beyond his powers to heal.

"Hello, Grimsoar," Darin said. "I always knew you were too big to be human."

The minotaur healer looked from Darin to Rynthala, and Darin was vaguely aware of having spoken without making sense. Rynthala made an imperative gesture; Darin wanted to remind her about not ordering minotaurs about.

For a moment he thought his reminder had come too late, as the minotaur drew a katar from an apron pocket. Then the minotaur jerked a pouch off his vest and let its contents—some sort of pinkish jelly—ooze over the katar. It was when the minotaur thrust at Darin's cheek with the katar that the knight became sure his wife had doomed them both with a mortal insult to the healer.

Then Rynthala clutched him, holding him motionless, and for a moment rage and pain nearly drove him to smashing her jaw with his good hand. In the next moment there was no room in him for rage, only pain. He was certain that the minotaur had driven the katar clean through his head, and wondered if the point would erupt through the other cheek.

Then the pain in Darin's cheek was gone. Rynthala was still holding him, and the minotaur was running the katar along the wounded hand, so the knight had no way to feel his cheek. Even when the minotaur stepped back and Rynthala released him, he did not quite dare to use his wounded hand to feel his cheek.

He was sure it would fall off if he used it.

But the left hand brought no pain from the wounded cheek, only brushing fingers over a ridged scar. He would have a barbarian's look to him if that scar did not heal, but for now he was content that it did not hurt.

And his sword hand was only stiff from its scar, not painful at all. He flexed his fingers; they all moved. No muscles torn, or at least none left unhealed.

He looked around for the minotaur healer. He saw only the backs of two minotaurs, one with bandaged eyes, walking down the hill. He also realized that the storm had died so completely that he heard the last rain dripping from the trees and little else. No, he heard distant moans, too deep to be human. Minotaurs did their best to die in silence, but some pain no being of flesh and blood could endure.

He now knew that better than ever before. He hoped that somewhere beyond the world, Waydol also knew that those he had left behind had some care for the human child he had fostered.

Then Rynthala was embracing him, so that his ribs creaked and might have broken had he not been wearing armor. As he bent to kiss her, the last thing he saw above was a flock of seabirds soaring in from the ocean.

Chapter 12

The night after the battle on Suivinari Island, Wilthur the Brown contemplated the future with distaste, although not yet with foreboding.

Certainly he had untapped powers for physical resistance to the invasion. Just as certainly, physical resistance would not be sufficient. The will of the gods was manifest in that matter. His aspirations came too close to upsetting the balance the deities cherished for them to tolerate his extending his attacks offshore—into the depths of either earth or sea, or into the sky. Wilthur privately thought that the gods feared his aspirations to enter among their ranks rather as a hall of nobles fears the petition of a wealthy commoner.

He would not petition. He would preserve his stronghold and, in due course, prevail.

But if physical means could not provide that defense, he knew he had to attack the enemy on a field that had not been forbidden him: their own minds. He had methods requiring spells so demanding that he could only set them upon one being at a time, that would yield poor or even dangerous decisions, without anyone knowing from whence those ideas came.

He had knowledge of the various leaders. After contemating that knowledge, he decided that the most vulnerable rget was the minotaur chief, Zeskuk.

* * * * *

Gerik was warm in bed and in a dream of riding through field of wheat so ripe that it almost glowed in the sun, hen he heard the knocking.

It took a moment for him to separate the noise from the eam. It took him much longer to reach full wakefulness, it he did not wait for that before reaching for his clothes. is hands instead encountered warm skin, and a giggle unded, almost as loud, and far more pleasant than the ocking.

He had a brief, almost overwhelming impulse to forget e door in favor of the owner of the skin and the source of e giggle. Then he felt a bare foot in the small of his back d suddenly he was rolling out of bed, jerking awake as if had been plunged into cold water. His clothes followed m, and he fought down a brief impulse to curse.

"Duty calls, my lord," came the voice from the bed. As if needed further reminder, the knocking grew louder. erik allowed himself one rude word about duty, then clad mself and opened the door.

Bertsa Wylum greeted him. From one look at her face, he ew this was no jest. What else it might be—

"You have come, Captain Wylum. Speak," he said.

Wylum wrinkled her nose and gave a mocking parody of e sell-swords' salute. "We have a sighting," she said. orty riders in Botsenril Woods."

That was to the south, in a direction from which neither bbers in past years nor ghost-riders this year had usually me. It was also within a half hour's ride of a number of e manor's tenant farms. And *forty* riders. Far too many anybody's jest, if the tale held truth. . . .

"One of my most trusted people," Wylum said. She did t describe the watcher further, which suggested to Gerik at he or she would be one of Wylum's secret allies. He

knew that she had such, she knew that he and his fath
had their own, and each trusted the other's judgment
secret matters. Names one did not know, one could n
reveal, either through too much wine or less pleasant i
fluences.

"I came myself with the message," Wylum went o
"Less noise before you give permission."

"Permission for what?" Gerik had thought he was to
awake to ask that sort of question. Wylum frowned b
held her peace until Gerik could command both wits ar
his tongue. "Yes," he said at last. "By all means take the s
riders of the ready guard. Take one or two more for me
sengers, if that will not delay you."

"Thank you, good sir," Wylum said. "The Botsenril's
tangle, and the roads more like trails. You can creep u
close unwatched, but it's not much help if you can't ser
back what you learn."

"No, and remember that two can play at the game
creeping through the woods," Gerik said. "If these visito
have anyone who knows Botsenril, they could surrour
you. We need your arm and your wits, and I don't want
hear what my father or Floria Desbarres would say if I a
lowed you to be killed."

"If it's my time, fathers and Florias have no say," Wylu
replied. "But I'll be careful just so you can sleep easy."

"Who said anything about sleep?" Gerik said. "Whe
you go out, sound the alarm. I'm mounting up the rest
the riders, and sending a patrol out to the Alsenor Cros
roads. Most of the ways out of the woods go by ther
sooner or later."

"Manors left undefended fall to attackers the lord didr
see—sooner or later," Wylum said.

Gerik flushed. "All right, *half* the remaining riders," I
acquiesced. "But you alert the village as you leave. This
not a night for anyone to spend abed."

Wylum's look spoke eloquently of her agreement. Sl
turned, drew her silver whistle, and blew hard.

Those not awakened by the whistle must have bee
awakened by messengers standing ready to pass the alarr

The whole manor was in an uproar before Wylum could walk from the door to the head of the stairs and disappear down them. Drums and trumpets had joined the neighing, clattering, and shouts before Gerik had even decently begun donning his armor.

It was only when he had finished that he noticed Ellysta was sitting on the bed, rather than lying in it, and was fully clad, rather than as she had been when his hands found her skin. She wore a man's garb, with several pouches on her belt that Gerik had not seen before. Beside her was a stout pack, oiled leather that looked like kender work. It bulged, and across the top was strapped a dagger Gerik had not seen since the day Ellysta came to Tirabot Manor.

To keep himself from having to speak and possibly say the wrong thing, Gerik started knotting his helmet cords.

"Let me play squire," Ellysta said. Her nimble fingers did up the knots in half the time Gerik would have taken. All of Ellysta's outward injuries seemed healed now, except a few that would need potent magic to avoid leaving scars.

As for the inward hurts . . .

"I have to take my place on the walls," Ellysta said. "For what good I can do, if only by being there and in danger along with the rest."

"In danger ahead of the rest, I should say," Gerik said.

"Sell-swords and household guards will not climb walls to carry me off," she said.

"Some might, promised enough gold, and have you never heard of archery?"

"That reminds me. Is there a bow to spare?"

Gerik held his tongue. If he didn't, he would insult her, and she seemed ready to tell the truth regardless of whether he spoke or not. Or even whether he wanted to hear it or not, but he had to want it. He was captain and lord, and being told other than the truth put everyone at Tirabot or under its protection in danger.

"Gerik, do not take this amiss, but if you do not return— if our enemies are ready to take knights' blood—I must take to the road," Ellysta told him quietly.

Gerik thought his face asked "Why?" loudly enough,

and perhaps he was right. Ellysta ran her fingers across his lips, then continued, "With you dead and me gone, there is no way to prove that my being here was other than your fancy. Without that proof, the laws against private warfare will weigh heavily against any attack on the manor. Against any harm to your folk."

She laughed. "Also, the kender and I and certain friends can lead anyone who does want my blood on a merry chase. They may still be turning over fallen logs and rotten mushrooms when the snow flies, too busy to think of Tirabot Manor—even if it is not guarded by the Solamnics."

Gerik looked at the ceiling. "Why do I have the feeling that the hens of this flock are wiser in war than the rooster?" he sighed.

"Because we are, for now," Ellysta said, with an unrepentant laugh. "But that will change, if the young cockerel lives long enough. So don't get killed, Gerik."

She kissed him decisively. "I came where some women might have seen or even expected a boy. But I looked with open eyes and mind." She kissed him again. "And I found a man."

Gerik walked steadily as they left the chamber, for all that his head was spinning.

* * * * *

The horsemen awoke Horimpsot Elderdrake from a sound sleep in Botsenril Woods, one that he had intended to continue until dawn. So he was in a worse mood than usual for a kender when he started counting them. Before he had finished his count at forty, he had heard a human watcher slipping away along another path. A warning was on the way to Tirabot, so he could do as he pleased.

It pleased him to make these fumble-witted humans pay for their silliness in making trouble for Tirabot Manor. It was going beyond what he or any other kender might owe to Sir Pirvan and all of his people. It was reaching the point where the humans needed to be taught a lesson about making nuisances of themselves.

Really, they were killing each other over things that no kender would have considered worth a quarrel, let alone a fight. Oh, there had been the time when his aunt put a lock on her biscuit cupboard, and half the village vowed not to dine with her or even speak to her for a year. The vow hadn't bound anybody that long, because somebody (Elderdrake suspected who, but would never tell) had picked the lock within a month.

But killing for the freedom to break one's own laws, even if some of those laws were so stupid that no kender would have lived under them for five minutes—this was "virtue"?

Elderdrake used a kenderspeak word that was usually translated as "idiots," in Common.

The kender unslung his pack and pulled out a glazed pottery jar wrapped in straw. He undid the wrapping and held the pot up to his ear. Good. They sounded all right.

One of the Spillgather guests was someone Shumeen hadn't told him about at first. Like many kender priests of Branchala, this one had chosen a practical joke for his masterpiece. It had gone a little far, and his friends had told him to hide out until they had forgotten it, then come back and try again. That was ten years ago and the priest had been with the Spillgathers ever since.

They hadn't asked him to stay away ten years, but like Imsaffor Whistletrot (and how was the old fellow doing, Elderdrake wondered) or Sirbones (who was really too old to be climbing aboard ships and sailing off to fight wizards at the rim of the world) this priest liked the road. He could also make more of his masterpiece, anytime anyone asked, without being paid—although people didn't ask very often, for obvious reasons.

Now it was time to turn the joke loose on Tirabot's uninvited guests. That should keep them from spoiling Gerik's party.

And afterward? Elderdrake studied the riders. They had fine horses and much better weapons and armor than such starved-looking, unkempt sell-swords deserved, or were likely to be able to pay for. Somebody was giving them all this, but there wasn't anybody to the south for quite a distance. So these men had to be like the ghost-riders. They had to have their supplies piled somewhere that wasn't on anybody's land.

That meant it wouldn't be protected by anybody's house guards. It might be protected by that fat little wizard who'd been with the ghost-riders, but Elderdrake would worry about him when he turned up.

The riders were talking now, as if nobody could be within a mile. In the intervals between loud boasts, Elderdrake thought he heard gurgles. He hoped it was wine or ale they were drinking, not water.

Dwarf spirits did even more than ale or wine to increase the power of the priest's masterpiece, but it was too much to hope for that this band of starvelings would be given dwarf spirits—or stay in their saddles at all, if they drank any.

* * * * *

Gerik led twelve fighters down the road to the Alsenor Crossroads under a cloudy sky that made him glad for the five villagers who had volunteered to play scout or messenger. He had accepted them on the condition that they would ride for their lives if it came to a serious fight, and look to their families and homes first.

He hoped they would keep their oaths. The fight might be no more than his twelve, Bertsa Wylum's six, and the odd roving spy against forty or more. It might be fewer, if Wylum's luck was out and she and her people were down before the fighting started.

If it started. Gerik vowed to keep his hand off his sword and use his tongue first, remembering many admonitions about how the best way to win a fight was not to have it at all.

One came to memory, in his mother's voice. "Only leeches, mosquitoes, and vampires *must* shed blood. The rest of us prefer to see what a little sweat or wine will do first."

However, he suspected that the forty riders would be in

a mood to talk only if they were here on some completely legal task, with no connection to Ellysta's being a guest at Tirabot Manor. Gerik would not bet a worn-out sandal thong that this was so.

Choosing speed and sure footing over secrecy, Gerik used the High Road. He reached the crossroads before too many of the curious routed from their homes by all these nocturnal comings and goings could come out and ask silly questions. This let him array his men for battle, with himself and three others mounted on the road, four more on the road behind, and four dismounted ahead in ambush. The villagers were farthest to the rear, and Kiri-Jolith grant that they would stay there!

Fighting for Ellysta was something in which he was honor-bound, both in his own right and as the son of his father. Getting unarmed loyal villagers killed was not. Indeed, honor demanded that he protect them from their own enthusiasm if he could, so that they would not be enslaved or imprisoned, their children sent to labor as "children of virtue" in certain secret temples, and the like.

He had not believed the stories of kidnapped children, until Rubina told him that two of her friends had lost kin that way, one of them a half-brother. He had then written down what she told him, and left the tale in a safe place, where his father might find it if he returned.

The night wind piped faintly in Gerik's ears. Off to the right and up the hill, a stand of templebeams twisted and dwarfed by something in the soil were mere shadows. It was easy to imagine them as the clawing hands of buried giants, bursting through the ground, reaching for the light and air.

It was also easy to frighten oneself into a fit with such imaginings, like a child in a dark room.

Gerik had just reined in his fancies when a sudden uproar broke out to the south, toward the woods. He heard horses neighing and screaming, men shouting and cursing, then a great many fast-moving hooves and even the clatter of steel on armor. It sounded as if someone there *had* frightened himself into a fit.

Gerik's men had made ready without his command; they had ears too. The young man's were now turned wholly toward listening for Bertsa Wylum's voice. A battle cry, even an oath, would help tell friend from foe.

Gerik realized that he should have had all the Tirabot fighters mark themselves somehow, with bands on their arms or patches on their backs. Something visible in the darkness, that would distinguish them from the enemy—

The enemy was upon Gerik before he could think further. His sword leaped into his hand. He had cut two men out of their saddles and was engaging a third when he realized that the man's comrades were not fighting. They were fleeing, as fast and as far as their horses could carry them.

Not all of the horses were willing. Gerik saw one rider, with a hairy chin and a balding head, somersault over the head of his mount as it stopped suddenly. The horse then fell as another, running loose, crashed into it. Both went down on top of the man. Frantic neighing and hideous human screams made a din that might have daunted the Dark Queen.

Before Gerik could see another such horror, the last of the riders had thundered past. A few riderless horses cantered off in various directions, trampling fallen horses and fallen men. Gerik was now more frightened than he would have been in a battle at odds of ten to one. In the darkness, amid the fading cries of maimed men and panicky horses, the Abyss seemed about to gape at his feet.

To spare his own steed, he dismounted. The horse was tossing its head nervously and whickering. Gerik stepped up to the gelding's head and whispered in its ear. Nothing that would have made sense, in Common, but in some horse-speech it seemed to say what the horse needed to hear. Gerik had just decided to mount again, when for a second time the darkness spewed movement.

This time no one died. A torch flared behind the movement, showing them to be eight or ten armored but unarmed men, all on foot and most looking as if they had been used as kickballs by giant trolls.

Behind them rode Bertsa Wylum. She held a torch in one hand and her sword in the other, guiding her mount with her knees at the head of her band.

"Take and bind them," Gerik called to his people, pointing at the men on foot. His men looked relieved at having something to do. The new prisoners looked almost relieved at being taken, as if their captors could protect them from what was abroad tonight. What that was, Gerik hoped Bertsa Wylum would know.

But when he rode up to her, all she said was, "Their horses went mad on them. I think a certain kender we chased off had something to do with it."

"I thought the kender had turned on you," one of the men whined.

Wylum grinned. Only Gerik saw the mockery in her bared teeth. "Of course they did," she said. "But you know kender. They can't tell friend from enemy when they're up to a joke. How much do you want to wager that he aimed at us and hit you?"

The man's curses said that was no wager, but certain knowledge.

"I suggest, good sir, that we leave some of our people here to bring these along after us, while we ride for the village," Wylum added.

"How so?" Gerik said, not minding at all sounding as if he did not know what was happening. He was one of many.

"Well, the rest of these witlings are heading straight for Tirabot," Wylum said. "I'd not wager they'll all fall off their horses before they reach it."

Gerik nodded and turned his mount.

*　*　*　*　*

Grimsoar One-Eye found himself second among the captains in the manor itself, after Gerik rode out of sight. So after a decent interval he asked the senior's permission to go down to the village and ask Serafina to come up.

She was spending the night in their house, and probably

would not come up to the manor even for its greater safety. Her duties to the village would come first, but he had to try. Also, if he could help her pack along more healing material, perhaps that would persuade her that she could do useful work in the manor. After all, no one could tell where the attack would come.

Grimsoar presented his case to the senior, a retired sellsword who called himself Orgillius, which could hardly be his proper name. He seemed even more seasoned a fighter than Bertsa Wylum, but his manners went far to explain why he had less rank.

"I thought you were too old to need a woman every night," Orgillius said.

Grimsoar shrugged. He wanted to do something rather more eloquent, such as knocking Orgillius down. He only said, "If the woman thinks I'm young enough, what odds? Wait until you're my age, then complain if a woman wants you!"

"We can't open the gates or give you a horse."

"I'm also young enough to climb down a rope," Grimsoar warned. "One never forgets that. And don't you forget that I can walk to the village faster than any horse here could carry me."

"On your head be it," Orgillius said. His tone suggested that he hoped Grimsoar's head would next be seen flung over the walls by an enemy siege engine.

Grimsoar turned away, vowing to make sure that Orgillius never got behind him in battle.

Pirvan's old companion had not in truth felt so young and vigorous in years as he felt tonight. Perhaps he would stay in the village a bit longer than he had planned, even if Serafina was willing to come. The manor was a trifle crowded, unless you were Gerik and Ellysta, and the gods knew they deserved their good luck.

It was easy going over and down the walls, and Grimsoar was halfway to the village before he realized that he had company. He thought at first he was being stalked by one of the kender, to keep up the game of their being enemies, then realized that the figure was only kender-sized.

When he knew who it was, the journey to the village began to seem less like a good idea.

"Rubina?"

"*Ssssssh.* If you shout like that, they'll hear you in the castle."

"They won't open the gate or send out riders."

"Not for you," Rubina hissed. "But maybe for me. And there's the village. They do have horses, and people who won't let me come with you."

"What makes you think *I* will let you come with me?" Grimsoar hissed back.

"What makes you think you can stop me?"

Grimsoar recognized the total deafness to the word "No" that he had encountered often enough in his own life. No doubt Rubina had it from her mother.

They came up to the village from the south, and the first thing they saw was Pel Orvot's wagon, still at the wheelwright's even though it had been repaired two days ago. Or so Rubina said, but she admitted that she might not be wholly fair where the farmer was concerned. Grimsoar was about to praise her for that sense of justice when he heard the sound of riders coming up from the south, so fast that they threatened to overtake their own din.

Somebody on the road challenged. The reply was nothing any Tirabot fighter would have given. Grimsoar pushed Rubina hard. "Run out of the road, now," he ordered. "Get behind a house! Enemies coming!"

"I am the daughter of two warriors and do not obey orders to run from danger!" Rubina shot back.

But she was addressing Grimsoar's broad back, as he bent to grab the wagon's yoke pole. One heave and it moved. Another heave and sweat broke out on his brow, and the wagon rolled. A third heave and it rolled out of the wheelwright's yard and into the road.

Grimsoar had just time to use a fourth heave to center the wagon on the road when the riders came storming up. They were no Tirabot folk, looking more like cheap sellswords, and not one of them had any command over his horse. All fifteen or more of them crashed straight into the wagon. Fast-moving flesh and bone met solid, immobile wood. The wagon tipped up on edge, then one wheel cracked beyond any wheelwright's craft to repair it, and the wagon fell over on its side.

Most of the riders and horses fell on top of it or around it. They piled up in a hillock of writhing, screaming human and animal flesh. Grimsoar came near to losing his supper at the expressions on some of the faces, both men and horses.

Then a man was before him, with an expression on his face that Grimsoar knew too well. It was the tight, angry look of a seasoned killer, one common among the old Servants of Silence. That unwholesome order, it was said, no longer existed. The same could not be said of the men who comprised it.

Grimsoar reached for his dagger, but the man struck first. Fire blossomed in Grimsoar's right arm, and the man snatched another dagger from his boot and drove in, ready to gut the old sailor like a flatfish for broiling—

—when a smaller figure leaped onto the man's back. The man was off-balance for his thrust, and, under the sudden weight, fell facedown on the road.

Grimsoar stamped on the man's wrists in turn. He wanted a prisoner, but it would help if no one had to worry about the man's daggers for a while.

Nobody would. Not only had Grimsoar broken both the man's wrists, but Rubina had reversed her dagger and knocked the man senseless with the butt.

"I told you I would not run," she said, panting. "And a good thing for you I did not. They would not come out of the houses—and you're bleeding!"

After that Rubina chattered so busily while she bound Grimsoar's wound that he could not have put a word in if he'd driven it with a shipyard maul. She only broke off when more riders loomed up. The pile of men were being bound by the villagers, and horses who were injured were being put out of their pain.

"Kiri-Jolith defend us!" came Bertsa Wylum's voice.

Then, another and more familiar, even if less welcome

voice called: "Grimsoar, what in the name of the hundred ghouls are you doing taking my sister into battle?"

* * * * *

"Fifty brass bits that he says Rubina came herself," Bertsa Wylum whispered in Gerik's ear.

"I don't have that much to spare, and anyway, I know my sister," he replied.

He did not find this much of an occasion for jesting. The Tirabot folk had lost no men and only two horses tonight, but their enemies had a dozen dead, as many hurt, and all their horses and war gear gone. Somebody would ask a price for that—House Dirivan, out of sheer pride, if no one else—and that price might yet end being paid with friends' blood.

But Rubina stepped forward. "Brother, apologize to Grimsoar," she demanded. "He pulled the wagon into the road and brought down all the riders. He is hurt, and I did not ask to come with him."

"No, you just came," Gerik said.

Rubina nodded solemnly, then spoiled the occasion by thumbing her nose at him. Laughter rose into the night, and even Gerik had to smile. He looked up. The clouds were breaking apart, although since Nuitari was the only moon high enough to benefit, they had little light from above.

"Very well," Gerik said. "Grimsoar One-Eye, we thank you."

"*We*, O exalted chief?" Grimsoar said, bowing deeply, then wincing at the pain in his arm.

"My lady and I—"

"She's your *lady*?" Rubina exclaimed. "I didn't know you had asked her about that. And don't Father and Mother have to know?"

Gerik knew he must have turned scarlet. Bertsa Wylum was ready to fall out of the saddle in her efforts not to laugh. Some of the other onlookers were not being so polite.

Gerik finally arrayed thoughts and tongue. "I will," he said evenly, "as soon as I return to the manor, ask her to grant me the great honor of her becoming my lady. I am of age, and can ask her this without permission. If she says yes, I will write to Sir Pirvan and Lady Haimya, and hope they will be here to bless Ellysta and myself. I hope that you will all be here, too, when we take our oaths and vows, sing our songs—"

"Dance!" Grimsoar roared.

Serafina pushed her way through the mob. "If you try to dance, my old dear, you will fall down and break something important," she said. "Tonight, you lie down . . . and *sleep*, so take that look off your face."

More softly, she added, "You're full-blooded enough for five men, so this little nick won't keep you down long."

Now the laughter was bawdy. Gerik wondered if Rubina understood all this, then decided that she probably did, nor would it do her any harm.

Tonight a little war had begun in deadly earnest. How deadly, he would know when they spoke to the prisoners.

But other things besides a war had begun tonight.

Chapter 13

Zeskuk was hosting this meeting in his personal cabin aboard *Cleaver*, so it was hotter than usual and as crowded as it could be, with three minotaurs. There was Zeskuk himself, there was Thenvor, leader of those who disputed his leadership (more precisely: those who wanted him food for sharks or magical monsters), and there was Lujimar, chief among the magicworkers with the fleet of the Destined Race.

Zeskuk would gladly have had a fourth—his sister—but her post of duty was with the humans. He had allowed himself to feel some happiness that after her feats in the battle she would have less need to guard her back. Not that she would lack enemies ready to thrust steel into it, but she now had human friends who would stand against their own kind even for a minotaur.

The chief judged that his guests were waiting for something. He doubted it was the servant bringing a second helping of supper, although Lujimar clearly suffered no lack of appetite. If he was ill, as rumors babbled, it was not in the stomach.

"We have done—"

"Not well enough," Thenvor said.

Zeskuk raised a fist as politely as one could execute tha
gesture. "Pray be silent until I am done," he said, "*then* cal
what I say nonsense. If you consent, you have leave tc
speak freely."

He hoped Thenvor would not interpret that as freedom
to question Zeskuk's honor. Even here, in such privacy as a
ship afforded, that meant a challenge; a challenge mean
lost time. That concerned Zeskuk more than the possibility
of losing to Thenvor, who was a formidable fighter anc
might carry the bout to the death. Whatever course the flee
might steer, it had best not wait to turn on to it until after a
challenge bout.

Vivid images of the fleet perishing on the reefs had come
to Zeskuk several times during the night. Once he had beer
sure he was asleep and having a nightmare. Once he hac
been sure he was awake, but perhaps uneasy in his mind
About the other times, he could not be sure, but the images
had been just as vivid, including even the cries of the
drowning.

Zeskuk was a sensible minotaur, which was to say tha
he believed in prophetic dreams. Lying awake in the dawn
he had seriously considered whether or not he had received a warning. A warning, perhaps, that he risked thou
sands of lives over mere curiosity about the mysteries o
Suivinari Island.

Had he been sure he had received a warning, and from
some source he could trust, his course would have beer
clear. As it was, he thought he could wait a few days, sending no more warriors ashore to die, but remaining off the
island to see what happened—in the waking world and ir
his dreams.

Thenvor's jerk of the head might have been a nod. Lujimar's eyes said that it would be taken as such. Zeskuk
went on. "We have done less well than I had hoped. We
have sent stores and reinforcements to our comrades on the
Green Mountain. We have made no path that we can use
day after day."

"The humans did not even do that well," Thenvor said
as politely as he ever spoke.

"No, but their magic allowed us to do as well as we did, y breaking the storm and slowing the attack of the mage-onsters," Lujimar said. "They may well have done this ore to save themselves than to aid us, but honor requires e to acknowledge a gift, even if unintended."

"I know the scrolls as well as you do," Thenvor said, re-rting to his usual pettishness. "Perhaps I know the scrolls *war* better than you. I acknowledge that we owe them mething. Not killing them outright would seem to be ough."

"Are you thinking, as I have been, that Suivinari Island too useless to anyone except the mage who calls it home r us to fight anyone over it?" Zeskuk asked. "That we ould withdraw, giving that as our reason?"

"Yes," Thenvor said.

"No," Lujimar replied.

Such needle-horned contradiction was rare for Lujimar. ot only had he never questioned anyone's honor, but he ad seldom publicly questioned anyone's judgment.

Perhaps he did not consider this public.

"You think we should remain?" Zeskuk asked Lujimar.

"I know that we should," Lujimar replied.

"The gods have told you?" Thenvor sneered.

"It may have been the gods, speaking to me or to others nong us," Lujimar said, with the bland confidence of one ho sold horn-strengthening potions in the stands of the ena. "But the message was clear."

Zeskuk wondered if Lujimar had received one of the reams, or sendings, or prophecies. This was not the time place to ask, however—certainly not when it would ean he and Lujimar comparing dreams in Thenvor's earing.

"The danger to the fleet is also clear, if we are here for the ext storm and no magic can stand against it," Thenvor id. "We had enough trouble on land when we went med and by intent. Cast away, we will be doomed."

"You croak," Lujimar said, which was the strongest ord Zeskuk could ever recall him uttering to another. For moment it seemed that Thenvor would ask for Lujimar to

173

appoint a champion for a contest of honor.

"We will remain here three more days," Zeskuk said. H would give Thenvor a cup of water if he were dying thirst, if only to prevent challenges from his kin. He woul not give his rival the satisfaction of watching an open qua rel between war chief and magic chief.

"That is not enough," Lujimar said.

"I say it will be," Zeskuk said, as firmly as the prie "We shall not leave later, unless a way is found around th mage-monsters to cleanse the island of their creator. W shall not stay that long if we learn that the humans hav knowledge that they have withheld from us."

"Ah, that witling Captain Torvik," Thenvor said.

"Not quite," Zeskuk concluded. "Captain, yes. Witlin hardly. Unless he is no true son of either his father mother."

*   *   *   *   *

Two of the three Wayward Knights met with Sir Niebz in Sir Niebar's cabin. Pirvan would have preferred a bo with no one else but them in it, and he and Hawkbroth would gladly have rowed. But even with Tarothin's healir spells fighting it, ship fever had left Sir Niebar too weak leave *Wavebiter* and barely with the strength to come o deck. Even if no unwanted ears would hear, on deck u wanted eyes might see. So they stayed below.

"They will leave if they can't do better than we can Hawkbrother insisted.

" 'They,' as in the minotaurs?" Sir Niebar asked.

"Of course."

"I would take that better coming from Sir Darin," Nieb said. "Although I must admit that you are as right anyone could be, Sir Darin included."

"The secret may lie with Torvik," Sir Pirvan said. H crossed one leg over the other and crossed his hands on th upper knee. The others in the cabin knew this meant h was uneasy; he did not care.

He was about to use private and personal knowled

about someone to whom his only ties were old friendship, not the Oath and the Measure, to advance the cause of the knights. Also of the knights' allies, and many others, the minotaurs probably included. But his honor would have been as much engaged if only one person was to be saved, as if it were a multitude. The Measure of the Knights of the Rose distinguished between public and private obligations; Pirvan himself had not grown accustomed to doing so.

"Now, my wife has old sell-sword comrades aboard nearly every ship in the fleet," Pirvan said. "All but those who worship the kingpriest in place of the gods will speak to her. They will also speak to the old fighters and sailors of Torvik's father Jemar the Fair.

"Haimya learned that Torvik's sister Chuina has been promoted to sergeant of archers aboard *Windmaster's Gift*. She sent Chuina a generous purse—from our own funds— for celebrating that promotion. She also sent a letter, saying how worried we were about Torvik, as friends of his mother, his father, and his stepfather. Unless Chuina is a witling—"

"Or enemy to Torvik," Hawkbrother said. "As the last of four brothers, I can assure you that kin are not always friends."

"Chuina has never had Threehand's reasons to quarrel with you," Pirvan admonished the young knight. "But I am grateful for the reminder. Another time, we should think on it."

Hawkbrother looked gratefully at his wife's father, for sparing him embarrassment over interrupting with something the older knights knew perfectly well. Pirvan's reply was a grin. Young Eskaia had chosen well, even if she'd wed in haste; he would not have unmade her choice if he could.

"Sister spying on brother?" Sir Niebar said, frowning.

"Sister taking counsel with brother," Pirvan replied. "Knowing Torvik, who is no more a witling than his sister, he would not be silent unless he held a secret that was not his to reveal.

"But everyone possessed of such a secret needs to

unburden himself to someone he trusts, to see if he must truly bear that burden. I do it with Haimya. Torvik has no wife, but I judge him to be willing to speak to Chuina and to hear her as well."

"But she is even younger than—" Hawkbrother began.

"—you?" Pirvan said. "Yes. And no older than your wife, my daughter Eskaia. I hope that does not mean you doubt Eskaia's wisdom."

Hawkbrother suddenly took on the air of one staring at a loaded and cocked crossbow ready to fling a bolt into his chest. His mouth opened.

Sir Niebar laughed, and then spoke quickly, to save the young knight further embarrassment. "Sisters can be positive oracles, if the secret involves a woman. I know. I was the youngest of five, and the elder four were all girls."

"No wonder you joined the knights," Pirvan said.

* * * * *

The sun had just begun to swell to the vast orange ball that would float on the horizon for a while before sinking into the sea when Zeskuk heard two sets of minotaur footsteps on the deck behind him.

He turned to see, instead, one minotaur and one human. Although the error was not surprising; the human was Sir Darin, who could look at least a third of *Cleaver*'s crew in the eye. Zeskuk was enough taller than Darin that the knight had to look up at the minotaur. When the minotaur looked down, he saw something that he did not enjoy.

Darin wore no armor, but he wore sword and dagger. He also wore all his marks of rank as a Knight of the Sword, over a sleeveless jerkin in the minotaur style. This left his massive arms bare but for minotaur-work arm rings. Waydol's gifts.

The minotaur was Lujimar. In spite of the heat, he wore his full priestly robes, red with the spiked yellow borders, broad studded leather belt, dragon-wing bracelets, and white paint on his horns. All of this gave Zeskuk such a sense of foreboding that it was almost painful. The dreams of the fleet's perishing on the reef had not made him half so uneasy.

Being of a warrior race taught to triumph over pain, he let none of this show on his face. Instead he took the most formal stance, arms crossed on his chest. To use any other, he suspected, would be taken as suspecting treachery—and then he would be questioning Darin's honor, instead of the other way around.

Darin raised both arms, hands held with fingers spread to show that they were empty. "By the Oath and the Measure," the knight called, "declaring me Knight of the Sword in the Knights of Solamnia. By my prowess as a warrior. By my fostering by Waydol, a minotaur warrior of unequaled honor.

"Zeskuk," he continued, "chief over the minotaur fleet at Suivinari Island, wishes to depart and leave evil possessing the island save for what humans may do.

"That to do this is a wish that evil triumph.

"That to wish this, if one is not oneself evil, is a betrayal of the true gods of both men and minotaurs, of those sailors, both men and minotaurs, who may come to the island in the future, and to all those whom evil magecraft may put in danger, be they men, minotaurs, or any other race upon the face of Krynn.

"By wishing this, Zeskuk has betrayed his own honor. I call challenge upon him, that he may prove with his own arm and by his own blood his unimpaired honor."

Zeskuk doubted that he could learn anything by looking further at Darin or Lujimar. He would have given ten years off his life to be able to speak to them, but the laws bound him too tightly for that.

He could not inquire what Lujimar might have told Darin without first meeting Darin's challenge. Otherwise his honor would be in question for refusing a lawful challenge, and that would be handing the fleet over to Thenvor.

He would also have to defeat Darin. Otherwise the charge against him would stand, and Lujimar would have the right to refuse to answer any of his questions, or to appoint a champion if Zeskuk was foolish enough to question the minotaur mage's honor. Zeskuk had the sense of having been outmaneuvered and surrounded with sublime skill, on the deck of his own flagship. He looked around, wondering how the audience for this little drama was taking it.

He had never seen so many minotaurs so silent or so still aboard a ship, not since he first stepped aboard one when he was seven. He tried to calm himself with steady breathing, knowing that his reply would reach not only Thenvor's ears (which he could endure) but would be read by minotaurs for five generations to come.

Minotaurs, ha! "Men, minotaurs, or any other race upon the face of Krynn," or at least any who could read and knew war and honor. The thought of the scrutiny of that much posterity nearly clogged Zeskuk's throat. He waited until he could speak clearly before replying.

"I accept the challenge of Sir Darin, Knight of the Sword and fosterling of Waydol, to prove my honor unimpaired, with my own arm and my own blood.

"Those who speak for us shall set a time and a place, not farther from here than one hour's sailing from the shores of Suivinari Island and not later than four sunsets from this time. I further swear that if it is the judgment of this duel that my honor is flawed, I shall remain at Suivinari Island until my death or the defeat of the enemy. I shall also invite all sworn to me to remain with me, and do battle at my side."

He had thought of promising more, but even the most honorable and knightly minotaur-fostered human deserved only so much. Also, he could hardly have promised more in good faith. To try to bind Thenvor, for example, would have made challenges and mutinies sprout about him like weeds in an untended tomb-field, and would have undone any good that came from the match.

When he saw the tightness in Darin's face and stance, Zeskuk almost laughed. The knight was as little at ease over this challenge as he was.

"One sign that this fight is honorable, I think all can see," Zeskuk said. He raised his voice to be heard or at least to break the silence on deck before it played further havoc with his peace of mind. "Sir Darin is minotaur-sized, and also taught to fight by a minotaur who was not the least warrior of his day. So I acquit Sir Darin of any intent to make me look as ridiculous as a minotaur usually does, fighting a human."

Darin actually smiled, which made Lujimar frown. "In time, perhaps, you should hear the full story of the fight between me and Waydol on the one hand, and Sir Pirvan and his lady Haimya on the other," he said. "I assure you that no one and nothing in the fight was ludicrous, and it was only by the gods' favor that we all lived to fight again."

"Then let us hope for such favor this time as well, whoever stands first," Zeskuk said. He knew that was close to binding himself not to carry the fight to the death, but that was his firm intent anyway. The more people who knew this, the better.

The fewer people who knew why, however, also the better. And accidents could claim the most accomplished duelists. Zeskuk hoped Fulvura would understand it all, and not mourn in any unseemly fashion if his luck was out. He also hoped that the humans would attempt no treachery against her if the minotaurs did sail, but did not expect to need to avenge her.

By the time Fulvura went down, there would be such a pile of human dead atop her that the little ones would need to dig out her body before they could take her horns for trophies!

*   *   *   *   *

The flute and drums from *Red Elf* floated over the water, out past long bowshot to the boat where Torvik sat facing his sister Chuina.

She was a year younger than he and had not spent as much time afloat, but somehow looked older. Perhaps it was just her new sergeancy, that the flutes and drums (and the wine and the ale, the fish, the pickles, and the cakes, all bought with Lady Haimya's bounty) were celebrating aboard both *Red Elf* and *Windmaster's Gift*.

Certainly she had grown since he last saw her. If she had any more growing to do, she would be taller than he, with long arms well made for archery. She was also darker, and her hair grew in tight curls that she had now tied up with red and silver threads that did not quite match her heavy dwarven-work gold earrings.

"Those are new," Torvik said, for lack of anything else.

"A parting gift from a special friend," Chuina said, with a reminiscent smile.

Torvik frowned. She caught the change of expression. "What, brother mine? Surely you did not expect me to be a maiden after all this time?"

"Well, it has not been quite enough time to forget the little sister who wanted me to take her out in my first boat," he said. "This reminds me of that day. Thinking of you as a grown woman comes a trifle hard."

Chuina patted his cheek. "There are rumors that thinking comes hard to you at all these days," she chided. "From some people I would believe nothing of the sort, but the tales have reached Lady Haimya. When *she* worries, only a fool ignores the tales."

Torvik had indeed been thinking since before dawn, but about only one thing, and that was not his sister's promotion. The message had been inscribed with a rock on a large fluted trumpet shell that he had found on his cabin deck in the pale gray of early morning. He had memorized it before the change of watch, and had not dared leave it lying about, so he had it in his belt pouch now. He silently pulled it out and as silently handed it to Chuina. She turned it over and over in her hand several times, then took a while to read the message. Torvik wondered if she doubted her eyes, needed to know the rest of the story, or could not make out Mirraleen's writing. The Dimernesti's talents did not include a fine, fair hand.

Without waiting for the question, Torvik told his sister the full tale. She listened in silence, holding the shell, then asked only: "Is this a trap, do you think?"

It was a question on which Torvik had pondered much

without finding an answer. He spoke what he believed to be the truth. "There may be a trap along the course I take to her, but I do not think it will be she who sets it."

"Have you lain with her?"

This time Torvik was ready for his sister's frankness. "No, and not because I have not thought of it," he told her. "In elven guise she is very fair, although rather taller than I."

"That was not idle curiosity," Chuina persisted. "If rumor got about that you had—"

"I know what rumor will say," he cut her off, "and what those who listen might do. I am unclean, have lost my virtue to a lesser breed, and on and on like that to no purpose. Would you have me afraid of small-minded rattle-jaws and arrant witlings?"

"No, but you cannot keep me from being afraid for you." She licked her lips and said, "Could I come with you, to guard your back and summon help if a trap does spring?"

Torvik pondered again, then shook his head. "Mirraleen would suspect betrayal. She would also suspect it if I did not come, and consider what she offers."

"A way into the mage's stronghold, outflanking all his magic and monsters," Chuina said. "Yes. That is precious, if only to keep common folly from setting men and mino-taurs at odds to no purpose."

"Then we agree, and you can help. Stay at your party, be seen by everybody, and hide as best you can the fact that I am gone. Lady Haimya doubtless thought she was doing us a service with that purse—"

"I saw you eat five helpings of the clams pickled in onion juice," Chuina joked. "You're a fine one to talk!"

"—but she made sure that both of us would be much sought-after. So you have to do the work of both of us," he finished.

"Well and good. I've always wanted to dance on the cap-stan."

"Dance on the capstan or the bowsprit. Dance in armor or starlight. Dance where and how you please, but keep everyone ignorant that your brother Torvik is—"

He broke off. From seaward, the breeze had carried to his ears the barking of sea otters.

* * * * *

Zeskuk hurried to *Cleaver*'s aftercastle, and the crew made way for him without turning their eyes from the sea.

He followed where they were pointing and saw at least twenty, perhaps twice that, sea otters swimming rapidly eastward. They were staying just out of harpoon range of the ships, and Zeskuk sent a message to hail the few boats in the water, reminding them against any otter hunting.

He had warned the fleet on the matter after Torvik's tale reached him, but there were always fools who forgot the taste of the first drink by the time they ordered the fourth. He did not want to have to clap too many minotaurs in irons for the rest of the voyage, especially not any of Thenvor's folk.

Moreover, he was sure of one thing: If Torvik had any secrets the minotaurs needed to know, their killing sea otters would close the young human captain's mouth as thoroughly as if he were dead.

The sea otters swam out of sight and out to sea as the swift darkness of a tropical night came down on Suivinari Island.

Chapter 14

The humans had not only put the tent in a clearing deep in the forest, they had tied down the edges all around it, except for the front, which was guarded. So Horimpsot Elderdrake went in from the back of the tent, using a sharp knife. He did not cut the canvas because it was tough and this was his best knife. Also, the cut would show. Instead, he cut the ropes and vines tying down the edge of the tent, then lifted the canvas and crawled in. If he could get out again before anyone came by, he would pull the canvas, ropes, and vines back into place. Then nobody would see anything until daylight, when he would be far away.

The opening in the front of the tent let in enough light for Elderdrake to see that the guard was on duty but did not have his mind on it. He and a local farm girl seemed to be much more interested in each other than the guard was in watching the tent.

So Elderdrake could wander around the tent the way he sometimes wandered around a potter's shop in town, at least until the potter saw him and chased him out. He found every kind of horse gear, including saddles, bridles, and even some horse armor. There were helmets and breastplates for more men than the kender wanted to think about, also swords, knives, waterskins, boots, belts, and bandages. He found crates of hard bread, salted meat, and dried fruit, barrels of wine and ale, and even a few bottles of dwarf spirits.

Whoever had put all this here was obviously putting together a private army. Elderdrake could recognize the House Dirivan marking, and saw it on the crates and barrels. But why put the supplies here when the men were somewhere else?

Down here to the south of Tirabot, there were fewer eyes to see. If they saw the supplies with no men about—well, crates and barrels without men didn't make an army. If they saw the men coming, unarmed and walking, that also would not look like an army. Only when the men reached the tent would Tirabot Manor's enemies have an army. By then it would be too late for the manor.

Quite ingenious, for humans. In fact, Elderdrake was growing more impressed by the ingenuity of humans every day. Not their judgment—they were using all this ingenuity in a cause that no kender would have thought worth a cup of the cheapest wine—but their ingenuity.

A kender can be noisier than a dozen minotaurs or more silent than falling snow. Elderdrake was the latter, as he slipped out of the tent, covered his tracks, and hurried off to warn his friends.

* * * * *

Torvik had taken the smallest boat from those tied up around *Red Elf*. It was still intended for two pairs of oars, and muffling the one pair he was using made it slower still.

The only other choices would have been company, when he'd rejected even his sister's, or swimming. The second course didn't risk betraying Mirraleen so much as it risked his not reaching her at all. She had assured him that Wilthur's Creation would not strike near the fleet, but there was plenty of empty water between the fleet and where he was to meet her.

Also, Wilthur's pet might not be the only thing with a

taste for human flesh swimming around in these dark
waters. Sharks, giant eels, nagas, and dwarf kraken could all
have appeared by now, drawn by curiosity about the noise
or the offal regularly flung into the water by the sailors.

The oars made only the faintest of thumps as the boat
slipped across the smooth water. From time to time Torvik
halted to tighten the sweat band that kept his eyes clear
and to look over his shoulder for the landmarks.

Mirraleen had given him marks to steer by, whether the
night was dark or clear. Tonight it was clear, but Nuitari
was the highest of the moons, with Solinari only a faint
glow from behind the Smoker. He had more light from a
vent on the Smoker's flank, which every few minutes
glowed yellow. By the yellow glow, he could see ash,
steam, and hot gas spewing into the air.

Was it his imagination, or had the Smoker been working
harder at earning its name lately? He knew that spells cast
outside common laws and customs governing magic could
have unpredictable effects on nature. He also hoped that
somebody with the fleet, even a minotaur, was making it
their business to predict what the Smoker might do.

The boat was grinding its way past the jutting teeth of a
reef before Torvik was aware of it. He jerked his mind from
a pleasant image of Mirraleen standing waist deep in the
water, with flowers in her hair—white ones would go best
with that auburn, he thought—and started to back water.
Then he realized that, barely thirty paces away, phosphorescence glowed a dim green around a rock shaped like the
head of a goat with one horn. That was the last mark. Stand
on the rock, Mirraleen had said, then wade in the direction
the horn points until you reach a beach of black gravel.

Torvik swung his boat around and found a place where
for now it would be hard to see from either landward or
seaward. The tide was at the ebb, of course, so in time it
might rise out of its hiding place. So he gave the boat a good
long mooring line, to keep it at least from drifting away.

The water was almost milk warm. When Torvik stepped
off the rock and began wading, it was barely up to his
chest. He tried to move silently, but was sure that he was

making more noise wading than he had in the boat. He saw the phosphorescence glimmer about his torso, and reached down for his dagger.

With the knife unsheathed and in his hand, he felt better. It seemed a long way to the land, and a little rust on the blade seemed a small price for an easy mind as he pushed through the water.

* * * * *

Zeskuk was drowsing when he heard the knock. Wrapping his kilt hastily about him, he opened the door.

It was Juiksum, Thenvor's son. Fortunately, he did not look as if he was bearing a challenge. He might be sober, even grim, but he was not showing the ritual anger of a challenge-bearer.

"Message from Sir Darin," Juiksum growled. "Is sunset tomorrow acceptable for your match?"

Zeskuk nodded.

Juiksum coughed. "It must be written," he said.

"Then bring me pen and paper—no, wait, I keep some here."

With sleep-slowed hands, Zeskuk laid out paper, pen, and ink on the folding table beside his bed. With sleep-blurred eyes, he wrote his acceptance and handed it to his visitor.

Juiksum read it, then asked, "You did not mention torches."

"We can decide that at the time," Zeskuk said. If he was going to end a busy day tomorrow by fighting a human warrior fully equal to a minotaur, he did not want to spend any more of tonight chattering like a squirrel over trivial matters.

"You have faith in Darin's honor," Juiksum said. It did not come out like a question.

"Yes," Zeskuk said. "Do you?" He almost added, "If you have no more wits than your father . . ."

Juiksum smiled. "I do. Neither of you need fear treachery, and Darin's night vision must be equal to yours or he would not be a warrior of the Solamnic Orders."

Having night vision equal to Zeskuk's was no great achievement. If they fought without torches, the minotaur chief knew he might end with a few aches and bruises he would otherwise have escaped. But honor was worth more than a few broken bones, let alone aches and bruises.

"Lujimar is sacrificing tonight, that this fight bring justice and honor," Juiksum said. "He did not say to whom."

With ears ready to carry tales to Thenvor, that was probably wise.

"I hope we can also have peace with the humans, for here, for now," Juiksum added.

"How so?" Zeskuk said. "Is that not arguing from fear?"

By instinct, Juiksum's nostrils flared and his fists clenched. Then he shook his head. "It is arguing from a desire to win the great victory rather than the small one," he said. "Cleansing Suivinari needs human and minotaur both. It is a coward who runs from a fight or counts the odds, when another forces it upon him. But it is not a coward who refuses to fight one weaker than he, who has not challenged him, and may even help him."

Zeskuk pushed the desk in and lay down. "Juiksum," he said, "I wish you prowess in the arena equal to your wisdom. Surely then you will become Emperor."

"Do you not fear that my father will then try to rule through me," Juiksum asked, "or at least gain my ear?"

"No. I think you are more likely to have his ear—in a gold frame, hanging on the wall of the throne room. To warn those who offer unwelcome advice. Good night, wise young warrior."

"Good night, sagacious war chief," Juiksum replied.

It was pleasant, Zeskuk reflected as the door closed behind Juiksum, to deal from time to time with those who presented no mysteries.

* * * * *

Mirraleen crouched behind a boulder as Torvik stepped out of the water. It seemed as if the night was holding its breath. Even her acute hearing could make out no sound louder than the water dripping from the young man.

He looked like a pirate, with his well-crafted dagger in his hand. The only way he could have looked more like one, indeed, was to have the dagger clenched in his teeth. In spite of what it did for his appearance, the dagger spoke of his good sense. No one could have followed her underwater, at least not without detection, or crossed the magic-haunted island to come up on her from landward. Torvik was not so fortunate.

She must have made a sound, or Torvik had hearing like an orca, because he suddenly stiffened and went into a fighter's crouch. The dagger gleamed dully, reflecting the last of the phosphorescence. His movements, she could not help noticing, were sure, graceful, and spoke of his being both strong and dangerous in spite of his lack of height.

Also, in spite of his lack of years. By human measurement he was young, by elven measurement a child, but by what Mirraleen saw he was a man in strength, skill, and wisdom. She could safely trust him with much, beginning with the secret of the underwater way into the heart of the Smoker.

She stepped out from behind her boulder. His dagger darted up, and she realized that he had the skill and the dagger had the balance for throwing. She raised both hands, palms outward, then touched a finger to her lips.

He said nothing until they were well inside the boulder-strewn approach to the beach. Even then, he first kissed the finger she had held to her lips, with a smile that made him look much younger or much older—perhaps both at once.

Then she put both hands on his temples. She realized she wanted to play with his dark hair, now damp, soon to be stiff with salt. She furiously mastered an impulse that she knew arose from too many years of celibacy, and would keep more important work from being done tonight.

Torvik was a gentleman. He did not reply to her touch by more than a smile that told her that touch was not unwelcome.

"We cannot be here long, or talk much aloud," she whispered. "If I touch you like this, I can put into your memory the way to enter the caves below the Smoker, where Wilthur's Creation lives. Once it is slain, the back door to the mage's stronghold is open, and no spells he can cast in front of it can save him."

"He has worn three robes, so can he not cast spells in three ways?" Torvik said, sensibly. "Moreover, killing the Creation will not be easy work."

"You will have help," she said. "I hope."

"Best if you can do more than hope," he told her. "Mirraleen, should you not come out to the fleet, and speak to at least a few others? There are some whose silence I would swear to, and who would hide your coming and going. Then whether the help you hope for comes or not, you and I will not be alone."

"I thought young men always wished to be alone with fine women," she teased.

"Yes, and the finer, the more alone. Much more alone than we could ever be on Suivinari Island, where only a few thousand humans and minotaurs, the odd wizard and his pet monsters, and the gods know what else disturb our peace.

"But jesting aside, what do you say?" he said. "I know it will be even more dangerous than the common waterfront tavern, but—"

She laughed in spite of herself, trying to muffle it with her hands. When she could speak plainly again, she shook her head and said, "Not until after the way is in your memory. There have to be two of us who know the way from the sea to deep in the rock. Two of us able to speak to the friends I hope will come to help. This is knowledge that cannot die with me."

"Then what we are doing is much more dangerous than a tavern," Torvik said. "I always thought there was a reason I stayed out of them." He raised one hand and twined the fingers in her hair with the touch of one who would gladly let his hand linger, or even wander.

She warmed to that touch, but took his hand and pushed it down into his lap. "Be still," she whispered. "This will not take long, and when it is done . . ."

She herself did not know what would come after. For now it was enough to press her hands to his temples again, and feel his memory ready to listen to her message and hold it.

* * * * *

The Dimernesti known as Medlessarn the Silent flopped ungracefully on the rock. As swiftly as he could, he flowed upward and outward into his elven form.

He sometimes wished the gods had made the Dimernesti's animal form something other than a sea otter. The creatures were splendid in the water, hardly less so than the porpoise-form of the Dargonesti, but they were only a trifle less awkward than a porpoise on land as well.

With his head some six feet above a rock already that far clear of the water, Medlessarn could hear, smell, and if necessary see much farther. He also had less natural senses at his command but only moderately, and these might be too dangerous to use until he learned what the enemy here could sense with his own magic.

The breeze was toward the land, so scent and hearing both failed him. In his home waters perhaps he could have picked out a fellow Dimernesti against wind and water alike. Amid this riot of new sensations (for Suivinari was long unvisited by his clan), he could hardly have smelled a rotten fish.

At least he had come this far unmolested. It would be as well to wait until at least a few more of those who heard the call swam up. Then if they met danger farther inshore, someone would surely escape, to warn the rest of the shallows-dwellers. Certainly the sea otters here had not of late been hunted nearly as much as one would have expected, from a fleet of this size. That gave them the right to any assistance the shallows-dwellers could give, without danger to themselves.

As for more—well, that was why Medlessarn had swum so far in so little time, to answer a warning so full of mystery and menace. To whom, he had yet to learn.

* * * * *

Torvik had just put into words for the third time the way to the beast's lair. He was now ready for the next test of his memory—drawing a map.

He wondered what else he might be ready for, afterward.

If he was not back aboard *Red Elf* by dawn there would be uproar, confusion, and a search for him that might undo all his night's work. Reluctantly, he concluded that there would most likely be no "afterward."

He hoped that Mirraleen would not be offended.

He reached for his pouch, to see if the paper and charcoal in their fishskin wrappers had survived the journey. As his hands undid the straps, his ears caught the faint *click* of pebbles. It came from inland, not the way other Dimernesti would come to help, if they came at all. Inland swarmed with Wilthur's creations, likely enough to bar any human or minotaur passage, so it could not be a friend who made that noise.

Torvik put a finger to Mirraleen's lips, then to his own. She nodded. He stood up—and the night was shot with raw fire in half a score of hideous shades, as something tried to tear his skull open.

He reeled back against the rock, clutching at Mirraleen's arm to draw her with him to safety, as he imagined. Instead she was down on her knees, clawing at her temples, as if the same pain was tearing at her skull. He thought he heard her cry out.

Then the pain ebbed as the darkness around them turned into a wall of human forms. Most were garbed like sailors. All were armed. Two stepped forward, and what these wore was no garb an honest sailor ever had.

They wore short, sleeveless black tunics and boots that even now Torvik thought must have been hideously awkward and uncomfortable on rough ground. Over their faces they wore masks, with prominent eyes and noses, but no mouths. The masks were white, in startling contrast to the black tunics.

The masks and tunics together had been the ritual garb of the Servants of Silence, the bloody-handed terrormongers of the kingpriests. The order had been formally abolished; no one had ever said that all who had served it were dead, though. Now even its abolition seemed doubtful.

Torvik endured, as if it were happening to someone else, the sailors binding him and Mirraleen. They were skilled. He knew he could not break out of his bonds and doubted that Mirraleen could do so swiftly enough to escape notice.

Two sailors jerked Torvik to his feet and held him, as one of the mask-wearers stepped forward and stood above Mirraleen. He held a tapered piece of hardwood in one hand.

"Now," an unfamiliar voice echoed from behind the mask, "you who call yourself captain, yet consort with abominations—do you know her secrets?"

"No," Torvik lied. "She keeps them close—"

The mask-wearer backhanded Torvik across the face. "Your light punishment for what I think is a lie," the masked man said. "Now, witness hers."

The wood—the club—came down across Mirraleen's shoulders.

Presently she was screaming. Long before that, Torvik had wished he could close his eyes, then his ears. Now he wished he could knock himself senseless or force these—their own word "abominations" was good enough—to do it for him.

At last he realized that easy escape would be a dangerous course. It would assure the enemy that he was weak, or lying, or worst of all, both. Then Mirraleen's torment would go on until one of them broke and confessed, or until she died.

He stared straight ahead and tried doing navigational calculations in his head, to keep his mind busy. He succeeded well enough that he only heard the reply to something a sailor muttered.

"No, we came here to punish consorting with abominations. Not to do it ourselves."

From that answer, Torvik knew what the question must

have been. Mirraleen was spared that particular horror, at least. But his vengeance for what she was suffering would be just as bloody. He suspected hers would be, too, if she was fit to take it.

* * * * *

"Pirvan, Pirvan! Wake up!"

The knight realized that Haimya was no longer in bed beside him, but standing over him and shaking him. She was not yet dressed, but fully awake.

She also looked as if her wakefulness at this hour—it would hardly be dawn yet—came from no good news. Her face was grim enough for an image of Takhisis.

"Wilthur the Brown has fled to the fleet, asking us to save him from his own pet?" Pirvan asked. He had to say something.

Haimya looked ready to slap him. "Torvik is gone," she said.

"Gone? How? Where?"

"If I knew that, I would have said that he is dead or abducted or sprouted wings and flown away like a pegasus," Haimya grumbled. "No one knows. What is certain is that trouble is coming because of it."

Haimya told her husband the crisis the fleet faced, briefly but still so completely that Pirvan only had to interrupt her twice with questions. Torvik had not slept aboard *Red Elf* last night. His sister Chuina had admitted seeing him, but not seeing him depart, nor would she say what they had talked about.

So Istarans had arrested Chuina on suspicion of guilty knowledge of her brother's disappearance. This had led to a protest aboard *Red Elf*, whose crew refused to release Chuina into Istaran custody. In this refusal they were supported by many elsewhere in the fleet, particularly those who had once sailed with Jemar the Fair or his kin. They were certain that Chuina could not have done it.

Equally certain were the Istarans. Chuina might not have done it but surely knew who had. Protecting her did her brother no service, nor her mother, nor her father's memory.

Indeed, it was mutiny. The penalty for mutiny could be death, enslavement, or at least losing ship, weapons, property, and all hope of sailing with Istar's blessing.

The people of *Red Elf* had told the Istarans what they could do with their blessing. In detail, and at some length.

Pirvan frowned, and asked, "You say, *Red Elf*'s people?"

"Yes."

"The Istarans among the fighters, too?"

"I have heard that some of them at least signed the proclamation," Haimya told him.

Pirvan sat up. "Well, that's some good news, that *Red Elf*'s crew is united behind their captain and his sister," he said. "Fewer heads for us and Gildas to send home to Eskaia, if Torvik does not come back."

Chapter 15

Pirvan had not approved of Darin's challenge to Zeskuk, but neither he nor Sir Niebar had interposed their authority as Knights of the Rose to prevent the bout. They both doubted that they had the authority in the first place, and Niebar's doubts carried particular weight with Pirvan. The tall knight had forgotten as much about the laws governing conduct between races as Pirvan had ever learned.

Also, Pirvan refused to believe that Darin had suddenly lost his wits and forgotten everything he knew about minotaurs. If Darin died tonight, Pirvan knew the younger knight would die in his right mind, with his face to the enemy, and believing that what he did served his honor, the knights' honor, and the purpose for which they had all come to Suivinari Island.

Pirvan had told himself this so often that he had begun to believe it. Now, all that remained was to be able to persuade the other humans of these simple truths, if indeed Darin had seen his last sunset.

The last of that sunset's light had faded from the sky when Pirvan and Haimya disembarked from their boat. The torches marking the boundaries of the arena were set so close and burned so brightly, however, that a beetle could hardly have crawled unseen across the arena.

The arena was a patch of hard sand beach dug, tamped, and scraped until it was as flat as an apprentice thief's purse and as hard as a pawnbroker's heart. It was sixty paces on a side, large enough not to make a minotaur feel confined, and small enough that a nimble human could not rely on evading Zeskuk's charges forever.

Of course, Darin knew more than enough about minotaur fighting arts to expect more than simple rushes. Zeskuk undoubtedly knew what Darin knew—and that a minotaur-sized human could reply with his own variations on minotaur skills. If one had only a dispassionate observer's interest in a rare matching of opponents, one could look forward to an enthralling evening.

After the stinging loss of Sirbones—a loss Pirvan had forced himself not to succumb to until the completion of the task at hand—he was more nervous about the possibility of Darin's demise than he wanted to admit. Pirvan expected to be biting his lip when he was not urging healers forward.

Inland of the arena stood a cordon of minotaurs and humans, each in several solid, well armed, and alert bands adequately separated from one another. At least a hundred sets of eyes were watching the darkness inland. The minotaurs had clearly been burning off the last bit of undergrowth as well, and both minotaurs and humans had set more torches and laid watch fires all along the cordon.

There was nothing left close to the arena for anyone short of a god to animate. Nor could anything approach the arena from inland without being seen a hundred paces away—and from the sea, the arena was guarded by half a dozen ships of each fleet, and two dozen boats rowing or sailing guard.

Had the arena been the tent of an emperor, it could hardly have been better guarded, but what most heartened Pirvan was the presence of both Lujimar and Revella Laschaar. They stood between the cordon and the arena, each with two attendants and a ceremonial stool, although both were standing and looked ready to stand for a year.

Both of them wore their most formal robes, but were bare-headed and barefooted. Lujimar had an amulet hanging from his stool, while Lady Revella had leaned her staff against her own seat.

All the healing power needed for anything short of necromancy was present in those two. Also, perfect memories and acute senses of honor. Possibly Lujimar saw farther, to the future of both races, instead of merely wishing to repay a favor done some ten years ago.

Or perhaps not. Neither would let either fighter or themselves know dishonor to save their lives. As long as such watched the fight, it would be fair and the outcome as skill and the gods allowed. And as long as such existed on Krynn, the bloodthirsty Thenvors, kingpriests, and ghostriders could not have the easy victory that was all their kind ever wanted.

Pirvan and Hawkbrother had both offered to attend Darin, but he had chosen Rynthala instead, as she already could come and go freely within minotaur territory—and this arena was on territory that even most humans conceded to the horn-headed ones.

So it was Rynthala who ritually shook out each of Darin's garments as he disrobed, until he wore only a loin guard. It was Rynthala who rubbed oil into Darin's skin, partly to ready it for healing spells and partly to keep Zeskuk from getting an easy grip.

It was also Rynthala who must have rubbed oil into her husband's skin a hundred times before, in more intimate settings. Pirvan could read that easily enough in her haunted eyes.

On the opposite side of the arena, Thenvor's son Juiksum was doing the same honors for Zeskuk, although the minotaur had only to remove kilt and sandals to be garbed for the bout. He seemed to be favoring one leg a trifle, but that was an easy trick for a skilled fighter to play, and Darin would probably have an edge in speed anyway. He would still be facing an opponent who could strike with twice the force and endure three times the punishment of almost any human.

Fulvura stood close by, her arms crossed on her chest. She wore only a simple tunic, with leather straps on her legs and forearms. She was, as law required, unarmed, but Pirvan hoped no human was fool enough to think her an easy target for vengeance if Darin fell.

"Do not worry, good knight," Fulvura said. "When Zeskuk says that a fight is not to the death, it is as good as an oath."

"I did not doubt that, nor fear for Darin," Pirvan said stiffly, to keep Haimya from saying something less polite.

"I would think no worse of you if you did fear for Darin," Fulvura said. "Had I a fosterling like that, who could go into the arena with a good chance of leaving it emperor—well, I would not love anyone who might even by chance put him down."

"We also do not love those who—" Haimya began. She might have said something unfortunate, except for what came next.

Lightning should come before thunder, but this thunderclap came with no warning. It was loud enough to make everyone's ears ring, and if it came without warning it did come with a blast of wind as solid as a giant's fist. Between those deafened by the thunder and those blinded by flying sand, few saw what appeared in the arena, seemingly out of thin air.

Pirvan was one of those few. He saw a ship's boat, about a six-rower size, he judged. It carried four armed, masked men forward, and one aft. In between, a man and a woman were both tied to the thwarts, with both chains and ropes that twisted them into contorted positions.

The five armed men wore the black tunics and white masks of the supposedly disbanded Servants of Silence.

The bound man was Torvik. The bound woman Pirvan did not recognize, but she was tall, auburn-haired, and her ears had elven points to them.

The man in the stern of the boat stepped out onto the sand and drew his sword. It was another piece of ritual garb—a short sword with an ugly saw-toothed blade, like a smaller version of a minotaur clabbard. He raised his sword.

"Hear us, O servants of iniquity, while we speak for the virtue you know not," the masked man called. "Heed our words, and virtue may come to you. Give no heed, and death shall be the portion of these beslimed folk, while ignorance and defeat are yours."

The man halted, to be sure he had everyone's attention. Pirvan thought the halt was needless. Even the sea breeze seemed to be holding its breath. But the silence gave him a chance to study all those around the arena, and two in particular:

Revella Laschaar, who seemed less surprised than she should have—but also angry, as though she should not have been surprised at all.

Zeskuk, who had made his face so unreadable that Pirvan thought he must have taken great pains to do so— for reasons that no human might be able to guess.

* * * * *

Zeskuk could not quite read Lady Revella's face, but did not need to. Lujimar was closer, had a better view, and commanded magic.

What the minotaur priest's face said was a plain accusation: Lady Revella had guilty knowledge that might bring her spells down on anyone who attempted to end this farce before it brought dishonor to all here.

Or at least what Zeskuk hoped would remain a farce. That saw-edged blade and the ritual garb of the Servants of Silence were not encouraging. Nor was the ability of the abductors of Torvik and the elf-woman to appear out of nowhere a good sign. She was Dimernesti, and was she the young captain's secret?

Had he been anywhere else, with any sort of weapon in his hand, Zeskuk would have felt freer to choose what to do next. Had he been here and ten years younger, with shatangs ready, he would have held the abductors' lives in his hands.

As it was, he deemed it wise to listen for a trifle, to hear what course these gutter scourings intended to steer. The leader was one of those, wearisome in any race, who could never use two words when five would do half as well. In spite of this, and the fact that he spoke with an accent that Zeskuk did not recognize except that it was not pure Istaran, he somehow made his intentions clear, saying, "Torvik Jemarsson stands guilty of treason, uncleanliness, lack of virtue—" and a whole list of other offenses. Zeskuk could have sworn he heard "spitting on the decks," but doubted his ears.

The tirade ended with "—and for all these offenses against men and gods, his life is forfeit. But mercy is a virtue. I and my followers, defenders of virtue, may be persuaded to show mercy, if the fleets accede to these terms I set forth:

"All at Suivinari will acknowledge the leadership of these five men . . ."

Zeskuk recognized only two of the names, and those because they were such blatant lapdogs of the kingpriest that even minotaurs had heard of it. Andrys Puhrad, with his reputation for diplomacy toward all, was not one of the five. Nor were any of Sir Pirvan's friends. Zeskuk wondered what army these virtue-defenders had, to impose their preposterous demands. Or did they care if the demands were met, as long as making them caused trouble?

"All at Suivinari shall also swear to fight side by side until the island is cleansed. Torvik has, though it be through his uncleanliness with the Dimernesti female Mirraleen, learned of a way to victory. Once all have taken oaths to the new leaders, that way shall be revealed. Then Torvik shall be set free, to redeem his honor as a human by leading his fighters in the cleansing of Suivinari Island. Mirraleen shall be held closely, as a hostage for the continued help of the Dimernesti. She may hope for freedom once victory is gained, but only for the hardest of deaths if she seeks to escape or her folk turn against the fleet that champions virtue."

A number of further thoughts ran through Zeskuk's mind, foremost among them the utter ignorance of these people about minotaurs. The leader seemed to think that the Destined Race would either abandon Suivinari Island (and their share of glory), fight (and be defeated), or tamely submit to being led by the new council (who probably had neither knowledge of war nor any other virtue).

Zeskuk's second thought was that perhaps the leader knew minotaurs better than it at first seemed. This farce would most likely sow quarrels between human and minotaur that no contest of honor could settle.

Then victory would be impossible, or at least so costly as to be hardly worthwhile. The only one to gain from leaving Suivinari Island under its present ruler would be that ruler himself. Did the Servants of Silence know that they were unwitting servants of Wilthur? Did Lady Revella suspect as much?

Questions to be answered later. Zeskuk realized that for now it was necessary for those who knew the truth to act to end this farce. Since he was the only one such . . .

For a moment, the minotaur chief would gladly have stopped breathing if that would have drawn less attention. He shuffled his feet, trying to look like one testing the muscles of a weak leg rather than one testing his footing for a leap.

He snatched the towel out of Juiksum's hand, took three running strides, and leaped over the torch-line into the arena.

* * * * *

Wilthur's scrying glass had just given him a clear enough image to see the arena when the minotaur chief leaped over the torches. The wizard's curses would have peeled paint off the walls of his stronghold, if any of them had been painted. Only chips of rock and fine dust fell instead.

His thoughts plunged downward—to find his Creation as unwilling as ever to seek the open sea. No diversion from that quarter.

No diversion from plant or animal close to the arena, either. Human and minotaur had done their work too thoroughly for that.

Nor could he openly work magic that would make the Servants of Silence wonder if they had help beyond Lady Revella's. They were proud and foolish; they would rather die than knowingly serve him, for all that he could cleanse Krynn of those without virtue as well as any mage in history and better than nearly all.

If someone killed Zeskuk, however, and in such a way as to make it seem to come from human dishonor—

Yes. Peace always had enough enemies, and hatred enough friends, for such work.

Nor would it be necessary to hide the traces of his mind-tampering spells, this time. Those whose minds he had twisted would be dead soon enough in the fighting, or have no coherent memory of Wilthur's invasion of their thoughts.

*   *   *   *   *

Pirvan was as surprised as anyone at Zeskuk's running leap into the arena. He also thought the bemused, gape-mouthed faces all about him were images of his own. Then Darin moved, so quickly that Pirvan realized here was one man who was not surprised. Which did not explain what he was doing.

Darin's movements were an almost exact copy of Zeskuk's, allowing for the human's being a much better jumper than the minotaur. Darin's leap over the torches seemed to carry him halfway to the boat. Then both man and minotaur were running toward the boat, and toward each other.

Knowledge burst like sunrise in Pirvan's mind. Whatever Darin and Zeskuk might intend, they would do it while so close together that no one could strike at either from a distance, for fear of hitting the other. Spears, arrows, stones, anything shot or thrown was useless.

Anyone wishing to aid the Servants of Silence would have to do so close at hand. That meant violating the sacred precincts of the arena, and also coming within reach of a large man and a large minotaur, both trained fighters and neither friendly to unwelcome visitors.

Someone was foolish enough not to see what was plain for everyone else. Only a few paces from Pirvan, someone unslung a bow and nocked an arrow. The man had also not seen Fulvura, standing right beside him. As if reaching to scratch an itch, she thrust one massive arm downward. It caught the man on the shoulder, knocking him sprawling. Before he could rise or anyone come to his aid, Haimya darted behind Fulvura and knelt, inquiring earnestly of the fallen man if he was hurt.

She had one knee on his right arm and the other on his chest. In the crowd, no one but Pirvan and Fulvura saw that she also had a dagger drawn, with the point at his throat.

It would have been too much to hope for, that the archer was the only fool present. The next fool threw a spear—but by now others were alert.

A shielding spell slammed down into the arena, so violently that sand flew where the edge struck it. The shield extended some ten paces in all directions around the boat, the five Servants and two captives in it, and the two would-be duelists, who were now nearly close enough to shake hands.

The spear bounced off the spell-shield and hurtled back the way it had come, whirling end over end. It would have been too much to hope that it would strike down its thrower, but it did the next best thing, sinking harmlessly into the sand.

Pirvan saw that it was Lujimar casting the spell, if the minotaur's stance with his eyes cast down and both hands on the amulet now hanging around his neck meant anything. He also saw Lady Revella staring from the arena to Lujimar—then toward her staff.

The knight's feet were only just behind his thoughts. Pirvan dashed from the ranks of the onlookers, cut across a corner of the arena, and flung himself at Lady Revella's staff just before her hands closed on it.

He rolled with the agility of a younger man, only slightly hampered by the staff, then came up with it in one hand

and a drawn dagger in the other. Lady Revella gaped at the knight and raised her hand.

Pirvan raised the dagger, thrusting the point under the rune-marked silver ring at the head of the staff. A silver ring, Tarothin had taught him, often meant that the spells within it or the whole staff could be countered with cold iron. From Lady Revella's expression, Tarothin had the right of it in this case.

"Pirvan, you cannot use my staff," she said. "You might die if I tried to use it while you held it."

Laughing in the Black Robe's face did not seem a wise idea, so Pirvan said simply, "Could you use it afterward, if so?"

"No, but do you wish it useless?"

"Until I trust you," he replied, "yes."

Revella looked as if he had struck her. He briefly considered handing the lady's staff to Lujimar, but knew that might cause her spells and the minotaur's to battle each other.

Also, seeing a minotaur given a human wizard's tools might drive some wild-headed human over the edge into attacking Pirvan. That could make a bad situation even worse. Pirvan saw that he had an advantage, and pressed it.

"Lady Revella," he said, "I do not know what you plotted, or with whom. I know even less what you intended, or how far what happened has gone beyond that. I do know that whether intending it or not, you have helped endanger peace between men and minotaurs, our work here on Suivinari Island, and the lives of most of those whom you once thanked for helping your daughter Rubina."

Lady Revella's mouth opened, without a word coming out (or at least any Pirvan could hear over the uproar). Then she knelt and put her face in her hands.

Pirvan wondered if he should applaud his own lucky guess or let the Black Robe cry on his shoulder. Haimya took the matter out of his hands by hurrying up and kneeling beside the wizard.

"Is the archer—?" he started to ask.

Haimya's reply was a bleak look, as if Pirvan himself were responsible for Revella's misery. The knight decided that five lifetimes was not enough for a man to understand how women could lock shields. He also realized that he would have no sensible answer from Revella now, and that Lujimar was too busy to answer anyone's questions about anything.

Pirvan resigned himself to letting the fight inside the shield take its course. At least he could guard Lujimar's back.

* * * * *

The fight was brief but bloody. Against Zeskuk and Darin, five trained human fighters of the common sort would have normally been no contest. The Servants of Silence were not mere bullies, however, and they both had their saw-edged ritual swords and long daggers against larger but unarmed and unarmored opponents. The contest might indeed have gone to the kingpriest's hirelings, except that Zeskuk and Darin were thinking alike almost from the moment the shield closed around them.

Zeskuk was briefly surprised at how swiftly he and Darin became a team, then realized he should not be. Darin was minotaur-trained, spoke the minotaur tongue, and had doubtless been watching Zeskuk and listening to talk about the chief's fighting style from the moment after he conceived the challenge.

Or had the challenge been suggested to him? Lujimar's swift creation of the shield might be only life-saving good sense. It was also a potent spell for even Lujimar to cast with no more than a few breaths' notice.

As for Zeskuk, he had to admit that he had been studying Darin's movements, on the battlefield and off it, to see how Waydol's training was reflected in a human. He had sharpened his scrutiny after the challenge. Preparing to be opponents, he and Darin had ended by all but training to fight as a team.

So Zeskuk lunged in under the prow of the boat and heaved it up and back, putting all his strength into making the heave as high and violent as he could. Darin sprang backward, ducking under a sword slash, and took his place at the stern as the boat tilted up on end.

Only in champion tales would the five Servants have fallen headlong and broken their necks or skulls, as the boat rose to the vertical. All of them did fall out; only the two captives tied to the thwarts remained in the boat.

However, all five of them landed on their feet, hardly even off-balance. Zeskuk also supposed that such as they were too thick-skulled and stiff-necked to be hurt even if they had tumbled out feet over fork.

Zeskuk and Darin were both ready for fighting opponents, however. Zeskuk let one Servant sink his edge into the minotaur's left arm. Before the man could draw the blade back, Zeskuk chopped his other hand down on the man's sword arm. It shattered; the man screamed; Zeskuk turned the screams to gasps with a punch to the stomach. As the man fell forward, he exposed the back of his neck, and Zeskuk struck again, the edge of his right hand scything down on the exposed spine.

Meanwhile, Darin had taken two steps backward, stood on one foot like a stork, then wheeled and slammed the other foot into the chest of one opponent. Sword-steel ripped Darin's leg, but the foot was the size of a minotaur's hoof and nearly as hard. Zeskuk heard ribs shatter and saw the man fly backward into a comrade, knocking him down. Zeskuk had to take only two steps and fend off only one sword slash before he could kick the man in the head. The man's head nearly parted company with his neck.

This left Zeskuk and Darin with only one opponent apiece. Darin picked up a fallen sword and tossed one to Zeskuk, to further improve the odds. Zeskuk grinned, having somehow expected the knight to finish the bout barehanded, out of some notion put in his head by the Oath or the Measure or Sir Pirvan.

Instead, Darin proved that he knew the minotaur principle of not wasting honorable fighting on a dishonorable opponent. He feinted, let the leader unbalance himself with a wild lunge, then struck together with sword and fist. The leader described a bloody arc in the air and toppled, one arm all but severed.

By the time Darin had knelt, ripped off the leader's mask, and begun binding the captive's ruined arm with it, Zeskuk had finished his opponent. The man tried to run, but Zeskuk still had one good arm and a loose oar from the boat. He also had most of the skill that had won him prizes at throwing the shatang.

The oar was not as well balanced as a shatang, but it did its work. Zeskuk heard the man's teeth slam together as the oar hit him in the back of the head. The oar struck so hard that the man skidded into the churned sand at the base of the shield, with his head facedown and half buried in the sand.

In that position he doubtless could not breathe. Zeskuk doubted that the man would breathe again anyway. The minotaur turned back to Darin and saw the human finish binding the leader's arm and sit down beside him.

"He'll do for a prisoner," Darin panted, "if we can find healing for him."

"There are healers aplenty outside the shield, if they can make up their minds to take it down," Zeskuk said. He would not name Lujimar to Darin, for all that he doubted minotaur priest and human warrior had that many secrets from each other.

"Then let them," Darin said. "I would not care to sit for long tonight, and you need both arms."

"True, but we did swear challenge, and we are still in the arena," the minotaur reminded the knight. "Should we not fulfill our oaths?"

"Of course," Darin said. He limped over to Zeskuk, knotted both fists into a single weapon, and tapped the minotaur at the base of his left horn.

The token blow alone made Zeskuk's head spin. He replied by punching Darin in the small of the back with his good hand.

"I declare that Zeskuk meant no dishonor in anything he planned," Darin said.

"I declare that Darin proved courage in all he did within the arena," Zeskuk replied.

Then both of them had to sit down again, so as not to fall senseless. They were trying not to do so anyway when the shield went down, letting cool sea air and a wall of sound from voices, human and minotaur, burst over them.

* * * * *

For moments after the shield-spell ended, Lujimar swayed, seemingly about to fall even more helpless than those he had saved.

Pirvan resolved to protect the minotaur priest, by standing over him with a drawn sword if necessary, and to the Abyss with scandal. Lujimar might have made any number of enemies tonight. If one of them reached him with steel, all the good done so far might yet be undone.

But Lujimar steadied himself, and walked into the arena, past where humans and minotaurs were busily relighting blown-out torches. The crowd that had rushed toward the fighters and the fallen Servants gave way before the minotaur's presence, and the size of the fists he held up before him also eased his passage.

Lady Revella was now standing again, turning red eyes toward the arena. "I wonder if Lujimar has a place for me in his household," she said softly. "As a kitchen slave, if no more. I hardly deserve better."

"That is for the gods to judge, and perhaps men if they know what you have done," Pirvan said. "Can you tell me a little of it, so that I may seem as if I knew what was happening?"

"Gladly—no, not gladly," Revella answered. "Never gladly. This has cost too much blood. But I will tell you. Someplace quieter, though, and after you tell me how you knew Rubina was my daughter."

"You were prepared to go against the kingpriest to befriend those who saved Rubina," Pirvan said. "I would do many things to repay those who helped a friend or distant kin. But something like that—something against Oath and Measure—only for Haimya or my children."

"I thank you," Haimya said, in a tone half tart and half

tender. "But look closely at Revella, and see if she does not remind you of Rubina."

"Tarothin also saw the blood tie," Revella said. "But he chose to respect a fellow wizard's secret."

"At the wrong time, I fear," Pirvan said. "I judge that Rubina favored her father more than you?"

"Yes, but one who seeks can find the resemblance."

There was no place to be truly private, not without going dangerously far from light and protection, and Pirvan could not go far even were it safe. Until Sir Niebar and Tarothin landed, he was as close to a leader as there could be on this shore.

He listened intently as Lady Revella explained how she had helped certain men who wished to test a spell allowing them to travel inland undetected. It might not work, and if so they were lost. If they succeeded, it was a step toward victory.

But she had not spoken to these men directly. She had dealt with them through an intermediary, who, it appeared, had also taken Lujimar into his confidence. The intermediary also knew or guessed that the men's plans went far beyond what they wished him to admit to Lady Revella.

"So he told Lujimar, but not you, and you were surprised but Lujimar was not?" Pirvan asked.

"That seems as good a way to put it as any," Revella said.

Pirvan muttered curses. "I should like to speak to this—person. It will be useful for all to know that the kingpriest's Servants of Silence are not only thriving again, but taking into their confidence minotaur spies and trying to corrupt high wizards."

"The name is not my secret to—"

This time Pirvan's curses were not muttered. "There has been too much thinking of others' secrets, and not enough thinking that our honor also lies in keeping them safe!" he snapped. He pointed at the boat, where Lujimar was now untying Torvik and Mirraleen—snapping the ropes with his bare hands, and twisting the chains off the oarlocks.

"If Torvik had said just a trifle more, would he and Mirraleen have suffered tonight's ordeal?" Pirvan continued.

"Would Zeskuk and Darin have put themselves at risk in the arena? Would I have had to threaten to break a wizard's staff, which makes a man look foolish if he can't and dead if he can?"

Torvik and Mirraleen were now staggering to their feet, each holding on to one of Lujimar's arms. Even from a distance, Mirraleen showed a ghastly array of cuts and bruises. Torvik's pain seemed more within, judging from his face, and he clutched Mirraleen's hand as if by so doing he could take her wounds on himself.

Revella looked ready to weep again, and Pirvan wondered if he had dealt too harshly with her. He would still learn the spy's name, even if he had to ask Sir Niebar to devote the secret matters office entirely to that purpose. When one finds the vital spot in a hitherto mysterious opponent, one does not humbly petition for the right to drive in the knife.

But there was Sir Niebar coming up the beach, surrounded by guards, and with Tarothin dropping away from the rear of the procession to join Lujimar in healing the two fighters and keeping the prisoner alive. Pirvan sent some of his own guards to guard the healers' backs. There had to be many in the crowd ready to use steel on the Servants, for vengeance or to silence them.

Then came a long, weary time of reporting to Sir Niebar just what had happened, dividing the report into what Pirvan had seen and what he suspected. Sir Niebar was full of praise and also of questions, and asked some of them of Haimya and even of Fulvura.

By the time Sir Niebar was done, Torvik was on a litter, bound on the shoulders of *Red Elf*'s folk to a boat and his own cabin. The dead Servants had been removed with the rest of the offal and the prisoners healed and bound. Rynthala had taken command of Darin's care, and Zeskuk was deep in a conversation with Lujimar that Pirvan would have given ten years off his life to overhear, if he'd thought there was any hope at all.

Mirraleen, however, seemed to have utterly vanished.

* * * * *

Wilthur the Brown raged.

Certain highly-placed servants of the kingpriest did the same. There was no silence anywhere near them, that night off Suivinari.

Out to sea, five Dimernesti crouched low on a rock, waiting for a sixth to swim into view. They knew that she was alive; they could wish that they knew when she was coming.

Deep within the waters, Zeboim's thoughts moved like the currents. The goddess was everywhere, except when she was nowhere, or (as very rarely) in her turtle form.

Habbakuk listened to those thoughts of Zeboim's, but found nothing in them to disturb him. Lady Revella might have heard Zeboim, too, except that she was too deeply asleep.

Far to the south, Horimpsot Elderdrake scrambled up the wall of Tirabot Manor and almost fell into Shumeen's arms.

"You must bathe before we bring your news to the young lord," she said. "You look as if you had crawled all the way, most of it through a midden pit."

"I ran most of the way," the other kender said. "But I suppose I didn't watch where I was going. My uncle—the one on the Rootslicer side—no, there were two, but it was one of them—he always said hurrying too much ends up making you slower in the end."

"I thank your uncles for saying it," Shumeen snapped. "I would thank them more if they had been able to make you listen. Now get out of those clothes before I slice them off you with a dagger, and if I take some of your hide with them it will be no more than you deserve!"

Chapter 16

Torvik slept the sleep of exhaustion until nearly dawn. He then awoke under the ministrations of Beeyona, whom Yavanna had escorted over from *Kingfisher's Claw* on Sorraz's orders. He awoke fully when he learned that Mirraleen had disappeared. Indeed, he leaped out of bed and began to dress himself. Beeyona finally told him that if he ran wild after Mirraleen, she would have to put him to sleep again. This time she, rather than nature, would say when he awoke.

"But something could have happened to her!" Torvik said.

"There are as many sea otters in sight as ever," Beeyona said. "This would not be so if a Dimernesti had come to harm."

"There are also as many who hate peace as ever," Torvik replied.

"Unfortunately, this is also true," Beeyona said, emptying two phials into a wooden bowl and stirring the resulting mixture with her thumb. "But I am not one of them, for all that you look at me as if I were."

"I beg your pardon, Beeyona," Torvik said. "But understand that the peace is fragile. Not all of those who attacked us last night have been taken—"

"This is true, and known to all," Beeyona said, licking her thumb to test the mixture. "It is even the subject of a proclamation, signed by Sir Niebar, Gildas Aurhinius, Zeskuk, and Andrys Puhrad. It appoints Sir Pirvan of Tirabot 'War Chief of the Fleet Off Suivinari,' and promises a pardon to all of your abductors who submit peacefully and confess fully within two days. After that they are outlaws, and any man or minotaur may slay them on sight."

The proclamation was encouraging news, if true, and Beeyona was as likely to lie in such a matter as a ship made of iron was to float. Torvik still made one last thrust.

"Then all the more reason to find Mirraleen," he said. "She has a better memory for faces than I do."

"Truly. It took you three weeks to stop calling me 'Berylla.' But when she wishes to be found, she will be. Until then you cannot make her well by making yourself sick, or bring her here by going everywhere else. Drink this."

An order from the kingpriest would have had less force, one from a god hardly more. Torvik drank.

It did not taste like something stirred by someone's thumb. Indeed, Torvik was not sure what it tasted like.

He was still wondering when his eyes grew heavy and his breathing slow. His last memory was of wanting to laugh at how neatly Beeyona had tricked him.

*　*　*　*　*

A summer-hot day at Tirabot Manor was coming to an end with the heat fleeing before a howling gale. Rain hammered on the shutters of Gerik's chambers, nearly loud enough to drown out the thunder. The lightning was so bright that it crept in around the edge of the shutters, outshining the candles hanging above the table and rising from its center.

"I still call it a bad idea, both you and Bertsa going to burn the supplies," Grimsoar One-Eye said. "We've not only got the manor to defend now, we've the villagers—and anybody else who wants to go—to get across the border into Solamnia. That's one more caravan, maybe two. We've work for two captains here. I may be two men in bulk, but not two captains in skill. Nor can I be in two places at once."

"You're one good, trustworthy captain," Gerik said. "If we can make our enemies stumble before they attack, one will be enough. If we do not, twenty will be too few."

"Then send Bertsa and stay yourself," Grimsoar said. "With you here, attacking the manor is attacking a knight's blood and property, if not the knight himself."

"If House Dirivan cared about law, they would not have lent themselves to the kingpriest's schemes," Wylum said. "Nothing will keep their troops from the manor, save the coming of those Solamnics Dargaard Keep was supposed to be sending." Her tone said that she expected them to come when snow fell on Midsummer Eve.

"But the sell-swords they have hired are a weak spot," she continued. "We must first destroy the supplies the hirelings trust to make their work easy. Then, when they have grown reluctant, Gerik and I must both play on their fears of scant reward and dire punishment. Gerik has the right. I know sell-swords' law. I may even know some of the captains."

Her tone implied that under other circumstances, she would not have admitted knowing any sell-sword who would stoop so low as to serve House Dirivan.

Grimsoar growled deep in his throat, like a bear feeding on salmon too long dead. Serafina patted his hand and said, "Do not doubt yourself, my love. Who was it who, single-handed, saved the village?"

"And who afterward had to be saved by a girl not yet twelve?" Grimsoar muttered. "A fine captain he was."

Rubina's escapade was clearly still a sore point with the old sailor. Gerik tapped on the table with his signet ring.

"It must be as we have planned it," he said. "Unless the Solamnics ride up to the gate before sunset, and even then I may ask some of them to join us as witnesses.

"But now, there is something else. It would be proper and just to give Lady Ellysta betrothal rights over me and mine, even had I not called her 'my lady' with half a hundred witnesses. I am of age, and so is she. She has no kin, and none of mine of lawful age would disapprove. Will you all be witnesses to our betrothal oaths?"

If anyone at the table wished to be elsewhere, they were not bold enough to say so. Gerik rose, walked to Ellysta's chair, knelt beside her and said, "My—my lady. this betrothal is my wish, more than anything ever has been. Is it your wish also?"

Ellysta put her hands on Gerik's shoulders. "With all my heart," she whispered.

She rose. "I, Ellysta, of lawful age and birth, here under the roof of just folk and the sky of the true gods—"

For a moment, thunder rolled so that the sky seemed about to be falling on the roof, gods and all. Ellysta tightened her grip on Gerik.

"—in the presence of honest witnesses, declare that I am in my eyes and the eyes of the gods, the betrothed wife of Gerik of Tirabot, with all the duties and rights belonging to that office, and may I meanly perish if foresworn."

It was a short form of one of the standard betrothal oaths, and Gerik noted that Ellysta had put "duties" before "rights," instead of the way his mother would surely have preferred. However, "rights" had little meaning in a battle to the death, and they had no time for long oaths.

At least the betrothal had long since been consummated. That gave Ellysta even more rights than she perhaps realized, including making any child she might bear entirely legitimate.

Now, if the rain would just stop before the roads turned to swamps—or else go on until it washed away the enemy's supply tent and all its contents, and maybe send a few-score sell-swords bobbing downstream after it. . . .

* * * * *

Torvik awoke to see ruddy sunset light filling his cabin. He also awoke to hear a faint scraping close to his ear.

He had just remembered that one of the cabin ports lay

there when the port flew open. It nearly hit him on the head. In avoiding it Torvik rolled out of his bunk. So he was on the floor, reaching for steel he was not wearing, when Mirraleen crawled in through the port.

She plucked a splinter of wood from under one finger nail, then swung her feet onto the floor, bent over, and began wringing out her hair. More water dripped from her impartially onto the floor and the bunk. Apart from the water and her old dagger on a new belt, of shells linked together with bronze wire, she wore nothing.

Torvik was annoyed briefly, that she would spend so much time grooming herself before explaining her return from the dead. Then he remembered his mother's words, "Even the fiercest woman will groom herself when she is uneasy. Or when she wants to look her best for her chosen man. In that, we are a trifle like cats."

What moved Mirraleen now? Torvik's heart was not to his throat; indeed, he could not have said precisely where it was. It did seem to be beating faster.

"Welcome aboard, dear friend," he said at last. "I did no command a search for you, because I thought you migh have reasons for hiding."

"Also, because you wanted to search for me yourself," Mirraleen said. She unhooked two links of the bronze wire and hung the belt of shells on a peg, then stood up. "It is as well. I wanted to come to you with none knowing."

At that moment, Torvik knew that he would someday tell his sons: "Remember, desire can make the nimbles tongue turn to stone." Certainly his had.

Mirraleen stepped close, then closer still, and kissed him. Her lips tasted of honey and salt, and of something that Torvik could only compare to a summer meadow somehow blooming under the sea, with fish browsing on kelp instead of sheep on the fresh grass.

His arms took on a life of their own. He drew Mirraleen tightly against him, without caring whether either could breathe. He was dimly aware of her hands moving, until he was clad as she.

Then, for a long time, he did not know—or care—where

he was or who he was or even if he was a person separate from Mirraleen.

* * * * *

Wilthur the Brown had learned the spell he was now using under the name of the Eye of Uchuno. Whether it still deserved that name, the mage did not know. Certainly Uchuno himself (a Red Robe) would have disapproved of Wilthur's use of this scrying magic, if Uchuno had not been dead for five centuries.

Wilthur, however, was alive. So were a good dozen or more of those who had been led by the Servants of Silence in the abduction of Torvik. Abandoned by their masters, they had fled inland, preferring death amid the magical monsters to what they suspected awaited them in the fleet.

They would have been right, had the mage not unleashed the Eye of Uchuno. The spell needed a large amount of melted volcanic glass as its material element, but in Wilthur's new home that was as abundant as moss in a forest. Sent abroad, it took the form of a gigantic red eye that could blaze with all-consuming fire when its master wished to cease scrying and feed.

Through the Eye Wilthur could feed on many things. Just now he wished to feed on the terror of the man whom the Eye was pursuing. The man had spent all of the previous night and all of today stumbling ever higher on the Green Mountain. Sometimes he wondered why neither animals nor plants attacked him, and once he halted and tried to drink at a stream.

Wilthur promptly turned the stream boiling hot. The man ran off like a mad thing, and his cries nearly warned the minotaurs in their outpost. But there were only five of them now, and they wisely did not step outside Lujimar's warding spell. They had arms and food in plenty to stand off any material attack, or so they thought. Their time would come. Meanwhile, it was the time of the pursued man.

He was a lean, scant-bearded fellow, who from his balding pate had to be older than he seemed. But he ran well, and now that he saw the cliff at his back, he seemed ready to turn and fight.

It would be a pathetic spectacle when he did, one that Wilthur intended to prolong as much as possible. He sought fear now, as some men sought ecstasy.

With a few syllables and a wave of his lesser staff, Wilthur brought a faint crimson glow to the crystal sphere hanging from the ceiling. It was now ready to receive, bind, and preserve the man's fear as a root cellar preserves a sack of turnips in the winter.

Some of Wilthur's more potent spells needed fear, just as others needed blood—in amounts that no necromancer would have countenanced for a moment. But the opinions of others had not bound Wilthur even before he came to Suivinari Island, and still less here.

On Suivinari, he was far more than man, more even than mage. Not yet a god, that he knew, but within his own borders (both physical and magical) all but immune to the gods' attacks.

A good first step.

The Eye began spinning a web of fire around the man, giving pain to lend savor to the fear. The man drew his knife—and the fire melted it in his hand before he could have hoped to slay himself.

Biting his lip against the pain of his charred hand, the man strode toward the cliff, pushing his way through the web of fire as if it were gossamer. Wilthur readied a further tightening of the web, to melt the rock under the man's feet and hold him in place.

Then the ground quivered. It was no more violent than the quivering of a crystal glass touched by a spoon. But the quivering found a fault in the cliff. The whole face of rock, higher than the mast of the tallest ship, peeled away, and the man went with it.

The last sensation Wilthur had from the man was relief, mingled with joy at going to meet his long-dead wife again. Somehow a ghastly death had become a welcome boon. It was no work of his, Wilthur knew. And he doubted that the answer lay on the island.

But if the earthquake came from somewhere else, how had it entered the island's defenses?

He was ready to send the Eye scrying farther afield, when the crystal globe, ready for the dead man's fear, dropped from the ceiling. The table was stone; the crystal shattered. Wilthur saw blood start from a cut on the back of his hand, drop onto the table, and vanish as if it had fallen on sand.

The mage was glad that no other crystal spheres were ready. Otherwise one might have sucked in and held ready his own fear.

* * * * *

Torvik thought that a god might have felt as he did, if the god had taken human shape and joined with one like Mirraleen—if there were any like Mirraleen. The god would also find something missing from his life afterward, as Torvik knew he would find missing from his.

The difference, the sailor thought, was in his favor. He would not have eternity to miss Mirraleen. A mere fifty or sixty years, and he and his memories would be dust, while she still swam sleek and fair through the seas of Krynn.

This hardly worried him now. Indeed, very little could worry anyone in Mirraleen's arms. But something was worrying Mirraleen. She had stiffened in his embrace, then slipped entirely out of it. With the silence of a spirit, she padded across the cabin and opened the port by which she had entered.

Torvik briefly contemplated her, as fair in some ways from behind as she was in other ways from in front. Then he decided that what made her this uneasy might have to do with the sea—and he was still *Red Elf*'s captain.

There was only room for one at the port, and when Mirraleen made way for Torvik, he did not know what he expected to see. Storms, monsters, portents, or Dimernesti swimming openly in their elven form among the ships?

Instead he saw only gleaming slack tidewater, the loom of the island with the two peaks only just falling into shadow, and the lights coming on in the ships. Nothing he had not seen for a score of nights before this.

"Can you hear it?" Mirraleen said.

"Hear what?"

"The—the cry of the mountains, and the sea calling back."

Torvik knew that Mirraleen commanded magic. How else would she have healed herself of the bruises from her beating at the hands of the Servants of Silence? But this went beyond what he was ready to believe.

Or rather, would have been ready to believe before he came to Suivinari for the second time.

He still saw and heard nothing, however. He stepped back from the port and put an arm around Mirraleen, thinking to lead her back to the bunk. There was no such thing as "all passion spent" with Mirraleen.

Then the night was riven by fire, spreading out from the island across the water, lighting up the fleets as all three moons together could not have done. It looked as if a slit had opened in the flank of the Smoker, allowing mortal eyes to see the forges of the Abyss behind it. In the light Mirraleen's skin took on the same hue as her hair.

Torvik also welcomed the glow. It hid the sudden pallor of his skin, as he realized just how close the gods might be—and other powers as well, less friendly to men.

* * * * *

Drums thudded and the sixteen sailors on the line hauled away. It was usually twelve on the line to hoist a fleet leader aboard, but this fleet leader was a minotaur. Even Thenvor could not have been more eloquent than Pirvan in reminding the sailors what would happen to them if any "accident" befell Zeskuk.

Pirvan stood facing the gangway of *Shield of Virtue*, just aft of the mainmast. Flanking him were Gildas Aurhinius and Sir Niebar, who really did not look fit to be out of bed but was determined to second Pirvan if he died for it.

Those who would flank Zeskuk were already standing facing Pirvan and his companions. They were Lujimar and

Juiksum, and the priest looked ill at ease. Pirvan knew some of the reasons for that and suspected more.

Standing side by side, farther aft, were Fulvura and Sir Darin. Both were fully armed, but for once their role actually matched their name. They were to observe this ceremony of welcoming Zeskuk aboard the Istaran flagship.

Behind the observers stood Sir Hawkbrother and a young Istaran captain, at the head of a dozen guards drawn equally from Vuinlod, Istar, and the Solamnics. Torvik's sister Chuina was one of the dozen. The meeting would not only be observed, it would be guarded.

Not that the meeting would serve much purpose, unless or until Torvik's newly-revealed connection with the Dimernesti offered an equally new way of attacking the island. Torvik had still said nothing, so while Pirvan trusted Jemar's son as much as he could trust anyone, that trust could not be evidence of coming victory.

But Zeskuk had asked to be received aboard *Shield of Virtue*, if only to repay the humans for their coming aboard *Cleaver* for the first meeting. It was a matter of honor—and with suspicions still rife and spies probably not yet all run to ground (or fled to sea), no matter of honor could be handled too delicately.

The drums reached a crescendo. Zeskuk in his chair rose above the railing. The sailors shifted their footing and hauled away again. The chair swung inward. In the lanterns' glow, Zeskuk looked somehow shrunken, and as pale as a minotaur could.

That was not entirely a trick of the light. Lujimar had healed his outward injuries, but Zeskuk had refused to be abed long enough for the balance of blood and other humors to restore itself naturally, or to submit to the exhausting spells that would speed that healing.

Darin would have done the same, out of honor. But once released from Lujimar's hands, he was under the care of Tarothin and Rynthala. They would not take no for an answer when it came to completely healing him. So Darin looked ready to fight any minotaur or any three humans on Krynn.

It was in the last moment before Zeskuk touched the deck that the fire blazed on the flank of the Smoker.

True to their discipline (or fear of Pirvan) the sailors did not flinch. They set Zeskuk down as gently as a baby into its cradle or an egg into straw, then they all rushed to the side, staring and pointing. A mate finally outbellowed a minotaur, driving all the sailors back to their post by the aftercastle.

Even then, Pirvan overheard mutterings.

"Reorx's forge is working," one man said.

Another uttered an obscenity, coupled with the name of the dwarf's blacksmith god.

"*Hunh*," a third man grunted. "I'll take Reorx seriously. The dwarves do."

"You mean you take dwarves seriously?" That sounded like the second man.

Yet another man said, "This is dwarf-work you'd better take seriously, before it's between your ribs. Where I come from, speaking against the dwarves is bad luck, worse than spitting into the wind."

The threatened man made no reply. Now Pirvan led his companions to Zeskuk, and all turned toward the land.

"That is no natural volcanic fire," Lujimar said.

Pirvan wondered if all clerics of every folk had to study how to utter meaningless profundities. From Zeskuk's expression, he thought the same.

"You may do anything you wish, to learn the nature of that fire," Zeskuk said. "Then tell us what it is, not what it is not."

"Anything?" Pirvan would have sworn he heard almost youthful anticipation in Lujimar's age-deepened voice.

"Almost anything," Zeskuk said, then added what sounded like prohibitions, in the minotaur speech, using words Pirvan did not understand. He wished Darin were within hearing—but then Darin might feel that it would be dishonorable to translate.

The simplicity of rejecting all who were not like oneself was very real and appealing, Pirvan knew. So was drinking oneself into madness and wrecking everything in one's path. Some temptations were harmless; hatred was not one of them.

The fire now had sea, island, and fleets so brightly illuminated that one could have read a scroll with ease. Pirvan saw Lujimar fumbling in the pouches on the vest he wore over his robes, with a look also universal to priests: the look of one who needed paper, pen, and ink, but had forgotten where he put them.

Pirvan snapped his fingers at a sailor and ordered, "My cabin, and hurry. Bring back writing materials—everything you find. Lujimar needs them." The sailor gaped, thought better of saying anything, and ran off.

By the time the sailor returned, the fire on the Smoker was fading, like hot coals turning dark under a light rain. Pirvan wondered if the fire was natural after all, but did not dare ask Lujimar.

The minotaur was far too busy asking questions of everyone within hearing, and writing down every answer, whether they made sense or not.

* * * * *

As the blazing light from the Smoker slowly died, Torvik noted that Mirraleen's skin now seemed to be glowing. It was as if she had soaked up the light like a sponge, and now poured it back like phosphorescent seaweed.

As if by their own will, Torvik's hands moved, to find comfortable places on Mirraleen's skin. She looked down and laughed.

"My hands were cold," Torvik said. "This is an uncanny night."

"So it is," she said. "But I can warm more of you than your hands." She lowered her mouth as he raised his, and for some time they were occupied warming each other.

For some while after that, they slept. A long while, because when Torvik awoke, the first light of dawn was turning the eastern horizon a translucent green.

Mirraleen, who had fallen asleep in his arms, was crouched on the deck, garbed again in her belt and knife, and contemplating an unrolled chart. Torvik wondered how she had come by it, then saw the picked lock on the chest opposite the bunk.

"I need the human name for what we—I—call Quillfish Lair Reef," she said. "It is just under two leagues to the southeast of the Smoker's Tail, in a straight line. It's hard to recognize unless the wind is from the south, when there's surf over it, but—"

Torvik sat down beside Mirraleen and they both studied the chart. It was noticeably lighter outside when they finally agreed that Quillfish Lair Reef was the same as the one humans called Yuon's Woe.

"Be there at sunset tonight," she said. "Yourself, and enough trustworthy captains to lead—oh, a hundred picked fighters. You need not bring all the fighters, of course."

Torvik doubted that any trustworthy captain would promise his people's service without letting the people see for themselves what was afoot. But he would face that problem when he knew whether or not it would be one.

At last Mirraleen uncoiled gracefully and kissed Torvik, a gentle brushing of lips that seemed to content both of them. Then she squeezed through the port and plunged into the sea.

Watching after her, Torvik saw one arm raised in farewell. Then she was gone into the morning calm, and he turned back into his cabin, to face the work of raising a band of fighters ready to befriend Dimernesti, and with those friends slip into a mage's lair.

Chapter 17

It would have been as well to ride out against the enemy's supplies, on the very night of the betrothal. The weather argued eloquently for delay.

"The roads will be too muddy for horses and just barely too solid for boats," Bertsa Wylum said. "Also, nothing will catch fire, or go on burning if we can set it alight to begin with."

"The sentries will all be hiding with hot cider and warm peasant girls," Elderdrake put in. "We could surprise them much more easily tonight than tomorrow."

"If we could find them at all, maybe," Gerik said. "But remember that mounted humans can't move as silently as kender. Don't take that as permission to go off and try to do the work yourself, either," he added, as a familiar smile crept across the kender's sharp features.

"Oh, I swear to do nothing that you would not do were our positions the other way around," Elderdrake said. He started to swear by both the human and kender names of the true gods. Gerik let him run through all the ones whom kender could lawfully swear by, while thinking that Elderdrake's oath might not be as confining as one could wish.

Were a kender to tell him to sit and wait while enemies

gathered, bent on gorging themselves on the blood of those he loved, he might find some excuses for doing something else. But all the kender conducted themselves properly, and now it was the next night, and Gerik of Tirabot was walking downstairs from his chambers to ride out.

In the courtyard outside, he could hear the horses already stamping restlessly. It had seemed a windless, overcast night when he looked out the window, rising from bed and Ellysta's last embrace.

She walked down the stairs behind him, wearing her traveling garb and now hung about with as many pouches and bottles as Serafina. She also openly wore two daggers, and said she had others hidden in various places.

"You are the only one who will ever learn those places, without having one of the knives thrust into you," she had said, grinning. It was a relief to him that she no longer talked of fleeing so as to draw the wrath of Tirabot's enemies after her. It was not a relief to suspect that nothing could now turn that wrath aside.

Where were the promised Solamnics? Not even a letter from them had come, although to be sure they might not be willing to use the ciphers for Gerik. So their letters might have gone astray or been read, and ambushes or laws or both placed in their path. There were any number of places where even a band sent from the Keeps could vanish without a trace sufficient to raise suspicion in anyone, and enough laws for a shrewd counselor to cheat Takhisis out of her rule in the Abyss.

Gerik had written of this, in cipher, to his father. He only hoped he still had a father to receive the letter. The fleet could not have met disaster; that word would have flown about the land as if on dragon's wings. But one knight more or less could be another matter.

Time, once more, to put away fears. Gerik walked out into the courtyard, Ellysta now beside him, matching stride with him, her hand on his arm. Some of the fighters started to raise a cheer; Bertsa Wylum silenced them with a furious gesture.

He turned to Ellysta and their lips met without thought. This time the cheers could not be silenced. Even Wylum smiled.

"All that we need for you to be something out of a hero tale is a garland of flowers for me to put about your neck," Ellysta said.

"That, and nobody dying, or at least those who die, departing without pain or fear," Gerik said. He could not force out of his memories the faces of the men who had died the Night of the Runaway Horses, even if they were enemies.

"We'll find that rose garden," Ellysta said softly. "We will find it, and there we can forget death."

If he kissed her or even spoke to her again, Gerik knew he would fumble his leap into the saddle. To avoid that evil omen, he turned away, slapped his hands down on the bow of the saddle, and vaulted high.

His horse made a rude noise that seemed to sum up the complaint of all horses against all men who wearied them with fine gestures. But Gerik also felt his mount as taut as his own nerves, with readiness to go.

The gate opened with scarcely a murmur from well-oiled hinges. Gerik bent low and whispered in his mount's ear, and man and horse together broke into a trot toward the gateway.

*　*　*　*　*

Torvik was quickly proved right in his suspicions that few good captains would come without bringing at least some of the men they might be leading the gods knew where. Mirraleen also knew, but everyone seemed to be painfully cautious about mentioning her name in Torvik's presence.

Every fighter and sailor aboard *Red Elf* wanted to sail to the reef. So did all of Chuina's archers. So did two captains and twenty fighters from Vuinlod, who called themselves volunteers but whom Torvik suspected were carefully chosen by Gildas Aurhinius.

There was a good band of the most seasoned fighters among the sea barbarians, come forward to follow Jemar the Fair's children in honor of their father. There was a smaller band of Karthayans. There were more folk from *Kingfisher's Claw* that Sorraz the Harpooner was happy to see go, with Yavanna at their head and Beeyona prepared to heal their wounds.

There were even a few from Istar, whether to garner for their city a share of whatever glory this enterprise might bring or to spy on it, Torvik did not know. He would not refuse them, however. They would be too badly outnumbered to cause trouble even if they wished it.

The minotaurs did not send fighters, but they sent a boatload of salt provisions and another, smaller boatload full of bottled healing potions. The last came with a note from Lujimar, hoping that at the end of the battle Torvik would have a name equal to what his parents had gained in the battle of *Golden Cup*.

So *Red Elf* carried nearly two hundred armed fighters and sailors when she dropped anchor off Quillfish Lair Reef, and waited for the coming of the Dimernesti.

* * * * *

Gerik had not expected any kender to ride with him tonight except Elderdrake, so he was surprised, and at first less than pleased, when six more kender slipped out of the woods into the road, halting the advance with a request to accompany the riders.

He was not, however, entirely surprised to discover that one of them was the kender priest of Branchala, whose gifts to Elderdrake lay behind the Night of the Runaway Horses. Or at least Elderdrake assured him that the robed kender was the priest, and the other five just as trustworthy in fighting if not in magic.

The priest's five companions were roughly clad for kender, well armed (two daggers at least, plus a chapak or hoopak), and almost as grim as dwarves. The priest wore a robe of fine linen and sandals of stamped leather. He carried nothing except his staff, and wore an unvaryingly polite smile.

None of the newly-come kender would give their names, but that hardly mattered when it became plain that they would obey no one but the priest. It did matter that the priest would not give his name either, but at least there was a solution for that problem.

The priest was the only bald kender short of old age whom Gerik had ever seen. He had luxuriant sideburns and a long plait hanging below his shoulder blades, but from just above the ears he had no more hair than the new granite blocks in the walls of Tirabot Manor.

So Gerik named the priest "The Shorn One," and so addressed him. It was, after all, a politer name than "Baldy," and Gerik suspected that politeness to this priest would be wise. He might not be carrying any visible magicworking materials besides his staff, but if he was a master of practical jokes as lethal as the allergy spell, he probably did not need them.

The kender climbed onto various horses, behind various uneasy riders (the horses seemed to take the kender in stride). With emphatic gestures they refused to be tied on, so Bertsa Wylum declared that the march would not stop to pick up the fallen. It might not even slow to avoid trampling them if they fell off at the wrong time.

For all the response this warning drew from the kender, Wylum might as well have spoken in Old Ergothian. Gerik put his band into motion again, hoping that he still had enemies only to his front.

* * * * *

Medlessarn the Silent must have found a deep hole in the reef, then swum furiously toward the surface. When he broached, he soared from the water until his toes barely touched the surface before plunging back cleanly. When he rose again, Mirraleen thought she heard an approving chorus of shouts and whistles from *Red Elf*.

The newcomer Dimernesti on the rock beside her, whose name she could not recall for now, looked much less agreeable. "Showoff," he muttered. "And from where did he take the name 'Silent'? He hasn't been silent since we gathered at noon."

Medlessarn, Mirraleen thought, was quite probably and quite simply nervous. She had labored hard to make it clear that while she had been here at Suivinari for many years as the Red Walker, he was her master in the knowledge of war. Which meant that he led, however reluctantly, and however much in need of her knowledge of the island and of the assembled humans and minotaurs.

The plain truth was that she did not know war. It was equally true that this was of her own will, and she would have been far happier if Wilthur the Brown had never come to Suivinari. But he had, and at least the human fleet coming to smite him had brought with it Torvik Jemarsson, so she had something to take with her from this war, however she fared afterward.

Also, even those of the shallows-dwellers who grumbled about Medlessarn would accept his leadership. Several of the newcomers would have fought her to the death had she claimed the first place, and in so doing ruined any hope of further Dimernesti aid for the humans. She still hoped that Medlessarn's accent in Common did not make him a figure of fun to the humans. Few warriors will follow a leader who makes them smile the moment he speaks.

"Greetings, brothers and sisters in this battle for all our folk," Medlessarn began. At least his choice of words was flawless. He still had such a strong flavor of Old Kagonesti in his accent that Mirraleen heard murmurs and some laughter from the ship.

"Silence!" from the foredeck. That had to be Torvik. Nobody else could have such a young voice and so much authority. Proof of that authority: when he commanded silence, he won it.

Medlessarn went on to explain how Dimernesti and humans working together could penetrate deep within the mountain called the Smoker—

"Into the volcano?" several cried.

Medlessarn continued without needing Torvik to command silence. "Through the passages where the sea flows deep within the mountain. Those passages give us swift entry to the mage's lair. Attacked from the rear and the front at once, his fate is sure."

"What about that cursed thing that munches minotaurs?" somebody asked, to a chorus of agreement.

"What about it?" Medlessarn replied. Mirraleen smiled and her hands told him that he was doing splendid work.

"What about it?" he said again, so quietly that a hush fell on the sea as everyone aboard *Red Elf* strained their ears to listen. "It is a monstrosity. Not even Wilthur can trust it, and the gods hate it. It will have no friends when it is faced by true warriors, of the shallows-dwellers, the humans and other dry—other land-dwelling folk, aided by true magic worked by wizards of honor. Without friends, not even Wilthur's Creation can prevail."

Everyone seemed so taken by this prophecy of victory that no one asked how many of them would be alive to celebrate it. But then that was not a question warriors were supposed to ask themselves on the eve of battle. Another reason, thought Mirraleen, that she was not much of a warrior.

Medlessarn continued, describing how each band must have at least one captain who knew the intricacies of the passages into the Smoker, past the Creation, and upward to Wilthur's lair. Torvik had already taken this knowledge into his memory, through the true magic of the shallows-dwellers. Who would be next?

A slim figure leaped onto the railing of *Red Elf*, tossed something to a friend, then plunged gracefully into the sea. When Mirraleen saw that the friend was holding up a bow and quiver, she suspected who was coming. When she saw a female version of Torvik climb out of the sea and wade toward the rocks, she knew she faced Torvik's sister Chuina.

Before she could greet the young archer, Mirraleen saw a scuffle on deck. Someone else went over the side, but not diving gracefully. He landed sprawling, and floundered about until someone threw a rope and hauled him back aboard.

"What was that all about?" the grumbling sea-elf said. His name came back to Mirraleen. "Kuyomolan—!" she snapped.

Chuina grinned. Her grin, also, was a near-twin of her brother's. "My guess is, one fellow who's been rattling on about Torvik and his elven lady. He said something like, 'a taste that runs in the family, I see,' and one of my archers threw him overboard. As long as he's not hurt, we've no need to fear," she said.

"Speak for yourself," Kuyomolan said. "Can we trust foul-wits like that at our backs? And I see no minotaurs aboard that barge."

"My brother's ship is not a barge, minotaurs do not swim well through narrow passages, and I will never stab you in the back," Chuina said. "But I may take you on face-to-face, if you blather like that again."

Kuyomolan was too stunned to reply, which was as well. An idea had just leaped into Mirraleen's mind like a porpoise leaping into the air. She turned Chuina around and whispered into her ear. The grin stayed on Chuina's face as she listened. It broadened as Mirraleen continued.

By the time the Dimernesti was finished, Chuina was laughing. They both turned and watched fighters scramble down into a boat alongside *Red Elf*.

"Better send that boat off quick, once the captains are here," Chuina said. "Torvik'll have to write a note too, not just you. Darin and Rynthala see far and think deep, but they don't know you and they hardly know me."

Mirraleen nodded. She could not help noticing that Medlessarn had his eyes firmly fixed on Chuina, whose wet garments hugged her skin tightly.

Would that rude jester aboard *Red Elf* be so far wrong, if Medlessarn and Chuina were much in each other's company? Perhaps—and there lay yet another reason for the message to Sir Darin and his lady.

* * * * *

Gerik was only two places behind the lead when his band rode into a clearing already held by an enemy patrol.

This saved his life, for one of the others was alert and skilled with a crossbow. The bolt took a Tirabot fighter in the throat, tumbling her from the saddle without a cry. Only the thud of her fall marked her passing from the band's ranks.

Before her mount could panic at the loss of its rider, the Shorn One leaped down from behind Gerik. He raised his staff and tapped the horse lightly across the throat.

Instead of frightened neighing, the horse seemed to utter a bawdy chuckle. A second crossbow went *spung!*, but such unnatural sounds from a horse put off the archer's aim. The bolt sank deep into a tree well above Gerik's head.

Then Gerik spurred his horse forward, taking the lead, drawing his sword as he did. His body did all that it was trained to do without any commands from his wits, which had their own work. He had planned to dismount and slip the last mile or so to the supplies on foot, but this early fight would mean riding in all the way.

Arrows whistled, horses and men screamed, and suddenly Gerik's left flank was free of mounted enemies. One man was still on his feet, but a kender's bollik sailed out of the darkness and three lead-weighted thongs wrapped the man's legs into a single unsteady support. He toppled over, and a kender tapped him firmly on the jaw so that he stopped moving.

Gerik was relieved to see the kender's mercy. Kender fighting as much as they had in defense of Tirabot Manor was unusual in itself. Kender turning bloodthirsty would unsettle the mind of Paladine himself!

To Gerik's right, the enemy patrol was riding or running off down the nearest path. The Shorn One raised his staff and fire flared at its tip. The fire took flight, a ball the size of a kender's fist, racing down the path after the fugitives. Gerik's stomach churned, as he took back his thoughts about kender and blood.

Instead of scything down the fleeing enemies, however, the fireball bounced off a tree, hit the ground, bounced again to hit a branch beyond the men, bounced yet one more time to strike a very high branch and plunge vertically among the men, to bounce and emerge *again*—

The fugitives stopped, as if the fireball was weaving a

cage of iron bars around them.

"That will halt them and dazzle them," the Shorn One said, breaking his silence for the first time. "Now we must ride on swiftly, so that the guards will only be frightened, not alert, when we come.

"Oh, I almost forgot. Those fellows must not hear us ride off, either." The Shorn One raised his staff again, this time pointing it at the kender who was retrieving his hoopak.

The hoopak leaped into the air and sailed off the same way as the fireball, so fast that its owner nearly went with it. He threw a black look at the Shorn One, which faded to a frown, and that turned into a smile as he saw his hoopak begin to whirl in the air, just short of where the bouncing fireball still wove its cage around the men.

A hoopak whirled by ordinary kender muscles was a formidable bull-roarer. This magic-driven one filled the night and the forest with a cry like a city of minotaurs gone mad. Gerik turned his horse, but let Bertsa Wylum and one of her scouts take the lead, for they knew the rest of the way better than he did. Then he spurred his mount to keep up with them.

It was, he decided, just as well that kender did not add bloodlust to their ingenuity. Then even the minotaurs and the Silvanesti might find that they had other rivals than the human ones, for the mastery of Krynn.

Chapter 18

There wasn't room on the trail for all the riders to outpace the warning the fight with the patrol had given. So Bertsa Wylum picked six riders who knew the ground and told them to cut across country.

"Get close enough to let the sentries see you, then retreat to draw them off," she said. "When you've lost them, cut through the woods to the Mine Road. We'll retreat that way and pick you up as we come."

Gerik signaled to Wylum to ride close.

"They'll have a better chance with you leading them," he said, "and you won't miss any of the serious fighting."

"I might miss sell-swords who will listen to me."

"You might also find them more easily," Gerik said. "You certainly won't find me complaining about being left alone."

"I might find your parents having a word or two on the matter."

"When they return, and find out, and we are all alive to hear what they say, *then* you can worry."

Wylum's smile told Gerik how much desire and duty had been clashing. She turned her mount, fell in at the rear of the six, but had worked her way up to the head before they vanished in the darkness.

Left alone at the head of twelve humans and six kender, Gerik ordered everyone to rein back to a trot. The ground here was well drained; it was soft from the rain, rather than muddy. Wet branches still slapped faces, and in the distance they could hear the enspelled hoopak still bellowing.

If Gerik had allowed himself to fear getting lost, that fear would have ended moments later. From ahead the shouts of fifty men and the clashing of twice that many weapons burst through the trees.

Gerik heard soft laughter behind him. Without turning he muttered, "Your doing?"

"A simple, quick illusion spell," the Shorn One chuckled. "There's another camp between us and the supplies, but it should be empty before we come through it. Nobody will be hurt, though. Not unless they are too careless to have any right to name themselves sell-swords."

The camp lay barely half a mile farther down the trail. It was indeed empty of human life when Gerik led his people into the clearing, but not for long. As he signaled for a new advance, a pack train came out of the trees on the far side of the clearing, harness jingling and creaking and guards prodding their mules and horses with cracking whips and shouts.

Indeed, they were so intent on their work that it was a moment before they realized that the camp was empty. By then, Gerik had spread out his riders and ordered the charge.

Enemy riders appeared as the charge went home and Gerik's fighters sliced through the pack train in half a dozen places. Gerik himself suddenly found that he was fighting two mounted swordsmen, while a man on foot with a spear tried to get between the swordsmen and join the fight.

It was Gerik's first time at real heavy cavalry fighting, a thought that lingered in his mind for all of about two heartbeats. After that he was too busy parrying and slashing, wishing he had a shield, and hoping that the spearman would be trampled by one of his own allies before he could bring down Gerik's mount.

Tonight, he had warned his people, they might not have the luxury of bringing out their wounded. He hoped none would sacrifice themselves trying to make an exception for him.

One of Gerik's people rode up behind one enemy and cut him out of the saddle. An arrow took the second's mount, and Gerik slashed down as the man leaped clear, cutting through helm and skull both.

The spearman was now close enough to thrust, but again a kender bollik came to Gerik's rescue. This time the thongs wrapped themselves around the spear, jerking it aside from its deadly line to the chest of Gerik's mount. The spearman stumbled, and Gerik's mounted comrade slashed the man across the back of the neck, between helmet and backplate.

That was as much detail of the fight as Gerik remembered. For the next few minutes it dissolved into a chaos of sword strokes ringing on armor or sinking through into flesh and bone, war cries, death cries, a hundred animals neighing and screaming, some of them trampling the fallen . . .

The first thing Gerik noticed afterward was kender on foot, busily exploring the packs of the fallen animals and the pockets of the dead enemies. It was an odd sort of relief to see kender indulging their usual curiosity about anything left unclaimed or even merely unattended.

The Shorn One stormed at his people in language that Gerik did not understand but doubted would bear translation, at least in polite company. Gerik counted empty saddles, and discovered that his band was down another two fighters. But torches gleamed through the trees, and beyond them Gerik saw the looming bulk of the tent. The pack train must have been the first issue of supplies to the men in the camp routed by the Shorn One's illusion spell.

"I can do most of what is needed now," the kender said. "Just guard my back." Then he dismounted and ran into the trees.

Not knowing what else to do, Gerik followed, but without dismounting. The trees here grew close-set, and by the time he and his band had squeezed their way through the last strip of forest, the Shorn One was at work.

He was running around the tent, leaping over the supporting ropes, vaulting pegs and poles, and generally behaving like the image of a witless kender. But Gerik saw that every few paces he touched one end of the staff to the ground. The guards who had not run off, in fear or to aid comrades, were staring at the kender priest. They were still staring when their eyes set forever in their heads, as human arrows and kender knives put an end to them.

By then the Shorn One had run completely around the tent. As he completed the circle, he tossed his staff high into the air. It flew like a spear to the peak of the tent then floated down as gently as a mother bird settling on a nest of eggs, to perch beside the pole now openly flying the banner of House Dirivan.

"Oh," the Shorn One said. "You'll want the banner." He made a pass with his hands; smoke curled around the pole, and it snapped like a twig. A moment later it thrust itself into the ground beside Gerik.

Then the Shorn One gave a single loud cry, and from the ground upward, and from his staff downward, heavy, thorn-laden vines began to sprout. They climbed up and down, met, entangled themselves, and exuded a pungent odor of resin.

Gerik did not remember breathing during the time it took for the vines to completely enshroud the tent, so that one could barely see the canvas and leather through the thorns. Then he gasped as the Shorn One made a final series of gestures and the resin-laden vines burst into flames.

They were only the ordinary bright orange flames from anything rich in resin, but they roared up in a pyramid of fire whose light blinded and whose heat scorched. Gerik shouted to the Shorn One to retreat, and began backing his own mount.

His warning was either too late or never heard. The base of the fire-pyramid widened, a wall of fire advancing outward in all directions. The Shorn One stood his ground, still gesturing. For a moment he was a dark silhouette against the orange glare—then the glare swallowed him up.

If the kender cried out, Gerik did not hear it over the roar of the flames. What he did hear was hoofbeats, as mounted enemies rode up—too late to save their supplies, but not too late to block Gerik's retreat.

Or so they must have thought, from the casual way they sat their saddles, weapons slung or sheathed. They had no warning of the flight of arrows that suddenly leaped from the darkness, to pierce both armor and exposed flesh and topple four men straight out of their saddles.

Bertsa Wylum's scouting party was only six. But surprised as they were, their enemies were in no state to count. The arrows might have been a shower from a war party of Kagonesti, from the effect they had on those facing Gerik.

They were already looking about wildly, at everything except their enemies, when Gerik ordered the charge. He wished briefly for a lance; he could have spitted the leader like a goose before the man saw his death coming. Then Gerik's riders crashed through the ranks of their enemies and straight past Bertsa Wylum, who was drawing again.

At the same time she was shouting, "Kender, to us!" and "Sell-swords of House Dirivan, this is not your fight. Look at the pyre we've made of what they promised you for this unlawful war! Think what you'll win here besides a dishonored grave!"

Gerik counted three mounted kender and ten riders, two riding double. A nod from Wylum, and one of her scouts led a riderless captured horse forward. The double-mounted rider was remounted in a moment, and then the whole band put in their spurs and turned south.

Behind them, the flames had begun to die down. But it would be morning before the ashes of House Dirivan's storehouse were cool enough to sift through, and those who sifted would find little enough for their pains. Even House Dirivan might have trouble sustaining four hundred fighters with supplies for fifty. The kingpriest doubtless had his own well-stocked storehouses, but would he be as free with their contents a second time, to those who had lost so much so swiftly?

On the answers to those questions, many lives might

hang. One life that Gerik was glad to see had been spared was Elderdrake's; he was now riding behind Bertsa Wylum. Gerik would have just as gladly welcomed the Shorn One, but all he could do for the kender priest was remind Branchala that he should remember and reward a good servant.

It was what Gerik hoped others would do for him, if he followed the Shorn One in the next few days.

*   *   *   *   *

After the duel, Pirvan quickly grew thankful that half the warriors off Suivinari Island were minotaurs. They were in theory under his command, but in practice he had to give them very few orders and those he passed through Zeskuk, after consulting with Fulvura.

The minotaurs did not expect him to hold their hands, console, counsel, or solve problems that he thought grown men and women should be able to solve for themselves. For this, Pirvan the Wayward blessed them exceedingly. The human half of the fleet was not so self-reliant.

As a result, by the second dawn after the duel, Pirvan had enjoyed perhaps three hours of fitful sleep in two days. He did not sway as he listened to Tarothin explain why Sir Niebar could safely land with the fighters, but that was because he was sitting down. Haimya had brought him a camp stool, and was standing guard behind him with a look on her face that was more effective than a drawn sword at keeping the unwanted from approaching him.

Tarothin, however, had the right to approach, to talk, even to try persuading Pirvan into letting Sir Niebar commit folly. No man of honor could deny so old and valuable a comrade those rights, and more. What Pirvan wanted to deny was that any amount of help from Tarothin could give Sir Niebar the endurance for the final battle on Suivinari. It might last for days, even a week, before they penetrated Wilthur's stronghold and cast him down—or before Torvik's band and the Dimernesti did the same from seaward.

For his own part, Tarothin was newly dedicated to the fight against Wilthur the Brown. The loss of his friend and comrade Sirbones weighed heavily, visibly on the mage. Wilthur had made another powerful enemy.

At last, Pirvan raised a hand. It did not shake, much to his surprise. Even more to his surprise, Tarothin stopped in midsentence.

"Will you be needed to watch for further—schemes—by the Istarans?" Pirvan asked the Red Robe.

"Lady Revella has asked all Istaran wizards and priests to swear to peace and honor, or be spell-locked until the island is seized," Tarothin said. "She says she can face open enemies, weak as she is, but not false friends. She herself is, I think, trustworthy. Even if she is not, there is always Lujimar, who—"

"Do not even think that aloud," Pirvan cautioned. "All the good we will have gained toward the minotaurs could go in a moment, if a minotaur priest were to smite a human wizard."

"As you wish. But if I have as much work in hand as I suspect I shall, some strong arm to aid Sir Niebar would be welcome. Sir Darin, for example, or Sir Hawkbrother."

Pirvan opened his mouth to forbid mention of Hawkbrother, then closed it again. His impulse had come out of knowing that Young Eskaia would insist on joining her husband in the honorable duty of guarding Sir Niebar on the battlefield. Honorable, and likely to be one of the more dangerous duties in the coming fight for Suivinari.

"Sir Darin should have first refusal on that post of honor," Pirvan said.

"Then we can settle the matter swiftly," Tarothin said. "I see a boat approaching, with both Sir Darin and his lady aboard it."

Tarothin had lost weight in the tropic heat, and his grin had something of a death's-head quality to it. But the wry twinkle in his eyes at putting across a good jest was undiminished.

Pirvan rose stiffly and walked to the railing. A boat rowed by four minotaurs was indeed approaching, with

Darin and Rynthala aboard. A pile of baggage lay at their feet, and both wore armor.

The knight decided that the only way to make sense of this was to wait and ask Darin. So he sat back down and tried not to fidget, without great success, until the boat bumped alongside and Darin sprang up the gangway. When Pirvan saw the expression on the younger knight's face, and saw that Rynthala held back, he knew that he was about to hear bad news.

"Let us walk aside, Sir Darin," Pirvan said formally, raising his hand in salute.

Well up on the foredeck, out of anyone's hearing, Darin told Pirvan the story of how Lujimar had contrived the duel between Darin and Zeskuk by revealing the minotaur chief's plans. It had been done for honorable reasons, to smoke out the Istaran treachery of which Lujimar had heard through his own agent, but it had required withholding true knowledge from Lujimar's chief, as well as others to whom he was bound in lesser degrees.

"So Zeskuk fears that Lujimar will seek death in the coming fight," Darin concluded. "Remaining among the minotaurs, I would need to guard him against his own wishes."

Pirvan thought that lack of sleep must be affecting his ears. "Why you?" he asked. "I cannot imagine that only you among all the thousands of minotaurs off Suivinari can guard one aged priest."

"I am the only one who knows his secret, other than Zeskuk, who has other duties," Darin said. "For another minotaur to do the work, he would need to know Lujimar's secrets, which would add to the priest's dishonor and might help Thenvor's intrigues."

Neither, Pirvan agreed, was a desirable outcome. But Lujimar's death was hardly one, either.

"Minotaurs do not fear death, least of all when it frees them from dishonor," Darin continued. "Zeskuk will not wish to stand in Lujimar's path."

Pirvan suspected that was as much from wishing Lujimar forever silent as from wishing him an honorable end.

He also knew that the accusation would be a mortal insult.

"Darin, you were led by impulse as much as by honor in doing Lujimar's bidding. You are lucky to be alive, and your lady is lucky not to be a widow. Consider, next time, that however long your legs may be, you cannot stand with one foot among the minotaurs and the other among the humans."

Pirvan sighed. "At least having you back among us solves one problem," he continued. "Sir Niebar is determined to go ashore with the rest of the fighters, to have one last battle. He is not seeking death, that I know, but he may find it unless well guarded. Tarothin will give him some warding against magic. If you can do the same against steel . . ."

Darin was actually shaking his head. He was doing it so mournfully that Pirvan's impulse to snarl at the younger knight died swiftly. He still had an edge in his voice when he said: "Guarding the back of a knight of Sir Niebar's rank is commonly considered a great honor. Who has offered you something more?"

Then Pirvan's mouth fell open as Darin replied: "The Dimernesti."

Pirvan's mouth remained open long enough for Darin to explain the message he had received at dawn, from Torvik, Mirraleen, and a Dimernesti named Medlessarn the Silent.

"They believe entering the Smoker from beneath will be costly but successful," Darin said. "It will cost less, they feel, if a seasoned captain in war, and trustworthy for elvenfolk to follow, leads."

"I see," Pirvan said. "I suppose proof of your respect for elves is your lady's blood. You realize that the proof will not be wholly convincing, unless she accompanies you?"

"That might not matter to the Dimernesti," Darin said. "But it would matter greatly to my lady. Rynthala still envies you and Haimya, the number of times you have fought side by side."

Pirvan put both hands on the railing and looked into the water, as if the fish or the Dimernesti would spell out an answer. Seeing only translucent blue-green, he sighed.

"A problem with growing old, which I hope you will live to encounter yourself, is how you come to see your youthful deeds," Pirvan said. "They now as often as not chil your blood, while they heat the blood of those who see only heroism."

"I have never seen anything else in you and Haimya,' Darin said with dignity. "No, I have seen more. I have seen you be as generous with your wits as with your strength blood, and steel. That kind of heroism ages well, Sir Pirvan.'

The Knight of the Rose decided that he had been assaulted in front, flanks, and rear by overwhelming odds and that surrender was acceptable. He clapped Sir Darin on both shoulders.

"Lead our seafaring friends well, then. But both of you of yourselves well so you are not wedged in narrow passages!"

*   *   *   *   *

Gerik's reunited band made a brief camp at the edge of the forest, to drink watered wine and eat cold sausage, rest the horses, and allow pursuers to ride off in every direction but the right one. To reach the campsite they used a trail that even most of the band did not know.

"—so if anyone comes upon us, it will be luck or treason," Bertsa Wylum concluded.

"Not treason, by law," Gerik reminded her. "We are not servants of a king."

"Better a king than a kingpriest," Wylum said. "And coming on us tonight is going to be as fatal as treason ever if the law says otherwise."

They made no fires but took turns on sentry duty. Dawn was gray in the east when they broke camp, leading their horses until they were clear of the forest and had a good view in all directions. Seeing no enemies, they mounted and rode for Tirabot.

To further reduce the danger of pursuit, they followed a roundabout way home, though broken, partly wooded country to the southeast of the manor. On that road they began to see small bands of armed men, mostly too well dressed to be bandits but as furtive as if they were.

It was not until just south of Livo's Bridge that they came upon one of these bands so unexpectedly that the men had no time to flee. Archers held them staring down the shafts of a dozen arrows, while Gerik rode forward to speak to them.

"It's no secret that House Dirivan brought us in," the leader said. "It's no secret that our feet are taking us out. Don't know if you've heard it, but they say the whole pay chest went up with that kender-fire last night.

"So even if the chiefs are honest, what's there for them to be honest *with*? My advice is, take your people home, if they've got one, and keep your ears open. The kingpriest's likely enough able to settle the charge of private warfare for the Dirivans. If he can't, though, I'm for over the border into Solamnia."

Gerik thanked the man and handed him enough silver to divide with his comrades. Then he rode on, and by heroic efforts managed to keep from bursting into laughter before they were out of hearing of the retreating sell-swords.

"The gods grant you've panicked all the ones we didn't knock out of the fight," he told Bertsa Wylum. "We may win our home back yet."

Around the bend, however, laughter died and hope faded. The farm had not been burned; that would have left a warning trail of smoke in the sky. The warning lay in what else had been done. House, barn, and byre had all been looted bare, all the animals carted off or slaughtered and left to grow flyblown, farm implements smashed, manure flung down the well, and obscenities scrawled on the walls.

They found the farmer himself in the barn, his head smashed in, and a haying fork rammed through his belly. After that, Gerik could hardly bring himself to enter the house, and could not keep from vomiting the moment he ran back out.

"All dead," he said, when he could command his voice again. "Even the grandmother. They—the baby—and the mother—"

Gerik refused to give details. Bertsa Wylum went in, then came out milk-colored and faster than she'd entered, to also get rid of everything she'd eaten for a week.

After that, nobody was curious enough to go in. Gerik wondered what they were imagining. He doubted that they could imagine anything equal to the reality. Mercifully, everyone was silent, even the kender.

Some people, however, had both imagined this and done it. If they ever came within reach of Gerik's steel or even his bare hands, they were dead.

Meanwhile, it was home to Tirabot—which was about to be home no more. It had to be over the border into Solamnia for everyone, the women, children, and villagers so that they would not face this, with the fighters guarding them on the way.

As they rode out of the village, smoke scrawled a greasy mark across the sky to the east.

Chapter 19

Pirvan and Haimya were the first to wade ashore from the boat, and nearly the last. They had just reached the hard-packed sand below the tide line when they heard screams behind them.

They turned to see dark, sinuous forms rippling through the water. One was clinging to the calf of a man knee-deep in the water. He drew his sword and slashed down; the snake divided in two. Blood clouded the water for a moment—then the severed tail of the snake grew its own fanged head, and both halves returned to the attack.

Meanwhile, blood trickled from the man's eyes and nose. He stared wildly about him, then coughed, bringing up more blood. His eyes widened, he clawed at his chest, and fell into the water with one snake still clinging to him.

Another man who'd climbed from the boat behind Pirvan and Haimya had gone farther and was luckier. One of the sea snakes wriggled onto the sand, pursuing him, but only struck his boot. The heavy leather turned the fangs, and he spun about, bringing the other foot down hard on the snake's head. It went limp, and the head did not grow afresh.

Pirvan cupped his hands and shouted, "Strike for the heads! They can't revive if you take their heads!"

How many heard him, above the shouts and screams of wading fighters bitten and dying horribly, Pirvan never knew. But he saw boats backing oars, pulling wading people into them, while those in the water dashed frantically for land. Many of them reached it safely, but for those bitten on the way there was only one end. The snakes' poison worked too swiftly for healing, even had there been a healer on the beach for each bitten man.

In time, Pirvan stopped shouting and started counting. Close to four hundred fighters were ashore, with their weapons and armor but scantily equipped as to water and food. The knight doubted if there was anything to eat or drink on the island, or at least anything that Wilthur could not make poisonous.

Forty or more bodies washed back and forth in the low surf, some still trailing blood. Pirvan wondered how long would take the blood to attract some of the seaborne predators who would drive themselves aground, drawn by the scent of fresh blood. At least a school of sharks or sea pike might find the snakes to their taste.

Pirvan looked out to sea. The boats farther offshore were resting on their oars. Twice he saw steel flash in the water sunlight, as sailors fought sea snakes trying to crawl aboard.

Tarothin hurried up, followed by Sir Niebar, who actually looked fit to be out of bed and ashore, if not wielding a sword in desperate battle. The Red Robe looked grim. "Are we cut off from help from the sea?" he asked.

"I'm sure there's a spell that will end those snakes," Pirvan offered. "If you don't know it, then try to reach Lujimar or Lady Revella."

"I can try, and probably succeed. But what of Wilthur listening to what we say?"

"Do what you think best," Pirvan said. "Certainly we do not wish to make a gift of our secrets." He looked along the beach. "Better yet, can you levitate a few rocks and logs onto that sand spit, the one just below the grove of horn fruit?"

Tarothin frowned. "A very few, yes, but why—oh, I see

A pier, so the men can walk ashore dry shod?"

"Yes," Pirvan said. "Those snakes seem to be bound with water magic. They're slower and weaker out of the water, and perhaps they can't regenerate on land. If you can't make a safe pier without exhausting yourself, we can try boats lined up abreast with planks over them. The knights have used that for landing horses more than a few times."

"Why don't we try both?" Tarothin said. "Sir Niebar, if you can organize a floating pier, perhaps I can try levitating the materials for the other one."

Pirvan was about to caution Tarothin about giving orders to Sir Niebar, when he caught sight of the older knight trying not to smile. Niebar knew the ways of wizards, and besides, he was back on a battlefield. For that privilege, he looked ready to take orders from Pirvan's daughter Rubina.

With a safe landing once again in prospect, Pirvan turned his attention to the men already ashore. It would be as well to get them out of the sun, but anything large enough to provide shade Wilthur could also turn against them.

At least there were patches of ground, cleared in the last battle and not yet regrown. In these, the fighters would be out of reach of any remaining plants and could see any animals coming at them in time. But sooner or later they would have to break new trails, in the face of the worst Wilthur could hurl at both men and minotaurs. If either Darin's band slipping in under the Smoker or the fighters marching overland faltered, Wilthur could throw all his strength against the other.

* * * * *

Darin scrambled out of the water and reached down to help Rynthala follow. She did not need the help, but sprang onto the rock as if she were Dimernesti herself. The shelf of rock where they stood lay at the base of the inner wall of a large sea cave. With the tide where it was now, the cave's mouth rose twice the height of a man above the water.

Through the mouth, half a mile across the sun-gilt water Darin saw *Red Elf*.

From the ship to the cave mouth ran a waterborne train of boats and swimmers. The boats carried mostly humans although more than a few humans had chosen to swim. The boats also carried the supplies for the landing party. On either flank of the boats swam sea otters, most of whom could not be Dimernesti, unless the shallows-dwellers were far more numerous in these waters than Darin had been led to believe.

A sea otter shot in through the cave mouth, slid up onto a rock, and transformed. Mirraleen then dived off the rock and swam up to Darin.

"We have word from the beaches, human and minotaur," she told him. "Wilthur has conjured poisonous sea snakes."

"Can the sea otters guard our swimmers?" Darin asked. Then, at a cough from Rynthala, he added hastily, "That is, without putting themselves too much in danger?"

Mirraleen frowned. "Some are agile enough, I am sure," she said. "But it would be wiser for the humans to enter the boats, however well they can swim. Word is that the snakes are clumsy out of the water."

"Very well. Then we should send word."

Mirraleen crouched by the water and barked like a sea otter. Two furry heads broke the surface; she barked again. The otters flipped end for end like acrobats and dived for the cave mouth.

The news that Wilthur was striking back seemed to lend wings to the oars and new strength to the swimmers. They rushed toward the cave mouth, and within minutes Darin saw a mirror wink from *Red Elf*. The last of the landing party was coming ashore, but the ship would wait until all were safely within the cave.

Torvik was in the last boat. As it passed through the cave mouth, he sprang overboard and swam to the rock shelf. Then he and Mirraleen embraced, as chastely as possible considering how little either of them was wearing.

Darin himself would have preferred, if not armor, a

least more clothing between his skin and the rock. But he could not deny that wet clothing weighed a swimmer down, and there could be much more swimming between the cave and Wilthur's lair.

The black rock of the cave was now tinged with orange, as humans and sea-elves busily lit glowballs. They were a Dimernesti gift to the band, tightly-packed wads of seaweed soaked with some kind of oil that burned, seemingly, forever. They need not fear darkness even in the lightless bowels of the Smoker.

Darin studied the cave more closely, now that he had more light. Several cracks in the wall offered passages upward; one ran level, and a black mouth yawned behind one boulder, seemingly leading down. If the directions put into his memory by Mirraleen held the truth, it was that black mouth that marked the first part of their underground road.

A wave larger than usual washed in through the mouth of the cave, extinguishing several glowballs. Everyone who did not fall on the supplies and glowballs to drag them to safety drew steel. A wave that size came from no sea snake, not even a school of them. Had Wilthur saved his Creation for them?

Then the shriek of rock against rock tore at their ears, and the echoes went on doubling and redoubling the shriek until Darin and many others were clapping their hands to their temples. A crack appeared in the rock, just above the cave mouth.

It widened. A slab of rock the size of a small temple tilted, then fell free. It splashed into the water at the cave mouth. A higher wave rolled over the shelf, knocking some men off their feet. This time the sound was like a dwarf's pick striking rock, but ten times louder. Another slab of rock, even larger, fell atop the first one. A third followed, then boulders and gravel rained down into the swirling chaos at the cave mouth, until murky waves clashed and splattered all over the cave.

Humans and Dimernesti alike stood as far back from the water as they could, watching in horror and disgust as their retreat was cut off. Darin had drawn his sword, but now sheathed it as his band crowded more thickly around him. Only Mirraleen and Medlessarn remained close to the water, so close that murky water swirled about their ankles. Mirraleen even knelt, with her hand reaching into the dirty foam. Darin finally pushed through the crowd to join the Dimernesti, and drew his sword again. If the Creation did thrust a tentacle out of the swirl, neither Dimernesti had more than a dagger to meet it.

By the time the waves from the rockfall died away, a dozen other humans and as many Dimernesti had joined Darin, ready to fight whatever enemy might present itself. All stared at Mirraleen when she stood up and announced: "I do not believe this is Wilthur's doing."

Darin would never have lived down saying no more than "*Uh?*" if half a dozen others had not said it loudly enough to drown him out.

"If Wilthur wanted to send his Creation into the cave, he would not have blocked it," Mirraleen explained. "Whoever made the rock fall wished to guard our rear from the Creation, and from anything else that cannot slip through the last gaps in the fallen rocks."

"But the rockfall blocks off reinforcements and supplies," Torvik said. His voice sounded like that of a man who wants to gibber but knows he must be calm for the sake of those he leads. Darin knew the sensation.

"We shall not need either, with all we have here," Medlessarn reminded them. "As for water, there are fresh springs within the mountain, and we can even catch fish and you humans can cook them in the hot springs. For as long as we shall need to be here, we are well fitted. If Wilthur had wanted to use the rocks to defeat us, he would have brought the cave down on our heads, not closed its mouth."

That seemed convincing, except to one man, who voiced a question that Darin admitted was in his own mind: "If Wilthur didn't bring down the rocks, who did?"

"The passage of time, as like as not," Torvik said. "But also let us remember that the True Gods are no friends of Wilthur.

If Reorx made the fire we all saw, perhaps Habbakuk can work with sea-worn rocks to aid us more directly."

Torvik did not mention to all what he had mentioned to Darin, that the Dimernesti at least thought Zeboim herself was a foe to Wilthur. That would have unleashed panic, and even Darin found himself chill at the thought of that goddess at work anywhere near him. The name for Zeboim, in the minotaur tongue, was translated, "The Great Treacherous She-Turtle." It was also said that if one had her friendship, one should at once seek the safety of an enemy.

* * * * *

From the wall of Tirabot Manor, Gerik could see not only the smoke to the south and east, but closer by, the flames at the base of the smoke clouds.

At dawn the smoke had still been scrawled across the sky, like the runes of an apprentice wizard writing down his first original spell. Now, at noon, the sky looked more like parchment on which the apprentice had carelessly spilled the ink bottle. Blackness ate at the sunlight, and at Gerik's soul.

He remembered Rubina asking, as the last party from the castle—save for the rear guard—assembled at the gate: "Gerik, will we ever come back here again?"

His answer was the best he could contrive, and he hoped the truth as well. "When there is justice against our enemies," he said, "so that we do not have to live sword in hand and back to the wall every moment, we can think about it. Until then, we must think about making our homes in Vuinlod."

Rubina swallowed and blinked, looking for a moment as if she wanted to cry. Gerik would have been glad to see her let her grief and fear out, if it would not have unmanned him. Then Rubina said, "Is Lady Eskaia honorable?"

"She is, but why do you ask?"

"If she has married again, and there is no one else to give me a home until I am grown and can—"

"Hush," Ellysta said. "Don't speak ill-luck words. Your mother, father, and sister may be at war, but they were alive the last we heard. Your brother may ride with the rear guard, but he is a brave fighter and he will not be alone."

"No, but—oh, it would be ill-luck words again, I suppose." She stood on tiptoe to kiss Gerik, and said, "Take care, Brother. And bring Grimsoar back with you. He has promised to teach me the sailor way of knife fighting." She hurried off to join Ellysta's band.

Gerik stood looking after her when she was long departed. It had been the right touch, those last words, and worthy of one years older than Rubina.

"Good sir!" Wylum called from below. "It's time to ride."

It was indeed. The air was hot and still, with hardly a breath of wind, but Gerik could still smell the smoke of the burnings. He fancied he could even smell roasting meat—the gods grant it be trapped pigs or chickens.

Gerik nearly stumbled on the stairs when he saw what Bertsa Wylum had tucked in her belt.

"Zixa?"

"Is that what Rubina called it?" The sell-sword captain handed the straw-stuffed doll with an elven face to Gerik, saying, "I found her in a hall, when I was leading the final search for stay-behinds."

"It must have fallen out of Rubina's pack in the dark," Gerik said, clutching the doll as if for dear life. "No wonder she was trying not to cry. She's had Zixa since she was five."

Now it was Gerik's turn to swallow and blink. Wylum laughed. "I won't hold it against you if you shed a few tears, Gerik. But Ellysta will put a dagger between my ribs if I don't let you cry on her shoulder first."

Gerik straightened and said, "How is the village?"

"As we expected."

The village had largely emptied itself once the smoke clouds began rising, but not completely. There were those who thought they were in favor with the kingpriest, or even genuinely believed in the reign of virtue. There were those who thought they had knowledge to sell, or who knew they had children or parents too young, too old, or too ill to move. Finally, there were those who simply would not believe that private war could come again to Istar, and be dangerous to them as well.

Gerik feared they would learn otherwise, when House Dirivan or whoever was now sending the riders came. They might not survive the lesson, either. But he had done what he could for them. Four guards with kin among the stay-behinds had offered to join them, and some of the villagers bore arms as well. Anyone who wished had also had Gerik's written permission to enter the manor and barricade themselves behind its walls.

That might be enough to fend off the wildings and the blood-drinkers, until the enemy's captains restored discipline. If they did not wish to do so, then the gods help those who stayed behind, because Gerik could not.

"How is it on the wall?" Wylum asked.

"No one in sight to the east, everyone out of sight to the west."

"Good. I hope the kender were telling the truth, about knowing the whereabouts of all the bandits between here and the border."

"They would know," Gerik said. "But they might not have remembered to tell us everything they know."

* * * * *

Zeskuk took the lead of the main column when the minotaur advance divided on the slopes of the Green Mountain. It would encourage anyone shaken inwardly (no minotaur would show it outwardly) by the sea snake attack.

Minotaur hides were thick, and more than a few of the waders had worn leggings to fend off attacking thorns and branches on land. Two thicknesses of bull hide could defeat the fangs of anything short of a dragon, and those minotaurs splashed ashore angry but unharmed.

Others came ashore over an improvised pier of boats laid bow to stern. Very few of the Destined Race were bitten, and not all of those took a lethal dose of venom. One who had seemed to was Thenvor, but Zeskuk's rival had rallied amazingly with nothing but a home brewed potion his son gave him. He would not lead or fight today, but he would live.

The sea snakes were still darting about in the shallows, and Zeskuk only hoped that the sea otter friends of the Dimernesti would stay away. Fur was nothing like leather at keeping out fangs, and sea otters could die from a drop of something needed in cupfuls to kill a minotaur.

"Signal from Juiksum, lord," the apprentice wizard attached to Zeskuk said. "He is in sight of the outpost. They have lost only two fighters. The vegetation has regrown, but seems to lack its old vitality."

No surprises there. Wilthur was a mage, and a human one at that, not a minotaur, let alone a god. He would have more demands on his magic today than it could very well meet.

Juiksum would advance to the outpost and then down the north side of the Green Mountain. Zeskuk would lead his column along the south side. Meanwhile, the humans would be carving their own path up between the two mountains to meet the minotaurs in the valley.

So far the minotaurs had advanced farther, which was as it should be. The humans had not only suffered more delay from the sea snakes, but had a longer route with less of it already cleared. Zeskuk drew his clabbard. He doubted he would need it for at least a hundred paces or so, but it felt good to have it in his hand, and looked more fitting for a chief.

Bellows from half a dozen throats made him raise the clabbard and take a fighting stance by sheer instinct. He almost made a fool of himself, looking around, before he saw someone pointing. Then his first instinct was to shout for the archers.

In wedges of five or seven, more than a hundred great birds were flying in from the sea to the north. They flew over the outpost and Juiksum's column too high for the archers, then began slanting down as they crossed the island. Each bird shone with blue feathers so fine and so glossy that they seemed almost like scales, and had a long white crest and bright yellow bill and claws. They called to one another as they flew, and as they passed overhead Zeskuk saw they had sharp teeth in their beaks.

The whole hundred and more passed over the minotaur column as if they were no more than rocks on the slope. Zeskuk realized that they were flying for the human beach, and ordered the archers to make ready on the right. It would not look well if the minotaurs ignored the birds and gave them a free attack on the humans.

The birds flew on over the humans with the same sublime self-absorption as they had shown the minotaurs. Only when they reached the sea did they halt. Now they formed a vast semicircle, nearly blocking the human beach from seaward. Then, almost as if a single mind controlled a hundred bodies and a hundred pairs of ten-foot wings, the birds dived. They plunged into the water, then leaped skyward again in showers of spray.

"They're catching the snakes!" someone shouted.

In moments, Zeskuk could make out the birds dipping and rising, and each time one rose, it held a snake in its beak. Sometimes they gripped and crushed the head straightaway. Other times, they flew side by side in pairs, one bird holding the snake while the other crushed the thing's head.

Only two birds fell from the sky, bitten by their prey. The rest went on with their deadly dance from sky to sea and back again, and the shallows began to foam with snakes desperate to find safety.

"Forward!" Zeskuk shouted. With their rear freed of the snakes, the humans would be advancing faster than ever. It would never do to let them outpace minotaurs, even if the humans had Fulvura and six picked minotaurs at their spearhead.

A bush some fifty paces uphill seemed to quiver in a way Zeskuk did not trust. He had nothing to throw, but a fist-sized rock lay at just the right distance. His clabbard whirled, then sang through the air. The toothed blade hooked the rock and flung it up the hill, into the heart of the bush.

Branches writhed, showing white where the stone had broken them or stripped off bark. The bush tried to pull itself out of the ground, roots and all, but fell over like a kender drunk on dwarf spirits. It rolled down to within reach of more clabbards than Zeskuk's. When they were done, only splinters remained.

The birds were not circling over the human beach, as the human rear guard slaughtered the snakes. Zeskuk saw one human leap back, holding a spear on which wriggled no less than three snakes. Before they could wriggle up the shaft to bite him, he thrust the spear into a tar barrel someone had set afire. The smoke turned from black to the color of putrid wine, and the stench reached Zeskuk even far uphill.

He was still sneezing when a bolt of fire lanced from the Smoker. It held all colors and none. It struck one of the birds, and consumed it in a moment as the tar barrel had consumed the snakes. Zeskuk could not even be sure he saw ashes floating downward on the breeze.

"Do I have to repeat myself?" he roared. "I said, 'Forward!' "

* * * * *

Wilthur did not know from whence the birds had come, and would not have withheld his fire if he had. He did know that the birds' coming had doomed the snakes, but perhaps that could be the end of the injury they wrought against him. So the fire went out, and the birds drifted downwind as fine ash.

All his magic and all his wits aimed at the birds, Wilthur spared not a thought for his Creation. Nor did anything else on Suivinari Island now have more magic than he had already put into it.

Chapter 20

From the head of the human advance, Pirvan saw very little of the battle of the birds against the snakes, and not much more of the war of firebolts against the birds. He smelled a good deal—both the lightning-reek the firebolts left behind, and the charnel house smell of the birds' drifting ashes.

He even had to draw his sword once, to kill a snake that a bird dropped just before it died. A single clean slash clove the snake's head in two, upper and lower jaws flying in separate directions, and the body swiftly twitched itself into stillness. Haimya touched his arm, with a flash of teeth in a face darkened by dirt, sweat, and sun.

"Another ten years, and you will be a better swordsman than I ever was," she said.

"Another ten years, and the gods willing, we will neither of us have to wield swords, except to teach our grandchildren," Pirvan replied, returning her playful smile.

"Perhaps. Meanwhile, it does not hurt that we are both fit to take our place at the head of a column of assault."

Pirvan did not quarrel with the siegecraft term. The battle for Suivinari Island felt more like the siege of Belkuthas than any other battle he had ever fought, but he was less sure about their being at the "head" of anything.

To be sure, he could see no one ahead of him, which probably meant that the scouts were lost from sight in the dense foliage of the valley, or else lost to some trap of Wilthur's.

He also could see no one to his left, and precious few—too few to be properly named a "column"—to his rear. To his right stood a more solid block of fighters, mostly Vuinlod infantry, with a company of picked sell-swords just behind him. Gildas Aurhinius stood between the two bands, so that he could watch and command either, and would be ready to take over the lead if Pirvan fell.

Tarothin and Sir Niebar were also on the right, with a dozen even more carefully picked fighters, Solamnic and sea barbarian. They had not asked for this bodyguard, but Pirvan had sent it and they had not refused.

The Red Robe (actually now Sun-Bleached Pink Robe) staggered a trifle as he surmounted a sandy slope made treacherous by thorn-studded vines. The vines did not move, however, only lying in wait for the unwary to stumble and sprain or gouge themselves.

"Wilthur plays with fire, and that is not a jest," Tarothin said. He needed three breaths to get out the words. Sir Niebar, Pirvan noted, was silent, having either still less breath, more sense, or nothing to say.

"We are all in the gods' hands," Pirvan said.

"Yes, but some of us spurn those hands as a miser spurns a beggar," Tarothin replied. "Wilthur's striking at the birds seems to me to be such a spurning."

Pirvan had suspected that the birds were the gods' creation as much as the snakes were Wilthur's. He rejoiced. He would have rejoiced more if the gods' hands had been open to Niebar, Tarothin, or both, giving them at least the knowledge that they should be easy on themselves.

Niebar at least had the strength to climb in full dismounted knights' armor, but Tarothin looked hardly better than Sirbones had, the day he died. The Red Robe would never be as lean as the servant of Mishakal, being too heavy-boned for that, but there was not much of him left save skin and sinew stretched tight over those bones. His eyes seemed to have grown to twice their size, and his formerly bulbous, almost clownlike nose, was a thinning beak. As for his hair, what was left of it was as much white as gray, and only the odd strand here and there was still brown.

A horrible tearing of wood that sounded like a large ship running on a reef made Pirvan whirl. In climbing the last slope they had almost reached the point where the trail vanished into a stand of trees, fanleaf greenbarks or their near kin. They were tall as masts, either virgin timber or mature second growth.

They were also leaning toward Pirvan. Their branches writhed in a way that could have only one meaning.

As the greenbarks' roots began to pull free of the ground, Tarothin raised his staff. A wind blowing vertically down from the sky caught Pirvan, making him stagger so that he and Haimya needed to brace each other like the timbers of a doorframe. Two of the snake-eating birds plummeted from the sky, to be blown among the writhing limbs and vanish.

The wind blew on downward, stripping leaves from moving branches and still ones alike. It blew on the moving roots and the earth around them like a cold draft on a cup of hot tea. The roots now quivered instead of writhing, while the ground rose in clouds of dust that settled back into mounds as solid as sandstone.

For as far ahead as Pirvan could see, Tarothin's immobilization spell had frozen the trees against Wilthur's latest effort to turn them into lethal weapons.

Pirvan shouted off toward the left, to rally the unseen and (he hoped) unscathed fighters there. He shouted to Gildas Aurhinius to speed the advance. Then he turned to Sir Niebar, intending to ask him to send a guard back with a message for the remaining Solamnics to join the rush forward. They would have to put as many fighters as possible beyond the trees before Tarothin's spell wore off or Wilthur conjured some new menace.

Instead of commanding, Pirvan found himself keeping Tarothin from falling. The Red Robe had dropped his staff, and his hands shook so badly that he could barely make one last gesture at the fallen length of wood and ivory.

"There," he muttered. "Safe now. Can't leave . . ."

His voice trailed off into a silence that Pirvan told himself was only weakness or at worst fainting.

He told himself that as many times as he gave orders for healers, litter-bearers, and guards for his old friend and comrade. The orders, however, brought everything Pirvan wanted. The wish brought nothing, not even a blink of Tarothin's eyes.

By the time the litter-bearers shouldered their burden, Tarothin's only movement was the shallow rise and fall of his chest. A fly buzzed near to the closed, sunken eyes, and Pirvan nearly drew his sword to bat it away from the dying wizard.

"Better use for it up forward," he muttered. Then he sprang forward with such swift strides that Haimya could barely keep up and Sir Niebar quickly fell behind.

* * * * *

The minotaurs marched off the Green Mountain four abreast, stamping their feet to defy Wilthur's magic and also crush any stray snakes or roots in their path. They bellowed war cries and curses, they clashed shatangs and clabbards on their shields, they beat drums, blew trumpets, and played on the war pipes that Thenvor favored.

Altogether, they made such a din that Zeskuk thought the gods themselves must be stuffing hanks of wool into their ears, to keep from going deaf. No minotaur's courage needed the inspiration of this uproar, or at least no minotaur would readily admit it. All hoped that advancing into the valley in this manner would inspire even Wilthur's most potent conjurations with the urge to flee, or at least draw all of them onto the minotaurs.

Then the minotaurs would have the glory of the great killing, even if they lost the honor of first into Wilthur's lair. Zeskuk hardly cared who had which honor now, as there would likely be enough to sate a host three times the minotaurs' and humans' united strength.

Moreover, even without glory there would be the sense of a necessary work accomplished. Leaving Suivinari

Island, Zeskuk realized now, had never been really an acceptable choice. Not after minotaurs had spilled as much of their blood as they had, even in the first battle.

Thenvor would have gloried in calling him a coward.

Fulvura would have questioned his wits, if not his honor or courage, and in private.

Darin had done man and minotaur alike great service, even if he had done so through listening to Lujimar's blandishments, and without considering all the possible consequences.

Zeskuk hoped that Darin would survive his grapple with Wilthur's Creation, and that he and Rynthala would have many tall sons with the knowledge of minotaur ways bred into their bones. He even allowed himself to hope that Lujimar would think again about his march to death.

But hope was all the chief could do. Against a priest determined to wash out dishonor with his blood, even the Emperor stood as much chance as a babe matched in the arena against a full-fledged warrior.

Hiding it with his body, Zeskuk made a gesture of aversion, for Darin's and Lujimar's good luck. He had just finished it when a cry rose from ahead: "We've found a cave!"

"Big enough for minotaurs!"

"It has to lead into the Smoker!"

Zeskuk hurried forward. There was no such thing as "has to" in this battle; even caves could have a mind of their own. But it was promising news, nonetheless.

The only problem was that one of the first to discover the cave seemed to have been Lujimar. At any rate, several warriors said they had seen him entering it when they arrived, and no one had seen him since. Zeskuk himself walked about half a shatang-throw into the cave. The passage twisted, turned, rose, fell, and generally behaved like a snake drunk on bad ale. But it allowed minotaurs fighting room nearly everywhere, and its general course was toward the depths of the Smoker.

The chief strode back into the light, and called for volunteers to follow him and Lujimar over the final stage of the journey to Wilthur's lair.

* * * * *

Darin was not good at measuring distances underground, with few marks to guide him. Rynthala was better, the sailors better still, and the Dimernesti best of all. So he had plenty of trustworthy observers to tell him that the underground attack had covered perhaps a mile and a third, when they came to the barrier.

It was not an unconquerable barrier, bringing all their efforts to naught. It was merely that a rockfall had blocked part of a natural arch, leaving at the top a clear passage— but only for persons of moderate stature. At the bottom was a partly blocked opening that would allow a minotaur with a kender standing on his shoulders to march through without stooping—once it was cleared.

There could be no simple solution, either, because on the far side they could hear the lapping of water. Not where it would be released as by a broken dam when they cleared the passage; that was not the peril. But any large body of water in these depths might hold the Creation. Any party who passed through at the top would need to be fightingfit.

"I shall lead," Torvik said. "Chuina, I will need archers more than anything else. Archers and spearmen, and if they have fire arrows, so much the better. The more we can fight at a distance, the longer we can hold."

"What are you thinking, picking my people to help you die?" Chuina almost snapped.

Torvik said nothing, merely put an arm around his sister's shoulder.

"All right," she acquiesced. "Just be careful, or this could be a bad day for Mother."

Chuina's look said that a direct command from their mother could not have kept her from leading her people into this fight. Darin realized that if he had not already wed Rynthala, he might have begun to think of becoming Torvik's brother-by-marriage. Chuina had a sense of honor as fierce as a minotaur's, the discretion of a human, and such skill in war to make one reluctant to question either.

The knight and his lady stepped back. The tallest person able to fit through the upper gap was a good three inches shorter than Rynthala. Their task for now lay below, commanding, and, if need be, guarding the stone-movers.

He looked at the stones. The dwarves might not think much of his knowledge, but he had listened when they spoke, whether they knew it or not. Wise stonemasons always braced the upper stones before beginning work on the lower ones. . . .

* * * * *

Torvik scrambled down the last slope of rock, crested the miniature sand dune, and looked at the underground lake. Behind him he heard the vanguard spreading out, to keep watch in all directions. Then he heard a not-quite-muffled oath.

Mirraleen was still in the upper passage, not through it as he had expected her to be. Indeed, she looked as if she were stuck.

He scrambled back up. The rough rock had scraped her skin the color of her hair in several places.

Now Torvik cursed. "If I took your hands—" he offered.

Mirraleen groaned, saying, "Don't tempt me. I would likely as not block the passage for everyone behind me, until folk came up from below to pull me back. And I would have no skin left to speak of."

It was no use suggesting that she transform. She could not do that again for several more hours. Even if she had been able to become a sea otter now, she would have been trapped in that form—and nearly helpless on land—for even more hours.

"Well, I appreciate your skin too much to wish it marred," Torvik said lightly. "But we need one of your folk on this side. The water looks too deep for human exploring, at least not without a boat."

Indeed, the lake seemed to have no end and no bottom, but that might only have been the weakness of the glowballs. The band was not yet running short of light, but to avoid being cast into darkness they had to be cautious with the light that they had.

"Oh, stop panting for your lover and let one whose passions don't toss him like kelp in a whirlpool go forward," someone muttered. Mirraleen disappeared almost as fast as if she had been dragged backward. A moment later Kuyomolan scrambled through the opening. He was no more than a finger or maybe a thumb's breadth smaller than Mirraleen, but that was enough to make the difference.

Chuina squealed at the sight of the Dimernesti least fond of humans.

"You sound like a mating porpoise," Kuyomolan growled. "The first sign of pleasure at the sight of me I've heard in a good while."

Chuina looked as if her fingers itched to put an arrow through Kuyomolan, or at least spank him raw with her unstrung bow. The Dimernesti looked hardly fonder of her.

"Peace, both of you," Torvik said. At least that was what he tried to say. Echoes of what had already been said were still flitting about the cavern, and they trampled half his words into oblivion.

Then he heard a deep gurgling, like a barrel the size of Solinari emptying itself into an infinitely deep cellar. Something hissed like a clan of serpents, and an indescribable stench blew past him.

He turned, without surprise, to behold the Creation rising from the depths of the lake.

* * * * *

Gerik was thinking that the line of smoke plumes had reached the village when a kender scuttled out of the underbrush. It was one of the Shorn One's companions, looking as if he himself had been shorn of nearly everything but life itself—and a desire for vengeance.

"Riders on the yellow trail," the kender said. "That's from the yellow clay. Really, the fallen needles hide the yellow most of the time, but the name hasn't changed since my great-grandfather's time."

"Where is it?" Bertsa Wylum asked. Gerik was about to warn her not to be so impatient with a kender in a mood to chatter, when the kender knelt and began to draw a map in the dust.

Gerik and Wylum together were able to make sense of the map, and that sense was bad news. Some of the sellswords might have deserted House Dirivan's service. Some might have died or stopped to loot and burn. But some eighty-odd were coming on swiftly, clearly trying to find a place where they could strike across every path that those retreating from Tirabot might take.

Bad news, but not the worst. The enemy was starting in the south, so that Gerik's armed band was between them and most of the refugees. The southernmost ones had departed the earliest, were the farthest along, and had the best chance of hiding in the forests even without the help of the kender.

Also, a small band with good archers had several natural ambush sites against a larger force coming up from the south. To Gerik, the best seemed where the trail came up from Forge Vale, said to have once been home to a dwarven band working bog iron.

"Of course, that must have been in the time of Vinas Solamnus," Gerik added. "But then, the tales run that most of this land was bog then, so perhaps there's truth in it."

More important was there being truth in the kender's tale. Gerik would be risking not only his life and that of nearly thirty of his best fighters, but the last sure shield for Tirabot's people. Hiding in the forest was more likely to mean starvation than safety, and even kender might betray hiding places or cease to give help if enough of their homes were burned and enough of their kin slaughtered.

House Dirivan had gone too far to draw back, so the only target Gerik had now was the fighting spirit of their men. Kill enough of those, and the spirit might break, ending the pursuit.

He had begun with law and hoped to stay with it. Now it would end with killing. He said as much to Bertsa Wylum.

"I've never yet seen a sheet of parchment that could turn a sword cut," she said. Then she slapped his armored shoulder. "But I've never yet seen anyone get through a sword blade to tear the scroll of laws behind it, either."

Chapter 21

The gods (at least those named by men as True Gods) contemplated the battle unfolding on Suivinari Island.

Having held the balance, they had done all that was permitted them. Victory or defeat, life or death, now lay in the hands of those on the island.

Wilthur the Brown was far too busy to contemplate anything. Having gathered in vitality from so many of the dead, he could now choose whether to send it to his Creation, his defenses, or himself.

Taking it into himself would aid only his flight, and he sensed that his flight beyond the island would not be unopposed.

He had no further communication with the Creation. A pity it was so self-willed, but to live in the sea he had deemed that degree of intelligence necessary. Now, however, it was shutting him out, from pride at fighting its own battle against a foe ready to hand.

He trusted it would succeed. Strengthened as he could have made it, its victory would be certain. Now, the only certainty was delaying his enemies, perhaps at a great price. Of course, if the Creation gained victory by its own strength, it might be a menace to him until he brought it under control, or the gods dealt with it for their own purposes and in their own good time. Perhaps delay was enough.

Certainly it had its uses. Given time, he could pour the vitality into the other defenses. He had too few for comfort, but they should not be too few to halt his enemies.

* * * * *

Messages poured over Pirvan like a tropical downpour.

Tarothin was dead. This was no surprise. Grief, yes, but not a surprise.

The last of the birds were gone. So were the last of the snakes.

All minotaurs and humans who had intended to land had either landed or died trying.

The Smoker was emitting steam from both old and new vents.

The mouth of the cave where Darin's party had entered the Smoker had collapsed. Pirvan could barely keep a sober countenance at this. He swore the messenger to silence.

The minotaurs had found a cave in the flank of the Smoker, perhaps the opening to an underground passage into the bowels of the mountains. They were continuing their advance on the surface, but Zeskuk and Lujimar had led a strong party of warriors underground.

A minotaur brought this last message, going first to Fulvura. She ordered him to Pirvan, with a peremptory gesture that was nearly a blow. The messenger bridled; all six of Fulvura's companions glared at him; the messenger obeyed. No need to fear anything from Fulvura, Pirvan decided. But what were Zeskuk and Lujimar doing, plunging down into darkness that might already have swallowed up Darin, Torvik, and their company?

"If we follow them, at least we'll all be buried in the same grave," he muttered.

An eloquent look from Haimya told him that he had spoken nearly loud enough to be heard by others besides herself. Pirvan shook his head, which did not help. He drank from his water bottle, which was empty when he put it down, but that did help. With his head clearing and his throat capable of speech, he called to all within hearing.

"The minotaurs say they have a way into the mountain. Let us be quick to join them."

"Not so quick that we fall over from the heat," someone shouted.

"Quick enough that we can help them if they need it," shouted another with a Karthayan accent.

Pirvan and Haimya exchanged glances. Both seemed to wonder alike: would helping the minotaurs honor or shame them?

It hardly mattered. It would be madness to turn back from victory now. Also, minotaurs were always proud, much less often foolish.

Pirvan pushed his way through the crowd, toward Fulvura, to ask her counsel. It seemed as if the ground had sprouted messengers, so many that if all had been armed they could have fought for a none-too-small barony. Or, under his son's banner, driven House Dirivan back to the stews from which it should never have been allowed to rise. Gerik's last letter had not inspired confidence in Pirvan.

Pirvan never caught up with Fulvura. She bellowed a war cry, her standard-bearer strode to the front of the minotaur wedge, and the seven were off. The human advance was, briefly, a scramble to keep up with Zeskuk's sister and her warriors.

* * * * *

Sir Darin heaved at a rock that not even he could hope to move alone. Sweat streamed off him, and rough stone scraped his hands raw until others came to help him. Even then, they were all panting as if they'd run a race for life, before the stone moved. They were making a new passage. They would make it, however the battle above ended. But they might not make the new passage in time to do more than avenge their comrades.

Darin realized that they should have held back a few of the smaller fighters to act as messengers. He turned to Rynthala and said, "Find the smallest of those we have left. Tell them to crawl into the upper passage as far as they can. We need to relay messages, to and fro."

Rynthala nodded and strode off. From above a chorus of shouts warred with a heavy splashing. The Creation seemed to have no voice, but Darin could feel the shaking of the rock as it flung itself against the shore of the lake, seeking prey.

A rumble from above turned into a shriek of rock against rock. Then came a shriek of human agony. A man-sized boulder bounced down the barrier, clattering and crashing, trailing dust and rock chips. Behind it rolled a Karthayan fighter, his face a mask of dust and blood and one leg a crushed horror.

The man landed almost at Darin's feet, in a small puddle of water. Darin had not noticed the puddle before, nor the trickle from the rocks that fed it. He wished the lake wouldn't waste its time trickling through the lower passage. If it could just wash out the upper one—

But no. That passage was solid rock. If muscle or water or both together could do anything in time, it would be down here.

"Healers!" Darin shouted. The cave gave back echoes, twice- and thrice-distorted.

Then someone screamed from above. The Creation had found a victim. Darin scrambled back onto the rocks of the barrier. They moved under his weight, as they had not before. He rejoiced, even though they might tumble away under him, and send him to the fate of the fallen man.

Then the rocks moved again, and this time he knew it was the ground moving under them, not his weight atop them. He leaped back onto solid ground, as another scream tore from the throat of someone dying under the Creation's claws and tentacles.

On the back of his neck, Darin felt a brief puff of hot air.

* * * * *

The Creation had taken three fighters from Torvik's band in its first rush. The rest had given ground, and by Habbakuk's favor there was ground to give. The beach of sand, gravel, and boulders at the end of the lake was wide enough that those to the rear were out of the Creation's reach.

It could not crawl onto the land, either. It weighed as much as a whale, and its lobsterlike legs had not grown in proportion to the rest of it. But it had a whale's shrewdness, too—or perhaps more, the wits of an ape or a water naga.

It swam back and forth along the beach, as far to either side and as close inshore as the depth of the water would allow. There were places where deep water lay close by, and those places the fighters quickly learned to avoid. Twice a tentacle uncoiled from the water, snatched a fighter off his feet, and pulled him screaming down to the waiting claws.

Other times, bold fighters drew close to the water, trying to plant spears or arrows into vital spots. If the Creation had any. Even if it did, the odds against striking one were heavy, as long as it faced its foes.

Torvik saw feather-fringed breathing holes and a softer underbelly to either flank. But those flanks were seldom exposed, and then only to desperate fighters who either shot or threw at random and missed, or waited for an aimed shot and too often died screaming. Sometimes the Creation did not even bother to use its claws, but crushed its victims to pulp with the sheer strength of its tentacles, or flayed them alive with the hooks that sprouted around the suckers on some of its arms.

"Did Wilthur use only lesser krakens and lobsters to make this, or more?" Chuina asked. She had closed with the Creation three times, to shoot two arrows each time. She was still alive, but the Creation was likewise unhurt.

"There is all of nature and none of it in that monster," Torvik said. "But it is flesh and blood, however much Wilthur shaped them with magic. Flesh and blood can die."

Chuina did not say that many men and women might die first. Instead, she ran in for her fourth try at the Creation, going so far that spray rose around her bare feet as she reached the water before shooting.

She struck one of the breathing holes fair and hard, and the Creation shuddered. But she did not slow it, and a lashing tentacle knocked her down. Another wound around her ankle, while one claw reached out—

Torvik ran in, so blind to everything but saving Chuina that he hardly noticed the dozen fighters running with him. He ran far enough into the water to hack at the tentacle holding Chuina's leg and laid open blackish gray flesh.

The Creation shuddered. It still did not find a voice, but Chuina screamed for all, as half a dozen pairs of strong arms snatched her from the loosening grip of the tentacle. She struggled free as her rescuers reached the shore, to stand with one leg of her pants ripped free and ugly, free-bleeding cuts on both her legs and the top of her foot.

"A good thing there are no sharks in the lake," she said, as Torvik stormed out of the water to see how she was.

"No, this madman's Creation is fierce enough by nature, without any scent of blood," Kuyomolan snapped. "We must turn it, so we can take it in the flank."

"It will not turn to take someone from the land," Chuina said. "At least not enough."

"Then perhaps it will turn to follow someone in the water," the Dimernesti said, more quietly than Torvik had ever heard him speak. "I did not come this far to return knowing that the journey was in vain, and that I left companions whom I might have helped."

Kuyomolan ran down the beach, to a point above one of the deep holes. He soared like a bird as he dived, but made less noise than a diving kingfisher as he broke the surface.

"Quickly!" Chuina shouted. "Archers, spearmen! Make ready! He's going to try to turn the beast and give us a flank shot! Hurry!"

Everyone who still had spears or arrows rushed for the beach, briefly careless of the tentacles and claws. Even Chuina took a few halting steps, before the pain in her blood-slimed leg halted her.

Torvik knelt beside her, tearing off his shirt and ripping it into bandages. "Now be easy, until the bleeding stops!"

he said, as he wound the bandages around Chuina's leg. "You may dance again, but not if you try to fight again today."

"Oh, and what will you do if I do not obey?" Chuina said. She was doing her best imitation of a silly schoolgirl.

"I shall tell Mother," Torvik replied, doing his best imitation of the schoolgirl's pompous older brother.

It was only when they had finished laughing that they realized that both Kuyomolan and the Creation had vanished. Ripples and eddies told of something large moving below the surface, but where and in what direction, no one could tell.

The archers and spearmen, ready to strike, looked something between angry and bemused. Some of them cast dubious looks at the dark water, knowing too well how suddenly it might erupt in deadly tentacles.

Then the water roiled, foamed, and erupted. A wave as high as a man's waist rolled up onto the beach. A dozen fighters went down, some of them to be swept into the water by the backwash. They thrashed frantically, forgetting weapons, as did those who rushed to help them.

Then everyone leaped or struggled backward, as the Creation rose from the water. In one tentacle it held Kuyomolan, but not fatally tight. He had his spear in both hands, and was jabbing at the convoluted segments of the carapace covering the head, and the fringe of waving antennae all around it.

The tentacle tightened its grip. Torvik saw blood start from the Dimernesti's leg. He also saw Kuyomolan draw back both arms and fling the spear down into the Creation's head with all his remaining strength.

Tentacles lashed in frenzy. Two more wrapped themselves around Kuyomolan, and the cave echoed to his last scream as he was torn literally limb from limb.

But something oozed from the Creation's skull, and its movements seemed less certain. Kuyomolan had hurt it. The archers could hurt it more.

Chuina limped toward the water, unslinging her bow as she ran. Only her brother recognized how much pain she was keeping from showing in her face, as she shouted, "We have it! Finish it now! Shoot, shoot, shoot!"

Then earth and water seemed to speak for the Creation, as rock crumbled, sand and gravel flew, and the waters of the lake tore downward through the blocked passage.

* * * * *

Darin saw workers crushed by rocks, swept away by the rushing water, or dashed to bloody pieces in falls. He saw boulders and rushing water vanish behind a cloud of spray and dust, and waited for something to swallow him or crush him as well.

The gods worked here. Mere flesh-and-blood strength could not serve.

Still, he snatched at limbs when they flailed past, and heaved rocks aside or off the fallen, even if the fallen would never rise again. He stood waist-deep in the torrent like a rock himself, with desperate swimmers clutching at his clothes, and altogether behaved as if he could single-handedly turn aside disaster.

Darin had his reward, when the spray and dust subsided. The lake was draining through a passage in which lower and upper no longer had meaning. A small ship with its mast stepped might have sailed through the gap, although it would have been dashed to pieces on the rocks below.

Of the fighters at his back when the lake declared war, Darin counted all but twenty or so still on their feet. And to either side of the torrent was a broad stretch of tumbled rock, slick and dark with spray, probably none too secure as footing, but with room for the whole band to climb up and join the fight.

Darin was the first to move, but Rynthala was not far behind. The rest of the band chased their leaders all the way up the rockfall, at a pace that brought more than a few of them down with sprained or broken limbs. But they were not far behind their chiefs in scrambling up onto what was left of the beach, and seeing what had become of the Creation.

It lay with its left side toward the beach, its legs thrashing the water into still more foam. Its claws clacked and rattled aimlessly, but the tentacles still lashed out menacingly. Archers shot steadily into the breathing holes and at the skull, but the monstrous vitally diminished only slowly.

Rynthala had climbed with her bow slung, but had it ready with an arrow nocked when she struck the beach. Running along the hard-packed sand to just beyond reach of the tentacles, she crouched as the last few arrows from Chuina's archers flew overhead.

Then she rose and began shooting with the deadly precision of a blacksmith hammering a pattern into the blade of a sword. Five times her arrows vanished into the breathing holes. Each time the lashing of tentacles grew perceptibly less frenzied.

Darin realized that archery could kill slowly, but that they needed a swifter kill, or the Creation might yet take more victims. He would have given much for a minotaur battle-axe, but before him stood a man who'd climbed up still holding the pry bar he'd used on the rocks.

"Excuse me," Darin said, reaching. With the bar in both hands, he ran into the water, testing the bar's balance as he went. It was clumsy but it had weight and a sharp end, much more important now.

Even Darin was not so foolhardy as to climb on the carapace, to fall off where tentacles, legs, or claws could still do fatal damage. He waded out until any man much shorter than he would have been swimming, then dived.

He rose from the water with the force if not the grace of the Dimernesti, the bar in his hand. The sharp end tore up under the lower rim of the Creation's skull, bone cracked and peeled, and Darin drove the bar into the exposed brain.

The Creation found a voice then, an enormity of raw sound, corrupted nature roaring its hatred of all uncorrupted nature. Foam rose higher than *Red Elf*'s deck as the Creation churned out the last of its unnatural life.

Those nearest Rynthala were torn between leaving the widow alone and drawing near, lest she fling herself after

Darin. Then part of the foam showed a darker core, the core moved, and Sir Darin waded out of the Creation's death-maelstrom.

His hands were empty, and indeed he seemed to be favoring one arm. He wore rags of clothes and a painful array of scratches and cuts, and had he been able to find the breath to speak would have said that he preferred wrestling bears. But he walked out of the water to find Torvik hugging Rynthala. It was an odd pairing, as the young captain was a good six inches shorter than the knight's lady.

"You did it, you did it!" he was babbling. "You put those arrows exactly where they belonged. Magnificent!"

Darin tapped Torvik on the shoulder. "Excuse me, Captain. I agree that my lady is magnificent. But your sister had something to do with the victory, I think, she and her archers."

Torvik drew back from Rynthala, who looked ready to burst out laughing. "Very well," he said. "Then, Sir Darin, you can kiss my sister."

"Yes, and then we will all kiss you," Rynthala said, finally losing her composure. "The thing did not have many brains left, but those it had, you dashed out."

Torvik cheerfully refused to kiss Darin, but was amenable to kissing Mirraleen. This left Darin free to kiss Chuina, which he did quite properly, for all that he had to stoop considerably to meet her lips and she winced at the pain of standing on tiptoe to help him.

Stooping sent pains shooting up and down strained muscles and scarred limbs, but Darin did not believe in letting minor pains distract one from honorably kissing a lady.

What distracted him—and everyone else—was a shaking of the ground that was accompanied by a distant rumble.

Looking down the torrent, Darin saw a distant ruddy glow reflected on the foam. A similar glow seemed to be spreading ahead, in the darkness on the far side of the lake, beyond the reach of the glowballs.

"We'd best start looking for that last passage Mirraleen's directions describe," he said. "The lake may drain out, and that much water washing about here could bring down more rocks."

That was true enough, but earthquakes could yield bigger rockfalls than all the water under the Smoker put together. Also, water flowing down volcanic vents could reach molten rock and turn into steam. Seeking an upward passage, the steam might cook them and Wilthur alike, as if they were so many chickens on a tavern spit. Not finding that passage, the steam might build pressure until the entire mountain tore itself apart in one cataclysm.

Going up and getting out of the Smoker had just become a race with death. Nor was the magic of Wilthur the Brown any longer the only likely source of that death.

* * * * *

Zeskuk had come to the rim of a hole where another passage dropped steeply downward, when word came that the humans had caught up. He knelt beside Lujimar, who was lying on the rock, peering down into the hole as if his gaze could pierce not only the darkness but the rock itself. Zeskuk wished it could, and pierce Wilthur like an arrow when it found him. That would save a great deal of muddling about in the darkness, in passages that were becoming a tight fit for humans, let alone minotaurs.

"Do we let the humans take the lead from here?" Zeskuk asked. "We can always follow, to pull them free if they become wedged."

"I sense no barriers of rock between here and Wilthur," Lujimar said. He sounded no worse than tired, but his tone still chilled the chief. "Other barriers are as may be. For these, we will need human aid."

Lujimar stood, turned his back to Zeskuk, and held his staff out over the hole. He muttered something that the minotaur chief was very glad not to fully understand, and the tunnel was suddenly lit as by the noonday sun. Wind blew both up and down, and Zeskuk would have been prepared to swear that it blew sideways, through the walls

Instead, he cursed, as he suddenly found a small, bony human female flung into his arms as if by a siege engine.

"What do you fatherless minotaurs think you're doing? Lady Revella Laschaar screamed.

"A simple spell of transference," Lujimar said. Zesku could not see him over Lady Revella's high-peaked cap but would have wagered the priest was smiling.

A second thought chilled the smile. Teleporting anothe wizard of Lady Revella's strength, without her consent an without warning, was vastly potent magic. It had bee plain for some while that Lujimar knew more than priest arts. Now it was a question of how much more.

Zeskuk had no answer to that question, which neede none in any case. Lady Revella, on the other hand, neede many answers, as well as being put on her feet in a reason ably dignified manner. When she had shaken dust from he clothes and cap, and laced up her boots, she glared impar tially at the two minotaurs.

"I suppose you think I can do more good here than from aboard ship?" she asked.

"I know it," Lujimar said, in a tone that froze even Lad Revella's tongue. Zeskuk was glad someone else had an swered; he could not have spoken.

"Well, then," the Black Robe said. "I will be of much more use much longer if I do not have to walk every step of our road through this volcanic pest hole. Where I can ride in a litter, I would prefer to do so."

"Of course," Zeskuk said, finding his voice at last. His bellow of four names sent echoes ravaging everyone's ears

When Lady Revella had taken her hands from her ears she was glaring again. "I am to ride in a litter borne by minotaurs?"

"Free minotaurs," Zeskuk said. "Surely you have ridden in enough borne by minotaur slaves, a lady of your rank You must allow us to give you the gift of this new experi ence, trusting yourself to freeborn minotaur warriors."

Lady Revella's face said that she would as soon trust her self to ghouls, but prudence kept that message from he

ps. Before she could frame a more diplomatic reply, more-
ver, glowballs and hurrying footsteps told of the arrival of
he human vanguard, and nothing could undo her embar-
ssment now.

* * * * *

Wilthur the Brown was not embarrassed. He was en-
ged at the demise of his Creation and the destruction
rought around the lake. His defenses would surely pre-
il against flesh and blood, but would the mountain be
fe afterward?

Perhaps, perhaps not. He could still make a new abode
the Green Mountain, even if there was less magic to
raw on in it. He would not flee.

The gods were not embarrassed, either. They were quite
ntent with the progress of the battle. Some were not so
ntent with Takhisis's reminding them that Wilthur had
een White, Red, and Black, so was a balance in and by
imself, and should be carefully preserved.

Zeboim spoke rarely, but now said things about Takhisis
at the Queen of the Abyss had seldom heard even when
carnate as a human woman, from the most foul-mouthed
ales. There was silence among the gods for some while
ter that, except for some subdued laughter from Sar-
nnas.

Gerik was still less embarrassed. He had no time. When
e is within minutes of attacking eighty men with thirty,
e has no time for anything except the work that will soon
e at hand.

Particularly, one has no time for a kender tugging at
e's sleeve, even when he is being quiet about it.

Chapter 22

With the strength of fury, Wilthur flung spells at his defenses. T
spells contained the stolen vitality of the dead of Suivina
Fed into the defenses, that vitality would render them
vincible.

Instead, the spells went astray, some of them, or reach
the defenses but bounced off them, like arrows off t
finest plate armor. As the spells scattered, so did the stol
hoarded vitality. As the vitality failed to enter the defens
from within, and the enemies tore at them from witho
the defenses weakened.

At last Wilthur rested. He would have to find the po
in the defenses (or points, perhaps as many as three) whe
the enemy sought the final penetration. He wou
strengthen the defenses there, and there only, howev
much he could.

He might not break the bodies of all his foes, human
minotaur. But he might do enough harm to break their sp
its.

It was a sad decline in hopes, from being ranked near
the gods to merely disheartening foes who were close
victory, but the only alternative was still flight. And that
ternative was as futile as ever.

Wilthur girded himself with spells against despair and for greater concentration, and prepared for the final battle.

* * * * *

Horimpsot Elderdrake did not dare make more sound than came from tugging at Gerik's sleeve. When that failed to draw the young lord's attention or even make him turn his head, Elderdrake felt as close to despair as a kender can.

He still wanted to find out what would happen next; a kender's curiosity dies only when he does. But he did not expect that next event to be something he would enjoy. Not if a second band of enemies came down on Gerik's rear while his attention was fixed so completely to the front.

They would have to do something about that themselves, he and the kender who had brought the news.

Elderdrake slipped out of the bushes and back toward his comrade. The other kender greeted him with a sour smile. "What took you so long?" the other kender asked.

"Trying to keep us from having to do this all by ourselves?" was Elderdrake's reply.

The smile grew even more sour. Then the other kender nodded. "His name was Fujindor Staffbinder," he said.

It took a moment for Elderdrake to realize that he had just heard the name of the priest whom Gerik called "the Shorn One." He had only known the dead kender as "the priest of Branchala."

"You are as likely to get free of this as I am," Elderdrake reminded his comrade.

"Or as unlikely," the other replied. "But all the others of our woods band know, too. Our friend's name will not die unless all of us do."

It took the two kender no more than the time for hard-boiling an egg to slip through the trees to within reach of the second enemy band's trail. Indeed, it was more of a series of gaps between the trees than a proper trail, but the ground was damp, soft, and moss-grown in places; the horses' hooves made little noise.

Elderdrake briefly wished that they had a few more

packets of Staffbinder's horse-allergy powder. But ther
was little breeze to scatter it, and what there was migh
bring it down on Gerik's band as well. They didn't war
that. Gerik's enemies could still win even if on foot, whil
Gerik needed to be able to mount and ride.

There was no time for subtlety, so the kender used none
Elderdrake's friend simply whipped his hoopak over hi
head, flinging a stone from the sling-thong. The stone struc
a rider in the forehead, dropping him from the saddle. The
the first kender flung himself out of shelter, striking or stab
bing with his hoopak depending on which end was closes
to an enemy. Elderdrake followed, considering that neithe
he nor his friend would likely tell anyone much of any
thing—but if they did, it would be a far better story than jus
the priest's name, as deserving of memory as he was.

Something struck Elderdrake hard in the right arm, an
all sensation and use left it. Fortunately a hoopak was on
thing he could wield with either hand. He dived to retriev
his fallen weapon, rolled under the belly of a horse, an
prodded the belly as he came up on the other side.

The horse reared, throwing its rider. The rider landed o
his head, leaving his neck at an impossible angle to hi
shoulders. Elderdrake wasted no time, because a rider wh
hadn't seen that his friend was dead was coming in. Th
kender held the hoopak up with his good left arm, the
twisted aside as the shaft deflected a sword cut, whirle
the hoopak like a sea barbarian cutlass-dancer, an
rammed the spear into the rider's thigh as he swept by.

The thigh was armored, but the spear point had not los
its sharpness, nor Elderdrake's left arm its strength. Th
man shouted, swore, and twisted in the saddle. He wa
left-handed, so he had to bring his battle-axe around an
over.

As the axe blurred downward toward Elderdrake'
skull, he heard something that sounded like a kender'
death cry. He heard a hideous din that sounded like th
death cry of many humans. He even heard, for a singl
heartbeat, the whisper of cloven air as the axe completed it
downward arc.

Then he heard a sound that was not a sound, but the end of all things, as the downward arc ended in his skull.

* * * * *

Pirvan thought briefly that a few folk not eager to be in the vanguard would now be more help than the small army of those who were. The tunnel showed no signs of broadening enough to accommodate more than two humans and two minotaurs. Each folk wanted to have the greater numbers in the vanguard, and Pirvan and Zeskuk were too jostled, squeezed, and short of breath to take counsel and introduce a trace of order to this underground chaos.

It could have been as bad with the magicworkers, except that no one of either folk wished to deny Lujimar his place ahead of all warriors. Certainly not Lady Revella, who could not have kept up with the advance on foot and whose bearers took up the whole width of the tunnel where they were.

In his mind, the knight made gestures of aversion, that the tunnel not drop so low overhead that the bearers must set the Black Robe down. Trampling underfoot one of a host's two most powerful magicworkers was not a recipe for victory.

Instead of dropping, the ceiling rose further and the walls receded. Before Pirvan had fully realized it, the vanguard had spilled out into a vast underground chamber, taller than the highest tower in Istar and so wide that an entire regiment could have formed a line of battle across the floor. Or rather, they could have, if a vast expanse of white webbing hadn't stretched across the chamber from side to side. It hung a man's height off the floor, rose two men's height higher than that, and seemed to spread over at least half the chamber's area.

It also glowed, with a pearly light that recalled no kind of spell Pirvan knew of, and made him wish that Tarothin was alive or Lujimar not wholly lost in his own purposes. The knight was commander of this host; he needed to know his enemy.

One thing struck several fighters of each race at the same moment: the light made glowballs unnecessary. They dropped theirs and rushed forward. No one saw whether a minotaur or a human reached the webbing first, but everyone in the chamber saw what happened to the first of each

It was not without reason that Pirvan had thought of spiders when he saw the webbing. What crawled out of the webbing had twelve legs instead of eight, and poison-dripping hooks on the inside of the foremost legs instead of fangs. They also had more eyes than Pirvan dared count, all glowing a diseased blue that might have been found in the coldest part of the Abyss or in some nightmare cave on Nuitari.

To these not-spiders, the minotaurs and humans charging them were as flies. In moments all were reeling about the chamber, clutching where the venom from the foreleg hooks was eating into their flesh. Pirvan saw the envenomed slashes turning black and flesh crumbling as it turned the color of charcoal, pouring out blue smoke at the same time.

The victims fell to the floor, but their weapons did not clatter beside them. The tendrils of webbing had already wound themselves around the weapons and snatched them aloft. Now the same tendrils dropped to the chamber floor and began reeling in the dead and dying in an obscene parody of fishermen with their catch.

Pirvan kept his eyes firmly fixed on the horror, to not show weakness and to learn more of what they faced, if any untutored eye like his could see anything useful. To the side, Pirvan glimpsed Lujimar, standing as solid and as impassive as a boulder on a mountainside.

He wanted to shout at the minotaur to do something. He also wanted to shout at the murmuring humans behind him to show some pride before the minotaurs. The "Destined Race's" warriors were probably as uneasy about this deathtrap as their human comrades, but were certainly hiding it better.

It was then that Sir Niebar stepped forward, out of the ranks of the humans. He was wrapped in his cloak, all but his sword arm, and moved like a man just risen from a bed of near-mortal sickness. Behind him stepped Lady Revella—who had to be ten years older than the knight, but now walked as if she were twenty years younger—carrying only her staff.

A look passed between knight and Black Robe, of a kind that Pirvan knew he would never be able to describe. Nor did he wish to. Knights of the Rose were not supposed to share secrets with Black Robes, and there were those in the Keeps who would make a scandal if they suspected such.

Sir Niebar halted until the webbing had swallowed the last of the bodies. It now jerked and twisted, like blankets over restless sleepers, and Pirvan had the stomach-turning thought that it was digesting the bodies. Perhaps the spiders were only the servants—the hounds coursing prey for their master, the living web.

Niebar took the last three steps, to within reach of the nearest spider. For the first time, Lujimar seemed to notice what was happening. He raised one hand in an urgent gesture.

Before the minotaur could finish the gesture, Sir Niebar raised his sword. He raised it high overhead, held level, within easy reach of the nearest spider or the web. The spider did not take the bait. The web did. Tendrils as thick as tent ropes poured down and wrapped themselves around the web—and around Sir Niebar's sword arm. Pirvan saw his face twist in pain; there must have been something like acid on the tendrils.

Then the web lifted the knight clean off the floor. As it did, he came within arm's length of the spider. His free hand darted under his cloak and came out with a glowball. With an arrow-swift gesture, he thrust the glowball into the spider's gaping maw.

Then the web jerked the knight upward again, so violently that Pirvan thought—and hoped—that the motion must have snapped his neck. His close-cropped white hair vanished into the web; Sir Hawkbrother cried out in rage and despair. Close at hand, Pirvan heard Haimya fighting not to do the same—and Lady Revella raised her staff.

She said nothing, made no other movements, and indeed stood as if turned to stone. But behind the Abyss-fire in the spider's eyes, something glowed that had not been there before. It was a warmer color—almost the color of one of the glowballs, Pirvan realized, in the last moment before fire erupted from the spider's mouth and joints.

For a long moment, the spider seemed to be a wheel of fire: orange, crimson, wine-hued, and even a virulent green. Then the fire touched the web—and the spider vanished in a whirlpool of flame as the web burned.

Half-dazzled, Pirvan saw Sir Niebar's partly-consumed body fall to the floor. He was not too dazzled to see Hawk-brother and Eskaia dash forward to recover it. Nor did he fail to see Haimya drop her sword and run to join the younger couple.

Pirvan caught up with them by the time the web was fully ablaze. He never afterward recalled any of the details, nor at precisely what moment he heard Eskaia scream, nearly stumbled over a half-melted sword that seared through his boot, and caught a lungful of smoke of such gagging vileness that his breath wanted to leave his body for fear of another such.

Somehow, they found themselves standing behind Lady Revella. She now stood with her staff apparently planted in the solid rock, her arms crossed on her chest, and an implacable look on her face.

Her features softened as the four companions laid what was left of Sir Niebar down. Pirvan took only long enough to see that Eskaia was only burned about the arm and neck, before he faced the Black Robe.

"Did you send Niebar to his death?" he shouted.

"Take your hand off your sword when you ask one of my age a question," Revella shot back.

Pirvan did not move. Haimya came to stand beside him and practically spat, "Was he Rubina's father?"

The Black Robe's answer to that was an almost girlish shriek of laughter. "Oh, I wish he had been. But he was not." She sobered. "Only a man who saw that his time was near, and wanted to make his death worthwhile.

"The web could have stood off fire from outside for longer than we could stay here. But fire inside its defenses, inside a spider—neither Lujimar nor Wilthur could halt it."

"Lujimar?" Pirvan exclaimed. That had sounded remarkably like an accusation of treachery against the minotaur. But Lady Revella had not heard, nor would she listen.

Instead, she turned toward Lujimar and cupped her hands to shout, "Magic brother! Crack the roof, for the love of all gods and your own true death, before we stifle!"

* * * * *

The ambush of the first enemy band reminded Gerik of a tale he had heard about the Silvanesti. Once upon a time, an ambitious human king had claimed part of their forest. He could send ten thousand fighting men to enforce that claim, he blustered.

"They will be shot down like deer," the Silvanesti emissary replied.

"What if I send twenty thousand?"

"Then each of our archers will shoot twice," was the elven reply, or so the story ran.

Gerik commanded twenty archers against somewhere around eighty foes. That meant shooting four times—or would have, if his archers had been the Silvanesti of legend.

They were not. But four arrows apiece still did enough work to earn victory in moments. By the time Gerik's people had shot that many, they had killed, wounded, or dismounted a good half of their opponents. At least ten had died before they could have fully realized they were in danger.

The quivers were half-empty when a sell-sword Gerik recognized as one of the horse-holders ran out of the trees. He had an arrow through his forearm, and ran first to Bertsa Wylum, who pointed at Gerik.

The man came up to Gerik and said bluntly, "We're for it, young lord. They had a second band behind us. The kender sprang that trap, but they've ridden off."

"Are the horses safe?" Gerik asked, and felt a fool the next moment, knowing he should have asked about the kender.

"Aye. The other fellows were too hot to be off on the trail of our folk, when they knew they'd been heard."

Gerik slammed his fist against a tree. From behind her own tree, Wylum shot another arrow, then called, "Hoy, good sir. Don't break your sword hand. We're not even finished with these fellows yet, let alone chasing down the others."

Finishing the House Dirivan band at Forge Vale proved swifter than Gerik had dared hope. A few more arrows were all it took to start the men holding up swords hilt-first or unstringing their bows. Bertsa Wylum led five of her band down, to collect weapons, take oaths of neutrality from those sell-swords willing to swear, and bind those of the House Dirivan fighters who would not.

Wylum returned, wearing a grim smile and carrying an armful of captured weapons. "I left five daggers and a sword for the lot of them. If any of them change their minds, it won't do them much good until they rearm."

"They'll still be at our backs," Gerik said. In his mind a single dark thought thudded like a drum.

The enemy was between him and Ellysta. They would not have been if he had been alert or listened to Elderdrake.

"Perhaps, but a long way off and with no horses," Wylum said. "We're taking all the ones fit to ride to mount more of our people. Besides, if they break the oath of neutrality, they're dead meat if we see them again today, and no sell-sword company will have them."

"I suppose that's something."

"It's the whole cursed band off House Dirivan's roster, without our having to kill them all," Wylum snapped. "That could be half the battle right there."

She looked at Gerik sideways, then started to tousle his hair. She snatched her hand back when he all but bared his teeth at her.

"All right," she growled. "Have it your way. But don't fret yourself into uselessness. You've made one mistake today, but it's one every captain makes a few times. A nice fat target is hard to resist."

She was right, and too much worrying would be a second, less forgivable mistake. But Bertsa Wylum hadn't held Ellysta during her mercifully-few nightmares.

Gerik drew a deep breath and said, "Then let's go take another. Is anyone hurt past riding, but able to get about?"

"Two."

"Good. Let them find the kender's bodies and hide them. Everyone else, mount up."

* * * * *

Whatever Lujimar had done or left undone, he took Lady Revella at her word. He turned, lifted his staff, pointed it at the chamber's ceiling, and bellowed what might have been words.

He bellowed them loud enough to make Pirvan clap his hands over his ears. The bellow was a hush, though, compared to the sound of the rock splitting apart, then bulging and finally erupting outward.

Wind blew out of nowhere, into the chamber, and out through the ship-sized hole in the roof. It carried with it the charred remnants of web, spiders, and victims, half-melted weapons and unidentifiable bits of debris, enough ashes to turn the air black for a moment, and anything that anyone had set down on the floor and not retrieved or tied down.

Revella Laschaar might have gone with the wreckage, if her two minotaur bearers had not come up and each taken a firm grip on one arm. Pirvan saw her try to shake them off once, then seemingly resign herself to their help.

A few bits of rock, too heavy for the wind or the spells to lift, fell into the chamber, but struck no one. When the wind finally died, they could breathe in the chamber without feeling that they would choke to death in the next moment.

"Let us be off," Lujimar said, the moment even a minotaur's voice could be heard by half-deafened ears. "Wilthur is not far. Lady Revella, stand well behind me hereafter. This battle—"

"This battle needs both of us, and you know it, bull-brained oaf," Revella snapped. "I cannot—"

Zeskuk gave a wordless bellow, then shouted, "If you can't offer more than insults, old woman, then save your breath!"

"*Yessss,*" a voice said. It was a voice that could not have belonged to anybody, even the giant serpent it suggested. It was a voice from beyond any realm where life had bodies; from everywhere and nowhere.

From Wilthur the Brown, Pirvan judged—and then saw his judgment confirmed by the looks on the magicworkers' faces. Human and minotaur both looked as if they faced having a tooth pulled with no healer's sleep spell or even a brimming cup of dwarf spirits to ease the pain.

In the next moment, Pirvan saw Lady Revella's face contort with—surprise? Horror? Something for which there was not a word? He did not know. He only saw her contorted face, the unchangeable impassivity of Lujimar's, and the sudden snap of the minotaur priest's arm as he threw his staff like a spear to the far end of the chamber.

Rock crashed. A throat neither human nor animal gave forth a scream that some who heard it would have given years of life to forget. The staff returned, wound like a vine or a constricting snake around a slight form in a faded brown robe.

The figure's face was hidden at first, inside the hood of the robe. Then the wind of the staff's passage tore the hood back. Pirvan was not the only seasoned warrior who swayed or cried out at the sight of what Wilthur had become. Some fainted outright.

Lujimar's staff carried its prey all the way back to its master. He reached for the free end, Wilthur spat in his face, and those who saw Lujimar swore that his eyes turned red.

Then the wind from nowhere blew again. This time it actually knocked minotaurs off their feet and flung humans against stone walls hard enough to crack bones. Two fighters who struck headfirst would have died had they not been wearing helmets.

Pirvan himself forgot knightly dignity and clung desperately to an outcropping of stone that he hoped was strong enough to save him. He would have been more ashamed had he not seen Zeskuk curling himself into a ball of hide and armor—except for one arm that clutched a human warrior's ankle to keep him from taking flight.

Curled up as he was, however, Zeskuk could not see what Pirvan was doing. He saw Lujimar and his opponent rise from the floor, blue fire crackling around them as Wilthur tried to fight free of the staff. He saw them soar toward the hole in the chamber ceiling, now moving faster than the wind itself. He saw them vanish skyward. In the same moment, he felt the rock under his feet quiver, almost innocently, like a stout tavern table against which a minotaur has quite innocently bumped.

The word "innocent," however, had no meaning in this place. Not now.

* * * * *

From elsewhere on Suivinari Island, and from the fleets offshore, it seemed that the Smoker had started to erupt. First stones spewed outward, to fall as the dead birds had, but with rather more impact where they landed. Man or minotaur needed both hands and perhaps one foot, to count those killed or maimed by the falling stones.

Then, moments later, what seemed to be a shooting star soared from the flank of the mountain. It leaped upward toward the zenith, and it blazed a shade of blue that no one had ever seen, or at least would admit to remembering.

Everyone remembered what happened next. Some sharp-eyed watchers had just said the star was actually a minotaur and a human, closely bound together, and received only scornful laughter, when the zenith turned the same shade of blue as the "rising star." It blazed across half the sky before it faded. Before it faded, it had also blinded a few watchers for life, and left many seeing blue spots before their eyes for many days.

The most frightening thing about the blue star, however,

was that it came and went without a sound. The blazing light seemed to swallow even the sound of the two bodies soaring upward through the air.

Not so silent, however, was the rumble from the mountain soon afterward. Nor did the rumbling cease—and fear for those in or on the mountain spread through those who watched.

* * * * *

In the chamber, the rock above cut off all within from a view of the zenith. So the blue glare dazzled few and blinded none. It was being occupied with rallying his fighters that kept Pirvan's attention elsewhere, until he suddenly realized that the chamber was much more crowded than it had been.

His first thought was a foolish one, that Wilthur had left behind a further host of enslaved creatures, these with human form. Then he saw a human form he could not mistake—the towering one of Darin—and realized that the underground raiders had somehow joined his own party.

Darin actually picked Pirvan up in the course of their embrace, something the younger knight had never done before. Pirvan did not worry about his dignity, of which he had precious little remaining. He only hoped Darin would not drop him. The younger knight looked weary and filthy, Pirvan's legs were none too steady, and the floor was still hard.

"The Creation is dead," Darin said at last, then looked toward the skyward hole. "Is Wilthur—?"

"Gone," Pirvan breathed. "Lujimar with him, likewise Tarothin, Sir Niebar—this is a victory almost worse than a defeat."

"To the Abyss with your sorrow!" Lady Revella snapped. "Wilthur sought godhood. Lujimar knew that if the Brown One took in his strength, Wilthur might yet succeed. So Lujimar bound them together in such a way that what befell one must befall the other. Then he flung them both into the sky, so that if what came about was too violent . . ."

"Let no one ever say in my hearing that Lujimar was without honor," Darin said.

"My young friend," Zeskuk rumbled, "a minotaur should also say that. But it is enough for now that one taught by a minotaur has done so. We have more urgent matters, such as departing this mountain while we still can."

Pirvan noted that no minotaur used the word "flee" that day under the rocks of the Smoker of Suivinari, but they obeyed Zeskuk's command to depart with such alacrity that if they had been humans one would have said they were running for their lives.

*　*　*　*　*

On the whole, the gods were pleased with the outcome at Suivinari.

Takhisis was the exception, but the other gods, including her consort Sargonnas, sat back and let Zeboim speak plainly to her mother. It was the sort of mother-daughter quarrel which, among mortals, takes a heavy toll among the crockery and other household goods.

Among the gods, the quarrel entertained most, except Mishakal, too kind to wish disharmony even where mutual ill will made it inevitable. Among mortals, there were storms at sea and portents on land, including rumors of dragons waking from dragonsleep.

Also among mortals—specifically, the mortals fleeing Tirabot Manor—Ellysta was not pleased. Gerik was taking too long to join them, and she was thinking of sending messengers to the other parties, to see if he had been obliged to join them. It would be as well to know what stood between them and their enemies.

She had just realized that there were few riders to spare for messenger work, when Grimsoar One-Eye approached her, with an ill-sounding message of his own.

"Riders on the road. Coming on fast, and too many to be Gerik's," he said. "We'll have to get the folk into the woods and let the wagons go."

Chapter 23

"Your armor, curse you!" Serafina screamed at her husband. To Ellysta, she sounded more like a fishmonger with a scanty stock than a concerned wife. But Serafina was doubtless weary and frightened. They all were, here in the forest as they awaited the enemy's attack.

Ellysta pushed through a tangle of vines, to see Grimsoar struggling to lay yet another fallen branch atop the modest barricade they had built. It blocked the trail, and to the left the ground was marshy, while to the right a ravine would make mounted attacks difficult.

The barricade would buy time; they needed nothing more. Most of the enemy could not have their heart in this work, and Gerik would be up and striking their rear within minutes anyway.

Ellysta told herself this, as she hurried down the slope toward Grimsoar. She told herself this because if she believed otherwise she would be sitting under a bush, biting the back of her hand to keep from screaming or even whimpering. I am not of warrior blood, Gerik, she said to herself, as if she were speaking to Pirvan's son. Are you sure you want to breed up sons from me?

Being a warrior can be in the blood, she heard, in Gerik's

voice. Or it can be learned. Don't doubt that you can learn it.

Meanwhile, there was a barricade to strengthen.

Ellysta had just wedged a third stone in behind one log, when the thud of fast-moving hooves swelled farther along the trail. War cries joined the hoofbeats, and the trail seemed to rise in her face and hurl mounted fighters at the barricade.

Grimsoar snatched up Ellysta by the collar of her tunic and the seat of her breeches and flung her over the barricade. She landed sprawling, the breath knocked out of her, as the first rider set his mount at the logs and stones and took them without drawing rein. A hoof stamped down within a finger of Ellysta's skull, and she rolled desperately to one side, praying that it was the safe side.

The rider was lashing about him with a long-handled battle-axe, and two men and a woman of Ellysta's party were already down. She lurched to her feet, drawing her longest knife, knowing that she had small chance against the rider unless she could surprise him but sure that her friends had still less.

A scream behind her jerked her head around. Grimsoar had grabbed the second rider by the leg and bodily twisted him out of the saddle, shattering the leg in the process. The old thief and sailor had his sword up to greet the third rider, and crushed the skull of the rider's mount with one blow, before an arrow sprouted in Grimsoar's shoulder.

That was all Ellysta saw before she whirled again and ran blindly toward where the first rider had been. The space was empty, though, and an arrow whispered past her ear as she turned wildly, seeking the rider.

He and his mount were halfway to the trees, and a small dark-clad figure was clinging to the horse's bridle. The rider was flourishing the battle-axe like a wizard with a conjure-stick, but his mount was bucking and skittering; he could not aim a blow.

He also could not guard his unarmored thigh. His attacker leaped, slashing desperately, and the man's thigh opened in a long red mouth of a wound. The axe flashed down, but the attacker darted under the horse's belly. The

man was reeling in the saddle when she caught the off stir-
rup, heaved herself up, and thrust the knife in again, below
the rim of the man's helmet.

The man toppled, Rubina held up her bloody knife with
a shriek of triumph that made Ellysta's blood freeze in her
body, and someone from beyond the barricade shouted in
a cracked voice: "Fools! We didn't come here to fight children! Back, and pray for the gods' mercy. Back, you fools,
or be cursed forever!"

* * * * *

The rumbling from the Smoker and the swaying of the
ground underfoot made Torvik think of being aboard a
large ship in a moderate gale. But they were still on Suivinari Island, and it would be a close-call if they all made it
safely back to friendly decks before the mountain erupted
and scoured the island clean of life.

Except that there were no unfriendly decks. Word was
that the minotaurs would take humans aboard, and
humans minotaurs. They could sort out who belonged to
which ship when they were all safely afloat.

Torvik approved. He also approved of the next word that
came down. He and Chuina didn't understand it at first,
but Mirraleen, with her acute Dimernesti hearing, heard at
once.

"Spread out, Darin says. We are to search for anyone
who fell out from heat or wounds as we return to the
shore."

Torvik looked dubiously at the landscape. It was less
overgrown than it had been, before human and minotaur-
wielded blades had taken their toll of it. Also, Wilthur's
magic no longer turned thornbushes into monsters.

But the time—

"I'm not lagging to look for minotaurs," someone
growled.

"Fair's fair," someone else replied. "They're letting us
aboard their ships. We can look for their fallen."

"All right," the first speaker said. "But if the Giant

Knight orders it, he can cursed well come down and help us. He's the only one big enough to be hauling minotaurs about in this sort of country!"

Another rumble made Torvik halt until the ground was steady. The march resumed, with the fighters spreading out into a search line, and an unmistakable odor of sulphur in the air.

* * * * *

Lady Eskaia reined in and watched the two Solamnic Knights arguing.

"Are you sure those folk were from Tirabot, and trust-worthy?" the tall, fair knight was saying to his chief.

"Unless they misled us worse than I dare believe possible, we'll soon hear any fighting," the short, dark-bearded one said. "Which means we keep moving, and keep quiet."

Eskaia breathed a sigh of relief. After this fourth argument, she had been ready to lead her Vuinlodders onward by herself. They would have obeyed, too, even knowing that if they did not come back their town would hardly be able to keep watch against common thieves, let alone defend itself.

At least, that would be so until the fleet returned. *When* they returned. The news from the north had not been so dire that Eskaia feared disaster there. It had been a trifle of news and a great many rumors of affairs in Istar that had sent her out of town, riding hard and fast at the head of the fifty best fighters left in Vuinlod.

They had met up with the Solamnics, the promised two knights and forty men-at-arms, on the road two days ago. The knights were silent about why they had not been across the border long since, but Eskaia knew that two could play at the game of invoking laws to suit their convenience. Doubtless the Istarans had made convincing arguments, for those bound to listen to anything Istarans had to say, even in defense of murder.

It had been her threat to ride on alone, without even her Vuinlodders, that had moved the two knights. Sir Shufiran of Geel, the dark-bearded senior, had not needed movin so much as he had needed an excuse. But the reluctance c the younger knight, Sir Rignar, had been as plain as his fin looks.

"Sir Shufiran," Eskaia called. "Do we advance, or awa our friends here?"

The knight tugged at his beard. He had an uncommo share of such nervous gestures, but none seemed to kee him from reaching sound decisions swiftly.

"We had best divide," he said. "Two trails eases the ris of ambush."

"Very well," Eskaia said. "Which of us takes which trail?

"We could divide each band—" Sir Rignar began, bu Shufiran coughed. The younger knight fell silent. Eskai shot a grateful look at the senior.

It was as well not to have to say that she did not trust Si Rignar out of her sight, nor would she trust him in her sigh if he commanded as many men as she did and Shufira was elsewhere.

In moments, they agreed that Vuinlodders and Solam nics would each send ten fighters to the other's column, t act as messengers, and that they would advance at once, a the trot.

To Eskaia, it seemed that perhaps Sir Rignar might ye learn war. For now, it would be enough if he learned wha he might face if any deed or omission of his killed th daughter of Josclyn Encuintras, the widow of Jemar th Fair, and the wife of Gildas Aurhinius—with or withou any of her Vuinlod riders.

*　*　*　*　*

Gerik rode at the head of his band, vowing lifelong grat itude to those who had taken care of the horses even wher fodder ran short at Tirabot. The mounts seemed to have wings on their feet, and cantered along as light-pacing a pegasi.

It was still as well that they had time to breathe, wher Gerik finally led his band up to the rear of the enemy. Non of the horrors he had feared greeted him, nor did he see any sort of battle going on. Indeed, the enemy seemed to be milling about in front of a rough barricade, and some of them were arguing with their rear guard.

They were arguing so loudly, indeed, that Bertsa Wylum took off her helmet and Tirabot badges and rode close enough to eavesdrop. When she rode back, she was once more smiling.

"Those dozen fellows with lances and crossbows are trying to keep the rest from deserting," she said. "It looks as if they pushed one attack, but our folk fought it off, and they lost heart for another. If we can unplug that rear guard of lackwits—"

"You want the work?" Gerik joked.

"I could do it. I could also lead a few of our fighters to help our friends, in case there's another attack. I can shout insults to wavering sell-swords from either place."

"Then the gods hold you in their hands."

"As long as they just hold, and don't squeeze," Wylum said. "Don't worry, Rubina will have her doll before sunset."

The gods' grip must have been uncertain. As Wylum led eight riders down into the ravine to the right of the trail, a crossbow *spung*ed from the enemy rear guard.

Bertsa Wylum flew out of her saddle and landed thrashing. The riders with her turned as one, all thoughts but vengeance driven from their heads. They charged the enemy rear guard without waiting for Gerik to put his riders in motion.

Gerik lost no time in doing so. But it was too late for half of Wylum's people. Facing lances and bows on unfavorable ground, they were slow-moving targets, and only three of them closed with the enemy still mounted. Then two more of these went down—and Gerik stood in his stirrups and screamed more than shouted: "Follow me!"

His first fear was that the enemy would take heart from Wylum's defeat. His second was that the uncertain ground would dismount him before he came to grips with the enemy.

He was up with the enemy before he had time to form a third fear. Then he had no time for anything except swordplay. That, and trying to keep his horse from stepping on Wylum's fallen.

Wylum's people had bought Gerik the advantage, even though with their blood. Crossbows were slow to recock and lances had the advantage over swords in reach, but once inside that reach the swordsman regained the edge. Gerik led a solid mass of six or seven riders into the disordered ranks of the enemy's rear guard, lost only one man, then was in too close for archery or lancework.

He was also at just the right distance to deliver berserker's attack.

Nothing more than a horse's length from him affected him. Nothing that had happened more than a few minutes ago remained in his mind. The world had shrunk down to the enemy in front of him and the friends on his flanks.

Slash at a sword arm, and watch it draw back, limp and spouting blood. Thrust—clumsily, with this sword—at an unarmored leg, and see the opponent turn away, to have his head loll on his shoulders as another Tirabot fighter struck with a battle-axe. Ride straight against a third opponent, and the two grappled barehanded, until Gerik drew a knife and stabbed wildly five, six, seven times, and then was stabbing the air above an empty saddle.

A horse screaming. His horse. Gerik felt his mount's hooves slow and stumble. Blood sprayed over him from the poor creature's slashed throat. The horse was falling sideways. Gerik tried to fling himself clear of the fall.

Instead the horse came down hard on Gerik's right leg, pinning it, breaking it, driving it into soft ground but also against a hard rock. Gerik wanted to scream with the pain but held his cry down to a gasp.

Then a lance drove down into his temple, just before the last survivor of Bertsa Wylum's sell-swords cut the lance out of the saddle. Unlike Horimpsot Elderdrake, Gerik had a moment of pain, and another, longer moment of bewilderment.

Then he died.

* * * * *

They were nearly the last humans on Suivinari Island, but Pirvan and Haimya felt reluctant to shake the last of its sand from their feet. Too many friends lay on the island, under its rock, or in the waters around it.

The expedition to Suivinari would still be accounted a victory, by those who wrote down such judgments. They would not mention the dead, except with conventional formulas of honor. They might also not mention what seemed to Pirvan the greatest part of the victory—humans and minotaurs each seeing that the other had courage and honor in plenty.

The two races would surely meet again as enemies, but among both, there would be those who remembered Suivinari.

A rumble began again, then grew louder than any before it. Looking east, Pirvan saw a ragged gap open in the side of the Smoker. A great ball of incandescent gas and lava grew from the gap, to slump down and begin to flow toward the sea. The glare seared the eyes, the sound hammered at the ears, and Pirvan doubted that any lungs could survive the dragon breath of the Smoker when it blew over the beach.

"Into the boat, you fools!" came a bellow louder than the mountain. "Into the boat, or I'll pick you up and carry you myself!"

It was Fulvura. Bandaged in three places and bloody in four more, she still seemed quite capable of carrying out her threat.

"I warn you, I bite," Haimya said, trying not to laugh.

"Hard way to get a mouthful of beef," Fulvura said. "I'm not as young as the lads seem to think. I'd be tougher than thanoi hide!"

"We'll take your word for it," Pirvan said. He turned and waved. The boat that had been resting on its oars just inside the surf line shot forward to grate on the sand.

The surf boomed louder and foamed higher on the way out, but Fulvura herself took an oar in each hand, and that made the difference. By the time they boarded *Shield of*

Virtue, a third of the Smoker's side was an orange glare, and a wall of heat was growing around the island. Even the Green Mountain seemed to trail steam from its crest, and more steam boiled up along the shore where the lava struck the water.

Safety lay still farther out to sea. For all the lava that was pouring into the water, much more had to still lie below. When the sea reached that—

"Make all sail," Pirvan called to the captain. "Our work here is finished."

* * * * *

It had been prudent to march to the sound of battle.

Lady Eskaia led her Vuinlodders up to the Tirabot barricade within minutes after Gerik's fall. Furthermore, he had left her with much less work than he might otherwise have faced. His berserker's fight had slaughtered half the rear guard, made the other half easy prey, and removed all barriers to the swift retreat of the remaining enemy.

All but a few diehards. They still held the trail, where it led into a clearing. Behind them, Eskaia saw another twenty or so armed riders in House Dirivan colors. No doubt the arrival of friends had given the diehards fresh courage.

It was annoying to have to do Gerik's work all over again. She used that word, because the tightness in throat and breast since she learned of Gerik's death would not let her even think anything stronger.

Time enough for that later. Stronger words, tears, being held and comforted—all could come later, as she had come, too late, for her friend's son and his friends.

Eskaia arrayed her men and was about to order them forward, when the Solamnics appeared, at the charge. It appeared that the knights' patience with recalcitrant House Dirivan hirelings had run out at the same time as Eskaia's. Forty Solamnics were a match for thirty sell-swords even if the sell-swords had their heart in the fight. These sellswords did not.

Also, Sir Shufiran had arrayed the Solamnics with a master's skill. Sir Rignar led the actual charge, shouting war cries and making his weapons and mount dance, but, as Eskaia noticed, doing much more to frighten than to kill.

Whether it would have come to killing, Eskaia did not know. The sell-swords did not tarry long enough to permit an answer to the question. Only two of them remained behind, and those as wounded prisoners who were so frightened of Sir Shufiran's bleak looks that they babbled as if dosed with truth-poppy.

Eskaia left that work to the Solamnics. She did not trust herself within reach of any who might have her friends' blood on his hands. Besides, there was plenty of work to do, helping Ellysta and Serafina keep themselves busy with healing the wounded.

* * * * *

It was only toward sunset that the sea flowed into the lava chamber underneath the Smoker. By then the fleet was so far out to sea that the explosion did not touch them, and indeed was almost invisible in the veil of ashes and fumes the mountain had drawn about itself.

Pirvan knew that such eruptions might fling towering waves on distant shores, but that magic and timely warnings or even mere common sense would diminish the death toll. He still had enough to do here, keeping any of the yet living from joining the well-filled ranks of the already dead.

He did it until well into the night, until he was so tired that Darin had to guide his stumbling steps to his cabin. Even then, Pirvan did not sleep, until he felt familiar warm arms grip him from behind, and a familiar soft breath on the back of his neck.

* * * * *

Darkness had long since swallowed the forest, for all that it was one of the shortest of summer nights. The forest life, driven into flight or silence by the day's battle, was slowly returning.

Ellysta sat on a stump, feeling almost as wooden as her seat, and listened to the *chrrrr* of a bird as she worked on a man's wounded shoulder. Remove the old dressing, clean the wound, salve it afresh, then bind it with clean cloth dipped in yet more salve. The man would live, perhaps even have full use of both arms, for all that his shoulder was worse than Grimsoar's had been, from the arrow.

It had been his heart that took Grimsoar One-Eye, a heart finally strained once too often. The wound had not helped, but it was his labor from the end of winter to this day's battle that had weighed down his heart, more and more, until it collapsed like an overburdened mule.

Serafina had been dry-eyed until sunset, then gone aside to weep in private. Ellysta supposed she should find time to do the same, but Gerik was already dead. He would not die again from lack of her tears, while some of the living who had fought well might die for lack of her care.

The man winced and bit his lip. He did not cry out, because Rubina was seated cross-legged on the ground, holding his hand. It was a point of pride for all the wounded not to show weakness before the Little Warrior, as they had nicknamed Rubina. Some thought her a good luck charm, some a mascot, some touched by the gods, and some merely the blood of Pirvan and Haimya running true. None wanted to disappoint her.

A small figure took shape out of the darkness—Lady Eskaia, in male attire. She carried something in one hand that looked remarkably like a doll.

"Zixa!"

Rubina jumped up and ran to Eskaia, then snatched the doll and hugged it.

"The people who were laying out the dead found this on Bertsa Wylum's body," Eskaia said. "They thought it might belong to one of her kin."

"Well, they should have known better," Rubina said. Then she tucked Zixa inside her tunic. "I have to go thank Bertsa," she said. "Lady Eskaia, will you come with me?"

"The dead aren't—" Eskaia began.

"The dead are dead," Rubina said, and Ellysta heard savage self-command in her voice. "But I still have to thank them."

"I can come," Ellysta said. "Lady Eskaia looks tired."

"Well, you look even worse," Rubina said. "Besides, you might be carrying Gerik's child, and you should save your strength."

"Gerik's—" Eskaia began, in bewilderment. Ellysta vowed to strangle the Princess of Vuinlod, if she so much as smiled.

"Yes," Rubina said. "I hope it will be a girl, because then I will have a baby sister, even though I will really be her aunt. I can—I can—"

Silently, Ellysta held Rubina with one arm and Eskaia with the other. This was rather a public place for all three of them to cry at once, but all of them needed it and nobody in their right senses would say a word.

* * * * *

Two days' sailing had taken the human fleet into clean seas, and a night's rain had washed the deck of *Red Elf*. The planks were still damp under Torvik's bare feet when he and Mirraleen came on deck at dawn.

It was more darkness than light still, and they had the deck to themselves save for the steersman and lookout. Torvik wanted to put his arms around Mirraleen and use all his strength in the embrace, so that perhaps they might merge into one flesh and never be apart.

Instead, he put his hand over hers, as she stood by the railing.

"You—you seem to know that I am leaving," she said.

"I do not exactly know. But I did not want to ask anything."

"Afraid of the answer?"

Torvik shook his head. "Afraid to show that I was of two minds about your leaving," he said.

Mirraleen looked truly confused. "I think you owe me an

explanation," she said.

"After last night, I doubt I can pay any woman anything, but I'll try.

"I love you, and not only when we share a bed. I would have gladly gone about my life, known as the captain with the Dimernesti wife. Besides, it would have made sea otters even safer, at least around Vuinlod. Nobody would dare risk hitting one of my kin by marriage!"

That had been the right thing to say. Mirraleen's laugh was a gurgle, like a clear brook running over stones on a sunny day.

"I would walk apart, of course," he said, "but I would be near to my kin, or at least to my own people. You would walk not just apart, but alone."

"Save for you."

"Am I—that much?"

"Very nearly."

"But not quite?"

"No," she had to say.

Torvik hugged Mirraleen, in love, gratitude, relief, and desire all churning together. She returned the embrace. He thought warmth had left him, but now it seemed to be returning.

It was Mirraleen who broke the embrace, then kissed him lightly on the corner of both eyes. She sprang to the railing and snatched her tunic over her head. It floated to the deck, as the dawn breeze lifted her hair.

Then she was gone, with only a faint *cloop* in the water alongside. When Torvik could lift his head and stare dry-eyed at the wake, only the sea stared back at him.

Epilogue

On an island so far north of where Suivinari had been that the seasons were the reverse of what they were in Ansalon, Mirraleen sat cross-legged on a mat of fragrant dried seaweed. She was nursing her son.

Water rippled, then splashed, in the pool in the middle of the cave. Medlessarn the Silent rose from the water, swam to the shelf below where Mirraleen sat, and walked up to her.

"How fare you both?" he asked. His eyes, however, were fixed on the babe. The babe, it seemed to Mirraleen, was returning stare for stare. But perhaps it was easy to imagine things about those eyes. They were the same intense dark brown as his father's, so well remembered from love bouts and much more.

"I think the lad will be one to make Torvik proud, whether he ever learns of the boy's existence or not," Mirraleen said.

That was the plainest answer she had yet given Medlessarn. It was also somewhat of a test of his character. He wanted try not merely to be her mate but wed her in the old style. The rites and ceremonies of that old style, however, said nothing about the bride's having already borne a half-elven child to a far-distant human seafarer.

Mirraleen was not sure whether she wished Medlessarn to be equally silent, or to speak eloquently. She decided that silence or speech could equally well lie or tell the truth.

"Has he changed yet?" Medlessarn asked.

Mirraleen laughed. "At barely four months old? I have never heard of even the most potent of the Dargonesti changing before a year. We shallows-dwellers are laggards.

"He can swim, though," she continued. "That is not common in human babes of his age. They seldom have that much use of their limbs, or if they do, too much fear of the water. I could sometimes wish he had more fear in him, of the water and other things."

"It is easy for a babe with a good mother to grow without fear," Medlessarn said.

"Easier when the mother has as many friends as I do."

That was not merely flattery. Medlessarn's clan had taken Mirraleen in, swollen belly and all, and given her as much help with the babe as if one of them had sired it. This said plainly that they did not think like the Silvanesti or the minions of the kingpriest, when it came to mixed-blood children.

Medlessarn lay down on his belly, propped his chin on one hand, and waggled the fingers of the other to amuse the baby. He was rewarded by a formidable belch, then a squeal of laughter.

"Swimming that young suggests the blood breeds true," he said.

"Which blood?" Mirraleen asked.

"It could be either, I admit," Medlessarn replied. "More likely shallows-dweller, but Torvik was not one of those human seafarers who refuse to learn swimming because that will only prolong their dying if they fall overboard."

"He could swim like an eel," Mirraleen said. "But he was much warmer to the touch."

They sat in companionable silence for a while, each thinking back to the battle now over a year in the past. Medlessarn broke the silence with evident reluctance. "How long will you keep him?"

"If he runs true to the shallows-dweller blood, until he is grown. If he does not, I shall take counsel on the best way of returning him to his father." She looked at the water, seeing nothing.

"Grown men or women can live where they please, with whom they please, and as they please," she said. "But a babe should grow up with those most like him, who understand his needs."

Medlessarn laughed. "Tell that to Darin," he said. "A minotaur raised him from the age of three, and he has the best of both races in him."

"Yes, but he was not of mixed blood, with his mother a sea-dweller. Humans and minotaurs are both dryfeet. If the boy cannot learn to change—"

"What of the old spells that could give a dryfoot that power? They were known once, at least among the Dargonesti," Medlessarn offered.

"Indeed, the tales run so. But are they still known, anywhere?"

Medlessarn frowned, and said, "I have heard whispers, which may be nonsense, I admit. But would it not be worth asking about? I have traveled farther than many in these islands, but there are some who have traveled and lived longer."

Mirraleen was grateful to her friend for not adding that he could give the babe what Waydol had never given Darin—two parents to raise him. She shifted the babe and patted his cheek.

"It is too soon to decide our future, let alone that of a babe who is still too young to be named." She was observing the old custom of waiting to name a Dimernesti babe until he or she had changed for the first time. This did not keep her from calling him in her heart "Joimer," the Dimernesti form of his grandfather's name.

"Ah. But if you wait that long, he may know you well enough that he will sorrow to leave you even for a father. Also, by then Torvik may well be wed to a human woman who will not be pleased at his half-elven by-blow coming out of the sea to remind her of his past."

"Torvik would never wed such a fool," she said.

"Men are not that much wiser than women, when it comes to whom they will wed."

Mirraleen had to laugh. Medlessarn could have lost her forever by the smallest lie, but had somehow managed to tell only the truth. His ability to resist temptation would make it hard to resist him.

When the babe's future was decided.

"If the babe is a shallows-dweller, you may name him yours, with all due rites," she said. "This I swear. But if he must live a dryfoot, will you swear to help me take him south to Vuinlod?"

"If the kingpriest has not laid it in ruins by then, I do so swear," Medlessarn said. "I also swear to adopt the babe or return him to his sire, whether we wed or not.

"But I hope when this coil in your mind about the babe is done, you will think kindly upon me."

"I doubt that I shall ever think unkindly of you or your kin," Mirraleen said. "Only—do not presume to be too much in my company. Otherwise, he will grow to know you as well as me, and then will sorrow twice over if we must part."

"That is the hardest thing you have asked of me yet," Medlessarn said. He sighed dramatically. "But weak men are not worthy of strong women. I shall try to be what you demand." He grinned. "But, oh, what a tyrant I shall be after we are wed!"

They kissed, nearly squeezing the babe between them, but making him laugh again.

* * * * *

The monument was a simple curving wall of stone, built into the side of a hill outside Vuinlod. The names of the dead from Suivinari and Tirabot were carved there. No distinction by race, rank, profession, or even which side they had been on (at least in those cases where the names of House Dirivan's dead were known).

Pirvan and Haimya stood for a long time before the slab

with Gerik's name carved on it. A hot breeze puffed across the flagstones at intervals, carrying dried petals and bits of yellowed fluff with it. Pirvan shook his head. "There are times when I wonder what it was all for," he said. "I can't say there is less injustice in the world. I can't even say that anyone's life will be better for all the dying."

"Not with certainty, no," Haimya said. This had been one of the nights when in the deepest hours of darkness, she had wakened to weep silently by the window. Her eyes showed traces of it, but her voice and carriage showed none. Pirvan would let her guard her secret, as she guarded the secrets of all the times he had wept, save when he did it in her arms.

"But do you demand certainty?" she went on.

"If I did, would I have become a knight or wed you?" Pirvan said. He held her hand briefly. "No, I suppose it is the feeling of every father and mother who have lost a son like Gerik. That he was as precious to the gods as he was to us, so that his death ought to buy a whole new world, or at least cleanse the old one of much evil."

"Well, there is House Dirivan under the ban of the Orders," Haimya said. "That and the merchants' wrath should keep them honest or at least quiet for a generation.

"There is much more knowledge and even somewhat more trust among humans and minotaurs. It may last only as long as Zeskuk does, but he has a good twenty or thirty years left.

"There is more caution among the knights—"

"How do you know that?" Pirvan asked.

"By listening to what they say, even when I am not supposed to, and to what you do not say, even when I could wish you spoke plainly. The knights may be more cautious about Istaran schemes to allow private warfare, and other breaches of the Swordsheath Scroll."

"We may need not so much caution as plain speaking," Pirvan said. "Istar needs reminding that it is ill done to divide the knights. We are still their true strength in war, just or unjust."

"Then you have chosen your work," Haimya said. "I

think Niebar may have given his life partly so that you could take on the work Marod intended for you, while you were still young enough for it. Like Zeskuk, you may have twenty or thirty good years left."

Pirvan put a finger over Haimya's lips. "Not if I have to listen to you every waking minute. But you speak some truth. Gerik may not have bought us more than time, but he bought enough of that for us to put it to use within the ranks of the knights."

"Yes, and Rynthala is with child."

"What has that to do with Gerik?" Pirvan asked, startled.

"Nothing," Haimya said. "I just received the letter this morning."

"I should hope it has nothing to do with Gerik," Pirvan said wryly. "Our son was honorable. He would never have lain with a comrade's wife and begotten a child on her."

For a moment it seemed the jest would escape Haimya. Then she gave a small snort of laughter and hugged Pirvan. He could feel her thoughts, for they were very much his own.

They had both made their peace, that Gerik had not left Ellysta with child. She and they alike would have nothing of him but memories.

But they were good memories, of a son and a betrothed who had lived and died without being a knight, yet also done both as if he had sworn more oaths than all three Orders together might have demanded of him. Such memories were not a small thing.

Arm in arm, they walked away from the monument down the hill, until the shadows swallowed them.